Because We're Worth it

PAULINE LAWLESS

POOLBEG

This novel is entirely a work of fiction. The names,
characters and incidents portrayed in it are the work of the
author's imagination. Any resemblance to actual persons,
living or dead, events or localities is entirely coincidental.

Published 2009
by Poolbeg Press Ltd
123 Grange Hill, Baldoyle
Dublin 13, Ireland
E-mail: poolbeg@poolbeg.com

© Pauline Lawless 2009

The moral right of the author has been asserted.

Typesetting, layout, design © Poolbeg Press Ltd.

1 3 5 7 9 10 8 6 4 2

A catalogue record for this book is available from the British Library.

ISBN 978-1-84223-373-3

Typeset by Type Design in Bembo 10.5/14.5
Printed by
Litografia Rosés, S.A., Spain

www.poolbeg.com

Note on the author

Pauline Lawless was born in Dublin and now divides her time between Ireland, Belgium and Florida. She has five children and, as Pauline McCorley, spent many years running "SuperSlim" slimming classes in the midlands. This experience gave her the idea for this, her first novel.

Acknowledgements

When, on my retirement, I started to write the book they say is in all of us, I never dreamed that it would one day be published, but thanks to the effervescent Paula Campbell of Poolbeg Press, my dream has come true.

Many thanks to Paula, Kieran, Niamh, Dave and all at Poolbeg.

To my editor, Gaye Shortland, special thanks for her unstinting help and advice, which greatly improved the original draft. As a first-time novelist I had a lot to learn and Gaye was very patient with me. Hopefully you won't have as much work to do on my second effort, Gaye!

A big thank-you to my lovely daughter, Ciara, for her support and encouragement and for the many hours she put in reading the drafts I sent her as the work progressed. I always took your advice, Ciara! Without you, this novel wouldn't have happened.

I'm forever grateful to my mother, my family and my many friends in Ireland, Belgium and Florida for their support and encouragement.

To all my old friends – the past members of SuperSlim – you were my inspiration!

Finally, to Jean Marie, with all my love. Thank you for sharing this exciting life with me.

To Ciara –
With much love

Chapter 1

"Perfect!" said Kate O'Mara as she bit into the crisp, but gooey on the inside, meringue that she had just taken out of the Aga. "Mmm . . . delicious!" Too late, she remembered her diet. "Oh damn! That's at least another hundred calories. There goes my diet again! Suppose I may as well be hung for a sheep as a lamb!" . . . and another meringue bit the dust. She then turned her attention to the chocolate mousse – couldn't resist tasting it and then licked the spoon clean when she had finished. The brandy snaps and Bailey's ice cream suffered the same fate. After all, she reasoned, if I don't taste it how will I know if it's okay? She was busy preparing a very special dinner and everything had to be absolutely perfect.

Her husband, Danny, had stressed the importance of this evening so she had pulled out all the stops. He ran a highly successful building company and often entertained his business clients at home. He maintained it was better than any restaurant as Kate was a superb cook but she suspected that he also wanted to show off their lovely home, of which he was very proud. Kate was painfully shy with strangers and found it an ordeal having to make conversation with them at the dinner table. She would much rather stay in the kitchen all night. However, she knew how important these dinners were to Danny and so she tried her best to overcome her shyness. It had got a little easier since he had convinced her to have a glass or two of wine which helped her to relax but that was her limit. She could not risk having any more than that or she would be drunk and the meal would become a disaster.

Tonight there was a very influential Dublin property developer, Michael Traynor, coming with his two directors and their wives. They had plans to build a big development in Canary Wharf in London – luxury apartments, hotel, shopping centre to start with – and Danny was the front-runner to win this contract. Secretly he hoped to clinch the deal tonight. She knew how badly he wanted it so she had done everything she possibly could to make it a success.

* * *

Kate stood surveying herself critically in the dressing-room mirror. She didn't like what she saw. Looking back at her was a very attractive woman who could have passed for much less than her thirty-nine years – thanks to her dewy youthful complexion and a look of innocence in her big blue eyes. She had shoulder-length honey-blonde hair that was a mass of waves and curls that always had that 'just-got-out-of-bed' look. Although she often tied it up in an attempt to look neat, curls and tendrils kept escaping around her face which drove her crazy but only added to her charm. It was, however, the sweetness of her expression and the warmth and kindness in her eyes that drew people to her like a magnet. Men wanted to protect her – women confided in her.

Looking in the mirror, she saw none of this. She had so little self-esteem that all she could see was fat and bulges everywhere not to mention boobs that she felt were far too big. Piled on the bed were the entire contents of her wardrobe which she had tried on and discarded.

"Oh dear God, I look so frumpy and nothing fits me!" she sighed. "I really will have to do something about it. I suppose it'll have to be my black silk tunic and pants again! At least they hide my stomach and hips and they're comfortable."

★ ★ ★

Less than a mile away Diana Rafferty had none of these problems as she prepared for the dinner. She sat in front of the mirror in her dressing-room admiring her new hairstyle. Gary had excelled himself – the plum highlights, which he'd insisted on, looked terrific in her her sleek, black shiny hair.

Yep, I like it, she thought as she preened, turning her head this way and that. Very edgy and now – just what I wanted.

Appearance was everything to Diana and she devoured

all the latest 'crap magazines' – as Kevin called them – to see what all her favourite celebrities were wearing. How she envied these women and their lifestyles: jetting around the world in private jets, partying in all the best places, paparazzi following their every step, glamorous men lusting after them! She sighed . . . that was the life she wanted!

Diana had a typical hour-glass figure: tall, with long slim legs, a surprisingly small waist, curvaceous hips and big full breasts. 'Voluptuous' was the word that sprang to mind when people first set eyes on her. She was 'sex-on-legs' and she knew it. She flaunted her body at every opportunity and men fell for it every time. Consumed with lust, they never noticed her cold grey calculating eyes. Women disliked her intensely and none of them trusted her.

She'd spent the morning in Dublin getting her weekly manicure, pedicure, waxing, massage and spray-tan. Then, after lunch in the Shelbourne with some girlfriends, she'd spent the afternoon in the top hair salon in the city having her hair cut, highlighted and treated.

She was busy applying a bevy of make-up products to her face when her husband Kevin emerged from the bathroom, a towel around his waist and his dark curly hair sprinkling little droplets of water everywhere. Once upon a time, the sight of his toned muscled body and smooth tawny skin would have excited her and she'd have dragged him to bed. His resemblance to Antonio Banderas had been a huge turn-on for her but that was like . . . in another life! Now he was just annoying her as he bent to kiss the top of her head.

"Don't touch me!" she shrieked. "You'll mess up my hair!"

He pulled back.

"Do you like it?" she asked, turning to face him.

"It's different. It will take some getting used to."

"God, you haven't a clue! This is the very latest trend."

He saw the new coral silk dress lying on the bed. "Very nice," he whistled as he read the label on the dress. "How much did this cost me?"

"Don't be such a tightwad. You know you like me to look well!"

"You look great in anything. You don't need Gucci for that."

"Well, these women at Danny's tonight will certainly be in designer gear and I don't want to feel like the poor relation. By the way, I bought a pair of Jimmy Choos to go with it."

"I won't even ask. I suppose I'll need to take out a bank loan for those. You can bet Kate won't be wearing Gucci and Jimmy Choos tonight."

"Kate is such a frump," she added viciously. "She could well afford them if she wanted them. Danny is always on at her to go shopping but she has no interest. He even opened an account for her in Brown Thomas and she has never used it. Can you believe it? How I wish I were in her place. Money no object there!"

"Darling, you can't complain. When do you ever want for anything? Anyway, let's get a move on. I promised Danny I would be there early to lend some moral support. Tonight is very important for him."

"Oh sure, he needs you to hold his hand!" she replied sarcastically.

Kevin held his tongue. The last thing he wanted now was an argument with her. Why is she so resentful all the time, he asked himself as he dressed. She's never happy – always envious. Women! I'll never understand them!

★ ★ ★

Meanwhile Kate was laying out the titbits to have with the pre-dinner drinks – or the '*amuse-gueule*' to have with the '*apéritifs*' – as Diana insisted on calling them. God, thought Kate, Diana could be so pretentious sometimes. I hope she doesn't flirt too much with the men tonight. One of these nights some wife will clock her! She giggled as she imagined the scene. How on earth Kevin put up with her she'd never understand. He had the patience of Job.

She helped herself to another Parmesan crisp. Stop it, she chided herself. There'll be none left if I keep this up.

Just then the doorbell rang. Danny was delighted to see that their first guests were Kevin and Diana. He brought them through the foyer and enormous reception room and out on to the terrace which overlooked the romantically floodlit pool.

"It's such a lovely balmy evening that I thought we would have drinks out here."

"Perfect. I just love these sofas," Diana said as she sank into the butter-soft white leather while hoisting her skirt up as high as she dared so that Danny could get a good look at her long shapely legs. She was also aware that the contours of her nipples were highly visible through the light silk of her dress. Danny could hardly take his eyes off them. She loved the effect she had on men. It gave her a sense of power. He wanted her and she knew it and he knew that she knew it. Of course, out of loyalty to Kevin he would never make a move on her, much as he wanted to.

"And what can I get you both? I've made a jug of Wallbangers but perhaps you'd prefer champagne or something else?"

"Champoo for me, please, sweetie," she replied coquettishly.

Kevin opted for a Harvey Wallbanger.

Danny brought them their drinks and filled them in on the other guests who were coming and just how much the night meant to him.

"Michael is the main man. It will be his decision to give me this contract or not – so try and charm him for me, Diana, will you?"

"No probs, darling," she purred, crossing and uncrossing her legs. "Anything for you!"

As Kate came in from the kitchen the doorbell pealed again. Danny nervously straightened his tie and went to the door. It was Michael and his wife Marcia, with one of his directors and his wife. As Danny ushered them in the other couple arrived. They were all beautifully dressed and groomed and reeked of money – lots of it!

Danny led them out to the terrace and made the

introductions all round. He was so good at this sort of thing, Kate thought, whereas she was useless. People gravitated to him and he could keep a whole room entertained for the night with his stories and jokes. He wasn't tall but his personality was larger than life. He used to be devilishly handsome but now his dark-blond hair was thinning on top and he had the start of a double chin. Even so, he could still charm the birds off the trees, Kate thought fondly.

Danny got drinks for everyone and after they were all seated, with the men on one side and the women on the other – things never change in Ireland, Kate smiled to herself – Marcia turned to her.

"What a beautiful home you have! It's so big and bright and the view across to the mountains is fantastic. And what a glorious pool! I would love one but we get so little good weather here that it hardly seems worth it. And I must say I love the white leather sunbeds too."

"Thank you." said Kate.

I'm afraid I'm responsible for the pool. It's been my biggest extravagance," replied Danny suavely. "It's always been a dream of mine. Kate and I only use it in the really fine weather but the boys use it all summer long when they're home from boarding school, regardless of the weather. We do enjoy sitting out here in the evenings and in winter we can enclose the terrace with double-glazed doors and a sliding roof, so we can have the view while still being snug and warm." He smiled around the room.

"That sounds wonderful. How many children do you have?" Marcia asked Kate.

"Four boys," Kate replied shyly.

"We have two daughters," said Marcia, adding sadly, "Michael would have loved a son also but it wasn't to be."

Kate wondered what had happened but, of course, couldn't ask.

"Diana, I love your shoes!" remarked Amanda, the youngest of the wives. "I almost bought an exact pair of those Jimmy Choos last week but in the end I opted for these Christian Louboutin." She lifted a perfectly pedicured foot, clad in a very high beige-suede stiletto. Diana and Louise, the other wife, made a big deal of admiring the shoes. Kate wondered how on earth she could walk in them.

"I prefer Manolo Blahnik," Marcia said. "I find them more comfortable."

Kate felt like a complete outsider as they rattled on about shoes. Looking around at the other women's feet she realised that they were all wearing the same vertiginously high heels. She prayed nobody would notice her feet, clad in their €12.99 flat ballet pumps from New Look. They were the most comfortable shoes she had ever put on. Before they could draw her into the conversation she quickly made her escape to the sanctuary of her kitchen. She remembered Diana once telling her that she had spent €590 on a pair of Louboutin shoes. Is this for real, she'd wondered. How could anyone justify spending that amount on a pair of shoes?

Overhearing the ladies' conversation, Michael remarked, "I just don't get it with you women. What is it about shoes that sends the whole female race gaga?"

"Well, for one thing they always fit. Whether you gain weight or lose it - your shoes always fit," Marcia answered him, to the cries of "Absolutely!" and "Hear, hear!" from Amanda and Louise. "Likewise bags," she continued, getting really into it. "My bags always fit me!"

The women all pealed with laughter. They were really enjoying this!

"Tell me, Diana. How many pairs of shoes do you own?" Michael asked.

"Mmm . . . probably about sixty – not counting boots."

"See!" He asked Amanda and Louise the same question and got much the same reply. Then he turned to his wife. "Okay, Marcia. Honestly now. How many pairs? A hundred? More?"

"Gosh, this is embarrassing but eh . . . okay . . . I'll come clean. A hundred and five pairs, last count."

"See what I mean? I rest my case."

"Hey, I've had some of them for over thirty years!"

"It doesn't matter, still counts."

"Oh, get lost! You can afford it!"

This brought more guffaws.

Kate, who had come back in from the kitchen, felt completely out of her depth. Was there something wrong with her? She had four, maybe five pairs of shoes – and that included her gardening ones. Why would I need more, she wondered? Am I a total misfit in the female race? She made a quick getaway to the kitchen once again before Michael could ask her about her shoes. She would have been mortified to let them know the truth. She put this out of her mind as she prepared the asparagus hollandaise for the first course of the meal.

Meanwhile, back on the terrace, Marcia watched Diana in action, flirting with all the men and Michael in particular. Oh, she knew her type so well! How many Dianas had she met over the years? This one had very striking looks but there was a hard edge to her. She was the ultimate high-maintenance woman – the kind that made other women feel they needed a makeover – with not a hair out of place and groomed to within an inch of her life. She was a Jezebel who would take any man she wanted, married or not. With dismay, she saw the way Michael was responding to Diana. No doubt about it – she was just his type! Marcia felt helpless.

Danny led his guests into the dining-room and he was pleased with their *oohs* and *aahs* as they took in the beautiful elegant room with its red silk wallpaper and crystal chandelier. The snow-white place mats and napkins and the large centrepiece of white roses made a lovely contrast to the rich mahogany table and the red walls. The many candles reflected the lights of the Waterford crystal and the Old Irish Silver cutlery.

"It's really beautiful," remarked Marcia and the others all agreed.

Diana meanwhile was turning herself inside out trying to impress Michael, batting her eyelashes at him and laughing heartily at his jokes. She was talking in that little-girl voice which she reserved specifically for men. When they took their places at the table she plonked herself down beside him although Kate's name was on the place card. Not wanting to make a scene, Kate silently sat down in Diana's place. Danny saw what had happened and shrugged his shoulders helplessly at Kate.

As they ate the starter, Diana leaned in to Michael at every possible chance and kept laying her hand on his arm as she whispered to him. She ignored the other guests and Kate felt embarrassed for Kevin. Marcia appeared not to notice but she had to be aware of it.

After the asparagus, Kate served a fish course of coquilles St Jacques. "These scallops are heavenly, Kate!" said Michael. "They just melt in the mouth!"

Danny gave her a wink. The dinner was going very well and the conversation was flowing easily. There was much laughter which was getting louder with every glass of the superb Burgundy wines that Danny was so generously pouring. The main course of mustard crusted rack of lamb was very well received and Kate heaved a great sigh of relief.

Then, as she was clearing away the plates from the main course she almost dropped them all in shock when she saw that beneath the table, unseen by the others, Michael had his hand up under Diana's skirt. She was doing nothing to stop him and, from the look on her face, appeared to be enjoying it. Kate blushed with embarrassment and looked over at Kevin and Marcia to make sure they hadn't seen it. Apparently not, thank God, as they were deep in conversation with one another.

When she came in with the dessert trolley all the ladies groaned . . . "I couldn't eat another bite . . ." until they saw what was on offer: white and dark chocolate mousse terrine, meringue nests filled with raspberries, cream and toasted almonds, brandy-snap baskets filled with Baileys ice cream topped with spun sugar and finally oranges in Cointreau.

"I really shouldn't indulge," declared Amanda," but how can we resist this?"

"I think I've died and gone to heaven!" Louise remarked.

"Forget the diets, girls! We'll start again tomorrow," advised Marcia.

They tried everything, much to Kate's delight. Desserts were her speciality and tonight she had outdone herself. It always amused her that even when people claimed to be completely stuffed they still found a space for dessert. Over the Irish coffees and liqueurs the compliments were coming so fast that Kate could feel herself blushing.

"That is the best meal I've eaten in years," announced Michael.

"Wonderful!" said Kevin and Amanda in unison.

"Superb!" said Marcia. "You just have to give me the name of your caterer, dear. I will absolutely have to get them to cater for my next party."

"There's no caterer – Kate did all this herself," Danny said proudly. "She's a terrific cook. Everything you ate tonight is home-made."

"You lucky man!" remarked Michael as the women looked at Kate in disbelief.

13

"You did all of this yourself?" asked Marcia, admiringly.

"Incredible!" said Amanda.

"Don't you even have help in the kitchen?" Louise asked her.

"No way! I tried that – they were more of a hindrance than a help, getting in my way. I prefer to do it myself, though Danny doesn't agree with me."

"Well, you seem to be able to cope admirably, my dear," Marcia smiled kindly at her. "It was wonderful."

Diana was noticeably silent.

"Thank you," said a blushing Kate. "I'm glad you all enjoyed it."

"I'd like to propose a toast. To Kate! The best housewife in Ireland!" said Danny.

"Housewife?" asked Marcia archly, raising her eyebrows. "You mean 'wife', surely."

"Yes, of course," replied Danny with an embarrassed laugh. "To Kate!" They all raised their glasses to her.

Diana was seething at all the attention Kate was getting, especially from Michael. She grudgingly admitted that the meal was good and Kate was an okay cook. That's all she's good for, she thought. Look at the state of her in that old black tunic that she wears all the time! Danny must be sick of looking at it. He deserves better. To think she could have a full wardrobe of designer gear if she wanted it! Some women are downright stupid. And she really is piling on the weight . . . I'll take that smile off her face . . .

"Kate, I've something important to tell you."

Everyone turned to look at Diana expectantly.

"There's a new Slimming Club opening in Naas on Monday night," she said, smiling sweetly. "It's called Slimforever and seemingly the girl running it can work absolute miracles. I thought you might be interested."

Kate almost died with embarrassment and wished the ground would open up and swallow her. She felt self-conscious enough about her weight without Diana calling everyone's attention to it. How cruel of her!

She felt the colour spreading up her face as she muttered, "I must check it out."

"I've heard about that girl," Marcia chimed in. "I believe she's fantastic. Some of my friends are travelling all the way from Foxrock to Maynooth to her classes. They say she can talk the weight off you!"

"I wish," sighed Louise, to everyone's amusement.

* * *

After the guests had left, thanking her profusely yet again, Danny took her in his arms.

"What a great success! You did me proud with the meal. I think the job is mine. Michael hinted as much to me before he left. Let's go to bed and celebrate!"

Kate tingled with anticipation. Their lovemaking was as good as ever, even after nineteen years of marriage and four children, and she loved the intimacy and pleasure she derived from it.

But tonight she had a niggling thought at the back of her mind. For the first time ever she felt self-conscious about her body while making love. She couldn't quite relax and as they were drifting off to sleep she murmured,

"I was very hurt by Diana's remark about that Slimming Club."

"Darling, you're much too sensitive. Pay no attention to her. You know Diana well enough by now. Her nose was out of joint because of all the praise you were getting. She was jealous. Don't let it bother you . . ." Then, after a pause, he added, "But perhaps it might be a good idea to check it out and see if they can help you lose some weight."

Was he serious? She couldn't see his face in the dark, but she knew he wasn't smiling. It wasn't a joke. She felt dejected and hurt. Danny – who frequently told her he loved her curves and who discouraged her from all those diets she was constantly on – was he now saying she was too fat?

That decided her. I'll join that club on Monday, she vowed.

Chapter 2

The next morning, Kate drove over to her friend Lauren's house to collect her two youngest boys, Sam and Toby, who had stayed the night with Lauren's son Ben. Ben and Toby were great pals, both eleven-years-old (though Toby pulled seniority by insisting he was eleven and three-quarters!) and they both idolised thirteen-year-old Sam.

"They're having great fun on the trampoline," said Lauren. "Come on in for a coffee and tell me all about last night. I'm dying to hear all the gossip."

"Well, it was a great success and I think Danny will get the contract. I actually enjoyed the night very much. They were nice people – good fun and down-to-earth. Not a bit snobbish! I particularly liked Marcia, Michael's wife. Diana, of course, was up to her usual tricks, flirting like mad with Michael. It was really embarrassing!"

"That woman! She makes my blood boil. I don't know how you stick her, Kate. You're a saint!"

"I wasn't that saintly last night. In fact, I wanted to throttle her."

Lauren laughed. "I don't believe it! That's not a bit like you. You're always so kind to her. Tell me more! I'm all ears."

"Well, after the meal, they were all saying how much they had enjoyed it and what a great cook I was – it was a bit embarrassing, to tell you the truth," said Kate, blushing again at the thought. "Anyway, Diana wasn't too pleased."

"I'll bet she wasn't! You can be sure her nose was out of joint because she wasn't the centre of attention," said Lauren scathingly.

"For whatever reason, she humiliated me in front of everybody by suggesting that I should join the new Slimming Club that's opening in Naas on Monday night. I needn't tell you, I could have killed her! I felt mortified."

"What a bitch! She's so jealous of you. I can just imagine her saying it – ever so sweetly, in that babyish voice she uses for effect! I hope you gave her a smart answer."

"No! I was so embarrassed I just wanted to die."

"How on earth does Kevin stay with her? I can't bear to meet her in the golf club and try to avoid playing with her at all costs. You should see the shenanigans of her with the men there. None of the wives can stand her."

"Well, perhaps she did me a favour," Kate admitted. "I do need to lose weight and I hear this woman is fantastic. They say she can talk the weight off you. Mind you, she'll need to talk up a storm to get it off me, but I really want to lose it and I was hoping that you would come along with me, for moral support. I couldn't face in there on my own."

"I'll be glad to. Actually, I could do with losing a few pounds myself. You know I gained about ten pounds on our holiday in Sardinia. All that gorgeous Italian food and wine! Mmmm . . ." She licked her lips, remembering.

"Gosh, Lauren, I can't see it. You're so tall you can carry it."

Lauren was indeed tall – five foot eleven, in fact – but despite this she moved with the grace of a ballerina. She had been a model when she was young and now, at forty-two, still had a figure that most women would die for. She also had clear blue eyes exquisite cheekbones, a flawless complexion and shoulder-length, straight, naturally blonde hair which she sometimes wore up, but today was held back with a velvet hair-band. Kate thought to herself that on anyone else this would have looked silly, but on Lauren it looked classy. She had a look that reminded people of the late Princess Diana and, like her, she was the epitome of elegance. She was always beautifully and expensively dressed in a very classic way, which suited her. Although she was quite reserved, she was smart and witty and not slow about speaking her mind. Kate often cracked up at her clever, cutting-edge remarks about people and events.

As she watched her friend setting out the Limoges china for the coffee, she marvelled at her touch. Somehow, everything she did was just perfect. Kate admired her enormously and thought back to how they had become friends.

Lauren had always been very interested in interior

design and had realised her dream to study it when her daughter, Daisy, had started playschool eight years before. She had an innate sense of style and when, two years later, she started her own small interior design business, it became an instant success. Danny was very impressed with her work and had asked her to design his new home in Ballyfern. Kate appreciated Lauren's exquisite taste and was very happy with the result. The two women had hit it off instantly. When they moved into the house, Lauren had been the first to call and welcome her, giving Kate the lowdown on the comings and goings of the town.

"Penny for them?" Lauren asked, breaking into her thoughts.

"Oh, I was just thinking how lucky I am to have you for a friend," said Kate with a smile.

"Likewise!" said Lauren. "Now how about a nice slice of chocolate cake? Maggie made it for the boys yesterday, bless her."

Maggie Hanrahan had been with the Smithsons since before Jonathan was born. She was a spinster and was devoted to the family. She considered them her family as she had no relations of her own whatsoever. She was just over seventy but still insisted on working, taking great pride in keeping the house spick and span. She was also a superb cook – cakes her speciality. She lived in the gate lodge on the estate and Jonathan had promised that she could stay there until the end of her days. She was a blessing to Lauren as she was always available to baby-sit and the kids looked on her as their nana. She even had her own room in the main house and slept over whenever necessary.

"Why not? I adore Maggie's cakes. We'll be starving from Monday night on. I intend to eat my way through this weekend as it will be months before I can have all my favourite foods again."

"The feast before the famine!"

"Exactly!"

They laughed like conspirators together.

* * *

Lauren poured herself another cup of coffee and cut another slice of cake as soon as Kate had piled the three boys into her car and left for the riding stables.

What the hell, she thought. In for a penny, in for a pound! Kate's right. It'll be weeks before I can have chocolate cake again. Thank God Jonathan's not around to see me – he'd be disgusted with me. But I'm safe – he won't be back from Dublin for another hour at least.

She thought about what Kate had said and felt that she was the luckier one to have Kate as her friend. Lauren was a very private person whereas Kate was much more outgoing. Lauren had twigged at once that Kate was a real softie with such low self-esteem that she was always being put upon by others. When she came to know Danny better she realised that he was the cause of this. She tried, whenever she could, to get her friend to stand up for herself but Kate had such a sweet nature that it just wasn't in her.

21

To outsiders it appeared that Lauren had it all. A perfect marriage, successful handsome husband, two lovely children, beautiful home, great looks and plenty of money! Not a cloud on the horizon! Sadly, this was not the case. Lauren hid a dark secret from the world, one which she had never shared with anyone, although several times she had been tempted to confide in Kate. Somehow, something always stopped her.

Just then her ten-year-old pretty little pixie of a daughter, Daisy, burst in.

"Oh yummy, there's chocolate cake left! Can I have some?"

"Just a small piece or you won't eat your lunch."

Giving Lauren a big hug, Daisy asked, "Mummy, can you and I go shopping in Dublin this afternoon? Ben's gone riding and Dad's going to golf, so it's just the two of us. I absolutely need a new schoolbag and they've brilliant Harry Potter ones in Brown Thomas. After all, I'm going into fifth class and that's really grown-up! I'll have lots more books than last year and maybe we can even have afternoon tea in the Westbury. I love it there! Mummy, pleeeease?"

Lauren couldn't resist and agreed, laughing. "Okay, okay, I'd really like that too. Now go and change out of those jeans and put on something nice. Grafton Street, here we come!"

★ ★ ★

Jenny Murray was sitting in the Coffee Pot in Naas enjoying her second slice of its delicious banoffee pie when she saw the tall, glamorous woman come in and speak to Mary Brennan, the proprietor.

I bet she doesn't shovel in banoffee pie, thought Jenny. God, she's so slim! What I wouldn't give to have a figure like that!

Jenny was not quite five feet tall, yet weighed eleven stone. She had a mass of auburn curls which fell to her shoulders and which she tied back with many varied scarves and combs. Her eyes were her most striking feature. They were light brown with amber flecks and they seemed to light up her face as she spoke. The phrase 'a twinkle in the eye' was coined for her. She had a smattering of freckles across her nose, just like those little porcelain character-dolls that are so popular. All of these features made her a very pretty woman and the fact that she was always smiling and laughing made her extremely attractive to both sexes. Men found her sexy but women never felt threatened by her. Her style would probably best be described as hippy, if not downright eccentric. She wore long, floating dresses and kaftans which she reckoned best covered up her figure. She almost always wore boots as she felt her legs were not suitable for public viewing. Although she would never have believed it, she had a quite unique style, all her own.

She watched out of the corner of her eye as the glamorous woman spoke to Mary, who must have said something funny, because they both laughed aloud. She noted, with envy, how the woman's golden hair fell like a curtain of silk. Not a sign of a curl or a kink, thought Jenny ruefully while pulling at her own curls, in vain. She had

23

never seen hair that colour before. It wasn't gold and it wasn't red, it was a mixture of the two. Jenny searched for a word to describe it and failed. One thing she was sure of – it hadn't come out of a bottle! She took in the stunning emerald-green eyes and the glowing golden complexion. Wow, she was beautiful! Jenny watched as she hung a poster on the wall of the coffee shop and left.

"God, she certainly wasn't behind the door when He was handing it out," Jenny remarked to Mary, who had brought her another coffee. "What's she selling?"

"See for yourself," Mary replied. "It's very interesting."

Intrigued, Jenny screwed up her eyes but was too far away to read the poster. Putting on her reading glasses, she moved closer and read:

Slimforever Slimming Club
Naas Town Hall
8 p.m. Monday

"What a perfect place to advertise! She certainly knows where to look for customers," laughed Jenny. "It's a wonder you let her!"

"I know – bad for business!" laughed Mary. "But I hear she's fantastic – can talk the weight off you. From the sound of it the whole of Naas will be there on Monday night, myself included."

"I could certainly do with it too, but then you'll lose me – your best customer. She's certainly a great advert for it."

"Isn't she just? Maybe see you there then!" And Mary hurried off to serve another customer.

Just then, Kate entered the coffee shop. She waved to

Jenny, whom she knew well as she had been Toby's teacher in Ballyfern School, and made her way over to her.

"Hi, are you on your own? Can I join you?"

"Yes, and yes," Jenny answered. "How's Toby? He must be excited about starting boarding school."

"Yes, he is, very!" said Kate as she plonked herself down. "He can't wait to go although he is also a little apprehensive. As for me, I'm dreading it. He's always been my baby. I'll be lost without him."

"Of course, it's always difficult letting go. You'll have to keep busy."

"I really will."

"Hey, I've just decided to join the new Slimming Club in Naas on Monday night. Am I mad?"

"Not at all," replied Kate. "I'm joining too!"

"You are? That gives me some courage. At least I'll know someone else there. I hate facing into these things on my own."

"Me too. Look, my friend Lauren is coming in with me – why don't we meet you beforehand and we can all go in together?"

"Oh, that would be great," said Jenny. "That will make it much easier."

"I understand. We'll meet you outside the Town Hall, at eight on Monday."

"Fantastic! I'll be there."

"Now, seeing as how I'll be starving for the next six months or so," said Kate, "I think I'll have a slice of that gorgeous banoffee pie!"

"What the hell! You're right. I'll have another slice to keep you company!"

They chatted on and left together.

As she walked home Jenny was thinking what a nice person Kate was – so caring and thoughtful and a wonderful mother too.

She found herself looking forward to Monday night. God, maybe this is the answer to my prayers, she thought. I have tried every diet imaginable but nothing works. I know I am comfort-eating and I just can't stop.

Please, God, let this work!

Chapter 3

Diana was only just out of bed, even though it was past midday. She was on her fourth cup of black coffee which is all she ever had for breakfast. She was in a foul mood thanks to the heavy hangover she was nursing and had snapped at Kevin several times. He knew when to leave well enough alone and, munching on a biscuit, buried himself in the *Irish Times*. He loved Saturday mornings when he could relax and read the papers at his leisure.

"Could you eat a little more quietly, please? I have a headache," snapped Diana.

Oh Lord, this was one of her worst humours, thought Kevin. You had too much to drink last night, he wanted to say, but knew better than to say it out loud.

"That Kate really gets up my nose," she said. "Did you see how she was preening herself over her cooking last night?"

"Well, you have to admit it was pretty fabulous."

She threw him a withering look. "If it wasn't for Danny

and the interesting people he invites to his dinner parties, I wouldn't go near the place."

With a resigned air, Kevin put his paper down. She was obviously on a roll so his paper would have to wait

Diana wouldn't let go. "She really pisses me off!"

"What's new?" he murmured. Then deciding that attack was the best form of defence, he continued. "You made it fairly obvious last night that you found Michael very interesting – Kate was embarrassed."

"Huh! As if I care!" She shrugged her shoulders. "Anyway, I took the wind out of her sails. Did you see her face when I suggested she join that Slimming Club?" She snickered at the memory. "She almost had a seizure," she added gleefully, pouring yet another cup of coffee.

"I felt really sorry for her – you were being a bitch," Kevin admonished her. "Kate is always so kind to you. I think you should ring her and apologise."

She couldn't believe what he was suggesting. "Fiddle-di-dee! Why should I? I told the truth. She needs to lose weight."

"She's fine. Not everyone can have your figure. After all, she's had four children. You should be more sensitive to her feelings."

Diana jumped up. "Typical! You always stand up for her. She can go to hell, for all I care! I'm off to the golf club."

"When will you be home?"

"No idea. I'll be home when I'm home," and with a toss of her shiny black head, she stormed out.

Kevin sighed. Things were really getting worse between

them. No matter how hard he tried, there was no pleasing her. She had everything she could possibly want but, regardless of how much he gave her, it was never enough. She was envious and resentful of anyone who had more. He was at his wits' end. How had she turned into this vicious, jealous woman? Was he partly to blame?

He'd fallen in love with Diana, almost at first sight, and had been amazed when she had seemed interested in him. She'd been funny and irreverent back then, with a caustic wit, and she hadn't given a damn about anyone. He'd admired her spirit and, although he'd known from the outset that he loved her more than she loved him, he'd thought that he had enough for both of them and that by giving her enough love and TLC they could be happy.

And of course, the sex had been sensational! If there was anything Diana was good at, it was sex. Looking back, he realised that Diana had kept him so enthralled with her sexual expertise that he'd been blind to her faults. He'd been like a lamb to the slaughter, although in fairness they'd had some great times. She'd been softer then and he wanted to believe that she had really loved him when he popped the question and she agreed to be his wife. He now accepted that his love hadn't been enough. Things hadn't improved – they had gone steadily downhill. Sometimes, he got the feeling that she hated him and he often wondered if she was capable of loving anyone. He was seriously beginning to doubt it. Deep down, she didn't like herself and that, he thought, was the real problem.

Still, he wasn't ready to give up on his marriage, quite

yet, and wished that he had someone who could advise him. He'd thought of marriage counselling but he knew Diana wouldn't hear of it. He didn't know where to turn. He had considered confiding in Kate, who was such a rock of sense, but somehow hadn't been able to broach the subject with her.

Thinking of Kate, he decided he'd better phone her now, as Diana certainly wouldn't.

"Hi, Kate, I want to thank you for a wonderful evening. It was lovely and the meal was, as always, superb. I'd also like to apologise for Diana's behaviour."

"You don't have to do that, Kevin. I know Diana didn't mean to be nasty."

"I wish I could believe that. I'm particularly sorry for – eh, that remark about the Slimming Club. It was uncalled for."

"Don't worry! Maybe she has a point. I have decided to join that club, so in fact she did me a favour."

"Well, I think you look fine just as you are, Kate, so pay no attention to Diana."

"You're being kind, Kevin, but I do appreciate it."

"I'll pop over tomorrow, after Mass, to say goodbye to the boys."

"Do that. I don't know how I'll survive next week without them. I'll miss them so much. See you then."

★ ★ ★

On her way to the golf club Diana revved up the BMW

convertible which she had insisted Kevin buy for her, although she rarely put the hood down as it mussed her hair too much. Checking her mobile again to make sure she had a signal, she turned down the Justin Timberlake CD which she normally played at full belt, just in case Michael might call. He had certainly seemed keen last night and had rubbed her thigh deliciously under cover of the table. She had a feeling that bitch Kate had seen it but knew she'd never say anything to Kevin. Not that I care, thought Diana. Michael definitely fancied her and she had let him know that she was interested. She had slipped him her mobile number, with the message, *Call me! Maybe we can get together.* His sour-faced wife had almost caught her doing it. Good enough for her, thought Diana. He wasn't particularly good-looking but he was sexy and exciting and had an animal magnetism and charisma about him which she found irresistible. The only drawback was that he was not very tall and she hated it when a man was shorter than her. She would not abandon her stilettos for any man!

She felt not the least bit guilty and spared no thought for Kevin. The high life was what she wanted – what she deserved. She had married Kevin thinking that he could give it to her but that hadn't happened. She'd thought that, once they were married, she could persuade him to give up his job with Kildare County Council and take a high-powered job in Dublin. He could have done so – what with his first class degree in Engineering and all his family connections – but no, he was happy where he was so she was stuck in hick Ballyfern! He seemed utterly content there and couldn't understand her discontent. He assured her that she would come to love it too. He was earning a pittance in comparison to what he might have earned in the city but this didn't seem to matter one jot to him. To him, living in the city or even commuting to it was his worst nightmare. If it wasn't for her Friday trips to Dublin, she'd have gone stark, raving mad.

Even the golf club was beginning to bore her. Most of the women there were dragons and kept a close eye on their husbands when she was around. She knew they called her a 'man-eater' behind her back. She preferred to think of herself as a *femme fatale*. In this persona, she flounced into the golf club.

★ ★ ★

Later that afternoon, Kate collected the young ones from riding, dropped Ben off and drove home. She planned on having a lovely family night in and would cook them their favourite meal: Pasta Carbonara and Chocolate Mousse. All four would be heading to Hayworth Boarding School the following day, for the start of a new school year.

As they arrived home Danny met her at the front door and swung her off her feet.

"What the hell . . .?" she cried.

He waltzed her into the drawing-room where he had champagne cooling in an ice bucket, the boys following them in amazement.

"I did it, I did it!" he cried exuberantly. "I've won the London contract! Michael rang me this afternoon." He was beside himself with excitement. "This will mean millions for us, darling, and make me the most successful builder in the country. It's time to celebrate! I've booked Moyglare Manor for all six of us tonight. So, guys, go get dressed up in your best gear and put on the glad rags, Kate! We've made it, we've arrived! *Yippeee!*"

Kate was dismayed. "I was really looking forward to a quiet night in together before the boys go back to school. Do we have to go out? Can't we stay in?" she pleaded.

"Don't be a spoilsport! This is a very important night for me. This is the biggest deal of my life."

Not mine, thought Kate secretly. Now I'll see even less of him. He's made his millions – we have enough – why does he need more?

She tried to smile and put on a happy face, for the boys' sake, but her heart sank even further when Danny added, "I have to fly to London tomorrow evening, for meetings."

"What about your business here? Who'll take care of that?"

"James will, for the moment. He's bright and ambitious. I can trust it to him."

Kate didn't agree. She didn't like Danny's young assistant at all. He was far too arrogant and cocky. "I wouldn't trust him as far as I'd throw him," she'd told Danny. "He's only out for himself." Danny had laughed at her. He didn't believe in female intuition. Kate did and all her instincts told her she was right.

"I'll be home every weekend and I can catch up on business then," Danny added.

Every weekend! It starts already, thought Kate as she went upstairs to change and make-up.

She thought she understood his ambition and his need for success. He was the eldest of nine and they'd lived in squalor and poverty with a drunken waster of a father and a worn-out mother. Danny had been an excellent student at school but he'd had to leave at fifteen and go to work on the building sites in London. He'd worked day and night and saved every penny. Seven years later he'd returned to Dublin and started his own building company. He had been a workaholic ever since and Kate was very proud of his success. But it was never enough for him. However much success he had, he wanted more.

He was cock-a-hoop all evening – she'd never seen him so buoyant. The meal was wonderful, as always, but she still would have preferred to have been in her own home having a simple pasta. She tried, for Danny's sake, to be upbeat but the fact that she knew her sons would also have preferred to be at home didn't help. She knew that they were trying to make the best of it also, because it was what their dad wanted. It was always all about Danny, wasn't it, she thought, and felt instantly disloyal. She did her best to put a good face on it but her heart was heavy.

They made love, later that night, and Danny was on such a high that he didn't even notice her lack of response.

★ ★ ★

The next day, Sunday, Kate woke with a horrible anxious

feeling and it only took her a moment to realise why. Today the boys were going back to school. She had loved having them around for the summer. Although they were often busy with their friends and their many interests, they were always coming and going and more often than not they had a posse of friends in tow. She loved it when the house was full of young people and spent many happy hours in the kitchen, cooking and baking for them. They wolfed it all down as though they had never had a decent meal in their lives and were always full of praise for her cooking. She suspected that the majority of them survived on frozen or fast food, as most of their mothers were busy career women. She guessed that these mothers were delighted to be rid of their offspring whenever they got the chance.

Not Kate. She adored her four boys and would miss them dreadfully when they were gone.

She would soon have to stop calling them 'her boys' as Justin, the eldest, was almost eighteen and going into his Leaving Certificate year. David was going into fifth year, Sam into third and Toby, the youngest, just starting. It almost broke her heart to think of him leaving home. He was still only a baby at heart but was trying so hard to act grown up in front of his brothers and friends. His hugs and cuddles had become even more frequent in the past few days – always when there was no one else around, of course. And now Danny would not be able to accompany them to the school as planned because he had to catch his flight to London. She'd have to take them and drive back alone and didn't know how she would bear it.

In all of their married life, their sons' schooling was the only major thing that Danny and she had argued about. She had wanted the boys to attend the local Secondary School in Naas but Danny wouldn't hear of it. He'd had to leave school at fifteen and cut short his education. Now that he could afford it, he wanted his sons to have the best education available and Hayworth was where he felt they would get it. They had fought bitterly over this but, despite her pleading and tears, Danny had got his way. The boys were happy, she knew, but who knew whether they would not have been just as happy living at home?

She now dreaded the school term beginning and it didn't help that Danny would also be away. The week stretched endlessly ahead of her. She got up and headed for the kitchen and after a cup of coffee started to bake cakes and biscuits for the boys to take back with them. She let them have a lie-in, their last for a while, and at ten o'clock she started to cook a big Irish breakfast, with all the trimmings. She knew the smell of sausages and bacon wafting up the stairs would do the trick. One after the other her hungry teenagers – weren't they always hungry? – came sleepily into the kitchen.

Over breakfast, they chatted about the holidays and the coming term. Justin was full of excitement as he had been elected Captain of the Senior Rugby Team, which was a huge honour, and he couldn't wait to get back to training – although he was going to have to study really hard this year. He had set his heart on studying medicine and that would require very good results in his Leaving Cert Exam.

Kevin arrived, just as they finished, and Danny shared his good news with him as Kate made fresh coffee.

"Congratulations!" said Kevin. "That's great news. Does that mean you'll have to be in London a lot?"

"Probably."

Kevin saw the look of pain that crossed Kate's face. She was going to find that difficult what with Toby gone too, he thought. He shot her a look of sympathy and she shrugged her shoulders.

Toby was delighted with the going-away present Kevin had brought for him.

"A book about rugby, cool! Gee, thanks a million, Kevin. Look, Justin!" They all crowded around Toby to have a look.

"Thanks, Kevin," Danny said.

Kate smiled at him. "That was very thoughtful."

Kevin said goodbye to the boys and wished Danny good luck in London.

The three older boys went down the town to say a last goodbye to their friends. Toby stayed home as Lauren was bringing Ben over to say goodbye to him. Ben was even more upset than Toby as he had another year to do in primary school and would miss his best buddy. Much to Lauren's chagrin, he was already talking excitedly about joining Toby in Hayworth next year.

Lunch was a very quiet affair although Danny was in high spirits and tried to laugh and joke with them. After lunch the dreaded moment arrived for Kate as she oversaw the boys' final packing. There was bedlam for a while as they loaded all their gear into the car and said their goodbyes to Danny, who was heading off to the airport to catch his flight to London.

The journey to the school was over all too fast. All too soon, holding back the tears so as not to embarrass her sons, she was hugging them goodbye.

Feeling really down, she got into the car and drove off. Her heart almost broke when she saw the forlorn little figure of Toby getting smaller and smaller, waving to her until she reached the gates at the end of the drive. Please God, let him be happy here, she prayed. Otherwise I couldn't bear it.

She stopped at the local chipper and bought fish and chips for her supper. She couldn't be bothered cooking, just for herself. Back home, she watched television for a time, then she tried to read, but she couldn't concentrate on the words in front of her. She wandered around the empty house but its emptiness mocked her. Finally she opened a box of chocolates and a bottle of wine and set to, wallowing in her misery. She dragged herself up to bed two hours later. Mercifully the alcohol had done its work and she fell into a deep, troubled sleep.

Chapter 4

The following morning Kate woke with a dreadful hangover and an awful feeling in the pit of her stomach. The house felt empty and lonely, as did she. She tried to pull herself together and after numerous cups of coffee she helped Betty – the woman Danny insisted she have in every day to clean – to tackle the boys' rooms and their laundry, which kept her going all day.

Lauren rang that afternoon, to see how she was coping and to remind her of their date for the Slimming Club that night.

"Oh Lord, I'd clean forgot! Maybe I'll leave it till next week."

"You'll do no such thing," Lauren answered bossily. "I'll pick you up at seven thirty, and don't forget that you told Jenny we would meet her there."

"Oh God, I never felt less like it but I suppose I can't let her down."

"Dead right!"

"Well, if that's the case I'd better begin my last supper, which could possibly go on all day!" Kate had finally found something to laugh at. Lauren joined in. "That's my girl. See you then."

* * *

It was seven o'clock that evening and what Kate really wanted to do was open a bottle of wine, drink it up and then crawl into bed. She considered ringing Lauren to cry off but knew what little sympathy she would get. Besides, she felt that Jenny would be upset if she didn't turn up. She had seen the look of hope in her eyes when she'd said that she'd be there with her tonight.

How do I get myself into these situations, she asked herself. Then she remembered Diana's remark last Friday night and Danny's also.

Okay, she told herself. This is it! I need to lose weight and this is my chance. Get yourself together, girl!

And so it was that she was ready and waiting when Lauren called for her, as arranged.

"You can drive next week," said Lauren.

"If we last that long!"

"Don't be so negative. We're in this for the long haul." Lauren was taking no prisoners.

* * *

As Jenny set out to meet them in Naas, she could hardly

believe that Lauren Smithson was actually going to a slimming class. Why, every woman and man in Ballyfern, and indeed those who knew her in Naas, thought she was the most gorgeous creature ever. Tall, slim, elegant – definitely not fat! Yet here she was, joining a Slimming Club with her. Wonders will never cease, thought Jenny. She didn't know Lauren all that well but had always admired her from afar. She was impossible to miss – a very beautiful and imposing woman. Jenny sensed that she was a very private person. Mind you, if she was a friend of Kate's then she had to be okay.

She arrived at the Town Hall at the same moment as Lauren and Kate and they were all dismayed to find a long queue winding its way from the Town Hall down Main Street.

"Oh God, I can't face this," said Kate.

"Me neither," agreed Jenny.

"Let's go home!" suggested Kate.

"What cop-outs! We're here and we're bloody well going to stay!" Lauren cried. "Let's go into Fletcher's and I'll treat you two to a stiff brandy, which might give you some courage. I'm sure that when we come back the queue will be almost gone."

The other two readily agreed. A reprieve! They hoped that when they came back there would be an even bigger queue and then they could go home. Sadly for them, when they got back there was practically no queue left.

"There!" Lauren grinned. "See, told you so. Nothing ventured, nothing gained."

"I'm not here to gain, I'm here to lose," joked Jenny.

"Onwards and upwards, girls!"

Kate and Jenny looked at each other helplessly, realising that they were in the hands of a Godzilla. Their fate was sealed. They took their places in the queue which moved amazingly fast and entered the hall to find, to their shock, what looked like a hundred women already there.

Kate was shocked. "Oh my God, I don't believe this!"

Even Lauren looked a bit put out. "This is unbelievable. Where have they all come from? Are there really so many overweight women around?"

"Obviously," replied Jenny, who felt relieved to see that many of them were much more overweight than she was. She began to feel positively skinny. Why, the woman in front of her was more than double her size – twenty-four stone at least! She waved to Mary from the Coffee Pot who was sitting in the front row with a friend.

A woman registered them, took their details and their money and gave them membership cards and diet booklets. She then asked them to take a seat and told them that Tara would address the gathering shortly and would explain the procedures. They felt a bit like sheep as they took their seats and hoped that this was not all a big mistake and a pure waste of time and money. Ten minutes later the stunningly beautiful woman that Jenny had seen in the coffee shop in Naas got up to address them.

"Welcome, ladies! Sadly I can't say 'ladies and gentlemen', as unfortunately no man is brave enough to join us yet. But I live in hope. My name is Tara . . . and yes, my mother was reading *Gone with the Wind* just before I was born. Luckily, I'm not called Scarlett!"

They all laughed and, after a pause for the laughter to subside, Tara continued.

"It's wonderful to see so many here tonight. I'm sorry that it took so long to register you all, but to be honest I'm stunned by the huge turnout. I will now weigh you in, row by row, and give you your target weight. Then I'll give a little talk to explain the principles of the club – diet etc – and then we'll have a short exercise session, which I promise will not be too taxing."

Tara paused and then, allowing her gaze to sweep over the room, continued more earnestly.

"I don't offer a miracle but if you put yourself in my hands and follow my advice, I promise you, you *will* succeed. Tonight could be the night that will change your life forever. You are at a crossroads. Either you keep on the road you're on, overeating and under-exercising, getting fatter and fatter, or you let me lead you down the other road, eating less and exercising more and getting slimmer and slimmer. There's no secret to losing weight. It's as simple as that. Most of you know that already but you just need someone to help you do it. I'm that someone! I can help you but only if you want to be helped. It's up to you. If you're not serious about it, there's no point in wasting your time here. Why should you do it? *Because you're worth it!*"

"Wow!" whispered Kate to Jenny, looking apprehensive. "She sure means business."

"She certainly doesn't mince words," whispered Jenny back, giggling nervously.

Fantastic – just my kind of woman – tells it as it is, Lauren thought. If anyone can help Kate lose weight and regain her confidence, she can. Thank God I made her come here tonight.

Lauren was very impressed with this beautiful woman. She'd have made a super model, she thought, taking in the figure, the cheekbones and her colouring.

"She's stunning, isn't she?" said Jenny.

"Yes, indeed," agreed Lauren. "Her eyes are so intensely green they're the closest thing to emeralds I've ever seen."

"It's her figure that fascinates me," said Kate. "How does she keep it like that?"

The woman beside Kate overheard this last remark and leaned over to the three girls.

"She has seven children, can you believe it?"

"No, I can't. How does she do it?" Kate asked with awe.

"Discipline, I expect. Not like us. Where are you all from?"

"A town called Ballyfern, about ten miles from here. And you?"

"There are five of us, down from Dublin. We went to her Maynooth class last term, but this is handier. We've all lost over two stone. Wait till you see. She's fantastic. She'll motivate you like no one can. We've all tried every club and diet imaginable but Tara is the only one who works for us. We couldn't live without her."

"Gosh, I hope you're right," said Jenny. "We need something drastic."

And then it was their turn to be weighed in. By this stage Kate was shaking and almost afraid to face this paragon, who sounded very intimidating. But when her turn came she was charmed by Tara's friendly smile and the kindness in her eyes. She felt she had found an ally.

Tara weighed her and asked, "What weight would you like to be, Kate?"

"Ideally, nine stone, but I know I'd never be able to get to that."

"Of course, you will. That's less than three stone you have to lose, and you will. Trust me!"

Kate did and floated back to her seat.

"I don't believe it," she told Lauren. "She really thinks I can do it."

"Of course, she does. And so do I," replied Lauren.

Jenny came back beaming from ear to ear. "You know, she really makes me believe I can lose two and a half stone. It's incredible. I can't wait to start."

They stayed for the talk and the exercise session and left, buoyed up with hope. Lauren had only ten pounds to lose but, as she confided to the girls on the way back to the car-park, Tara had told her that the last half stone was the most stubborn, so she'd be likely to lose it very slowly.

"I nearly died when I saw that gossip Agnes O'Reilly there," said Kate. "I was hoping we wouldn't meet anyone from Ballyfern. Now it will be all around the town tomorrow that we were there."

"Why should we care?" replied Lauren.

"She can't have anything much to lose," remarked Jenny.

"I bet she was just there out of curiosity. The Nosey Parker! Anyway, we've nothing to be ashamed of."

"Isn't Tara amazing? Some women have it all," sighed Kate.

"Yes, she's beautiful," Lauren agreed "but I think it's her personality that makes her so attractive."

"She has an aura. I think it's what they call charisma," said Kate. "You know, the way some people just have this magnetic attraction. Bill Clinton has it, I believe."

"JFK had it too," Jenny chimed in. "Strange I can't think of any woman who has it."

"I can. Princess Diana had it," Lauren said with sadness in her voice. She'd loved Princess Di. "She was truly charismatic. Everybody adored her."

"She definitely had it," Kate agreed. "And now Tara has it too, lucky girl!"

"Seven kids – I just can't believe it!" said an astounded Jenny.

As they reached the carpark, Lauren turned to them. "It's too late tonight to go in for a drink but next week, girls, I suggest that we have no dinner before we go to Slimforever – after all, we will want to weigh as little as possible at the weigh-in, and then we'll go for something to eat after the class. What do you say?"

"Great idea!" chorused the other two.

They parted company and when Kate got home to the empty house she went straight to bed, just in case she would be tempted to have a drink or start munching chocolates. Strange, but she felt like a new woman. She was really determined to give it a go. For the first time ever, she felt she could see some light at the end of the tunnel.

* * *

Kate woke the next morning with the feeling that something important was about to happen. Then she remembered. Today was a big day for her. She would take the first step on the road to slimness. As she sipped a cup of coffee, she read through the diet booklet that Tara had given her the previous night and made out a list of all that she would need to buy from it. It didn't seem too difficult. No chocolates, obviously, and definitely no wine! The first thing she did was, as Tara had instructed, dump all the fattening goodies – crisps, chocolate, biscuits and cakes – in the bin. Tara's words were ringing in her ears: "Better in the bin than on your hips and thighs!"

She arrived at Behan's supermarket at nine, to find Lauren there before her, also holding a list.

"Great minds think alike!" laughed Lauren.

"And I'm sure Jenny would be here too, if she didn't have school," said Kate. "Did you dump all the goodies?"

"As much as I could. I have to keep some things for Daisy and Ben. Jonathan has a sweet tooth too but it will do him no harm to go without."

"I'm lucky that the boys are away at school and Danny is not there either, so I dumped everything, except the fruit cake, which I don't eat. And I measured myself, as Tara asked us to do, and got a nasty shock. I'm even bigger than I thought."

47

"Okay, let's go. And remember, 'if you don't buy it – you can't eat it'," said Lauren, mimicking Tara's words.

"Listen to us – we're quoting her like she was the Messiah!" Kate laughed.

"For now, she *is* our Messiah," Lauren replied, laughing too.

They did their shopping, buying almost identical items and were not happy to see Agnes O'Reilly behind them at the checkout. She was an insignificant, mousey-looking woman, with small squinting eyes constantly darting this way and that, in case she missed something. She reminded Kate of a ferret. Her probing eyes zoomed in on their baskets.

In her pipsqueak voice, but loud enough for the whole shop to hear, she announced to one and all, "I see the girls are starting on their diets!"

Kate found herself blushing furiously but Lauren was well able for Agnes.

"Hope you're going to stick to the diet too, Agnes, seeing as how you joined the Slimming Club last night."

Now it was Agnes's turn to blush, as Lauren drew herself up to her full height. She slowly, slowly, put each item on the counter, daring Agnes to remark on anything and when they'd paid, again excruciatingly slowly, she took Kate's arm and marched out of the shop, her head held high.

Once outside they burst into laughter and they were still laughing as Agnes brushed past them, her pointy little nose in the air.

"That's put her in her place," Kate said, wiping the tears from her eyes.

They decided not to go into the hotel for coffee as they normally would do as they felt the temptation of the cheesecake might be too much for them on their first day.

"Good luck! Ring me if you find the going too tough," Lauren advised Kate.

"Likewise! Tara said we were to give each other moral support."

★ ★ ★

Unknown to the two girls, Jenny was actually an hour ahead of them. She had been the first customer into Superquinn in Naas at eight that morning. She'd whizzed home and made the healthy breakfast on the diet plan before leaving for Ballyfern and school. She'd cleared out the cupboards the night before. She'd also packed a chicken salad for lunch and an apple for elevenses. No more chips every day in the Ballyfern Inn and definitely no more chocolate éclairs at break. She could almost see her halo glowing. She had never felt so positive in her life.

She had come home last night, full of enthusiasm, raving about the club and the diet but Tom, her husband, had laughed and said, "You'll never do it. You know you can't stick to a diet."

This had infuriated her. How dared he! If anything, his comment had given her the final motivation to succeed. I'll show him, she vowed.

★ ★ ★

That afternoon, as the girls were experiencing their first day of deprivation, Diana was in a quandary.

She had just started her Pilates class in the gym when her mobile phone rang. Despite the disapproving looks that Anna the instructor and the other students had thrown her, she had grabbed it and left the room. To her delight, it was the call from Michael that she had been hoping for. When he asked her if she was free that evening she tried to play it cool.

"Not this evening," she answered.

"That's a pity," he replied, "It could have been interesting. Well, goodbye, Di . . ."

Before he could hang up, she quickly cut in, saying in her sexiest voice, "But I could meet you Friday evening."

"Leave it with me. I'll see what I can do."

She was kicking herself. She could easily have met him that evening but, in an effort to play hard-to-get, she might have blown it. She knew from experience that men loved the chase and, if you appeared too keen, they lost interest. However, Michael was a different story. He could probably have any woman he wanted.

She went back to her Pilates but could barely concentrate on the exercises. For the rest of the day she waited for his call and when he didn't ring she went home in a thoroughly foul mood. Kevin tried to humour her but failed miserably and retired to his office in despair, on the pretext of having some work to do.

Chapter 5

On Wednesday evening, Kevin dropped in to Kate on his way home, to give her the latest John Grisham book that he'd promised her and which he'd just finished reading. He was keen to hear how things were going for Danny in London and Toby at his new school. She brought him up to date on them as she made coffee, but he could see that she wasn't her usual chirpy self.

"And how are you coping?" he asked her, when they were seated at the kitchen table with the coffee and a slice of fruit cake for him.

"Not very well, I'm afraid. I miss Toby dreadfully. The days are so long I don't know what to do with myself. I really wish I didn't have Betty coming in to clean every day – at least it would keep me occupied – but Danny would go crazy if I let her go."

"You really should consider getting a job, Kate. You could turn your hand to anything." He popped a piece of cake in his mouth. "Mmmm, this is delicious!"

"Glad you like it," Kate smiled. "Yeah, I've thought about a job. But you know Danny better than anyone – he'd hate me to be out working. He considers himself the breadwinner and he does that very well, I have to say. He's proud of the fact that he provides so well for us and that I can stay home but, honestly, I'm feeling so useless with the boys all away. It's as if I have no purpose in life any more. Now, with this new contract, I reckon I'll be seeing less and less of Danny too. I'm just so bored. Maybe I will broach the subject of a job with him."

"I know Danny is proud of what he has achieved," said Kevin quietly, "and . . . well . . . knowing where he came from – can you blame him? Funny, he never would invite me to his home even though I was his best friend in the school. He was ashamed of it. He wanted a better life for himself. He once told me that he wouldn't stop until he'd made his first million."

"Well, he made that a long time ago, and many more since, but he'll never stop. He'll never have enough."

"People who come from a very poor background often feel like that, Kate. I think they harbour a fear of being poor again. Like Diana. You know she had a dreadful childhood too?"

Kate looked surprised. "No, I didn't know that. She's never mentioned her past to me – not at all."

"No, I suppose not. She's very ashamed of it too. When we met, she told me that her parents were dead but that was a lie. It all came out one night when she was drunk but she has absolutely refused to discuss it ever since."

"That's terrible! But why would she lie about them?" Kate asked him, a puzzled look on her face.

"Well, like Danny, she comes from a very large family. She was the youngest of seven. Seemingly, her father was a drunken bully who abused the children, both physically and sexually, and Diana most of all."

"Oh my God, how dreadful! Poor Diana!"

"She never forgave her mother for allowing it to happen," he continued. "She ran away from home at fourteen and has never had any contact with them since. It's as if she has erased them from her life."

"Can't say I blame her! Where did she go when she ran away?" Kate was shocked by these revelations. How little we know of people, she thought.

"To Dublin," he answered, "where she got a job in a hairdressing salon. Her real name is Mary but that was much too ordinary for a swish Dublin salon. The owner gave her the name of Diana – Princess Diana was in her heyday at the time. Diana would have preferred to have been called Madonna, but seemingly there was already a stylist with that name."

Kate couldn't resist a smile. "I can imagine why – Madonna would have been more her type."

"In any case, she wasn't in a position to disagree – so Diana she became. Anyway, she has never laid eyes on any of her family since that day, nor does she want to."

"How unutterably sad! It probably explains a lot of her behaviour."

"Yeah, that's what I thought at the time. I thought that

if I made her feel loved and cherished, she would heal, but it hasn't worked. The scars are too deep. She's still bitter and resentful and I can't do anything about it. I sometimes wonder if anyone could make her happy, Kate. I'm seriously beginning to doubt it."

He let out a long sigh as he ran his fingers through his hair. "I'm really worried – I just don't know what to do. I'm not sure I can go on any longer. Our marriage is a sham." His voice was breaking and he had tears in his eyes. Embarrassed, he wiped them away and with a little laugh, said, "Any chance of another slice of cake? Just a small slice – comfort food – I need it!"

She cut another slice for him and poured more coffee. He looked so down and dejected that her heart went out to him.

"Oh Kevin, don't give up on her! Obviously her childhood has had an effect on her, just like Danny's. It has made them both so ambitious for the things that money can buy. They don't realise that money can't buy the most important things – love and security and peace of mind." She shook her head. "Have you thought of counselling for her?"

"I have, but Diana won't hear of it."

"What about a baby? Sometimes motherhood changes people completely."

"Forget that! She's told me she can't have children and she won't consider adopting, although I would love to. Diana's not exactly the maternal type. It would interfere with her social life too much." He gave a bitter smile.

Kate had to admit that he was probably right. "She always seems so driven. She and Danny make a good pair. You know, I've often thought that we four are mismatched. I would be perfectly happy living in a nice bungalow like yours, or even the semi-detached house we had when we were first married, if I could have my family around me. I'd swap this mansion in the morning if I could have the boys coming home from the local school every evening and Danny here with us for dinner every night."

"You and Diana are like chalk and cheese. She would love to live here and wouldn't care if she never saw me from one end of the week to the other. She'd spend her time entertaining and showing off to all her – cronies – I wouldn't call them friends!" Kevin snorted with disgust. "Well, enough of my problems. I hope you enjoy the book as much as I did. It's very similar to *The Firm,* which I loved. He's a brilliant writer. I don't know how he churns them out."

They chatted about their favourite books and authors as they finished their coffee and Kevin promised to lend her the latest Harlan Coben book that he'd just bought, when he finished it.

"Well, it's time I was going. I didn't mean to burden you with my problems but it's been good to talk about it, Kate – a relief, in fact. Thanks for listening."

"What are friends for? Take care, Kevin."

"You too, Kate. You're one in a million. Danny is one helluva lucky guy."

Kate felt sad when he'd left. I'm so lucky really, she

thought. I won't complain any more. Poor Kevin, he has so much to offer! And how tough it must be for Diana too, with no family and no children. Of course, I suppose she could adopt children, if she really wanted to, and she's lucky to have Kevin if only she would realise it. Please God she will, before it's too late. I hope their marriage can survive, for both their sakes.

* * *

Kate rang Jenny on Wednesday night.

"How's it going – finding it tough?"

"Surprisingly, no. I find that writing everything I eat down, as Tara told us, is a great help. If I've had a good day, then I don't want to spoil it. If I've had a bad day then I don't want to make it worse. And you?"

"Exactly the same. I find writing it down a great help too. The nights are the hardest, of course."

"Me too, and I'm dreading the weekend. I've invited seven of the teachers from school over for lunch on Sunday and I just don't know what I can serve without breaking my diet. Of course, I could cook something separately for myself but, apart from it being a hassle, it would be so embarrassing – for them as well as for me."

"It shouldn't be too difficult to plan a suitable menu."

"Maybe not for you, Kate – you're such a brilliant cook."

"Look, why don't you pop in tomorrow after school and in the meantime I'll rustle up some tasty, low-calorie recipes for you?"

"Would you, Kate? You're a gem!"

"No problem. See you then."

Kate then rang Lauren and recounted her conversation with Jenny.

"Would you mind if I come too?" asked Lauren anxiously. "Jonathan has invited people for Sunday lunch and I'm in the same boat. I can't decide what to give them."

"Of course, you're always welcome. There'll be no cake though – strictly coffee only. Bring the kids if you like."

"No need. Daisy has ballet and Ben is going to a birthday party, so I'm free."

"Looking forward to a good chat. See you then."

Chapter 6

It wasn't strictly coffee. When Lauren and Jenny arrived on Thursday afternoon they found that Kate had made beautiful little parcels of fresh fruit salad, topped with fat-free fromage frais. And they couldn't believe their eyes when they saw the selection of recipes that she had prepared for them.

"All guaranteed to let you stick to your diet," she grinned.

"Kate, you're a bloody genius!" Lauren told her.

"Your talent is wasted," said Jenny. "You could earn a fortune doing this."

"I wish I could. I'm going crazy here all week on my own. I have so much free time on my hands."

"God, Kate, anyone in their right mind would be delighted to have you. I'm just thinking – Mary from the coffee shop is looking for someone," Jenny informed her. "Her pastry chef is getting married and moving to Galway and she's quite desperate."

"Gosh, I'd love that, but Danny would never allow it."

"Excuse me? Allow it?" exclaimed Lauren with that cool, appraising look that only she could give. "You're almost forty years old, Kate – time to do what *you* want. Danny will get used to it."

"I don't think so. Maybe I'll try and broach the subject to him when he comes home tomorrow night."

"Well, I must be off," said Lauren. "Have to pick up Daisy from ballet." Then she added with a laugh, "I'm just a chauffeur for these kids. That's all mothers are these days!"

"Don't complain!" replied Jenny wistfully. "I'd give anything to be a chauffeur to my kids, if I was lucky enough to have them."

Lauren could have bitten off her tongue. She hadn't meant it of course. She adored being there for her kids but she had forgotten that Jenny was desperately trying for a baby, with no success. God, I'm so thoughtless, she admonished herself.

"Oh, I don't really mind," she said awkwardly as she gathered up her things. "I'm just moaning out of habit!"

"I know," said Jenny hastily.

Kate got up to accompany Lauren to the door.

"Jenny, I hope you keep the diet going over the weekend!" said Lauren. "Good luck!"

"Same to you!"

Kate had seen the hurt in Jenny's eyes at Lauren's throwaway innocent remark. She couldn't begin to comprehend what it would be like, not to have children in her life. She could only imagine how awful it must be for Jenny.

When she came back from seeing Lauren off, she said, as casually as she could, "Jenny, do you have anything on tonight? If not, would you consider having dinner with me? I've really had a goddamn awful week and would appreciate your company. I'll understand if you can't, of course, but –"

"Kate, I'd love to. To be honest, I'm alone most nights. Tom spends almost every night at either the rugby club or the golf club. He's on the committees of both and they see much more of him than I do, so I would be delighted to stay and have dinner with you. It sure as hell will beat having yet another dinner alone, in front of the TV."

"Great! I find it very lonely all week, what with Toby and the others gone and Danny away. I'm being selfish, feeling very sorry for myself."

"So you should be! And you're not being selfish – I'll be very happy to keep you company."

"Great. And don't worry, we're having fish and it's all low fat and low carbohydrate, to fit in with our diet. But I think a glass of wine is called for. I know it's not allowed but we've been so good and this is a crisis. I'll get it out of the fridge."

An hour later, Kate and Jenny were into their second bottle of Chablis.

"Oh, to hell with it!" said Kate. "We'll make up for it tomorrow. Anyway, it's strange but I feel slimmer already, after only four days. I know it's probably only in the head, but I really do."

"No, it's not in the head. It's in the knees," said Jenny giggling. "I really noticed it in the bath last night. My knees are definitely slimmer."

"Here's to skinny knees!" Kate was laughing so much she could hardly get the words out. "God, I think I'm getting drunk."

"Not 'getting' – *already* drunk," remarked Jenny. "Uh, uh, I think it's time for coffee."

"Jenny, could you stay the night? If Tom's not home he won't mind and the guest-room is always made up."

"Okay! I was thinking of getting a taxi as I'm over the limit. I'll give Tom a ring on his mobile and let him know."

By the time Jenny had spoken to Tom, Kate had made a decision.

She took Jenny's hands in her own, her eyes full of gentle concern. "Jenny, please tell me if I'm speaking out of turn, but I saw your hurt when Lauren passed that remark about being a chauffeur and I'm sure she didn't mean it but –"

Jenny cut her short. "Oh, please don't feel bad, Kate. I'm over-sensitive when it comes to babies." And without warning, she started to cry.

"Oh, sweetheart, I'm so sorry!" Kate put her arms around her. "There, there, I understand."

"I'm so sorry, Kate," Jenny said, sniffling. "I'm making a fool of myself. It's just that I've wanted a baby for so long. You can't imagine how awful it is to have this yearning inside you and not be able to fulfil it."

Kate couldn't begin to imagine what Jenny was going through. She only knew that she couldn't have borne it, if she had been in that position. She got up to get Jenny a tissue and helped her dry her eyes.

Her kindness touched Jenny and, as so many people

found with Kate, she found herself spilling out all her hurt.

"I was thirty-six when I met Tom and, to be honest, I thought that I was on the shelf. I thought that he was my last chance and, to be truthful, I married him so that I could have children. But it hasn't happened. I've been to a specialist and he says there's no reason why I can't have a baby, even at my age."

"Of course not," Kate assured her. "Women are having babies now well into their forties."

"I've tried to talk to Tom but he won't listen," Jenny continued. "He has an eighteen-year-old son, Mark, from his first marriage, but he takes no interest in him whatsoever."

"God, that's terrible! The poor boy!"

"If Mark was sporty, they would possibly be closer, but he isn't," Jenny continued, still wiping her eyes. "Tom expected to have a big macho son but Mark's a very sensitive, artistic kind of guy, into art and classical music – not exactly Tom's cup of tea! It's a shame. I feel so sorry for him – he's really sweet."

"The poor kid," Kate said. She couldn't understand how any parent could treat a child like that.

"Anyway, I've asked Tom to come to the specialist with me to see why I can't conceive but he won't hear of it. He maintains that it's not his fault, as he already has a son, and that it's my weight that's making me infertile."

"That's ridiculous!" Kate was incensed. "His sperm could have deteriorated. That happens, you know. It might not be your fault at all." She was disgusted that he should cite Jenny's weight for her inability to conceive – without at least having it checked out medically.

"Yeah, but I'm afraid it might be." Jenny started crying again. "That's what's made me so desperate for this diet to succeed. I really don't know where to turn. Sometimes I feel I would have been better off trying a sperm bank and bringing up a baby on my own if I conceived, than being where I'm at now."

Kate's heart went out to Jenny and she put her arms around her again. She was at a loss for words – what could she possibly say to ease Jenny's pain? "I wish there was something I could do to help," she said.

"You are helping, Kate, just by listening." It was so cathartic to be able to share her pain. She felt Kate, who was such a good mother, understood her need.

"I feel so selfish, complaining about Danny, when at least I have my boys."

"You're a wonderful mother, Kate."

"I hope so. Sometimes though, I wonder what my marriage would be like if I didn't have the boys to think about. This week has made me sit up and think. I'm beginning to feel so useless."

"Don't be silly!" Now it was Jenny's turn to take Kate's hand.

"No, really. I've been someone's daughter, sister, wife and mother, but really that's about it. I've never been *me*. I seem to have been living my life through other people."

"I know what you mean. I've often felt like that too."

"This week with the last of the boys gone and Danny

away, I've been asking myself if I have any purpose in life." Kate's voice was forlorn as she continued. "I seem to have become totally dependent on looking after others and now that they don't need me I feel like a waste of space,"

"Oh, don't be daft! You and Danny are obviously very happy together."

"Yeah, but he takes me for granted. Love only survives as long as it's nurtured and I'm beginning to ask myself if men know anything about bloody nurturing."

"Well, they sure as hell do when they first meet you and want to sweep you off your feet, but somewhere along the way they reckon you don't need to be nurtured any more. Big mistake!"

"Absolutely – I'll drink to that!" Kate raised her glass. She and Jenny had bared their souls to each other and she had a feeling that they would be close friends from now on.

* * *

Diana was certainly not thinking of her marriage on Thursday night nor of the need to save it. All she cared about was whether Michael would contact her again. She knew she was behaving like a teenager. She was furious with herself for being so stupid as to turn him down when he had rung. She now didn't go anywhere without her mobile phone and if she found herself with no signal, or in a noisy shop, she got out of there immediately. She'd even refused to play golf that day, which was Ladies' Day, just in case Michael might ring again. No way could she take her mobile on the course – the other women would lynch her!

This is ridiculous, she said to herself and just then, when she was despairing he'd ever call again, he rang. Her heart was racing wildly as she answered.

"Hi, sexy," purred Michael.

"Hi, sexy, yourself," she replied. Oh thank you, God, thank you! No more playing it cool.

"That's okay for tomorrow night. Can you meet me at seven thirty – downstairs in the Merrion Hotel bar?"

"Tomorrow, seven thirty. I'll be there," answered Diana, in a voice that she knew was throatily sexy, because that's how she was feeling. Really sexy and turned on!

"Can you stay the night?" he asked. "I promise it will be a night you won't forget."

"I don't doubt it," laughed Diana. "How could I resist an invitation like that?"

She couldn't believe it. Yes! Yes! Yes! Oh my God, I can't wait, she thought excitedly as she dashed upstairs to survey her wardrobe – and more importantly her lingerie drawer. It took her ages to decide between the coffee and cream La Perla set or the black Agent Provocateur one. In the end she opted for the La Perla. The black might be too much and she guessed Michael would appreciate the classy one more – for now, anyway. Plenty of time for the black one later, when she really wanted to drive him crazy. Not that the one she'd chosen wasn't sexy – it did have a suspender belt, which all men loved – but it was demure sexy.

She was so happy that she was singing as she swished around the bedroom. She heard Kevin's key in the door and just had time to put the stuff away before he walked into the bedroom.

"Are you okay?" she asked, noticing the droop of his shoulders and the grey look on his face.

"Tough day," he replied.

"You go have a nice shower and I'll fix you a drink and we can have a chat about it," she said, giving him a peck on the cheek and a big smile.

He couldn't believe his ears. She hadn't been this concerned about him for a long time. He wondered what had put her in such good humour. Women were a mystery!

Chapter 7

On Friday evening, Diana met up with her coterie of girlfriends, prior to meeting Michael, in the Horseshoe Bar of the Shelbourne Hotel. They were on their second round of drinks and she was in such good spirits that her best friend, Isabelle, asked, "Di, have you been snorting cocaine? You seem high."

"Of course not, I'm just high on life."

"Uh, uh! She's met a new man," Isabelle said.

"Not any man – *the* man," Diana replied.

"Poor guy – watch out!" said Lulu.

"Oh, my God! Kevin is so gorgeous," said Jasmine. "Can I move in on him, once you move out?"

"He may be gorgeous but he's boring," said Diana. "You're welcome to him. This new man in my life is exciting, rich and powerful, and very, very sexy."

"Tell us more!" said Isabelle. "What does he look like? Is he tall?"

"Hmmm. . . unfortunately not, but he looks taller

standing on his money!" This was an old joke of theirs and they all laughed uproariously.

"God, Di, where do you find them?" Chloe wanted to know.

"That's a secret but, if he has any brothers, I'll let you know."

To peals of "Please!" and "Me first!" Diana ordered another round of Cosmopolitans, the drink *du jour*, since the girls on *Sex and The City* had made it popular. This was her third one. I'd better take it easy, she thought. I don't want to turn up pissed for Michael – who will be my entrée to the good life! She sipped it slowly and was only halfway through it when it was time to leave her friends.

"Don't do anything I wouldn't do!" Jasmine said, envy in her voice.

"Call me tomorrow with all the glorious details," whispered Isabelle.

"Will do," she said, kissing her goodbye. She waved to the others, and left, feeling like a star. God, she was excited!

She went into the newly renovated Ladies'. It irritated her that she couldn't find her way around the Shelbourne any more. She used to know every stone in the place but they had gone and changed it all. She wasn't sure, like many others, that she liked it. She scrutinised herself in the mirror. The Armani suit that she had finally decided on was just perfect – expensive-looking and elegant, yet sexy. It was low enough to reveal a little of her substantial cleavage and short enough to show off her long shapely legs. She checked her stockings (to make sure they hadn't done an about-face, leaving the seam halfway round her leg), touched up her lipstick and kohl eyeliner, sprayed Chanel No. 5 on her pulse points, took a deep breath, and set out to face her future.

She had no doubt that Michael was her future and she had purposefully set her cap at him. He had everything that she wanted – money, position, power. The thought made her dizzy. *All the frogs I've had to kiss and now at last, I've met my prince.* Here goes, she thought, as she strode out of the Shelbourne on her four-inch Manolo Blahnik heels and up Merrion Row, to meet her fate.

"Do or die!" she said aloud. "Go for it, girl! You deserve it!"

★ ★ ★

At that very moment, down in Ballyfern, Kate's phone rang. It was Danny. She could hear voices in the background and a woman laughing.

"Where are you?" she asked, thinking that he should be halfway across the Irish Sea by now.

"I'm really sorry, darling, but I'm still at a meeting here in London and I think it will go on a while longer," he whispered. "I'm afraid there's no way I can catch a flight tonight. Please understand. I'll be home tomorrow. Love you!" And he hung up, before she could utter a single word.

She stood looking at the receiver stupidly. *I don't believe it! This can't be happening!* She had been so looking forward to seeing him and had prepared his favourite meal. Now he wasn't even coming home. Nobody works on Friday nights, she told herself. It hadn't sounded like work, what with glasses clinking and that woman laughing in the background. Doesn't he even think that I've been alone all week and am missing Toby? Does he even care?

She sat down as the tears slowly rolled down her cheeks. What has happened to us? We used to be so close but we're growing further and further apart. This job in London is the worst possible thing that could have happened. Danny just can't stop and it's not about the money any more. We have more than enough. He could retire in the morning if he wanted to, but he just can't give up. He's on an ego-trip now and it's all about power. What is it that drives him?

The telephone rang, breaking into her thoughts. Her heart lifted. Maybe it's Danny, saying he can make it after all, she thought, running to answer it. It was Kevin.

"Hi, Kate, how are you? Is Danny there? He said he'd meet me in the golf club tonight for a drink and I was wondering what time."

Choking back a sob, she replied, "No, he's not coming home until tomorrow."

"Oh, sorry, my mistake – I was sure he said Friday night."

"He did. He was due home tonight but he's just rung to say he can't get away and will catch a flight tomorrow."

Kevin heard the tears in her voice.

"I'm sorry. Kate, I know you must be disappointed. But look, why don't you come anyway? Diana can't make it as she's spending the night with friends in Dublin. It'll be the usual Friday night gang. You know them all."

"No, thanks, Kevin, I'll be fine. I wouldn't be very good company. This is our new life. I'd better get used to it."

Kevin thought, as he hung up, that she didn't sound a bit fine. Danny was a fool!

★ ★ ★

Diana was walking down the stairs of the Merrion, trying her best to look cool and sophisticated although a hundred butterflies were dancing reels and jigs in her stomach. Thank God I had those few drinks or I'd have been a complete nervous wreck altogether, she thought. Her heart did a little somersault when she saw Michael waiting for her. On the table was a bottle of champagne, on ice.

"Hello, my beauty!" he greeted her, letting out a low whistle as he took in her cleavage and legs. "Wow! Very, very, nice. Even sexier than I remember."

She had forgotten how blue his eyes were and how intensely he looked into her eyes. It sent shivers down her spine. He kissed her cheek and she could smell the clean masculine scent of him which mingled with an after-shave that she didn't recognise. It would probably have been way too expensive for any guy she'd been with before.

As she sat down, he rested his hand lightly on the small of her back and it felt like an electric shock going through her. What was it about him? No one had ever made her feel like this before. She watched him as he poured the champagne for her, which she noticed was vintage Dom Perignon.

"Well, do I pass muster?" he asked, with a twinkle in his eye.

Embarrassed that he seemed to have read her thoughts, she found herself blushing. Oh dear God, this is ridiculous – I'm behaving like a teenager. Cop yourself on, Diana!

"Dom Perignon, I'm impressed," she said, trying to mask her gaucheness.

"Only the best for you," replied Michael, as he raised his glass to her.

"A toast, to new beginnings," he said quietly as she found herself drowning in his eyes. "We have two lives to catch up on so we have a lot to talk about. Tell me about yourself."

"No, you go first," she said and he did, revealing himself, warts and all, making her laugh and putting her completely at ease.

They went to dinner in Patrick Guilbaud's where it was obvious he was a regular customer as all the staff treated him with great deference. He ordered for both of them and when he had finished his story, asked about hers. To her amazement, she found herself telling him all about her past; her hopes and dreams, her marriage, her disillusionment with life, opening up as she had never done before. It felt so right with him, like she had come home.

The time passed so quickly that she couldn't believe it when he announced,

"It's almost midnight and we're the last here, I think maybe we should let the staff go home."

He called for a taxi and gave the driver an address in the Financial Services Centre, north of the Liffey.

"Is there a hotel there?" she asked.

"No hotel for you, my beauty. I'm taking you to my apartment."

Apartment? What an understatement! It was a luxurious penthouse suite. There were butter-soft, black-leather sofas, stretching all around the enormous living room. She had never seen such a chic pad in her life. He took her out to the wraparound balcony and wrapped his arms around her waist, as he pointed out all the famous landmarks of Dublin.

"I thought you lived in Killiney?"

"I do. The family home is there but I use this place during the week, as I often have late night or early morning meetings. My office is here in the FSC. Commuting from Killiney at rush hour just isn't on."

"You should get a helicopter."

"I did think about it but the office doesn't have a helipad. This is a good solution. It also gives me some space."

"I'll bet! Doesn't your wife mind?"

"We have a very good arrangement. She has a very busy, full life of her own, what with her charities, lunches and clubs. But we always spend Saturdays and Sundays together."

Diana was in a state of high excitement. This was what she had dreamt about when she was growing up. This was what she had expected to find when she fell in love. But until now she had never experienced anything even close.

Oh God, please don't let tonight ever end, she prayed, as Michael started to nuzzle her neck. She turned around and put her arms around his neck and he kissed her so deeply and hungrily that she thought she might faint with pleasure. Lifting her up with ease, he carried her into the bedroom which was seductively lit with soft gold lighting. She glimpsed gold silk drapes and satin sheets and lots of cushions on a massive round bed, before she completely gave herself up to the delicious sensations she was feeling. He slowly slipped her top and bra from her shoulders and started fondling her breasts, circling her nipples gently, first with his fingers and then his tongue.

"What beauties!" he said. "What a luscious, sexy body you have! It was made for love."

She smiled. He then moved down over her body, arousing her to fever pitch, until she longed for him to enter her. But still he stayed, caressing and kissing her body, making her wait until she could stand it no longer.

"What is it you want?" he asked her, teasingly.

"Please, please, I want you now! Please take me!" she cried, her breath coming faster and faster. . .

He did as she asked. As he entered her, she felt waves of pleasure sweeping over her. She thought she would die as they took over her whole body, gaining in intensity with every thrust until she thought she could stand it no more. As he reached his climax, she experienced an intense explosion inside her which made her feel that she was sinking, down and down, drowning in pleasure.

When it had subsided Diana realised with a shock that

she had experienced her first true orgasm. This is what she had heard and read about but never understood. It was the most fantastic feeling in the world and for reasons she couldn't explain, she started to cry.

"Hush, hush, my beauty," he said tenderly, softly stroking her hair. He kept doing this until she fell into a delicious, warm, comforting sleep.

Sometime, in the middle of the night, she woke to find Michael caressing her breasts and within seconds they were making love again, but this time with even more wild, abandoned passion – both of them hungry for each other. She climaxed again, as powerfully as before, and marvelled at what this man could do to her body.

As she drifted back asleep, his arms wrapped around her, she whispered to him, "I've never in my whole life felt so alive. I could die, I'm so happy."

Chapter 8

Diana awoke on Saturday morning and rolled over, reaching out for Michael, only to find the bed empty. She looked at her watch: it was eight thirty. In a panic, she rushed into the living-room to find a note propped up on the coffee table.

Thank you for a wonderful night. I hope you enjoyed it as much as I did. I have to get home to Killiney. Please help yourself to breakfast and pull out the door after you. I'll be in touch. M.

Diana felt the tears prick her eyes. She had been so looking forward to making love again and maybe going out to lunch with him, and now this. She hadn't wanted it to end. What an anti-climax! She felt dejected and terribly alone as she checked the presses for coffee. Only Nescafé, but it would have to do. She made herself a cup and sat feeling sorry for herself. She explored the apartment but it gave up no secrets. It was a functional bachelor pad. There was nothing else for it – she got dressed and let herself out.

She didn't feel able to face home, or Kevin, as she

wanted to relive the night over and over again, so she went for a walk along the Liffey Quays, her mind full of Michael. Oh God, she thought, what's happening to me? I'm the cool one, always in control, but not this time. I've never felt like this about anyone before.

Eventually there was nothing else for it but to retrieve her car from the Stephen's Green carpark and head back to Ballyfern and boredom.

★ ★ ★

Kate was having breakfast on the terrace – a bowl of Special K and skimmed milk – when the phone rang. It was Lauren.

"Good morning. Just checking on how the reunion went. I didn't want to ring last night in case I was disturbing anything romantic."

"I wish. Unfortunately, Danny didn't come home. He had a meeting that went on late and is flying in this morning." Kate tried to sound upbeat but Lauren knew her too well.

"Oh Kate, I'm so sorry. You should have phoned me. You could have come here for dinner."

"Thanks, but I was okay. I could have gone out if I had wanted to. Danny had seemingly arranged for us to go to the golf club with Kevin and Diana last night – not that he even considered asking me if that was okay. Anyway, Kevin asked if I wanted to go but I said no. I was in no mood for social chat, I tell you! In any case, Diana wasn't going as she was seemingly staying in Dublin for the night."

"Doing what and with whom?" Lauren said, uncharitably. "I don't suppose you'll be coming to the golf club tonight then? There's a special charity night on. It should be fun though I imagine you'll both want to stay home and catch up."

"I hope so. I'll let you know one way or the other."

It was midday when Danny arrived home. Giving her a peck on the cheek, he exclaimed, "What a week! I'm exhausted but it was so exhilarating. This is gonna be one major project. First off I need to have a long shower and maybe you could rustle up a nice brunch, darling. I'm sick of hotel and restaurant food. I miss the old Irish bacon and sausages. I couldn't wait to get back to your home cooking."

Kate stood staring after him. Is this all I am, she thought – someone to cook his food? He hadn't asked how she'd been, how Toby was getting on, nothing! She rustled up some fried eggs with bacon, sausages, black pudding and home-made brown bread – all of which he wolfed down.

"That was delicious, Kate," he said, getting up from the table. "Right – I must give Kevin a buzz and catch up. I've brought a load of work home with me and I need to make some phone calls – James will be over in fifteen minutes and we'll be working through the afternoon. You and I can talk later and you can tell me all about your week then."

Before she could reply, he went into his office, banging the door behind him.

Kate stood looking at the closed door and had an

overwhelming desire to burst in and scream at him. I can't believe it, she thought. Does he think I'm just a doormat? Everyone had always told her that she was too soft and it was true – she would do anything for a quiet life. Because her mother had been an argumentative harridan who had made life hell for everyone – including her beloved father – she had learnt at an early age to give in, for peace sake. She was now doing the exact same thing with Danny. He made all the decisions and she never questioned them. She had been happy to bow down to his wishes. Why? Was she so gormless that she had no mind of her own? During this past week, when she had been on her own for almost the first time in her life, she had started questioning what her life was all about. More importantly, what *she* was all about.

She had been so young, only twenty, when she'd married Danny. She'd been very much in love, happy to have his babies, happy to leave all the money and business problems to him. And then he'd become so successful, so quickly, and they'd had no problems any more. But somewhere along the way, she sadly admitted to herself, she'd lost her identity. This past week had opened her eyes.

She marvelled at how she was managing to persevere with her diet. Somehow all this negativity had inspired her even more. This was something she was doing for herself. It would have been so easy to wallow in self-pity and comfort-eat, but she resisted the temptation.

As the two men worked through the afternoon Kate was called on every hour or so to bring in coffee. She did it with a bad grace but Danny didn't notice although she suspected James did. They finally emerged at seven and, when James left, Danny plonked himself down on the couch.

"Kate, darling, could you pour me a large whiskey and whatever you're having yourself and come sit down and tell me how your week was?"

"Pour it yourself and I'm not having a drink, thank you."

Danny looked at her, the shock registering in his eyes. "What's wrong, love?" He stood up and came close to her, trying to put his arms around her but she pushed him away. "What is it? This is not like you!"

"No, it's not – not like the person who's been waiting on you hand and foot for the past twenty years, anyway. But maybe this *is* me." Kate knew her voice was strident and had gone up an octave, but she couldn't help it.

"Please, Kate, I'm not in the mood for female histrionics. I suppose Lauren has been filling your head with all her feminist rubbish. You were never like that. You know I hate that type of woman." His voice was cold now.

"Of course, you do," said Kate. "They don't lie down and let you walk all over them. And this has nothing to do with Lauren. It's about me!" She wouldn't let him blame Lauren for how she felt.

"Kate, haven't I looked after you and the boys?" he asked, his voice wheedling. "What more do you want?" He came close to her once more. She moved away.

"I want a husband who loves me and cares about me. I need you here. I miss you. I don't want an absentee husband. I don't want to be alone all the time." Kate was almost in tears now.

"Don't you understand? This is the biggest deal of my career. You know I love you. You're my wife, the mother of my sons. You've got to support me in this because, yes, I will be away from home for long periods but it's for our future, our legacy to our children."

He looked so confident and self-assured as he spoke that Kate didn't know how to answer. She was at a loss for words.

"Come on, darling. Things will work out," he said. "Let's get dressed up and have a good night out." He tried once again to put his arms around her but she shrugged him off. "There's a charity night for The Samaritans in the golf club and I said I'd support it," he continued. "We can grab a bite there before it starts."

Kate said nothing but she walked out dejectedly. I can't win, she thought. I'm not clever enough. I can never find the right answer for him but I know I'm right. She didn't want to go to the golf club but she acquiesced anyway. As usual, Danny got what he wanted.

She pulled out her usual black trousers and tunic and found to her amazement that they were loose on her. With mounting excitement she decided to try on her peach coral suit and couldn't believe it when the zip slid up effortlessly. This is not possible. I can't have lost that much weight in one week.

She rang Lauren from the bedroom phone and told her the good news.

"That's fantastic. I can't wait to see you! I take it you're not staying in?"

"Well, that's what I would have preferred but Danny wants to go to the golf club."

"Okay, I take it we'll see you there so."

* * *

Lauren arrived at the golf club and, after greeting all her friends, chose a table in the corner where she and Kate would be able to chat, undisturbed. While Jonathan was ordering drinks she thought about her friend. She had sensed the disappointment in her voice on the phone and felt sorry for her. She hated the way Danny treated his wife. Kate was so shy and lacking in confidence and Danny was exactly the opposite. He was brash and forward and not at all Lauren's cup of tea. '*Nouveau riche*' described him exactly. However, she tolerated him because she was so fond of Kate. She saw how gentle and vulnerable she was and recognised, almost immediately, that Danny had sapped all her confidence. Her friend never felt good enough or worthy, which was ridiculous. She was a wonderful loyal wife, a fantastic mother and the truest friend anyone could ask for. She was worth ten of Danny but he was a control freak and had found his wife an easy target. Lauren treasured Kate and her gentle qualities and was determined to always be there for her, if she was needed. She strongly suspected that that day was in the not-too-distant future.

Jonathan had just returned with their drinks when

Lauren spotted Kate and Danny coming in. She waved and called them over. Jonathan asked what they were drinking and went off to order while Danny disappeared to circulate, as he called it.

"I am not in the mood to socialise tonight. Let's just sit here quietly," said Kate to Lauren.

"Absolutely. That's why I chose this corner," said Lauren.

Jonathan brought Kate the sparkling water she'd ordered and went off to find Danny and give him his drink.

Lauren was looking Kate up and down. "Gosh, you're being very good and it's paying off. I can really see the weight loss. That suit is gorgeous on you. Coral is really your colour."

"Yeah, I love this colour. I even prefer roses in this colour to red or yellow ones. As for the weight loss – it's the only positive in my life at the moment."

"Well, keep going, because you look great! I can't wait to see how much exactly you've lost. Have you weighed yourself?"

"No, I did as Tara said – I put away the bathroom scales and took out the kitchen one!" Kate said with a laugh. "I'm excited about tomorrow night. Wonder how Jenny has done?"

"We'll know soon enough."

Kate spotted Kevin and Diana at another table and waved over at them. Kevin waved back. No response from Diana.

"What's up with her?" Lauren said bitchily. "She's not

her usual self. In fact she's suspiciously quiet. It's not like her to be sitting demurely with Kevin."

"Yeah, that's pretty unusual," Kate remarked in a worried voice. "I haven't spoken to her lately. I hope she's okay."

"You're too kind. I, for one, am not about to go and find out why she looks like she's been sucking on a lime," replied Lauren wickedly.

★ ★ ★

Diana was feeling miserable. She had not heard from Michael all day and was wracked with thoughts of him cosily at home with his wife or, even worse, meeting other women at a dinner or party who would surely find him as attractive as she had done. Was someone, right now, handing him a note with her phone number on it? She knew that she had a very possessive nature but she'd never before felt this jealous about anyone. She couldn't even be bothered to join the men at the bar, as she usually did. Compared to Michael they were boring and provincial.

Kevin couldn't figure out what was wrong with her. She had been morose ever since she had come home from Dublin today. He had tried to find the reason for it but she wouldn't discuss it. He figured that she must have had a row with Isabelle or one of her other friends in Dublin. He wondered would he ever know. She was, most definitely, not herself.

"Why don't you go over and say hello to Lauren and Kate?"

"You're not serious! That pair – they hate my guts."

"Oh don't be ridiculous, Diana. They're our friends."

"Yours maybe – not mine!"

He gave up.

★ ★ ★

At eleven o'clock, as Lauren and Jonathan were leaving, Kate asked Danny to go home too.

"Not just yet, darling. I've just met two guys here who might be useful to me in the future. I need to keep them sweet. You look exhausted. Why don't I ask Jonathan to drop you home and I'll follow when I've had a talk with them?"

"Please don't be too late. I've something I'd like to discuss with you."

"I won't. See you later."

Kate went straight to bed, lying awake until she heard his key in the door.

It was five minutes to three.

"Sorry, darling," he mumbled as he fell into bed beside her. Within two minutes he was snoring loudly.

Kate tossed and turned and it was almost six o'clock when she finally fell into a restless, fitful sleep.

Chapter 9

On Sunday morning Kate came down to find Danny having breakfast. He was in his bathrobe and looked very fresh, considering how much he'd had to drink the night before. It's not fair, she thought. She'd only been drinking water, but she hadn't slept very well and was feeling wretched. He kissed her on the cheek.

"Sorry I was so late last night but you know how these things go. I couldn't get away." Danny was munching on toast and reading Saturday's *Irish Times.* He poured a coffee for her. "You said you had something you wanted to discuss. What is it?"

This really wasn't the time to discuss it, she thought. She knew she looked a mess and would have liked to shower and dress before having this discussion. She had no choice however, so she took the bull by the horns. Taking a deep breath, she said, "Well, I'm finding it very lonely and boring here during the week and thought that maybe I could get a little job." She paused, then continued with more confidence than she was feeling, "There's a vacancy in the Coffee Pot in Naas and I'd like to apply for it."

His slice of toast stopped its journey to his mouth, hanging in midair. "Kate, you can't be serious! You know my views on you working. You have more than enough to do here in the house, seeing as how you won't employ more staff than Betty to help you."

Kate took a slice of toast in the hope that it would give her some strength.

"There's not even enough work for Betty, with only me in the house!" she said. "And since you insist on having a gardener, I can't even do anything in my own garden. Johnny gets upset if I so much as pull a weed. He reckons it's his territory. But since you insist on them, I have no choice. I'd prefer to look after my own house and garden." She was past caring now that he would get annoyed. She had to let him know how she felt.

"For God's sake, Kate, what would people think if we had no staff? I'm surprised you don't want to let the pool cleaner go and do it yourself. You have such a bourgeois attitude." His face was suffused with anger.

"Bourgeois! We *are* bourgeois!" She was crying now. "*Nouveau riche*, that's what people call us and that's worse than bourgeois!"

"Calm down, calm down," he said. "Here, have another coffee." He was shocked at her outburst. What had brought this on?

As she sipped the hot coffee, he continued, "What about the leisure centre? We have family membership there and in the golf club. You could make use of those." He resumed eating his toast.

"Don't you remember how bad I was when I tried golf? You told me I would never make a golfer. And anyway, the women up there intimidate me. They're all so pushy and bitchy – with one or two exceptions, of course." She found her courage draining out of her.

"You'll have to learn to stand up for yourself. You're too sensitive." Danny reached over and took her hand.

"I'm trying to stand up for myself now," she said, "telling you I'd like to get a job."

He snatched his hand away. "Kate, you don't need a job! You have as much money as you could ever want."

"You don't understand! It's not about money. It's about me having a life, something outside the home." She heard her voice wobble and was afraid that she might start to cry again.

Danny stood up abruptly, banging his hand on the table. Her coffee spilt all over it but he didn't notice.

"Absolutely not! I forbid it! I don't want to hear this mentioned again. We have a status to keep up in this community. My wife working in such a menial job as a coffee shop – it doesn't bear thinking about!" He was beside himself.

She had never seen him so angry and she quivered under his furious gaze.

"Kate, you're not stupid," he continued, calming down a little. "You must realise it's out of the question. Now I must dash. I'm playing golf at nine o'clock. We'll have to take the two cars when we go to visit the boys this afternoon as I'll have to leave for my flight straight from there." He was already on the move.

"You're flying back to London tonight?" She thought she must have misheard.

"Yes. Didn't I tell you? I'll be spending most of my time there for the foreseeable future, at least until this project is up and running. I thought you understood that. This is mega bucks!" He was looking around for his keys.

"No, I didn't realise that. You never discussed it with me . . ."

Before she could finish, he'd found them, grabbed his jacket and was on his way out. She stood there, bereft, listening to his car roaring down the drive, wondering where it had all gone wrong.

She spent the morning baking for the boys and applauded herself for resisting all the goodies. Not a single bite did she take. A week ago she would not have believed it possible. She ate her lunch alone and kept Danny's warm for him in the oven. They barely said another word to each other before she left to go visit the boys. Danny went upstairs to pack and would follow on after her. Normally she would have packed for him but today she was in no mood to. She was upset but felt that he was being very unfair. Anyway, she was not going to let anyone, or anything, spoil this afternoon with the boys.

★ ★ ★

When she arrived at the school Toby was waiting out front with Sam.

They came running over and Sam said, "Hi, Mom, love you! I'll go get the others."

Toby jumped in the car and gave her a big hug. His words came tumbling out excitedly: "Oh Mom, I've missed you very much but this school is so cool! I'm on the first year rugby team and I've joined the choir and the swimming club and the canoe club and . . ." He had run out of breath.

She felt relief – happy that he had settled in – but also a little sad that he didn't need her as much as before. The circle of life, she told herself, remembering that beautiful movie *The Lion King*. We all must move on. Toby's done it and now, so must I.

She went into the school to meet up with Sam and her other sons. Danny arrived half an hour later and spent just forty minutes with them before he had to leave for the airport. She gave him a cool peck on the cheek and then joined the boys in the refectory for tea.

"Only bad thing is, Mom, the food is not nearly as good as yours," remarked Toby, pulling a face.

"Well, I'm afraid all school food is the same. I've brought you some cakes, biscuits and chicken sandwiches for later. And just think how much you'll enjoy my cooking on your weekends at home."

"Cool, Mom. And can I bring my new friend Miguel home at the weekend break? He's from Spain and it's too far for him to go home and I said I'd ask you . . ."

"Of course," she said, laughing at his enthusiasm. He ran off to find Miguel and Justin came and sat beside her.

"You don't need to worry about him, Mom. He's really settled in and we're all looking out for him. Are you okay? David and I are worried. We thought Dad seemed really strange today."

My God, how sensitive of them to realise things were not right, she thought. Sometimes you underestimated your kids.

"I'm fine, love," she reassured him. "Your dad really has a lot on his plate with this new London project. It was a bit difficult for me last week with you all back at school and your dad away but I'm fine – keeping really busy."

"That's great. David and I were a bit worried, what with Toby gone and then Dad off in London. We were worried you'd be lonely," he said, "but you look great – different – cool. Sure you're okay?

Absolutely!" she assured him, loving him for his concern, and David too. She kissed them all goodbye and made her way home thinking that they were really young adults now and how lucky she was to have them.

Chapter 10

Diana hadn't slept very well on Sunday night, although she had downed at least ten gin and tonics. She thought Monday would never come, sure that Michael would ring.

All day Monday she waited. Nothing!

"I don't believe it!" she cried aloud. "Who does he think he is?"

She felt sure he had enjoyed the night as much as she had. If so, why wasn't he ringing her? Was he thinking about her? She could think of nothing else. Was it not the same for him? She was dying to hear his voice. She went to her yoga class and left halfway through. Then she went for a swim but couldn't relax and left the pool after ten laps. She hoped a massage might help and, although she normally fell asleep in the middle of it, this time she was edgy and tense.

"What's up, Diana? I've never seen you so tense. Try and relax and go with the flow," suggested Zoe, the masseuse.

"Sorry, I have a lot of problems right now."

"Obviously! I can't really help you while your body is fighting me."

After her massage, Diana went into the bar of the hotel. She ordered a large G&T and while she was downing it the owner of the hotel, who was quite a hunk, came over to her.

"Hello, beautiful! What brings you here and all alone, today?"

Previously she would have flirted madly with him but today she wanted to tell him to piss off. "I just wanted to be alone."

"Oh sorry. Here was I thinking that maybe you and I could get together for the afternoon."

"Fat chance!" she replied getting up and leaving without paying for her drink. Let *him* do that, she thought, enjoying the look of dismay on his face. "You're too late, buster!" she said under her breath as she strode out. "If you'd asked me last week I'd have accepted."

She went home and poured another large drink for herself and by the time Kevin arrived home from work she was completely blotto. He was shocked to find her in this state and wondered what the hell was going on. He cooked dinner, made her eat some and put her to bed.

Later that night he sat nursing a whiskey trying to figure out what to do about her. Their marriage was dead – he accepted that now. She didn't love him and never would. Still, he didn't want it to end – he believed in for-better-or-worse and it was now certainly for-worse. But what could he do about it?

* * *

Kate was apprehensive but hopeful as she dressed in her lightest possible clothes and shoes for her first weigh-in at 'Slimforever'. She collected Lauren and then drove to Naas and picked up Jenny, who was in very high spirits.

"How did the lunch go yesterday?" Kate asked her.

"Brilliant! They all enjoyed it – even more so when I told them it was all low calorie. They're almost all on diets – with the exception of Miss Delaney who's in her sixties and naturally thin and the lads, of course!" she laughed. "Conor's as fit as a fiddle and Ciarán and Jimmy are mad into sports too."

"What did Tom think of it?" asked Kate thinking that he was certainly a meat-and-two-veg man and probably wouldn't have appreciated it.

"He wasn't there. He had an important Towns Cup match at the rugby club."

A rugby match was more important than your lunch party? Lauren wanted to say but held her tongue.

Kate was wondering the same thing.

"My lunch was a great success too," said Lauren, "but I didn't let on it was low calorie."

"Any idea how much you've lost, Jenny?"

"None whatsoever! I didn't weigh myself once all week so I'm dying to find out."

They were surprised that there were only half as many women in the hall as had been there the previous week.

"Tara has split the class in two," explained the woman in front of Kate. "The other half came at six o'clock."

"That's great – means we'll be finished earlier."

Finally, it was their turn to weigh in.

Jenny was dying to know how much she'd lost but Tara wouldn't tell her.

"You'll have to wait till the end of the lecture. But you've done well," she winked.

When Kate got up on the scales, Tara gave a little whistle.

"Excellent! I knew you'd do it." Nevertheless, she left Kate in suspense too. They could barely wait for her talk to be over. At last it ended and she started to read out the weight loss. It was very impressive. Women had lost from two to five pounds in the week and each one got a round of applause. Kate loved the sense of camaraderie and support from everyone in the room. Lauren was delighted when Tara informed her that she'd lost three pounds and then Jenny's name was called.

"Jenny Murray – fantastic! You've lost six pounds since last Monday. Congratulations!"

Jenny practically danced up to Tara, beaming broadly, as everyone applauded.

Kate sat with bated breath. I'm next, she thought, but was very disappointed when someone else's name was called out.

"What about me? I was after Jenny in the line," she whispered to Lauren. She couldn't understand it. She felt sick with apprehension.

"Finally, the last card belongs to our 'Girl of the Week' who has lost a staggering nine pounds!"

This can't be me, thought Kate. I can't have lost that much. She must have lost my card . . .

"Kate O'Mara! Congratulations! Come on up here!"

Kate couldn't believe it. She thought she must have misheard.

"Did she say nine pounds?" she asked a grinning Lauren.

"She did indeed. Go on up there. It's fantastic, Kate."

"Well done, Kate!" said a beaming Jenny, giving her a hug.

She was so dumbstruck that both Lauren and Jenny had to lift her up off her seat. All the other women were standing and applauding her as she received the 'Girl of The Week' trophy from Tara.

"This is just the start," Tara whispered to her as she presented it.

"My God, I can't believe it! Thank you so much."

"*You* did it – all by yourself."

Kate had never felt such a sense of achievement. No wonder her coral suit had fitted her. Nine pounds!

She put twice as much energy into the exercise session, feeling the difference the nine pounds made. God, she felt like a butterfly!

As they were leaving the class, the other women leaving with them called out words of congratulation. She felt as if she was walking on air. Lauren and Jenny were so happy for her.

"This calls for a celebration," said Lauren as they drove to Moorehill Lodge for a bite to eat. "I think a celebratory glass of wine is called for – because we're worth it!"

The others laughed and agreed with her.

"I think we've earned it," said Jenny. None of them had had anything to eat since lunch-time.

"A glass of wine would be nice. The only drink I had all week was with Jenny, on Thursday night," Kate told Lauren.

"Just imagine what we would have lost if we hadn't had that," Jenny replied, with a rueful smile.

"Forget it! Everyone breaks out now and again. We're only human. The main thing is to get back on track straight away," Lauren scolded them.

They ordered three steaks and surprised themselves by asking for three salads, instead of chips and onions.

"Crazy – but I thought I'd kill for chips tonight," said Kate. "Strangely, now that I can have them, I can do without them. I'm so thrilled with my weight loss that I don't want to spoil it – but I am enjoying this glass of wine."

The other two didn't reply but were staring at something behind her. Kate turned around to investigate what it was that had caught their attention. It was Tara, who was standing in the doorway. She spotted them and. with a wide grin on her face, walked over to them.

"Caught in the act! It's all right, Jenny, you don't have to hide your glass under the table!" she laughed.

Jenny felt her face reddening and, feeling like a six-year-old who'd been caught stealing, she put the glass back on the table.

"Do you girls mind if I join you?" said Tara. "I'm alone."

"Of course not. You're welcome," they mumbled.

Lauren was the first to compose herself. "It's not as bad as it looks," she explained to Tara. "We decided, last week, not to eat before the class but to go for a meal every Monday after it, as the treat of the week." She smiled her most charming smile.

Tara laughed. "Of course, that's a good idea. I have a class at six o'clock so I don't get to eat before, either. I normally come here to have something before I head home."

Just then their steaks arrived and they were very relieved that they had not ordered the chips and onions!

"That looks delicious. I'll have the same, please," Tara told the waiter. They offered her a glass of wine and she accepted it gracefully.

"I don't normally drink when I'm driving but I reckon this is a special occasion. I'd like to propose a toast." She raised her glass. "To my three stars! Do you realise that, between the three of you, you have lost eighteen pounds this week? That's a stone and four pounds. Not bad!"

The girls clinked glasses, giggling like schoolgirls. They were very happy indeed.

They settled in to enjoy their meal and the conversation flowed freely. Tara was great fun and they cracked up at some of her stories, mainly about the women she had come across in her classes.

"You did so well," Tara said. "Tell me, did you not find it a problem to stick to the diet over the weekend. That's when most women fall by the wayside."

"Without Kate, we'd have been lost," Jenny explained. "Both Lauren and I had lunch parties on Sunday but Kate made out menus for us which were easy to prepare and delicious but really low in calories. She's a genius with food."

"Really?" said Tara. "I've been looking for someone like you, Kate! Do you think you could give me these menus so that I could pass them on to my members? I would pay you, of course."

"Don't be silly, I'd be delighted to do it for free."

"No way would I accept them without paying you. Do you think you could do out a week of recipes for me for next Monday?"

"Sure!"

"Great. And then we must come to a business arrangement. This is stuff I would love to be able to do myself but, you know, with seven children, there's never enough time."

Lauren was intrigued. "How did you get into this business?" she asked.

"That's a long story," said Tara, "and I'm afraid I have to leave now but if you're coming here next week after the class, I'll tell you then."

They all thought this was a great idea. On the way home they all agreed that she was a lovely person. Beautiful *and* smart.

"Kate, you really must do out a week of menus for her. This is a great opportunity for you." Lauren thought it was just what Kate needed right now.

"Tara's so interesting and full of life. I'd love to be like her," Kate said wistfully.

"Don't be daft – you're very special too," Lauren shot back at her.

"Everyone loves you, Kate," said Jenny, "and you have a lot of talent that other people envy."

"You just have no confidence," added Lauren.

"Tara certainly has plenty of that," Kate said, wishing she had the same.

They dropped Jenny off and, on the way to Ballyfern, Kate told Lauren of Danny's reaction when she'd mentioned taking a job. Lauren rolled her eyes up to heaven. She had suspected that Danny would be reluctant to agree but had hoped that Kate would win him over.

"He's still living in the dark ages," Lauren said. She had no time for this macho behaviour. "He thinks domesticity and motherhood should be fulfilment enough for a woman," she continued, getting more irate as she thought about it. "He's meeting career women every day, even in the building business. Why can't he accept that his wife might need something more to fulfil her?"

"I don't know. It's a macho thing, I suppose. Anyway, he suggested that I might take up golf again and I thought maybe I'd give it another go, even though I was useless at it" Kate didn't sound very hopeful.

"You weren't any more useless than any of us were when we began. Your problem was that you went out playing with Danny and he demoralised you." God, Lauren thought, I don't think I can take any more of Danny and his chauvinist ideas.

"I suppose you're right. I remember you took me out and I played okay."

"Better than okay – for a beginner. You just have to keep practising and it all comes together. I was woeful in the beginning and I'm now playing off twelve, which is pretty good – if I say so myself." Danny's not exactly a single-handicap golfer, she thought viciously.

"You're one of the best ladies in the club, Lauren. I'd never be anything like that."

"You never know, Kate."

They had arrived at Lauren's house. When the car slowed to a halt, she turned to Kate.

"Anyway, I'm free on Wednesday morning," she said. "Why don't you come out with me and we'll play nine holes and see how it goes?"

"Why not? I've nothing else on and maybe I won't tell Danny until I can play decently. What a surprise that would be for him!"

Puh-leese! Lauren wanted to say, but she wouldn't have hurt Kate's feelings for the world.

"You're doing this for yourself, Kate, not for Danny," she said as she got out of the car. "Okay? Understood? That's a date then. Till Wednesday!"

★ ★ ★

Jenny was on cloud nine when she got home but she had

no one to share it with either, as Tom was still out. She was wondering when he'd be home and if she would wait up when she heard a car outside. She went to the door and opened it, dying to share her news and, if she were honest, to crook a finger at him for not believing she could do it. It wasn't Tom, however. It was Conor, her next-door neighbour and fellow-teacher in Ballyfern, who was pulling into their shared driveway.

"Hi, Jenny! You okay?" he asked when he spotted her, concern showing in his face when he saw her peering anxiously out.

"No, no, Conor, nothing wrong. I just thought you were Tom and I'm bursting to tell him my good news."

"What good news?"

Barely able to keep it in, she burst out, "I was at my slimming club tonight and I lost six pounds since last Monday night! Can you believe it?"

"Congratulations! I noticed you stayed in the staffroom last week at lunch-time and wondered what was up. Now I understand," he grinned.

"I couldn't trust myself to resist the chips in the Ballyfern Inn," she admitted.

"You shouldn't have told me because now every time you put something in your mouth, I'll be on your case." He was laughing as he issued this threat.

"You're a horror!" she said. "I'll steer clear of you, so. Goodnight!"

"No midnight snacks, now!" he teased, wagging his finger at her.

"As if I would!" she retorted, retreating back into her house.

She and Conor had been friends for fifteen years, ever since Conor had arrived at the school, fresh out of college. Jenny had taken him under her wing and, when he'd told her that he was getting married and looking for a house nearby, she suggested that he look at the house next door to hers which was up for a quick sale. That was the start of a wonderful friendship. She and Beth, his bride, had hit it off instantly and had become best friends. It had been a terrible blow to her when Beth had died of breast cancer two years earlier. Jenny, with her constant good humour, had been a godsend to Beth during her last difficult months and a fantastic support to Conor ever since.

There were quite a few ladies who had their eye on Conor but he seemed unaware of the effect he had on women. He was tall, six foot three, broad-shouldered and had the look of a guy who spent all his time outdoors. In summer he went sailing, surfing and rock climbing and in winter he took to the ski slopes every chance he got. As a result he had a perennial tan which made his blue eyes seem even bluer. These were framed by the longest lashes Jenny had ever seen. Beth used to laugh that they were wasted on him – any woman would have killed for them!

His hair was dark blond and long and he had a habit of raking his hand through it when he was thinking. He lived in jeans and denim shirts and Jenny often teased him, saying all he needed was a Stetson and some cowboy boots and he could make it as a country singer. She wasn't far out as he played a mean guitar and had a lovely, husky, country-style singing voice.

All of the female teachers in the school were crazy about him and Jenny used to giggle when even Miss Delaney, the prim spinster who was due to retire next year, became coquettish and coy in his company. As for his pupils – the eleven and twelve-year-old girls that he taught – there wasn't one of them who didn't have a crush on him. They thought he looked like Matthew McConaughey, the actor, and Jenny had to agree that there was a similarity between them. Conor confided in Jenny that his present class were so precocious, often flirting openly with him, that he thought he should consider going back to teaching five-year-olds again. Jenny laughingly suggested that arriving at the school on his motor bike, in his leather gear, wasn't helping matters.

He was a fantastic teacher and had a great rapport with the kids. He had a way of getting even the most hardened cases to enjoy learning and many of his former pupils would say that he had, indeed, changed their lives. Underneath that masculine exterior Jenny knew there was a gentle sensitive soul who genuinely cared for other people and was truly kind.

★ ★ ★

Lauren arrived home from the slimming club to find Jonathan watching television.

"You're late. What kept you?"

She heard the querulous tone in his voice and,

recognising his anger, said a prayer. Please, God, please! Don't let this start . . .

God wasn't listening.

"Please, Jonathan, you know where I was."

"Did you check out that report I asked you to do?"

"No, sorry, I didn't get a chance – I'll do it tomorrow," she replied, trying to mollify him.

She saw the telltale red colour suffuse his face as he stood up and, before she could run, he grabbed her roughly by the arm and dragged her across the room.

"Please, Jonathan! Please . . . no . . ." she pleaded.

"You have no time to do what I ask, yet you can spend the evening out gallivanting with your friends!"

And with that he slapped her hard across the face and threw her against the wall.

She felt the blood gushing from her nose and could feel its warm mineral taste in her mouth.

"Please, Jonathan, please . . ." she begged. "Think of the children asleep upstairs. They may hear us. I'm sorry . . . truly I am!"

He dragged her by the hair, slapping her face with his other hand. Wham! She couldn't escape. He threw her to the floor.

"I'll show you sorry!" and with that he gave her a kick that completely winded her. She lay there whimpering as he left the room.

She stayed there until she could find the strength to get up and crawl to the bathroom, where she threw up. Her nose was still bleeding so she ran the cold tap and then pressed the cold facecloth against it. It subsided. She looked at her face in the mirror – it was already swelling. How many times had she been down this road? How much longer could she take it?

She was lying down in the bedroom when she heard the inevitable footsteps. He came hesitantly into the room and knelt by the bed, his head in his hands. He reached out to touch her but she recoiled from him.

"Don't touch me," she whispered. "I couldn't bear it." She curled herself into the fetal position and moved to the middle of the bed.

"Oh my darling, I'm so sorry . . . forgive me, please . . . I didn't mean it . . . I love you and would never hurt you."

"And what do you call what you just did to me?"

He was prostrate with grief. She could hear the anguish in his voice.

"I don't know what came over me . . . it was your tone of voice. Please forgive me!"

She'd heard this so many times before. It was always her tone of voice, or a look she might give him that would set him off. She always knew when it was coming. She could feel the anger building up in him over a period of weeks and it always culminated in this explosion of violence against her. He never laid a hand on the kids, thank God. That she would never have accepted.

For the past fourteen years, from the very first year of their marriage, her wonderful husband – who was wonderful 99% of the time – had been violently assaulting her for no apparent reason whatsoever. After the beating he would be abject in his horror at what he had done, beg her forgiveness, swear he would never touch her again, and he wouldn't – until the next time. This was the history of their marriage.

According to all who knew them, they were the ideal couple. He was wealthy and successful, she beautiful and accomplished. What a sham, she thought. She had never confided in anyone, she was far too ashamed. She felt that somehow, it was *her* fault.

She had seen a programme on television recently about battered wives and had been shocked to find that she identified with them. There was this one woman in particular – a very homely, nice woman – who told her story:

"My husband has been beating me on a regular basis for the past twelve years. I don't know why he does it. He loves me and I love him, in spite of it. I've learnt to live with it. He's the nicest guy in the world most of the time. Then I notice the anger building up in him and I know that he will have to vent this anger somehow. He takes it out on me. Sometimes I pray that he will beat me up as soon as possible and get it over with, so that we can get back to being normal again. I know it sounds strange but I feel it's my fault that he's so angry. And afterwards he's full of remorse and so kind that I end up feeling sorry for him"

As Lauren had watched this programme she'd sat with tears streaming down her face. She could identify so much with that poor woman. It shouldn't be like this, she thought. We shouldn't accept this behaviour. This is not normal behaviour for a man. She had tried to get Jonathan to go for counselling but, like most violent men, he wouldn't hear of it.

"It won't happen again," he'd promised – but it had, again and again.

Now he made a second attempt to reach out to her.

"I said don't touch me!" she cried. "I can't stand it! I can't take it any more! It's never going to stop."

"It will. I solemnly promise. Please, Lauren, give me one more chance?"

She looked at him sadly. How many chances had she given him? She now realised it would never end. She felt so worthless and dehumanised. How could he treat someone he loved like this? It was incomprehensible!

"Can I get you a cup of tea?" he asked, his voice shaking.

"No," she replied tersely.

"What about a brandy? That would help," he suggested timidly.

"Nothing will help, Jonathan. Can't you understand?" she said harshly, getting angry now. "Just leave me alone and sleep in the guest-room tonight. Could you get the kids out to school in the morning? I don't want them to see me in this condition. Tell them I'm not feeling well and need to sleep."

"Oh Lauren, please, my darling! I don't blame you. I can't forgive myself but I'm begging you – please, give me another chance?"

She looked at him, disgust and revulsion in her eyes. "Leave me alone, Jonathan, I've forgiven you once too often." She turned away from him.

When he'd left the room she started crying softly and lay for a long time wondering if she would have the courage to do what she knew she must do. When sleep wouldn't come, she took a sleeping pill and fell into a fitful sleep which was peopled with nightmares.

★ ★ ★

After Kate had locked up for the night she rang Danny on his mobile. It was switched off so she left a message and then she tried his hotel. The receptionist said he was not in but she would leave a message for him to call Kate back. She was thrilled with her weight loss and she wanted to share the good news with him.

She stayed up waiting for Danny to call and, when he hadn't called by midnight, she went to bed. She read until about one thirty and when he still hadn't called she gave up and went to sleep.

She did wonder where he could be till that hour but then convinced herself that it was business and that could go on all night – or so he said.

Chapter 11

Diana woke up on Tuesday morning with a raging hangover. She got a shock when she saw the time – eight forty-five. Oh God, she was due to play golf with Mabel and Una at nine thirty! No way could she wield a golf club in this state! She rang Mabel and explained that she had a dreadful migraine.

"Are you sure it's not a hangover? I hear you were knocking back the gin and tonics in the hotel yesterday."

Bitch! Diana fumed. You can do nothing in this god-forsaken town without the whole world knowing about it.

"Of course not," she replied coolly. "I'm well able to handle my drink – not like some I could mention."

On that note, she hung up. That's put her in her place, she thought smugly. Diana was never at a loss for words. She could always go for the jugular!

She took two aspirin and crawled back to bed where she stayed until two o'clock. She kept her mobile right beside her but still no call from Michael. She was starting to despair. She couldn't face her Pilates class and didn't even bother to ring and cancel. She then sat in front of the television for the afternoon watching Oprah and Jerry Springer and all the other stupid chat shows that now made up the daily viewing of a large percentage of housebound women. She scoffed bar after bar of chocolate which was something she always did when she was depressed.

She had read somewhere that chocolate was an anti-depressant and that it contains phenylethylamine, or PEA for short, which is close to amphetamines. She had been fascinated to learn that you get a surge of PEA when you fall in love and that it also floods your system when you have an orgasm. Well, it had certainly flooded her system last Friday night but was having no effect now, despite the fact that she was eating chocolate non-stop. She considered ringing Michael's office but decided against it. Instinct told her that that would be a stupid move. He would not appreciate it.

* * *

Kate was also waiting for a phone call, from Danny, but by midday he still hadn't rung. She decided to try his mobile again and this time she got through to him.

"Oh, hello, love," he said. "I was going to ring you this afternoon. How are you?"

"Didn't you get my messages last night?" she asked coolly.

"Yes, I did, but I was in very late and didn't want to

disturb you. And things have been so absolutely hectic today that I didn't get a chance."

"Danny, I could have needed to contact you urgently. This is not on."

"It wasn't urgent, was it?"

"No, but that's not the point. It could have been."

"Oh Kate, stop playing games! What was it you wanted last night?"

"Nothing at all – it wasn't important," she retorted, hanging up.

She wasn't about to admit to him that she missed him and had just wanted to share her good news with him, as it was pretty obvious that he wasn't missing her, not one jot.

What was he doing out so late, she wondered. They seemed to be growing further and further apart. Danny didn't seem to care about her and she was unable to do anything about it. She put him out of her mind and started working on some menus for Tara. She was never happier than when she was immersed in her cookery books. The hours flew by.

Lauren rang at about four o'clock. She sounded very strange. She told Kate that she'd had a bit of a fall and was sorry but she couldn't keep their golf appointment the next day.

"You poor thing – can I get you anything? Shall I bring over some lasagne from the freezer for dinner?"

"No, thanks, Kate, I'll be fine. I just want to rest. Sorry to cry off like this but I promise, as soon as I feel okay, I'll ring you and we'll hit the golf course."

Kate didn't know what to think. This wasn't the first time that Lauren had said she'd had a fall. She'd been concerned that Lauren was suffering blackouts but now it was happening again and Kate was beginning to wonder if Lauren could possibly be the victim of domestic violence. It hardly seemed believable – Jonathan was such a gentleman and it was obvious that he adored his wife. However, Kate had had experience of this domestic violence before. Her sister, Teresa, had been through it and she prayed to God that it wasn't now happening to her friend. Until she could get Lauren to confide in her, there was nothing she could do, but she would do her best to help her, in any way she could.

★ ★ ★

Jenny was in such good form. She came into the staffroom at morning break, feeling on top of the world. The other teachers caught her mood instantly and brightened up themselves.

"You look like the cat that got the cream. Has something happened?" Miss Delaney wanted to know.

"Nothing special – it's just great to be alive."

But this wasn't true. Something special had happened. Maybe. Something wonderful.

Conor caught her eye and winked, thinking he knew her secret – the six pounds she had lost last week.

But the idea of slimming hardly mattered to Jenny any more. In fact, her concentration on losing weight had almost made her miss the most momentous event of her life.

But she hardly dared to hope yet.

"Well, if you find out what makes it so great to be alive, having to cope with these little horrors every day, do please share it with us," said Jimmy who had the unenviable job of teaching the dreaded fifth class.

"Oh, they're not so bad!"

"Oh yeah? Would you like to take them for the rest of the day – or even the rest of the year, if you'd prefer?"

"No, thanks, you're right. Then maybe it wouldn't be so great to be alive!" All the other teachers roared laughing at the truth of this remark.

★ ★ ★

Lauren was still in a state of shock and had to cancel all her appointments for the week. She just couldn't face people. And she couldn't risk meeting people who might suspect what had happened. She was terrified that Kate might call and see the bruises. She knew Kate's sister had been a victim of domestic violence too, and she was worried Kate might put two and two together. She hid her car in the garage, just in case, and felt awful doing this. She wasn't ready to tell her friend just yet but knew that it was only a matter of time before she would have to confide in someone and who better than Kate?

She knew her mother wouldn't have believed her. Mary O'Reilly had been overjoyed when her daughter had married a barrister, and a judge's son at that! She was a frightful snob and had lorded it over her friends ever since. She would never accept that Jonathan could do any wrong – least of all assault his wife. And perish the thought that Lauren might want a divorce! What would her friends and neighbours think?

Jonathan was, as usual, grovelling and being so solicitous for her welfare that she wanted to puke. He arrived home with roses, chocolates, champagne, and a gold bracelet that she had admired in West's on Grafton Street. When none of this seemed to move her, he offered her a weekend in New York: travelling Business Class, staying at the Waldorf Astoria, two Grand Circle tickets to The Metropolitan Opera to see Renée Fleming and Andreas Scholl in Handel's *Rodelinda*. She found this almost irresistible and would have jumped at it had she been able to go with Kate or any of her other friends. But she knew this was meant to be a romantic weekend with Jonathan and that she could not stomach.

She knew Jonathan couldn't believe that she was turning down this trip. Previously, she would have acquiesced and forgiven him but this time he had run out of luck. She could still feel his hands slapping and punching her and feel the force of the kick that he gave her as she lay helpless on the ground. No, thank you! This time she would not – could not – forgive him. Her friendship with Kate and seeing how Danny bullied her was making her stronger and making her think seriously about her own marriage and its shortcomings. For the first time in her life she began to think that maybe she didn't have to put up with this.

* * *

Kate tried ringing Lauren but her mobile was switched off and the answering machine was on. She decided to call by there and although she could see no car outside, she tried ringing the bell on the gate. She knew, instinctively, that Lauren was there but no one answered. Convinced more than ever that something was wrong, she was determined to get to the bottom of it. She would have to find a way to get Lauren to talk to her. With a heavy heart she drove home.

Chapter 12

By Wednesday evening Diana could stand it no longer. She had tried ringing Michael's office but when she refused to give her name and said that the call was personal, the snooty receptionist told her, in no uncertain terms, that he was unavailable. She didn't have his mobile number but she knew that she had to contact him somehow. Then she had a brainwave. Danny must have his number. She knew that he was in London for the week but she would ask Kate to give it to her. She rang her.

"Hi, Kate! Diana here. I need a favour. You know Michael Traynor who was at your last dinner party? Well, he offered to give us some advice about investments but, unfortunately, I've mislaid his mobile number. Would you have it?"

I'm fine, thank you, Diana, and you? – Kate wished she had the guts to say this but she didn't. Instead she replied, "Of course, let me look in Danny's telephone book. Yes, here it is – I have it," and she called it out. "Got that?"

"Yes, thanks."

"You're welcome. How are you anyway? I didn't get a chance to say hello on Sunday night at the golf –"

Diana cut her off. "Thanks, Kate, that's great! See you round."

Before Kate could reply, Diana had hung up. Strange!

Diana was whooping with joy. She felt sure that Michael must have lost her phone number otherwise he would surely have rung. She dialled his number and when she got his voice message she left a sexy message on it. When he hadn't called back three hours later, she sent him a text message: *Missing you. Please call me. Diana xxx*.

He didn't reply to this either.

Diana couldn't figure it out.

* ★ *

Lauren felt really bad about ignoring Kate's messages. Kate was such a good friend but she just could not discuss this with her right now. She had crawled into a cocoon and wanted to stay there. She couldn't face the world at the moment. She cancelled her golf tee-time on Thursday although she never missed Ladies' Day. She had even phoned Maggie, her housekeeper, and told her to go and visit her friend in Offaly as she would not need her for the rest of the week. Lauren did not want Maggie to see the state she was in. She also tried to act as normally as possible with the children but she knew they were worried. Daisy stayed close by her, not wanting to go out and play with her friends. She was so good, bringing her cups of tea and even offering to make dinner which made Lauren smile. Even Ben, who was normally so high-spirited, seemed very subdued. He wanted to know if she'd had a row with Daddy. How long more could she hide things from them? In another year or two she wouldn't be able to fob them off with the excuses she offered them now. She wanted to shield them from the harshness of life. But this can't go on, she thought. When I'm feeling better I will have to make a decision on what I'm going to do.

* * *

Diana was a total wreck by Thursday afternoon and began to think that Michael had only viewed her as a one-night stand. She was beginning to give up all hope that she would see him again when, out of the blue, he called her. She was so relieved that she could hardly speak to him.

"Sorry, I couldn't call you sooner but it's been a bitch of a week business-wise. How have you been?"

She resisted the urge to bawl him out which she certainly would have done with anyone else. She knew that Michael would not take such treatment and anyway, she was longing so much to see him again that she found herself softening. Careful girl, she told herself. Don't blow it.

"Michael, it's lovely to hear from you," she purred in her sexiest voice. "You poor thing, you're working too hard. What you need is some TLC and a nice long massage and

I'm very good at that . . ."

"That's exactly what I need," he said. "Can you make it tomorrow night? I'll meet you in the Fitzwilliam Hotel, at seven thirty."

"Lovely, I'll be there. I look forward to it."

What an understatement, she thought – I'm living for it! She felt like dancing. How can this man affect me so much? I wasn't just a one-night stand, thank God. I must understand what a tycoon he is and be more understanding.

She whirled around the room, drunk with anticipation. She poured herself a stiff gin and tonic and ran a lovely fragrant bath for herself where she languished for over an hour. There, she thought about making love to him again and wallowed in thoughts of the pleasure that awaited her tomorrow night. She couldn't wait to go to sleep so that the hours would go faster. Am I falling in love, she wondered. He could make her deliriously happy or downright miserable. She certainly had never had these feelings for anyone before now. She drifted off to sleep, dreaming of Michael's caresses on her body.

★ ★ ★

Jenny hardly dared to hope but couldn't keep herself from beaming. Her period was now a week late and her excitement was mounting by the day. It was ironic. Every month for years she had calendar-watched obsessively, waiting for her periods to come or not to come, counting days to calculate ovulation. Last week for the first time she had forgotten that her period was due. Excited about counting pounds she had forgotten about counting days. It wasn't until after the grand climax of Monday night that it occurred to her that her period was overdue. But isn't that what they said? 'A watched kettle never boils'? Slimforever had stopped her obsessing about conception and now it seemed she was pregnant.

Ironic too that she had only had sex once in the past month with Tom – she didn't call it making love any more. She was praying to all her favourite saints, particularly St Gabriel of Our Lady of Sorrows, and even St Jude, whom everyone said was the patron saint of hopeless cases.

Though she felt it was too early to say, she couldn't resist telling Tom.

"I think I may be pregnant, Tom. I'm a week overdue, and I'm always so regular."

"I doubt it," he said. "You're probably starting the menopause."

Great, she thought – just what I need to hear. She suspected he was being deliberately cruel but she was scared that maybe he was right.

On Thursday evening she had to return to the school for a concert and the staff had decided to go for a few drinks in the Ballyfern Inn afterwards.

"I'm driving Jimmy and Ciarán tonight – why don't you travel with us and that way you can drink with a clear conscience?" Conor had asked when she ran into him in the staffroom earlier that day.

"No, I'll drive and you can all drink," Jenny replied.

Conor raised his eyebrows, surprised. "That's not like you, turning down the opportunity for a piss-up." This was not the Jenny he knew.

"I'm on antibiotics," she lied.

Conor wasn't convinced. She hadn't mentioned being ill and she certainly looked in good health. Glowingly healthy, in fact. Women! They really were a mystery!

The concert went well. The kids were always so funny and some of them so talented. The proud parents smiled and clapped enthusiastically and Jenny even saw a tear or two being shed by the mothers.

Conor noticed that she was very quiet in the pub afterwards and when they had dropped Jimmy and Ciarán off at the house they shared, he said, "I know you too well, Jenny. Something's up. Out with it!"

Without meaning to, she blurted it out. "Conor, I think I might be pregnant. I can barely believe it. I can't think about anything else. You know how much I want children."

"Oh Jenny, I hope you're right. So that's why you're not drinking – I might have guessed! But honey, don't get your hopes up till you're sure. Beth went through this so many times but it was always a false alarm We eventually found out that Beth could never have children and at that stage her cancer had started so it was too late to consider adopting. But I do hope that you are pregnant. You'll make a wonderful mother."

"Please don't say anything to anyone. You're the only one I've told, besides Tom, of course."

"Your secret is safe with me."

"I don't know what I would do without you. You're a star."

When she got home, Tom was, as usual, out drinking with his mates. She didn't even know where, nor did she care.

He staggered in just as she was drifting off to sleep, reeking of beer.

"I know you're awake, Jenny," he said, giving her a shake on the shoulder.

"I am now," she replied sleepily. "Tom, you know I have to be up early for school in the morning."

"Ah, come on. I'm feeling horny. How about giving me a bit of loving?" He jumped into the bed beside her and, before she could realise what was happening, he had pulled her nightie up, tearing it, and despite her protests had forced himself on her. He thrust and grunted and three minutes later, he was done. She lay there feeling used and abused.

She remembered a discussion in the staffroom, some time ago, about marital rape and how most of the men thought that it wasn't possible. This had sure felt like rape. If this was her husband's idea of loving, it wasn't hers.

As he snored loudly she looked at him and wondered how she had ever believed she could be happy with him. Why couldn't she have met someone loving and caring? All she felt now was disgust and repugnance for the drunk beside her. Do I really want a baby with this man? It will tie me to him forever. She remembered the saying: 'Be careful what you wish for because it may come true.'

* * *

Kate knew that Lauren was avoiding her. She had phoned several times and got the answering machine. She had hoped to talk to Maggie to ask her if everything was okay but to her surprise Maggie wasn't there either. Lauren's mobile was turned off.

Then Lauren rang on Thursday night, telling what Kate was sure was a whopper of a lie.

"Sorry I missed your calls, Kate, but I had a meeting with a new client in Dublin today. How are things?"

"Grand, but I was worried about you. Are you okay?"

"I'm fine. Maybe we can get together tomorrow evening. Is Danny coming home?"

"God knows. I never know what he's doing nowadays. I'll call him tonight and ask him and let you know tomorrow."

Kate put the phone down wondering if she'd been imagining things. Lauren sounded her usual cheery self.

* * *

Kate rang Danny at about eleven thirty that night but as usual he wasn't there. And as usual his mobile was turned off. This was very strange because he always kept his mobile turned on, even when in restaurants. She had been mortified once when it had rung while they were at a concert in the National Concert Hall. She used to joke with him that it would be simpler for him to have it transplanted onto his ear. She couldn't figure out why it was now almost always turned off. She left a message on his hotel voicemail asking him to call her – no matter how late it was when he got in. At five minutes past three, he rang. She could tell – from the way he slurred his words – that he had been drinking.

"Danny, where have you been till this hour?"

"Kate, don't be cross. I know it's late but you know how it is. Wining and dining clients. What is it you wanted?"

She could hardly contain her anger but realised that, in his condition, it would be useless to try to have an intelligent conversation with him.

"Are you coming home tomorrow?"

"It's looking unlikely. Probably Saturday. Still a lot to do here."

"Fine, I'll go ahead and make my own plans for tomorrow night then. Obviously, if this goes on I will have to start an independent life of my own."

"Ah Kate," he said in that wheedling voice that she knew so well, "don't be like that. We'll have Saturday night together. Promise."

Great, she thought, after she had hung up. I get to spend one night a week with my husband and I should be pleased! Well, he can go to hell! If he thinks I'm going to put up with this for much longer, he's got another think coming. Things are going to change around here.

Chapter 13

On Friday morning an invitation arrived in the post:

Marcia & Michael Traynor
Request the pleasure of the company of
Kate & Danny O'Mara
For Drinks and Supper
*   On Friday, 28th September*
*   From 7 to 10 p.m.*

RSVP:
Island View,
Vico Road,
Killiney.
01 8447689

Kate was pleased to note that both her own name and
Marcia's were ahead of those of the men. Marcia's doing, no
doubt. She couldn't see Marcia putting up with the crap

that Danny was dishing out. She would certainly bring him to heel pretty quickly. Kate would have liked to go to the party but as it was a Friday night she guessed that Danny would be still in London. He seemingly was needed there every Friday night now. She would never have the courage to go to the party on her own if Danny wasn't with her.

It's exactly two weeks away, she thought wistfully, and I know I've lost another few pounds this week. This party would be a great motivation for me, to keep me going.

Kate was back wearing jeans again, for the first time in three years. For a laugh, she had taken them out of the closet yesterday and to her delight had been able to get into them. Okay, she'd had to lie on the bed to zip them up but everyone had to do that, even size zeros. Size zero! Kate couldn't begin to comprehend it. What was the world coming to? Although she would have loved a daughter, in a way she was relieved that she had all boys. She didn't think that she could handle the angst that seemingly went with raising teenage girls these days. Boys were definitely much easier, or maybe she was just lucky with her four. Certainly, some of her friends were having a nightmare time with their teenage daughters. She decided to stay in her jeans as the slightly tight waistband was a reminder every time she felt tempted to indulge. No more tracksuit bottoms and sloppy jumpers, she decided. The new me is about to emerge!

Danny had always been on at her to go shopping and buy new, fashionable clothes. Kate had never been interested. She now reluctantly admitted – if only to herself

– that the reason for that was because of her weight. She hated shopping because she found it so hard to get anything to fit her and even if she did it inevitably looked awful. Now that she was losing weight she thought that maybe a shopping spree would be on the cards, but not yet. She'd wait until she had got all the way down to her target weight.

Kate rang Lauren to tell her that she was free that night.

"How about trying out that new Japanese restaurant in Naas?" suggested Kate.

"Lovely. I've heard great reports of it."

"Would you like me to ask Jenny if she's free to join us?"

"Why not? The more the merrier. I really like Jenny. She's great fun." Jenny was delighted to be invited and said that she would make the reservation as she knew the manageress there. She suspected that it might be difficult to get a table as it was the latest trendy place to see and be seen. Lauren called for Kate and, though she appeared to be in good spirits, Kate could tell that it was an act. She noticed that Lauren was heavily made-up, which was unusual for her and, despite the make-up, Kate could see the shadows of bruising underneath. Kate was determined to get to the bottom of it and wrest the truth out of Lauren.

Kate couldn't believe how busy the restaurant was.

"Typical Irish people," she said to the others, surveying the queue and the people being turned away. "They all rush to any new and trendy place until the next new place opens and then they all desert *en masse*."

"Are you suggesting we're like that?" Lauren asked her.

"Of course not! We're here because of our diet," Kate replied grinning.

"Thank goodness you booked us a table, Jenny," Lauren said, as she waved at the local bank manager and his wife. "I wouldn't fancy having to queue."

"God, everyone who's anyone in Kildare is here," Jenny replied, spotting some racehorse trainers and big name developers at other tables.

"And it's far from sushi any of them were reared," Lauren whispered.

"More like bacon and cabbage!" Jenny said.

They were all laughing as they were called to their table.

Kate and Jenny had never eaten Japanese cuisine before but Lauren was an old hand and explained the menu to them.

"No raw fish, please," Jenny and Kate implored her.

"Okay," she agreed.

They finally decided on beef teriyaki while Lauren went for the sushi. They were amazed at how delicious it was. Lauren offered them a taste of her meal. It was so good that they wanted a taste of everything on her plate.

"Maybe next time you'll order your own," she said, as she slapped Jenny's hand away from her plate.

"Sorry," Jenny grinned, "but it is damned good."

Quite a few people stopped by their table to say hello to Lauren and she introduced them to the girls.

"My God, Lauren, you know everybody," Jenny said, amazed.

"Everybody wants to know her," Kate teased. "She refuses to get involved in their social rat race, so they all want to snag her."

"Get off. Don't be ridiculous!" Lauren laughingly punched Kate on the arm.

They had all agreed that it was a super evening and that Japanese cuisine was perfect for keeping the calories low.

They dropped Jenny off and Kate noticed that Lauren had gone very quiet. Maybe now was the time to have a talk with her.

As they came close to Ballyfern, Kate said, "Lauren, why don't you come back with me for a coffee?"

"I'd like that. Actually, would you mind if I stayed the night? Jonathan's away and the children have gone to stay with his sister Helen for the weekend."

Kate was delighted and relieved. "Of course. I'd be delighted. It's quite lonely on my own every night. That's settled then."

They drove to Lauren's house to collect her overnight bag and then back to Kate's.

Kate led Lauren out onto the terrace. There she lit some candles and switched on the lights around the pool. Then she put on her favourite Juliet Turner CD, before opening a bottle of Danny's precious 1985 Lynch Bages.

"To hell with coffee! We need something stronger."

She hoped that with a glass of wine Lauren might confide in her.

"Just what I need," said Lauren. "Some TLC. This wine is divine, Kate. It's so smooth."

"Now, would you like to tell me what's wrong? I have my suspicions but I'd rather hear it from you than jump to conclusions."

Lauren was silent for a few moments and Kate waited patiently. Eventually, Lauren started to speak in a whisper – so low, that Kate had to strain to hear her.

"I don't know how to begin, Kate. It's just so awful."

"Well, how about telling me what happened last week? Jonathan did something to you, didn't he?" she asked gently, taking Lauren's hand in her own.

"Yes," she hesitated, not able to get the words out.

"It is okay, Lauren. You must tell me," Kate said gently. "I won't be judgemental, I promise."

She waited until Lauren was ready. Lauren looked at her, tears in her eyes. "He beat me," she whispered.

"Oh, you poor darling," Kate said, stroking Lauren's hand. "I suspected something of the kind. Has this happened before?" Kate gently pushed Lauren's hair back from her face.

"Yes, many times. He's always so sorry afterwards that I forgive him, but it happens again and again."

"How long has this been going on?" Kate asked, horrified at what Lauren was telling her, afraid that she would cry and upset Lauren even more.

"Almost from the beginning," Lauren whispered, staring at the floor, not wanting to see the pity in her friend's eyes.

Once she had started, the floodgates opened and Lauren poured out the whole sorry tale of Jonathan's violence over the years. Aghast at what she was hearing Kate kept stroking

Lauren's hand, hoping to give her some comfort.

When Lauren came to what had happened the previous Monday night she started to cry gently and Kate put her arms around her, rocking her as she would a baby. Lauren continued through her tears and when she had finished Kate had tears streaming down her cheeks too.

"You poor, poor thing! How I wish you'd told me this before!"

"I wanted to, but I was so ashamed. You've no idea what it's like, Kate."

Kate got up to get a box of tissues and handed them to Lauren, taking some herself.

When they had dried their tears, Kate said, "Lauren, you know this can't go on. You can't let him keep doing this. These men never stop. I know. My sister Teresa was married to an abusive guy and he almost killed her." She gripped Lauren's hands. "Please do something before Jonathan does the same to you." Kate was energised with the need to get Lauren to see this.

"Yes, I know, and I'm so afraid for the children. They're beginning to understand and what kind of a message is this giving them?" She started to whimper again, thinking of Daisy and Ben, and how this would affect them.

"You have to think of them but, just as importantly, yourself. Would you consider leaving him?" Kate felt that she really had no other option.

"I don't know. Right now I hate him and don't even want to be in the same room as him but I have felt like this before and we've got back on track. But this time I don't want to. I have to do something to make it stop – but what?" She appealed to Kate for an answer.

"Jonathan is always such a perfect gentleman. You just never know, do you? It's true what they say: no one knows what goes on behind closed doors."

They talked late into the night, exploring every avenue, and eventually Kate persuaded her to take steps to stop it, once and for all. She suggested that she go to a solicitor and look for a barring order. Lauren knew that, as a barrister, Jonathan would be mortified and that the news would spread like wildfire through the legal world. It was an option, and a good one. Kate felt that it might shock Jonathan into seeking help.

"You have no idea what a relief it has been to tell you about all this," said Lauren. "It's been dreadful keeping it secret. Frankly, I didn't think anyone would believe me. My mother certainly wouldn't – and you know me, Kate – I'm very reserved. I often wish that I had a sister that I could share things like this with."

"I'll be your sister," Kate told her, giving her a hug.

"You're better than a sister. You're a great friend. I feel like a big weight has been lifted off my shoulders. Thank you for listening. Now that I've finally decided that I have to take some action, I feel better."

"I'm so glad you finally unburdened yourself. How awful it must have been for you, hiding it for all these years!"

It was three o'clock when they went to bed but both of them felt closer than ever – sisters together!

★ ★ ★

At that very moment, Diana was making love to Michael for the fourth time that night. She had been a bundle of nerves since his phone call yesterday and had not eaten a bite since. She'd had butterflies in her tummy just as she used to have when she'd hear her father's footsteps outside her bedroom door. These were anticipatory too – but anticipating pleasure, not abuse. She cried off her meeting with Isabelle and the other girls. She couldn't have made small talk. Instead she stayed longer in the beauty salon and had a facial and body wrap as well as her usual treatments.

She had decided to wear her Chanel suit today but when she had tried it on this morning, the zip wouldn't close. All that bloody chocolate she'd eaten! In a panic she jumped on the scales. Ohmigod! She couldn't believe it. She tried again – five times – but the scales told the same story each time. Although she was five foot eight, Diana prided herself on being less than ten stone and a perfect size twelve – or ten, American, as she was so fond of telling everyone. To her horror the scales showed her at ten stone three. No wonder her Chanel suit wouldn't fit her. God, I'm gross! Michael will hate it. I'll have to start a diet today. So she'd eaten practically nothing all day. A grapefruit for breakfast, a starter green salad in BT's for lunch with only one glass of chardonnay and nothing since. She couldn't risk drinking with the girls on such an empty stomach so she went straight to the Fitzwilliam at seven thirty to meet Michael.

When she got there, there was no sign of him. She panicked. What if he didn't show up? She ordered a glass of white wine and sat nervously, trying to look confident. It didn't help that she felt really fat. God, look at those models over there! Eight stone maximum and almost six feet tall! Just as she thought she might have a panic attack, Michael arrived.

"My darling, I'm so sorry. I was at a meeting which went on later than expected and then got caught up in the bloody traffic. Wow! You look sexy."

She stood up to greet him and as he pulled her to him she could feel his hardness against her.

"Is that a gun in your pocket or are you just pleased to see me?" She smiled as she gave him the old Mae West line.

"I'm just really pleased to see you," he answered, giving her a long lingering kiss which left her feeling weak at the knees. "Let's get the hell out of here. I need you desperately."

Her heart soared and she was giddy with excitement. He wanted her as much as she wanted him – she'd known it. She was exuberant!

She finished her wine while he ordered a taxi and she hoped that the taxi driver couldn't see what was going on in the back seat. He slipped her panties off – if you could call the wisp of material that – it was the tiniest thong imaginable. He then started to caress her slowly and she became so aroused that she thought she might come, right there and then, in the taxi. Luckily, she held off and once inside the apartment Michael continued what he had started. Inside the door, he went down on his knees and using his tongue brought her to the most fantastic orgasm that she could ever have imagined. He then laid her down on the plush carpet which felt like velvet and entered her with an urgency that made her feel like the most desirable woman in the world.

"Oh God, it's so good with you," he murmured.

"Mmmmm," she purred. "You make me feel so alive."

She hadn't known what love and sex was all about until now even though she had been married for so long. Poor Kevin, it wasn't his fault, and she felt an uncharacteristic sympathy for him. She was to blame. She should never have married him. She had never loved or even fancied him. Now she had met a man that she both fancied like hell and loved. Oh God, am I really in love? She'd never understood all the hype about love – in poems, books and love-songs. Now she did and she welcomed the pleasures of sex and love with open arms.

When they were both totally satiated Michael opened a bottle of champagne and handed her a menu.

"If it's okay with you, we'll order a takeaway from the local restaurant. I know the owner well. He won't mind delivering. What do you fancy?"

Diana couldn't believe her ears. "My God, this is a really upmarket restaurant and they even deliver for you! I don't believe it!"

"For you, my princess, everything's possible."

She felt herself getting aroused again. Michael noticed it.

"Let's order before we make love again or we'll never eat," he said with a laugh.

He recommended the lobster to start, followed by the duck in a cherry sauce. If he'd said sausages and chips, she'd have been happy. Nothing mattered except that he was there.

I can't believe it. I think I've died and gone to heaven, she thought.

After he had ordered, he started slowly peeling her top down and caressing her breasts.

"Wow! I love these beauties. Have I told you that you have the most beautiful boobs I've ever seen? They're sensational – big and heavy and soft – not hard and full of silicone like most women's nowadays. I can't keep my hands off them. That first night I saw you at Danny's house, I couldn't keep my eyes off them. They were straining against the silk of your dress and I could see the contours of your nipples. It drove me crazy and I wanted to rip the dress off you and caress them. I had a hard-on all night. I never thought that I would be enjoying them now."

Diana was afraid to tell him that she had been contemplating having a boob job to lift her breasts. Thank God she hadn't had it done!

After a wonderful meal Michael carried her to bed where they again made slow, sensual love – exploring each other's bodies and doing things that Diana had never even imagined. It all came so naturally.

They were lying in a happy haze when Michael playfully pinched her tummy,

"Uh, oh, what have we got here?" he teased. "Has somebody been overindulging, this week, or is it just contentment?"

She rolled onto her tummy, mortified that he'd noticed. She didn't dare tell him that it was the anxiety of waiting for his call that had caused her to binge on chocolate.

"Just coming up to that time of the month," she lied, determined to starve from tomorrow on. Maybe she'd join the slimming club that she'd told Kate about.

The following morning Michael was still sleeping when she woke up and she felt a rush of love for him. She sat watching him sleeping and when he stirred she moved closer to him.

"That was a wonderful night," he murmured, nuzzling her neck.

They made slow gentle love and she desperately wanted to tell him that she loved him but instinct told her to stay mum.

Over coffee, however, she had enough courage to say to him, "Michael, do you think that you could let me know earlier than a Thursday if you want to meet me on Friday night? You know I have quite a busy social life and I wouldn't want to have to say no to our meetings due to a prior engagement."

"Of course, my love, but I don't always know myself whether I'll be free or not. You know how it is in business. Unexpected crises often crop up. However, Fridays seem to be working out fine for us so far. Let's try and keep it Friday nights and I will try and ring you by Wednesday in future.

Okay? After all, I need my weekly fix of those beautiful breasts."

"Perfect," she murmured.

Diana felt much happier, and more secure, leaving him that morning. She knew that she was in love and, although he hadn't said anything, she suspected Michael had fallen in love with her too.

She couldn't wait for him to realise it – then they could be together permanently. She would finally get to live the life she'd always dreamed about.

Chapter 14

Lauren woke and for a moment didn't know where she was. She took in the large four-poster bed with the pale blue silk drapes and thought that she must be in some luxury hotel. Then she remembered – Kate's! She felt a sense of release flow through her as she recalled the previous night. Finally talking about her abuse had given her a sense of peace and taking the decision to do something about it had made her feel strong. She knew that she would have a long battle ahead of her and that Jonathan would be furious but, if their marriage had any hope of surviving, she had to take it in her own hands. She was snuggled down amongst the snow-white Egyptian cotton sheets and luxurious duvet when she heard the gentle tap on the door.

"Are you awake, Lauren?"

"Come in, Kate."

"I've brought you some coffee."

Kate carried in a tray set with freshly squeezed orange

juice, coffee, and toast, all on beautiful china. There was also a single yellow rose in a crystal vase.

"Kate, you're too good to me. This is beautiful. You've gone to so much trouble!"

"I think you deserve some TLC after all you've been through. I'm going to run a bath for you and, after you've soaked for a long time, we can have breakfast together on the terrace. It's such a lovely morning that I'm going for a swim before my shower, so take your time."

As she lay soaking in Kate's beautiful marble bathroom, Lauren thought how lucky she was to have such a loyal friend. Kate deserved the very best but she was not getting it from Danny. How could he be so heartless as to leave her alone, week after week? Lauren felt sure that he was not working as much as he pretended. Danny had always liked a good time and, away from Kate's watchful eye, who knew what was going on? Lauren didn't trust Danny and was afraid for her friend. Kate was so trusting she believed everything he told her and never doubted him. True, she was living in luxury but Kate didn't need that. She'd have been happy anywhere once she had love and Lauren wasn't at all sure that she had that any more. Life is never fair, not for anyone, she thought to herself.

They enjoyed a nice leisurely breakfast of poached eggs and grilled bacon.

"Sorry there are no sausages or Clonakilty pudding. We have to face Tara in two more days."

"Actually, Kate, I've eaten hardly anything all week. Some people comfort-eat when they have problems. Me –

I can't eat a bite. How have you done this week?"

"I've been very good, with the exception of the wine last night. I think I've lost some more. It's great to be able to get into my jeans again."

"I can really notice it on you. How are the menus for Tara coming along?"

"Almost finished. I've really enjoyed doing them. It's kept me occupied so I barely felt the week flying by."

"That's what you need. You really do need to think of something you can work at, regardless of how Danny feels."

"Yeah, well, we'll see," Kate replied without much conviction. "I'd better get a move on and organise something for dinner tonight. What are you doing for the rest of the day?"

"I'm thinking of ringing an old school friend of mine who specialises in family law, to ask her advice. Then I may pop into Liffey Valley for some retail therapy. Jonathan has gone to Paris for the weekend – for the Rugby World Cup. No wives allowed! Actually, Jenny's husband is also on the trip. Jonathan did offer to cancel it and stay home but that's the last thing I wanted. Tomorrow I'm going to his sister's for lunch and to collect Ben and Daisy. I'm not looking forward to it. I don't feel like facing his family."

When they'd finished breakfast, Lauren helped Kate clear up before leaving.

"I can't thank you enough for last night, Kate. You're one in a million." Giving her friend a big hug, she took her leave.

* * *

Jenny had really enjoyed her night out with the girls although she felt that Lauren was not her usual self and wondered what the matter could be. She had been sorely tempted to share her hopes of pregnancy with the two girls but somehow resisted the temptation. She was afraid that she might jinx things and in fact now regretted having said anything to Conor. She prayed and prayed and could think of little else. In fact, her initial mood of elation had passed and a kind of anxiety had taken over.

She decided to go into Dublin on Saturday to take her mind off things but, instead of that happening, she found herself looking at baby clothes and ended up in the nursery department of every shop she visited.

Her first priority was buying a pregnancy-testing kit in Boots. She could never have done that in Naas. The whole town would know about it by the next day. She resisted the temptation to go into Beshoffs for ray and chips – her usual treat when she visited Dublin – and instead went to a salad bar on Henry Street. She had been really good all week and didn't want to blow it now. Her clothes were all feeling loose on her although she secretly hoped that they would get tight again in the next few months – with baby fat!

She was on her own again this weekend as Tom had gone to France with his buddies from the rugby club, to cheer Ireland on in the Rugby World Cup. The World Piss-Up, more likely! She was looking forward to two weeks without him. Sad, she thought, to feel that way about your husband.

When she got home she rushed into the bathroom, hands shaking as she unwrapped the pregnancy test. She read the instructions carefully, did as they said, and couldn't believe it when the blue line appeared. Negative! It's not possible, she thought. I feel sure I'm pregnant. I feel so bloated. This can't be right. Miserably, she decided that she would give it another week and try again.

* * *

Diana was in such good form when she got home that Kevin wondered what had caused it. You never knew with Diana. Last week she had been in foul humour, today she was all smiles.

"I take it you made up with Isabelle?"

"What?" Diana didn't know what he was talking about.

"Well, last week you came home in such bad form that I assumed you'd fallen out with her."

"Oh . . . um . . . yes, everything's fine again." Phew, that was a close one! She really must be more careful. What if Isabelle had rung last night? Kevin obviously assumed that she had stayed with her. It won't make much difference soon, she thought. Michael and I will be together, forever! She gave Kevin a dazzling smile.

He decided to make hay while the sun was shining.

"I thought we might ask Kate and Danny over for supper tonight. What do you think? We really owe them one."

"Why not – as long as you do the cooking? I'm really too tired."

Too tired? Doing what? Kevin shook his head in exasperation but he was pleased that she had put up no objection. He knew that she didn't really like Kate, though how anyone could not, he would never understand. Kate was always so kind to Diana. He rang her and invited them over.

"Kevin, if you don't mind, I really want to stay in tonight. Danny and I have hardly had a chance to talk since the night of our dinner party. He's not going back till Monday, so maybe tomorrow night?"

Kevin turned to Diana and asked if this was all right.

"I suppose so," she answered in a bored voice.

"That's settled then. Eight o'clock. Look forward to seeing you both."

Secretly, Diana was looking forward to it as it would give her a chance to pump Danny for more information about Michael.

★ ★ ★

Kate got dressed in her favourite blue dress, which had not seen the light of day in over three years. She was thrilled when she'd tried it on and it had fitted. Danny had always said that it matched the colour of her eyes exactly. She made up carefully and couldn't believe her reflection in the mirror. I almost look my old self, she thought gleefully. I can't believe how losing a little weight can make such a difference. She was determined to make a big effort and get back to the old closeness that she and Danny had always shared. They had become so distant since he'd taken that goddamned job in London. She planned to share a nice romantic dinner together and then go to bed and make love like they used to. This was the longest time that they had gone without sex. She was really looking forward to it and hoped that it would help mend things between them.

When Danny arrived home he brushed her cheek and headed straight for the shower. She was disappointed that he had not noted the change in her appearance but she would not let this spoil the evening.

She prepared some smoked salmon on brown bread for him and just salmon for herself. She also opened a bottle of Chablis and put it on ice.

When he came downstairs he looked surprised.

"To what do I owe this? Is it my birthday? Don't tell me it's your birthday and I've forgotten it!" he joked. "I'm not so stupid as to forget my wife's birthday. Now that would be suicide! So, what's the special occasion?"

"I'm just happy to have you home."

"Now that is exactly what a good wife should say!" He raised his glass to her. "You look nice – is that a new dress?"

"Danny, I've had this outfit for ten years. Don't you remember it?"

"Well, I haven't seen it in a while."

"That's because it hasn't fitted me in a while."

"That's good. You've lost a little weight, I think."

Lost a little weight? I've lost almost a stone! she wanted

to scream at him. Was he trying to irritate her or did he just not see her any more? Before she could reply, his mobile phone rang.

"I'll take this in the office."

How strange. He'd never done that before. He always answered calls in front of her. He didn't speak until he had closed the door behind him. Twenty-five minutes later he reappeared.

"Who was that?"

"Just a colleague in London. She needed some information."

"God, do they work all weekend as well?"

"They're very dedicated."

You can say that again, thought Kate.

"How are the boys?" he asked, taking a seat and tackling his smoked salmon with gusto. "How's the rugby going? Is Justin pleased with his team? And has Toby settled?"

She gave him all the news of the boys as they finished their salmon and then Danny said, "I was hoping that I could touch base with Kevin later this evening."

"You can do that tomorrow night," she told him. "They've invited us round for supper."

"Great." He drained his glass of wine. "And what have you been getting up to all week?"

She started to tell him about the menus that she had been working on for Tara but she could see that he was only half listening. He had a faraway look in his eyes. His mind was a million miles away. As she was telling him about the sushi restaurant in Naas, his damn mobile rang again.

"I don't believe this!" she said. "Are we to have no privacy at all this weekend?"

"Sorry, darling, but it's important," and he headed for the office again.

Kate was getting really exasperated. She was trying hard to stay cool but it wasn't easy. Where had she gone wrong? They had no life together any more. Try as she might, she could not get back to the old, easy, loving relationship they had shared before this whole London thing began. Sighing, she headed to the kitchen to start cooking the steaks. Hopefully this phone call won't last twenty-five minutes, she thought, or his meal will be ruined. Well, it'll serve him right!

★ ★ ★

Lauren had passed a very pleasant day. She couldn't face the line of traffic heading into Liffey Valley so she continued on to Grafton Street, where she found it a simple matter to park in the Brown Thomas carpark. She then treated herself to a beautiful new winter coat from Paul Costello and a pair of Bally boots to go with it. She bought some Jo Malone candles and bath oil for Kate, as a thank-you gift, and treated herself to some also. Then, in a mad moment of extravagance, she splashed out on a pot of Crème de la Mer moisturiser. Because I'm worth it, she told herself. She was getting very fond of this saying and thought they should all adopt it as their motto. She grabbed a late lunch in Pasta Fresca, an old favourite haunt of hers from her modelling days. She had considered going to the Shelbourne but knew that she would be sure to bump into some of their friends there and that was the last thing she needed.

When she got home she closed the door behind her, revelling in the solitude. I get so little time to myself nowadays and I really need it, she thought. It was so rare for both Jonathan and the kids to be away that she was going to make the most of it. She rang the children who were waiting excitedly for a Chinese takeaway to arrive. They'd spent a wonderful day sailing in Dun Laoghaire with their cousins. They were obviously having a great time.

She wandered around the beautiful old Georgian house, lovingly touching the antique mahogany furniture that glowed in the lamplight. How could she bear to leave this house if she and Jonathan divorced? The house had been in Jonathan's family for three generations and when Jonathan's father, Benedict, had passed away his mother had moved to an apartment in Dalkey, to be closer to her daughter. This house would one day belong to Ben, the fifth generation to live there.

She put the answering machine on and ran a beautiful scented bath for herself with her new bath oil. Then she lit the candles, placing them around the bath and finally opened a half bottle of champagne that she had put on ice. Slipping into the bath she gave a deep contented sigh. She was feeling strong again. It would take more than a few knocks to keep her down! She had made an appointment with her friend Stella, a solicitor, for Tuesday and she would take it from there.

Lauren remembered the first time that she had come to this house. She and Jonathan's sister, Helen, had been school friends at Alexandra College, even though Helen was a boarder and Lauren a day pupil. She had been invited to Helen's twenty-first birthday party, held in this house, and here she'd met Jonathan. He could not take his eyes off her. He was completely smitten and followed her around all night. She quite liked his attention. She found his dark good looks very attractive and, at six foot four, he towered above her, which she didn't find happening too often. He had qualified as a solicitor three years previously and was much more sophisticated than the guys she usually hung around with. They started dating. He was a real gentleman and he made her laugh and it wasn't long before they fell in love. Jonathan would happily have got married there and then but her modelling career had really taken off and she loved every moment of it. She wasn't ready to settle down just yet. Her face graced the cover of every magazine and she was invited to every hot event in Dublin. He was busy establishing himself in legal circles so they agreed to wait a few years before settling down. Modelling had only a very short shelf life anyway, so why not enjoy it?

When Lauren was twenty-eight they tied the knot in what was dubbed 'The Society Wedding of The Year'. They made such a handsome couple. Lauren's mother, a dreadful snob, was beside herself with joy. Her daughter had landed the most eligible bachelor in Dublin. His father a High Court judge! She never stopped boasting about it to anyone who would listen. All her friends and neighbours were thoroughly sick of hearing about it. Two years later, Lauren became pregnant with Ben and packed in modelling for good. Her beautiful little daughter, Daisy, was born a year after Ben. Her world was complete, except for the violence, which had begun shortly after their marriage.

It was time for change.

* * *

Kate had been so looking forward to Danny coming home but the evening was turning out a shambles. Danny had stayed in the office until it was time for dinner and Kate couldn't help noticing that the whiskey bottle was emptying very rapidly. This wasn't like Danny.

Over the steaks, which mercifully were not dried out, she told him about the invitation from Michael and Marcia.

"I don't suppose you'll be able to get home for it as it's a Friday night."

"Of course, I'll come home for it. I want to keep Michael sweet and it will be good for networking. Ring Marcia on Monday and accept."

No problem there then! He can get home on Fridays if he wants to, she thought angrily.

She tried to keep the conversation light but Danny responded in monosyllables. They sat watching *CSI Miami*, one of their favourite shows, while Danny steadily emptied the whiskey bottle. This was worrying. Maybe he really is stressed out with this job, she couldn't help thinking. I'll have to relax him and try and get him to unwind. But when they went up to bed and she tried to make overtures to him – kissing his neck the way she knew he liked – he didn't respond.

Instead he said, "Please, not tonight, Kate. I'm not in the mood."

She was so hurt and felt such rejection that she wanted to cry. When had Danny ever 'not been in the mood'? He was always in the mood for sex. And she had been so hoping that he would notice the change in her body which she knew had toned up. What's happening, she wondered. He's changed and I can't get through to him.

Chapter 15

The next morning Danny was up early and off to play golf, refusing the breakfast she offered to cook for him. She prepared lunch and wondered if he would refuse that as well. Luckily, he didn't although he was so late home from golf that it was a rushed affair.

Danny was pretty monosyllabic throughout the lunch, not at all like his usual chatty self.

"Is the beef okay?" she asked, surprised he hadn't passed a comment on it, as he usually did.

"Mmmm, fine," he mumbled, through a mouthful of Yorkshire pudding. She gave up. There was obviously something on his mind – something he didn't want to share with her.

The drive to the school to visit the boys wasn't much better and they drove for the most part in silence.

The boys were in high spirits and Danny brightened up in their company and was his usual ebullient self. When he met some other fathers that he knew he was Mr Personality personified. Seeing him smiling and full of chat with others, she concluded that she was the problem.

She tried again on the way home.

"Have I done something to annoy you, Danny?"

"Of course not, Kate," he said, patting her knee. "Don't mind me, I'm just preoccupied."

Thank God, she thought with relief, it's not me. She let him be.

★ ★ ★

Jenny was feeling very down in herself. After that dreadful encounter with Tom, when he had forced himself on her, she finally faced up to the fact that she didn't love him any more. Her disappointment with the pregnancy test had left her feeling even more depressed. She went for a long walk down by the canal on Sunday. It was one of those, lovely, sunny Autumn days when one should feel good to be alive. She passed many couples, young and old, walking holding hands and talking quietly together. How I envy them, she thought. How I would love to be walking here, holding hands with someone I love. Not much chance of that! She was beginning to resign herself to a loveless future.

On the way home she passed a young couple eating chips. The smell wafting towards her drove her crazy and before she knew it she was standing in The Capri, ordering a large bag of chips. She debated having a spiceburger or sausages with it, but luckily she passed on them. Coming out of the chip shop, she went into The Gem next door and bought a Crunchie, a Mars bar and two bars of Cadbury's Fruit & Nut. She knew it was sinful but she didn't care.

She ate the chips on the way home, enjoying each delicious bite. Halfway home, with half the bag gone, the guilt set in. She rang Kate.

"Kate, I've been very bold," she confessed.

"What did you do?" Kate asked her.

"I've demolished half a bag of chips – I couldn't resist them," she said sheepishly.

"Did you have anything else?" Kate asked her.

"No."

"Good, now dump the rest of that bag in the nearest bin, okay?"

"Okay." Jenny had actually had enough. They didn't taste quite as good now that she felt guilty. "Okay, done," she said as she deposited the offenders in a bin . . . but . . . I did buy some chocolate as well . . . um, several bars."

"Oh, Jenny! Have you eaten it yet?"

"Not yet, but they're burning a hole in my pocket."

"Right, in the bin with them too," Kate ordered.

"Oh, Kate you're cruel!"

"I have to cruel to be kind. And think of the weigh-in tomorrow night!"

"Oh, God, you're right," and the chocolate followed the chips. "Thanks, Kate. I needed that. Bye."

When she'd put her phone away, she started home again but after a few steps, turned back and retrieved the Crunchie and one of the Fruit & Nut bars from the bin.

When she got home there was a string of cars outside.

Shouts and laughter were issuing from Conor's house. She remembered him saying he'd be having a few mates round to watch the rugby match on TV.

Great! Everyone has a life but me, she thought, feeling extremely sorry for herself. She just couldn't help it – she opened up the chocolate bars and demolished the two of them in three minutes flat.

When they were gone, Tara's words rang in her ears 'A moment on the lips – a lifetime on the hips.' Oh God, she thought. That's so true!

★ ★ ★

Kate was dreading the evening with Kevin and Diana but again, once they arrived there, Danny was his usual charming self. She felt she was married to a chameleon. How could he change so quickly? And they say women are moody, she thought with annoyance. .

They were barely in the door and finished saying hello when Diana pounced.

"Tell me all about London, Danny," she said, taking his arm.

"Hey, hey, let me get my coat off and a drink first!" He winked at Kevin. "God, you women are so impatient!" But he was smiling at Diana and admiring her cleavage as he spoke.

"What a lovely fire!" Kate said, as they took their seats in the living-room.

"The evenings are getting very nippy," Kevin remarked,

throwing another log on the already blazing fire.

Diana couldn't contain herself any longer. "Well, how is London, Danny? A lot more exciting than bloody Ballyfern, I'll bet!"

Kate looked at Kevin, who shrugged. Neither of them could understand how she didn't love the place. They did.

Danny was amusing and told some funny anecdotes about his time in London that Kate hadn't heard and which had them all laughing. Why could he not have shared this with me before, she asked herself, more than a little piqued. At least his mobile is not popping every hour, she thought.

"Tell me about Michael," gushed Diana.

"What about him?"

"Well, you're working for him. What's he like?"

"He's only been over once. Mainly we speak on the phone."

"Oh. Have you been to his home at all?"

"No, not yet, but we did receive an invite to a drinks party there the week after next."

Kate and Kevin were wondering what all the questions were about, but not Danny. He had a very good idea what they were all about. He knew Diana too well and didn't trust her as far as he'd throw her.

Then Kate remembered that Diana had called her looking for Michael's number.

"By the way, did you ring Michael about those investments?" she asked Diana.

"What investments?" Kevin asked, puzzled.

"Nothing important," said Diana quickly. "Just

something Michael was talking about the night we met."

Danny knew exactly what was going on and wondered how Kevin could be such a blind fool. He was just like Kate. They trusted everyone and thought everybody was as honest as they were. He had tried to warn Kevin about Diana but he wouldn't listen. Danny had given up.

Kevin went out to the kitchen to prepare supper and Kate went out to help him, which was funny when she thought about it. She was in Diana's house and yet here she was, in the kitchen, while Diana was pouring herself another gin and tonic.

When they were out of earshot, Danny hissed at Diana, "What the hell are you thinking of? I know what you're up to and let me tell you – you're playing with fire. You're out of your depth here and you'll only get hurt. This guy is a major player."

"I know. That's what makes him so exciting."

"Diana, trust me. You'll be like a lamb to the slaughter. What about Kevin?"

"What about Kevin?"

At that moment, Kevin came in with the food and said, "What about me?"

"Just wondering if you had supper ready," she lied glibly.

The lasagne was delicious but Kate refused a second portion much as she wanted it. She loved these informal evenings with no fuss – just friends sharing a simple meal in the kitchen. Supper was so much nicer than the grandiose dinners that Danny preferred.

Then, just as they were getting ready to leave Diana

asked, out of the blue, "When is Michael's drinks party by the way?"

"It's on Friday week."

"That's not possible."

They all looked at her, questioningly.

"What do you mean, not possible?" asked Kate, wondering had she missed something.

Kevin was also looking at Diana in a very perplexed way.

Diana realised that she had blundered. She was incensed that Michael should choose a Friday night for a party when that was *their* night and he had six other nights to choose from. However, she had better watch her step. Danny was looking at her with a knowing smirk and Kate and Kevin were looking at her very strangely.

"Well, what I mean is . . . eh . . . most people have a party either during the week or on Saturday night." She knew that sounded very lame but they seemed to buy it.

"Yeah, you're probably right," said Danny, giving her a sly wink.

Kate and Danny drove home in silence. She couldn't think of anything to say.

Danny went straight to bed and by the time she had locked up and come to join him, he was fast asleep.

The next morning he left to catch the eight o'clock flight back to his new life, leaving Kate alone again.

Chapter 16

Jenny and Conor were both very quiet and subdued in the staffroom at lunch-time on Monday.

Neither had any appetite and eventually Jenny said, "I know what's wrong with me but why are you so glum?"

He replied quietly, "Well, tomorrow is Beth's second anniversary and you know it's not a good time for me."

"Oh, Conor, I'm so sorry! I've been so wrapped up in my own problems that I completely forgot the date. I'll be at her anniversary Mass tomorrow night."

"I'm going to invite some people back to the house for drinks afterwards and I'd love you to come."

"I'd be delighted. Can I bring anything?"

"Just yourself. Everything's organised."

* * *

Kate managed to get all the menus for Tara printed off in time for Monday night but it wasn't an easy task. She had

167

to admit that when it came to computers she wasn't the brightest but then she'd always had Danny or Sam or David, who were all computer wizards, to help her. She often wondered – looking at these two boys that she had brought into the world – how they had become so knowledgeable. Having struggled with all this technology by herself, she finally had the finished product ready to deliver to Tara.

Feeling her self-confidence dwindle, she hoped that her work was up to scratch. She wasn't sure. Would Tara approve? Was it good enough or what she wanted? Should she tell her that she hadn't time and start again? Don't be stupid, Kate scolded herself. I've put a lot of effort into this. I've got to believe in myself, as Lauren would say.

She rang Marcia before lunch to thank her for the invitation and to say that they would attend the party.

"Kate, it's lovely to hear from you. We had such a nice evening in your home. How are you and how is Danny getting on with the London project? I was so pleased when Michael told me that he had won the contract."

"Thank you, Marcia. He's doing fine but it has changed our lives completely. He's in London all week and is only home from Saturday till Sunday. I'm finding it difficult. Lord knows how you've coped all these years."

"To be honest, Michael doesn't go away all that much and he doesn't work Saturdays or Sundays. That's family time. It's strange that Danny doesn't get home on Fridays. As far as I'm aware they all close down then for the weekend. I'll have a word with Michael about it, if you like."

"No, no, thanks, but please don't," said Kate, feeling really worried. God, Danny would kill her if he thought she was complaining to Michael.

"Very well," said Marcia. "I look forward to seeing you next week."

How strange, Kate thought. Even Michael doesn't work weekends. I'll really have to tackle Danny about this and sort something out.

★ ★ ★

Lauren was back to her old self. She could tell that the children were relieved. The break in Dublin had been good for them all. Jonathan arrived home on Sunday night and she could see that he was surprised and happy that she was speaking to him, yet she sensed that he felt a little uneasy. She guessed that he couldn't believe she had come around so easily and suspected she had something up her sleeve. His barrister's instinct probably told him something was up but he couldn't figure out what.

Lauren felt empowered as she never had before. She had finally taken things into her own hands and was doing something about it. Tomorrow she would meet with Stella, her solicitor friend, and she knew things would never be the same again. Meanwhile, she had a slimming class to go to tonight.

★ ★ ★

Kate spent the afternoon in the garden thinking of all the calories she was burning as she dug and weeded. Johnny, the gardener, had hurt his back and was out of action and she was delighted with the opportunity to do something without listening to him moaning about it. She loved gardening and got a great sense of satisfaction from seeing beautiful plants grow from little seeds and cuttings. The garden was still very young but every year she could see a big improvement and looked forward to the time when it would be fully mature. She hadn't wanted to hire Johnny at all, but Danny had been adamant.

"You can't possibly do all the work yourself," he'd said, and so she had Johnny under her feet, day in, day out, complaining non-stop. She had to admit, however, that he did have green fingers – everything he planted flourished.

As she worked she could see the gorgeous Tim cleaning the pool. He came in once a week and he also did any odd-jobs that needed doing around the place. Diana had tried to seduce him the first time she'd laid eyes on his gorgeous body, but he'd had enough sense to reject her advances. Kate could hardly blame her – he was a hunk.

He waved over at her and she waved back.

She was sure that she had lost more weight because the only time she had broken out was with the wine on Friday night. I'll have to stop having my friends around for counselling, she thought, smiling. They are my downfall! Last week Jenny – this week Lauren. Maybe it will be my turn next week. Hopefully not – touch wood!

★ ★ ★

They all met up in Naas, as usual, and after they had been weighed in, they took their place in the class beside the Dublin girls that they had met the first week. They were great craic altogether and were in the middle of another hilarious story when Lauren gave Kate a nudge in the ribs.

"Holy God, I don't believe it! Get an eyeful of who's just walked in."

Kate and Jenny both turned to look and Kate almost fell off her chair when she saw Diana marching up to Tara.

"What's she doing here?" asked Lauren.

"No idea. She never mentioned a word to me last night."

"Well, I never!" remarked Jenny, who was equally gobsmacked.

The girls from Dublin had followed their gaze.

"Do you know her?" they asked. "She has a great body. Don't know why she wants to lose weight."

"Boy, do we know her!" came back the reply from Lauren, making the others laugh.

They all watched, intrigued, as Diana arrived at Tara's weigh-in point.

They could see Tara talking with Diana and obviously something unusual was going on. It looked like a confrontation. After some more discussion, Diana stormed out of the room, her nose in the air.

"Go after her and find out what's up," Lauren urged Kate.

Kate slipped out but was too late. Diana was nowhere to be seen. The class was just starting as she came back in and she shook her head at the others.

Lauren had lost four pounds. "I'm not surprised, seeing the week that I've had!"

Jenny had lost only two pounds. "Those bloody chips," she said to Kate, slyly omitting to mention the two chocolate bars she'd scoffed as well.

To Kate's delight she had lost another three pounds, to make it twelve pounds in the two weeks. Mary from the Coffee Pot was 'Girl of the Week'. She'd lost five pounds.

They were all in very high spirits, despite all their problems, as they made their way to Moorehill Lodge. Tara arrived promptly, having arranged to pick up the menus from Kate there.

They ordered the same steak and salad but this week decided to forego the wine.

"It really is difficult to lose weight without giving up alcohol. The problem is that it slows down your metabolism," Tara explained. They all agreed that the wine would have to be kept to a minimum in the future.

She also told them that they couldn't expect the big weight loss of the first two weeks to continue and that they might have to settle for just two pounds a week from now on.

"I'll be happy with that," Kate said. "That means that I'll have lost three stone by Christmas."

"Me too," said a delighted Jenny.

"I'm feeling a little guilty because I left the hall so quickly tonight," Tara told them. "There are always women who want to chat after the class but tonight I just wasn't in the mood," she admitted, shaking her head. "I think they're just lonely and need someone to talk to but, honestly, I'd be there till midnight if some of them had their way. Anyway, I just left in a hurry as I'm bushed and hungry and wanted to meet up with you."

"It's sad that there are so many lonely women out there. I think maybe that's the reason they overeat," suggested Kate.

"How right you are," said Tara. "So let me have a look at the menus, Kate."

Kate shyly handed them over, praying that they were good enough.

"Kate, these are fantastic! You're a genius. How did you do it? Look, girls!" She showed them to Lauren and Jenny. "Baked Cod with a Parmesan and Chive Crust – Prawns wrapped in Smoked Salmon – Chicken stuffed with Mushrooms and Fromage Frais. This all sounds so delicious and I can see how low-calorie they are. I'm so grateful. We'll definitely be doing business together. Can you meet me on Thursday and we'll discuss it?"

Kate was chuffed and Lauren and Jenny were grinning broadly.

"She just has no idea how good she is," said Lauren. "We agree with you – she's a genius!"

"She is – an absolute genius," Jenny added and they laughed as Kate blushed an even darker crimson.

"Let's change the subject!" she said.

"Okay!" said Lauren and seized her chance. "Tara, can you tell us what happened with that girl who walked out? Diana. What was she up to? We know her well." She was dying with curiosity to know what Diana had been doing there.

"Well, she's a strange one," replied Tara as their steaks arrived. "I could see that she has a fabulous body, curves in all the right places. She's not overweight at all."

"I couldn't agree with you more," Kate butted in. "I'd die for her figure."

"Anyway," Tara continued, "when I asked her to get up on the scales, she refused. I'm very conscious of people with eating disorders using the class to lose even more weight."

"I can imagine," Jenny agreed. "You can't be too careful."

"Well, I refused to accept her into the class unless she agreed to be weighed in. She was, to put it mildly, furious and, as you saw, left in high dudgeon. She's something else!"

"You have no idea!" Lauren couldn't suppress her delight. She was enjoying this immensely.

"Yeah, well, I don't need problems like her," Tara told them. "I've had my share of them over the years. One can't be too careful, what with anorexia and bulimia so prevalent, especially with young girls. Anyway, she stormed out, talking about discrimination and threatening her lawyers on me."

"That's our Diana, all right!" Lauren found this whole thing hilarious and couldn't stop laughing.

"God love her. Imagine her thinking she needs to lose weight." Kate, with her soft heart, was feeling sorry for Diana.

"Oh, you're such a softie!" Lauren exclaimed. "She doesn't deserve your sympathy."

They tucked into their steaks with gusto, savouring every mouthful. Kate and Jenny couldn't help but envy the couple at the next table who were tucking into chips but they tried to ignore them and thinking of the weight they'd lost helped a lot.

"Tara, how on earth did you get into this business?" Jenny asked. "You promised you'd tell us."

"It's a long story, as I said last week. I studied dietetics at college and met Seán in my first year. He was studying medicine. We qualified together and Seán wanted to go to Canada to specialise in obstetrics. We were very much in love so after graduating we got married and headed for Canada.

"My God, how brave!" Kate said. "Leaving everything, just like that."

"Yeah, it was scary. My first baby was born a year later and four more followed, one after the other. By then we'd decided to come home as we wanted to raise the children in Ireland and Seán had qualified as a consultant and been offered a job in The National Maternity Hospital in Dublin." She paused to take another bite of her steak. "Gosh, this steak is fantastic!"

"They're as good as you'll get anywhere" Kate told her, spearing another piece of tender, rare sirloin on her fork.

"Five kids in five years! How wonderful! How on earth did you manage?" Jenny asked, her admiration for Tara growing by the minute.

"You just do," Tara replied. "You have no other option, and Seán was great. Anyway, as I was saying, I had always been very slim but with each baby came another few pounds and on the fifth, I really gained a lot."

"I can imagine – I gained loads on the boys." Kate grimaced at the thought. "But I only had four and they were more spaced out – sorry, go on, Tara – what happened next?

"Well, when we got back to Ireland, I decided to tackle this weight so I devised a diet to help me lose it. To help motivate myself, I asked a few friends to join me. We met in my house once a week and I weighed them and gave them some dietary advice. I was pretty housebound, as you can imagine, with five children under seven, so it suited me."

"Golly, I can't even begin to imagine it," Lauren said with feeling, admiration in her voice.

Tara continued. "Word spread quickly of our success and I was inundated with calls from women wanting to join our group. In the end I had to move the group to the local school to accommodate them all and so Slimforever was born. I had always wanted to work but also wanted to be with the children during the day so this suited me down to the ground. Four years later I had the twins and kept going with the classes, right up to the end. This also forced me to control my weight."

"You are an absolute advertisement for making a success of your situation. I take my hat off to you!" Lauren said, tipping an imaginary hat. The others laughed. "Go on, please."

"Are you sure I'm not boring you?"

"Are you joking?" Kate said. "It's fascinating and very motivating."

"So what happened next?" said Jenny.

"Well, in my innocence I thought that I would get everyone slim within a year and that would be that – but it hasn't worked out that way. They lose weight and then go back to their old eating habits. As a result, they regain all the weight they've lost and the following year I see them again."

"Why does this sound familiar?" Jenny turned to Kate, looking for confirmation that she felt the same. Kate nodded her assent.

Tara smiled at Jenny, knowing just what she meant. "In the beginning I felt that I was a failure because they were regaining the weight, but then a regular client of mine said, 'Tara, if it wasn't for you, I would now weigh twenty stone. You're my lifeboat – without you I would sink.' That made me feel much better and here I am, fifteen years later, still doing the same thing and a lot of the women who started with me still keep coming back, year after year." She stopped, looking somewhat embarrassed. "God, I haven't talked about myself so much in years. I'm sure I'm boring you all to death!"

"You must be joking. It's a wonderful story," Lauren assured her.

"It makes me feel that I should get off my butt and do something," Kate admitted.

"And seven children!" said Lauren. "How did you cope? I find two a handful!"

"It wasn't easy, but they're great kids." Tara smiled a secret smile, thinking of her children. "The twins will be sixteen next month and my eldest daughter has two little girls. I don't know where the years have flown. One minute they're babies, and the next . . ."

"Who are you telling!" agreed Kate.

The waitress came to clear their plates and asked if they would like to see the dessert menu. They all declined. No surprise!

"You a grandmother – I can hardly believe it," Jenny said. "You have to be Ireland's most glamorous granny!"

"You should see me at seven in the morning," Tara laughed, making a face. "Trust me, I'm not very glamorous then . . . God, look at the time! I really must dash. Sorry for rattling on, girls!"

"Not at all!" said Kate. "Honestly, you're an inspiration to us all!"

In the flurry of goodbyes, Tara said she'd be in contact with Kate about their meeting. The girls couldn't believe that Tara was a grandmother. She could easily pass for thirty-five. They decided that, because she had such a good figure, she looked years younger and they looked forward to shedding some years, along with the pounds, themselves.

* * *

Diana was furious as she drove, much too fast, back to Ballyfern. How dare she – that stupid cow – refuse to let her join the slimming club! Who did she think she was, telling her what weight she should be? Insisting that she get on the scales in front of all those dreadful women! Was there no privacy law that could stop this kind of thing? The nerve of her! Who did she think she was dealing with here? And those green eyes – like a cat's – nobody had eyes that green. They were obviously contact lenses. The nerve of her and in front of all those women! They looked like a bunch of sheep, all overweight and expecting that woman to work miracles. Tara, she said her name was. Huh! Definitely made up! Her real name was probably Mary or Ann.

She'd conveniently forgotten that her own real name was in fact Mary and that she now called herself Diana.

Worst of all, she had seen Kate and Lauren and their hippy friend staring at her as she left. Well, to hell with them! She'd think of a good reason to give them for being there. She'd say she was doing research for an article she was writing. What a great idea!

It was at that moment that she saw the flashing blue lights in her rear-view mirror. Oh, damn! This is all I need. What speed am I doing? She very soon found out. The squad car pulled her in and the policeman ambled over to her.

"Well, miss, you're in a big hurry."

She fluttered her eyelashes at him and gave him a sexy smile.

"Sorry, officer. My husband is ill and I'm in a hurry to get home to him." She'd seen this in a Cameron Diaz movie once and it had worked for her before.

"Must be a mighty sick man you've got there because when I stopped you last year you were rushing home to him as well. This year he must be even more ill, as you're in even more of a hurry. You're doing ninety in a sixty-kilometre zone."

"I'm so sorry, officer," she said in her little-girl voice – trying to squeeze out a few tears.

"You will be indeed, Miss, because I'm giving you a ticket."

After giving him her details she drove home in an even greater fury, but within the speed limit. She flounced into the house and with barely a hello to Kevin, poured herself a large gin and tonic and went straight up the stairs and ran herself a bath.

What's up with her now, he wondered, going back to his television programme. This was getting ridiculous. He couldn't keep up with her tantrums and moods any more. She should change her name to Diva, or Donna – Prima Donna! He had finally come to the conclusion that he couldn't help her any more. He'd had enough!

Chapter 17

When the very grand, new hotel had opened halfway between Ballyfern and Naas, Danny had been among the first to take out family membership in its brand new leisure centre and spa, despite the fact that they had their own pool and neither of them was remotely interested in the other facilities offered. When Kate had queried the huge annual membership fee, in view of the fact that they would probably never avail of it, Danny had silenced her with a look and said, "Have you no sense, woman? Can't you see the benefit of being a member? It doesn't matter a damn whether we use it or not. The main thing is that we are members. It gives us a certain standing and I can always network through there." Kate couldn't see why they should pay this crazy amount of money for something they would never use. Now, at last, she felt she could justify it. Her friend Hilary had inveigled her into trying out the Pilates class at the centre and when she saw the indoor pool and sauna and the fantastic gym equipment, she vowed that she would avail of these facilities to help her get back in shape.

* * *

Diana popped into town to pick up the *Irish Times* and as she was paying for it was stunned when Mrs Behan, the shopkeeper, remarked with a snide grin, "I hear that you were seen at the Slimming Club in Naas last night and that you had a little trouble on the way home. Naughty girl!"

"Have you nothing better to do than gossip?" she snapped back.

She was furious. How dare that old bag talk to her like that! She was equally furious with Kate. She was sure that Kate was the one to have told Mrs Behan although, on second thoughts, it was more likely Lauren. Lauren hated her guts. Either way they were certainly the ones. It must be all around the town by now. She knew how they'd all be gloating. Peasants, all of them! She knew they were just jealous of her.

* * *

Lauren was early for her appointment with Stella and wondered whether she was making a dreadful mistake. Before she could bolt, Stella came into the waiting-room and hugged her.

"Lauren, you look fantastic. As slim and gorgeous as ever!"

"You don't look too bad yourself," Lauren grinned at

her old friend, remembering just how much she'd always liked her.

They went into Stella's luxurious office.

"Wow! Very impressive!" Lauren said as she entered. "Obviously, business is booming." She sank into the comfortable leather sofa.

"Can't complain," Stella admitted as she poured coffee from the silver coffee pot that her assistant had just brought in.

She sat beside Lauren on the sofa and they made small talk for a few minutes.

"Well, what brings you here?" Stella asked then. "Not just to see an old friend? Do you have a problem?"

Lauren was very hesitant to open up but her friend was quickly able to get the full story.

"You know, I've been practising family law for twenty years and you wouldn't believe the things I've seen and heard, Lauren. Marriage is a crazy institution, which is why I've never ventured there. I've seen too much of the bad side. You've no idea how many women have come to me with the same story as yours – middle-class, respectable wives who've been putting up with this treatment for years. I've had wives of men from every profession, solicitors and barristers included, in the same boat as yourself, so don't think that you're on your own, or that it's your fault. And yes, it has to stop. Do you want a divorce or do you want to stay married to him?"

"I don't honestly know what I want," Lauren replied with a sigh. "If I could get him to stop then things might be okay again."

"There is help available that you may be willing to try. There are now specialists working in this field who are achieving amazing results but, of course, Jonathan would have to agree to attend one of these spousal-abuse anger-management programmes." Stella sipped her coffee as she watched Lauren digesting this information.

"That will be a problem," Lauren said, shaking her head.

"You'd be amazed what the threat of a barring order might do to change his mind. I can send him a letter notifying him of your intention to apply for this but I think that if you tell him that you've taken legal advice and that we've advised you to apply for one, it should be enough to do the trick."

Lauren put her head in her hands as she weighed up how Jonathan would react to this.

Stella took her hands down and held them in her own. "You have to be brave if you want it to stop."

Lauren knew she was right. After a minute or two she acquiesced. "Okay, I'll talk to him although I dread his reaction." Now she'd decided to start the ball rolling, she was going to see it through to the end. Because I'm worth it, she thought, with a wry smile.

"Good girl," Stella said. "There really is no other way." She felt sorry for Lauren – she didn't deserve this – but then did any woman? Her heart almost broke sometimes when she saw broken, terrified women and heard their horrendous stories. And now it was Lauren. Stella knew Jonathan well and met him often in the courts and the law library. He was such a gentleman. Who would ever have believed it possible? Thank God, she said to herself – for the millionth time – that I stayed single.

They chatted on for a little while, talking about old school friends, as Lauren left Stella said she would be in touch.

Then Lauren decided on the spur of the moment to pop out to see Helen, Jonathan's sister, even though she'd been there to lunch the previous Sunday when she'd collected the kids.

"What a nice surprise!" said Helen when she opened the door. "Why didn't you call? I might have been out and missed you."

"Oh, I was just in the neighbourhood . . ." She stood there awkwardly, trying to control her agitation.

"Is everything okay, Lauren?"

"Well, yes and no. No, actually. I . . ." She couldn't go on.

"Come in and sit down," said Helen gently, "and tell me all about it."

Seated opposite Helen in the living-room, Lauren forced herself to continue. "I've just come from a solicitor, Helen, and . . . you're not going to like this . . ."

"Oh my God, what is it? Is it Jonathan?" Helen's face had gone as white as a sheet.

"Yes." Lauren's voice was almost a whisper. "We have a problem – well, that is, he has a problem and . . . oh, God! . . . I don't know how to say this." She knew it was coming out all garbled. How could you put this into words – and to Jonathan's sister who adored him. She could see the shock on Helen's face.

"Is he hitting you?" said Helen.

Now it was Lauren's turn to look shocked. "Yes," she replied in a whisper. "How did you know?"

"You'll have to talk to Mum about this."

"Oh no, no, I couldn't possibly! I wouldn't like to upset her and Jonathan would never forgive me. You know how much he adores her."

"Trust me. You have to talk to her. I'll come with you if it makes it any easier."

Before Lauren could object further Helen was dialling her mother's number.

"Mum, Lauren is with me and there's a problem. She needs to talk to you – can I bring her over?" Helen's voice was taut.

It appeared her mother didn't ask any questions but immediately agreed that they should come to see her.

Lauren still wasn't so sure of the wisdom of this but Helen was insistent so she found herself, ten minutes later, being ushered into Nana's luxurious apartment, overlooking Dublin Bay. Lauren had never been able to bring herself to call her mother-in-law by her first name, Nancy, so when the kids arrived 'Nana' had seemed the easiest way to address her.

"Helen, Lauren, come in. Come in," she said, kissing them both. "What a surprise! I'm so glad I didn't go to play bridge today or I would have missed you. You're looking lovely, my dear, as always," she said to Lauren. "Have you lost a little weight?"

She fussed about making tea for them and when they

were all seated, Helen said, "Mum, Lauren has something she wants to talk to you about."

Lauren blushed, not knowing where to begin. She was reluctant to upset this lovely lady with what she had to say.

"No, really, it's nothing. I don't think your mother needs to be bothered with my problems."

"Yes, she does. You have to tell her."

Lauren was amazed at the vehemence in the usually gentle Helen's voice.

"It's Jonathan, isn't it?" Nancy's hands gripped the table and her face went a deathly pale. "What has he done?"

Lauren didn't answer but started to cry.

"Has he been violent?" Nancy asked her, her voice shaking.

Lauren couldn't bring herself to speak but nodded her assent.

"Oh no, my dear! Oh, no! How dreadful for you!" she said, coming to sit beside Lauren on the sofa, putting her arms around her.

"I'll pop out for a stroll along the seafront and leave you two to talk," said Helen quietly and she quickly disappeared.

"Tell me about it, dear – has it been going on for long?" said Nancy, holding Lauren's hands.

Lauren told her story again, anguish in her voice, and when she'd finished, Nancy was quietly crying.

"You poor darling, you can't let him go on or it will continue until you come to hate him. I know, because you see, my dear, his father was also violent with me and I regret so much that I did nothing to stop it, many, many years ago. It destroyed my life."

Now it was Lauren's turn to be shocked. She couldn't begin to comprehend that Benedict, her gentle father-in-law, had also been violent with his wife.

"I understand how you feel," said Nancy, "but for your own sake and the children, you must do something to stop it. I know Jonathan's my son and I love him dearly but he must not be allowed to continue with this."

Lauren was really glad that she had talked to Nancy. Who was it had said that a problem shared was a problem halved? They were so right! She was discovering that sharing this problem was helping her. First Kate, then Stella and now Nancy.

"I'm very concerned that this violence may be hereditary," Nancy continued. "I know Benedict's father was a very aggressive man and I'm quite convinced that he was violent towards his wife, but, of course, Benedict would never talk about it, out of loyalty to his family, I suppose. Still, three generations – makes you wonder."

"I do so hope you're wrong," said Lauren, for she did not want her darling son Ben to behave as his father and grandfather had done.

Nancy excused herself and put the kettle on for another cup of tea which, Lauren thought, is what all Irishwomen do in a crisis.

"So what do you plan to do now?" Nancy asked.

"Well, I've been to see a solicitor friend of mine today and she suggested that Jonathan undergo a course of treatment – what did she call it? – spousal-abuse anger-management."

"Well, there was nothing like that in my day, unfortunately," Nancy replied, "but there is so much help out there today. Do you think Jonathan will agree to it?" She looked at Lauren intently.

"I honestly don't know but I have to try."

"Go for it, girl!"

Lauren was amazed at Nancy's very hip saying.

"I'm not dead yet," Nancy smiled, seeing Lauren's surprise. "*Sex and the City* is my favourite programme, you know. But don't tell Helen."

Lauren laughed, for the first time that day.

She left Nancy shortly afterwards, before Helen got back. What an amazing woman, my mother-in-law, she thought, at seventy-six years old!

★ ★ ★

When Diana saw Kate arrive at the leisure centre that afternoon, she made a beeline for her.

"Thank you very much! With friends like you, who needs enemies?"

Kate looked bewildered. "Diana, I'm really sorry but I don't know what you mean." She started nibbling on her thumbnail which she always did when she was nervous.

"Oh really? Well, when I went into Behan's shop this morning the old biddy was able to tell me that I'd been at the slimming club last night and that I'd been stopped for speeding on the way home."

"I didn't know that." Kate's face was, as always, transparent, and Diana knew she was telling the truth. "I stayed in Naas until after eleven o'clock."

"What about Lauren?" Diana demanded.

"She was with me." Kate was on the defensive but she didn't know why.

"Who could have spread the gossip then?" Diana was really angry and aggressive.

"Possibly Agnes O'Reilly. She was there and left early, so maybe it was her."

"That bitch! She pokes her nose in everywhere. I'll give her a piece of my mind when I see her!"

Diana turned away without so much as an apology to Kate.

Kate was quite shaken. Diana sure could put the boot in when she wanted to. Kate wished she had a fraction of her courage – Diana was afraid of no one – but, not for the first time, she wondered how Kevin put up with her. She was quite impossible!

★ ★ ★

Kate enjoyed the Pilates although she knew she wasn't very good at it. She looked with envy at Hilary and Diana and wondered how they could get their bodies to bend like that. Anna, the teacher, was very encouraging and told her that she would be as good in a couple of weeks.

"I wish!" Kate replied.

She was aching in muscles that she hadn't known existed.

She got home just in time to have a shower and change and make it to the anniversary Mass for Conor's wife in Naas. Although she hadn't known Beth very well, Conor had taught three of her sons for many years and she was very fond of him.

As she drove to Naas her thoughts were with her boys. They were coming home for the weekend and she couldn't wait! Toby was bringing his new best friend, Miguel, with him. She hoped Ben wouldn't be jealous. Lauren had said that he was counting the minutes till he saw Toby again and had asked if he could stay over on Saturday night.

But the rest of the week would fly by. She had agreed with Lauren to give golf another go on Wednesday and on Thursday she was meeting with Tara about the menus.

Gosh, thought Kate, it's crazy, but my life has suddenly become very full and busy. I love, love, love it!

* * *

Jenny was getting dressed to go to Beth's Mass when she felt the dreaded bleeding start. She rushed to the bathroom and her heart sank when she discovered that the pregnancy test had indeed been correct. She was not pregnant. She felt the bottom drop out of her world. For one brief week she had allowed herself to believe her dream had come true. Now she was scared that the reason she had been late was because she was starting the menopause. This meant she would never conceive the baby that she so longed for. She went along to the Mass with a heavy heart.

She was pleased to see Kate there. How nice of her to come, she thought. She felt tempted to tell Kate of her disappointment but thought better of it. This is something I have to bear myself.

While they were waiting, Kate told Jenny of Diana's accusations. Jenny had to stifle her laughter at the thought of Diana's discomfiture. Then she spotted Agnes O'Reilly in the church.

"God, nothing passes her," she whispered to Kate, dissolving in a fit of the giggles again.

Conor wanted Jenny to come and sit with the family but she thought it better if she stayed with Kate.

She couldn't pray during the Mass but railed at God for her childless state when she had so much love to give a child. It angered her when she heard of the teenage mothers giving birth to babies they didn't want. She saw red when she read the statistics of women having abortions. She felt that there was no justice in this world. Here was Conor and herself, who both wanted children, unable to have them.

There were quite a few people in the church as both Conor and Beth had been well known and very popular in the area. He was so grateful to everyone for coming and invited them back to his house where he had put on a big spread. Jenny was furious that Tom hadn't seen fit to make an effort to be there, even though she had asked him especially.

Kate had not intended to go back to the house but Jenny persuaded her. When they arrived they saw Agnes O'Reilly was there and making a beeline for them.

"Here comes Her Ladyship, Chief Gossip of Ballyfern! This should be interesting," whispered Jenny, grabbing a glass of wine.

"Did you hear what happened to Diana Rafferty last night?" Agnes could hardly contain her excitement and her piggy eyes were aglow with the thrill of spreading such succulent gossip, particularly about Diana, whom she detested. Diana had always treated her with disdain so she was delighted to be taking her down a peg or two. 'That one' was much too big for her boots, in her opinion.

"No," said Jenny with an innocent look in her big brown eyes, giving Kate a dig in the ribs. "Do tell us."

Agnes recounted the story again but with even more embellishments, as her stories always got more exaggerated with every telling. Jenny and Kate tut-tutted and when Agnes had moved on to spread her news elsewhere they burst into giggles.

"Well, that's priceless!" said Jenny. "Agnes has it in for Diana. It will be all over Kildare by tonight. Lauren is going to love this."

"Poor Diana," Kate said. "That woman is really dreadful. We shouldn't encourage her." But she couldn't help smiling.

"Don't be such a softie!" said Jenny. "Diana was horrible to you today. She really has it coming!"

When Kate saw all the glorious food she was sorely

tempted but resisted all but one canapé of smoked salmon. She resisted the wine also and settled for a sparkling water. Jenny showed no such restraint and tucked in. She really wasn't in the mood for dieting tonight. Jenny lost count of how many glasses of wine she'd had and when Conor saw that she was drinking, he raised a questioning eyebrow at her. She raised her glass to him. Kate left after an hour saying that she was aching so much from the Pilates she would need to soak her poor body for two hours at least, if she were to contemplate lifting a golf club the next morning.

"You look great, Kate," Conor smiled as he kissed her on the cheek. "Thank you so much for coming."

★ ★ ★

Kate tried Lauren's number again when she got home and this time she got her. Lauren couldn't stop laughing when Kate told her Agnes O'Reilly's news.

When she'd finally calmed down, Kate asked her, "Well, how did things go with the solicitor?"

"Quite well, considering. Stella says there are programmes for spousal-abuse anger management that can be very beneficial but, of course, the problem is getting Jonathan to agree to it."

"And how would you do that?" Kate asked, thinking Lauren had no chance of getting him to agree to go.

"Well, Stella says that if I tell him I've been for legal advice and that they advise me to apply for a barring order, it should do the trick." Lauren sounded hopeful.

"That's great. I imagine that would be the last thing he'd want. This should give you courage. Are you going to talk to Jonathan?"

"Yes, but I need to pick the right time and think first about what I'll say to him. I'm not looking forward to it."

"I can imagine. Still, it has to be done. I think maybe after a few drinks, when he's mellow, would be a good time. Just be honest with him. Tell him you won't take it any more."

"You said it, Kate. I won't. I'm amazed at how determined I am. Hopefully, he'll see that too. I'll tell him that if he doesn't agree then our marriage is over. Simple!"

"Lauren, I'm proud of you and I know you're doing the right thing. It has to stop. Listen, if you need me to take the kids or if anything goes wrong . . . I'm just a phone call away."

"I know that . . . and Kate . . . thanks. You've given me the courage to do this."

"Good luck, sweetheart! I'm here if you need me."

★ ★ ★

When all the others had left Conor's, Jenny stayed on to help him clear up.

"What's with the drinking?" Conor asked her.

"False alarm. You were right. I shouldn't have got my hopes up." She knew she was a little tipsy.

"I'm so sorry, Jenny, but I'm sure it'll happen for you, someday. I feel it."

"God, I hope you're right. Sometimes I despair that I've missed the boat," she said with a grimace.

When they'd finished clearing up, Conor poured them both a brandy and they sat down by the fire to reminisce about Beth. Conor talked quietly and Jenny listened.

"It's so easy to talk to you, Jenny. Beth was the only other person that I could ever talk to like this. She was very fond of you, you know." He was tempted to tell her something that Beth had said to him some time before she died, but he resisted. Jenny was single then – she was married now. That changed everything.

"I loved her too," Jenny said quietly, missing her friend more than ever tonight.

"She was very unhappy about your decision to marry Tom, you know," Conor continued. "She felt it was too sudden – that you didn't know each other well enough."

"Yeah, I sure didn't hang around! I made a big mistake rushing into marriage like that and I was bloody old enough to know better. But there you are. I've made my bed, now I have to lie on it." Jenny was beginning to feel very sorry for herself. "And what about you?" she asked Conor. "Two years on – how do you feel?"

"Strange. Everyone told me that the first year was the hardest and that after Beth's first anniversary I'd start to feel better and move on, but that didn't happen – obviously I'm a slow starter!" He gave a little smile. "But somehow, at the Mass tonight it hit me – Beth's gone – for good. We had a wonderful life together but she's gone – and she's not coming back. I like to think she's in a better place now, but the fact is I'm still here and I have a life to live. Beth has moved on. Guess it's time I did the same."

Jenny listened, her heart aching for him. "Life is cruel," she told him, tears welling up in her eyes. "Beth was a very special person. I've never known the kind of love you had together, so I can only imagine how devastating it must be to lose it."

"It's been hell," he said quietly, "and you've helped to keep me sane at times, Jenny, but as I've said, life goes on and so must I."

"Well, time I was going," Jenny said, uncurling from her armchair.

Conor got up. "Thanks . . . for everything," he said, kissing her on the cheek. "You're the best friend anyone could have, Jen."

She crossed over the patch of grass between their houses, into her empty loveless home. She climbed the stairs, thinking how wonderful it would be to be going to bed to make love with a man she loved. Dream on, Jenny, that ain't gonna happen, she told herself, as she snuggled down in the big lonely bed.

Chapter 18

Kevin was worried about Diana. She had been acting so weirdly lately and now she appeared to have stopped eating. Every evening when he came home she claimed to have eaten already, which was unusual. Although their marriage was a sham they at least tried to have some semblance of normality and sat at table every night together. No longer! He asked her if she was dieting – which seemed ridiculous given that she had a figure most women envied. She denied this but he knew something was up. Why was she so complicated? Why couldn't she just be normal, like Kate or Lauren for instance? He immediately felt guilty at such disloyal thoughts.

★ ★ ★

Kate dragged herself out of bed on Wednesday morning, aching in every possible place. Despite soaking for an hour in the bath last night she was still stiff as could be.

"I'm so unfit," she told Lauren when they met at the golf club at nine.

"Don't worry. Eighteen holes will soon cure you," laughed Lauren.

On their way to the driving range, Kate asked, "Did you speak to Jonathan?"

"No, he was not in good form last night so I didn't dare broach it. He had a big brief on today so he spent most of the night in his office." Lauren made a face. "I have to be very careful to pick the right time to discuss it. The night before a big case is definitely not the right time."

"Yeah, you're right," Kate agreed.

At the driving range Lauren made Kate hit a few balls. Then she corrected her grip and swing and let her hit another bucket of balls. It was beginning to go a lot better.

"Okay. Golf course, here we come. Are you ready for us?" sang Lauren, as they took their place on the first tee. The first few holes were abysmal but Kate very quickly got the hang of it and Lauren was very encouraging.

"We'll make a golfer of you yet, Kate!"

Kate was exhilarated. She felt that she could really get into this game.

"I think you should maybe have a few lessons with the pro here," said Lauren. "He's really good and will help you much more than I could."

Kate went straight to the pro shop and booked a course of lessons for eight weeks, starting the following Monday morning. She had really enjoyed herself. She decided to say nothing to Danny and then to surprise him with her new skill.

They had lunch in the clubhouse and Lauren introduced her to so many women that her head was spinning trying to remember all their names. She found them all very friendly and wondered how she had found them so intimidating before.

When she mentioned this to Lauren, she replied, "You've changed, Kate, since we started with Slimforever. You're much more confident and you've got your own life now outside of Danny and that's good."

"I suppose you're right. Losing weight has given me much more confidence. Long may it last!"

★ ★ ★

Diana normally went horse-riding on Wednesdays but cancelled her appointment as Michael had promised to ring that day and there was no way she could take his phone call while cantering around the Curragh plains. Besides that she was feeling light-headed from this crash diet she was on. She had got it from Isabelle who swore that she would lose half a stone in a week on it but Diana suspected it wasn't very healthy. She was only having smoothies – no solid food at all – but although it was torture it would be worth it to lose the weight. Kevin was giving her grief about the dieting. He was such a pain.

Today she had felt quite confident that Michael would ring but as the day wore on she became less sure. She had intended launching into him about having his party on a Friday night but now she was thinking twice about that.

She would just be so relieved if he rang. She could always tackle him about it in bed – that way he'd be more compliant. Yes, that's what she'd do.

She had almost given up hope of hearing from him when he rang her later that night. Kevin was watching the News so she took the call in the kitchen.

"Sorry I'm so late, sweetie, but I was stuck in meetings all day. However, it is Wednesday and I am ringing as I promised. Are you on for Friday night? I have something special planned for you so meet me at seven thirty in the Merrion and we'll go on from there."

"How exciting, Michael! I love surprises and I really do appreciate you ringing. I can't wait to see you. I'm getting hot just hearing your voice and bed sounds like somewhere special to me."

"Please, Diana, you're giving me a hard-on right now and I've got to face these guys in the bar! You're a vixen!"

She laughed. "Till Friday, my love!"

She was over the moon. What power did he have over her that he could make her feel this happy? It wasn't just the sex, though, of course, that was great.

She soaked in a long bath and then got her golf gear ready for the morning. She just knew that she would play a blinder tomorrow.

I can't wait to see smarty-pants Lauren's face when I win, she thought happily.

★ ★ ★

Kevin didn't know what to make of her. He had no control over her any more. She did just what she liked, without a thought for anyone. He was only needed to provide the necessary cash to keep her in the style she required. He knew he was a fool and that she was walking all over him. He could see no way out. They did less and less together as a couple. He was lonely. He had rung Kate a couple of times but she was never home. In truth, he was also missing Danny. They had been friends for such a long time and had played golf twice a week for years but now he hardly saw him and, besides, he felt that Danny had changed since taking that job in London. He couldn't put his finger on it, but yes, he had changed. He wasn't confiding in Kevin as he had always done. He barely spoke about his days in London at all.

Everyone else seems to be moving on but me, he thought. Maybe Diana's right, I am an old stick-in-the-mud. What to do about it? Am I too old to change?

★ ★ ★

When the kids were in bed, Lauren sat down beside Jonathan.

"Could you please turn off the TV? I need to talk to you." She was quaking inside but she wouldn't let him see it.

"Of course, dear." He switched it off immediately and looked at her expectantly.

"Jonathan, I don't want you to get angry but we need

203

to talk," she said calmly. "I've been to see a solicitor about your behaviour last week and I've been advised to apply for a barring order."

She saw the shock on his face and the fear in his eyes.

"Lauren, how could you do such a thing?" he cried.

"I could ask the same of you regarding the way you treated me last week," she replied firmly.

He started to protest. "You know I didn't . . ."

She stopped him, holding up her hand. "No, Jonathan, please hear me out."

He stopped talking and buried his face in his hands, waiting for the next bombshell.

"I would be willing not to apply for this, but on one condition."

He looked up at her, hope in his eyes. "Anything, I'll do anything. Please, darling," he pleaded with her.

"There is a programme that you can attend for people who abuse their spouses . . ." He winced as she used this term and loosened his collar. "If you're willing to attend this programme, then there may be some hope for us. If not, then I'm afraid I'll have no choice but to apply for a barring order and file for divorce."

She looked at him sadly as he struggled to take this in, amazed at how calm and detached she felt. Jonathan was shaking, gripping the sides of his chair.

"Lauren, please, I beg you. I promised you – never again!" His eyes were pleading and she could see the perspiration on his forehead.

"No, Jonathan. Your promises mean nothing any more.

I mean what I say. Either you agree to see this therapist and follow the programme or it's over for us. It goes without saying that the children will stay with me." Lauren had expected to be upset and emotional but she felt completely in control.

Jonathan left his chair and came over to her, kneeling on the floor beside her. "Lauren, Lauren, you're my life, you and the kids. I couldn't survive without you. You're my family. I'll do whatever you want but please don't leave me!" He buried his head in her lap.

"Are you saying you'll join this programme?" she asked him.

"Yes, yes, anything you say. I'll do anything to keep you."

He was distraught and she felt pity for him but still she kept in her mind how she had felt with his blows raining down on her. That memory kept her strong.

"Okay, I'll set up the appointment with the therapist. Now I think we both need a drink." She gently pushed him away and went to the drinks cabinet. She poured two large whiskeys and, giving him one, sat down facing him.

Jonathan was back in his chair, somewhat composed, and as he sipped his whiskey Lauren spoke again, looking him straight in the eye. "There's something else. I went to visit your mother and told her about your violence and discovered that she'd been a battered wife also."

"You went to my mother? You told her? Oh, my God! How could you do that? What did she say?" he whispered, cringing at what his mother must think of him.

"She told me that I can't let it go on and she regrets that she didn't do something about your father years earlier because it destroyed her life."

"Oh my God!" he said again, wringing his hands. "I can't believe this is happening."

"It's happening, Jonathan, and you brought it on yourself."

"I'll do anything you want, Lauren," he whispered.

She saw he was close to tears. She believed him. He looked like a broken man. She had to give him one last chance.

"I will never let you touch me again. If you do, I will apply for a barring order the very next day and you'll lose us all. We can only hope that this therapy will work and then we can put all this behind us." She was starting to feel sorry for him.

"I love you so very much, Lauren. I know I don't deserve this chance. Please tell me you still love me a little." His eyes beseeched her to say yes.

"Yes, I suppose I do but you're killing my love a little bit more every time you hit me. This is your only chance, Jonathan. Please make it work, for all our sakes."

She put her arms around him and he crumpled in them and then she saw him crying – something she had never seen before – not even when his father had died. She comforted him as she would the children and when they went to bed together she held him close until he fell asleep. She realised that taking matters into her own hands and taking action had subtly changed their relationship. She was now in control, she had found strength, and somehow she believed that he would change and that those awful days were behind her.

Chapter 19

Tara rang Kate on Wednesday night to confirm their meeting for the following day. She suggested meeting in the Ballyfern Inn but Kate said, "They're renovating it at the moment so it's not the quietest place. Why not come out to my house? We can talk in comfort and privacy and I have my cookery books here so I can show you a few ideas."

She gave Tara directions and the code for the gate and promptly at two the next afternoon, Tara arrived. Kate marvelled at how elegant and glamorous she looked although she appeared to be wearing no make-up whatsoever. She had that natural glowing skin that always looked tanned and it accentuated the stunning emerald of her eyes.

She moved with such grace that Kate asked her, on impulse, "Were you ever a dancer?"

"Well, actually, that was always my dream. I went as far as I could with my ballet exams but my parents were adamant that I go to university and foolishly I gave in – instead of following my dream. I've often regretted it and

wondered how I would have fared, but I'll never know."
She had a sad faraway look in her eyes as she spoke.
"Funnily enough, my youngest daughter, Melissa, one of
the twins, is a really good dancer and is determined to be
a professional. I certainly will encourage her to follow her
dream even though I know it's a very tough life."

Kate led her out onto the terrace.

"What a beautiful home you have, Kate, and, oh, my
God, the pool!"

It did look very beautiful in the warm September sun. The
leaves were beginning to turn golden and everything sparkled.

I am indeed lucky, thought Kate.

They got down to business, discussing menus and
recipes. Tara told her what she would require and then,
despite Kate's protests, they discussed money.

"Kate, you're doing me a favour. I need this stuff and if
you won't take payment then I won't take them from you
and we'll both be losers. I suggest that I pay you €70 for
each week of recipes."

"That's too much," Kate started to protest.

"No, it's not. It's a once-off fee but I'll be using them for
years. Okay, that's settled then." She was so forceful that
Kate just nodded agreement.

"I've invited Lauren and Jenny to join us for coffee,"
Kate said when business was concluded.

"That's nice. They're lovely women and great fun and I
can see you're all very close. You're lucky to have such good
friends."

"Yes, I'd be lost without them."

Lauren arrived, looking chic and beautiful, as usual.

Kate couldn't resist saying, "Here I am, sitting between the two most elegant women in Ireland and, you know what, I don't feel too bad!"

"Kate, don't be crazy! You shouldn't feel bad about anything," Tara admonished her.

"I agree," Lauren said, turning to Tara. "Actually, Kate has grown in confidence since joining your class. It's good to see." She smiled at Kate, who was blushing.

"It's funny," Tara replied. "I've noticed that a woman's confidence goes up and down in direct relation to her weight. It really does have an effect on your personality.

"I feel so good," said Kate. "I've so much more energy since I lost that stone."

"Just wait till she loses the other two, she'll be bounding around the place like a monkey!" laughed Lauren.

Jenny arrived just then and Lauren let her in while Kate went to rustle up the coffee. They all marvelled at the delicious, low-calorie canapés that Kate had prepared. These were followed by little ramekins of fresh fruit with *fromage frais.*

"Kate, if I had you as my personal chef, the weight would fall off me even while I ate gloriously," Jenny joked, her mouth full of some delicious salmon and cream cheese.

"Well, with the recipes that she's preparing for me, you'll be able to prepare these scrumptious goodies yourself," said Tara.

They chatted on for over an hour, enjoying each other's company as only a group of like-minded women can. They discussed men, children, make-up, fashion, films, restaurants and even the latest Hollywood gossip. Lauren was sorry to break up the party but she had to go to collect Daisy from her riding lesson.

"What a lovely afternoon! I've really enjoyed it. We should do this more often," said Tara.

★ ★ ★

Kate spent the rest of the afternoon preparing for the boys. She made their favourite pasta sauce and pizzas and also cookies and chocolate cake. She was so looking forward to having them home again. She rang Danny on his mobile and was surprised when she got through straight away.

"Oh Kate, hi – it's you. Sorry, I was expecting another call."

So that's why you answered on the first ring, she thought.

"Just checking when you'll be home. You know the boys are coming home tomorrow lunch-time. Can you make it tomorrow night?"

"I was going to ring you later. I don't know how to break this but I won't be able to make it home at all this weekend. Things are really hectic here. The chief architect is flying in from Italy and he can only come Saturday and will be going back Sunday."

She was so angry she could hardly speak. "Danny, I don't believe this! The boys will be so disappointed. It *is* Toby's first weekend home and he'll be bursting to tell us all his news. He's bringing his new Spanish friend with him and, besides, Justin is so excited about the rugby and will be dying to discuss it with you. Please don't do this to us!"

"I can't do anything about it, Kate. I have to be here to meet this guy. You know I'd come home if I possibly could. Anyway, I'll be home next Friday for Michael's party and we'll have a long weekend."

"Oh yes, you can make it for that all right but you can't get home to be with your sons!" She banged the phone down on him.

She expected that he would ring her back and apologise or at least try and cajole her but he didn't.

The phone rang twenty minutes later and her heart was hammering as she answered it, but it wasn't Danny, it was Kevin. She tried to keep the disappointment out of her voice.

"Hi, Kate, I'm on my way home from the gym and I have that Harlan Coben book for you. I'd also like to borrow your hedgecutter, if I may, that's if Johnny can spare it."

"No problem, Kevin. I'll put the kettle on and open the gate for you. I've finished *The Associate.* I loved it. See you soon."

Five minutes later he was at the door.

"Hi," he said. "You're looking good ... and ... different." He looked at her, perplexed, trying to figure out what it was.

She just smiled at him and said nothing. Her weight loss *was* making a difference. Kevin's reaction confirmed it.

"You're such a busy bee lately I'm surprised to get you in." He followed her into the kitchen where she put the kettle on.

"Tea or coffee?" she asked him.

"Tea, please. I've had enough coffee today to last me a week." He took a seat at the table. "So, tell me, how are you?"

"Not well, Kevin," she told him as she began to set out the tea things. "I'm furious with Danny. I was talking to him earlier and he's not coming home this weekend even though it's the boys' first weekend home. I just can't believe that he would do this!"

"That's most unusual. He adores them and it's not like him to miss seeing them when he gets the chance. Is anything wrong?"

"Everything is. I feel like my marriage is falling apart and I can't stop it." She took a small jug of milk from the fridge and put it on the table. "You know, everyone used to envy us and say that we'd be the last couple to ever divorce, but look at us now. I barely see him any more and all because of this stupid job. He's changed, Kevin – he doesn't seem to care about us any more."

"Oh, I'm sure he does, but you're right – he has changed. I was only thinking that last Sunday night. He certainly doesn't confide in me much any more and he always used to. I don't know what it is but he seems obsessed with this new London project."

"I'm scared, Kevin. I don't know what to do."

He watched her silently as she made the tea, then said tentatively, "Maybe you should have a long talk with him next weekend and tell him how you feel."

"He doesn't want to listen to me. He's always preoccupied with something or other."

"Would you like me to have a word with him?"

"God, no! He'd go mad if he thought I was talking about it to anyone, even you!"

"Well, if I thought Diana would listen to you, I'd ask you to talk to her but we have two chances of that happening – none and nil!"

"What's wrong now?" she asked as she poured the tea.

"Where do I start? She appears to be on some kind of starvation diet. I'm worried about her. She has a fabulous figure. She doesn't need to diet."

"You can say that again," Kate said enviously. "I'd give anything to have her body!"

"She says she's fat and that size twelve – which is apparently what she is – is unacceptable. Can you believe it? She's informed me that all the top stars and models are size zero." He shook his head in disbelief. "What's the world coming to? She wants to look like those celebrities, who look, to my mind, like they've been in a concentration camp. To top all this, I heard in the gym this evening that she was stopped for speeding last Monday night in Naas. She didn't even tell me about it!"

Kate hadn't the heart to tell him that the whole town knew about it. Poor Kevin, he really didn't deserve this. Not for the first time she thought how badly matched they all were. Diana would never have put up with Danny's absenteeism – she'd have been in London with him, buying up Bond Street, and Danny would certainly not have put up with Diana's shenanigans – he'd have been able to control her. Meanwhile, she and Kevin were quite happy just plodding along in Ballyfern.

As they drank the tea they discussed the book she was giving back to him and then talked about how much they enjoyed Harlan Coben's books. They both loved reading and liked the same authors. Kevin left shortly after, saying he'd drop in over the weekend to say hello to the boys. Kate settled down with her new book.

★ ★ ★

Lauren had contacted Stella to tell her that Jonathan was willing to seek help.

"That's wonderful. I was hoping that he would. Leave it to me. My friend is secretary to the best psychiatrist in Dublin. He is a specialist in anger management and works on this spousal-abuse programme. I know he's very busy but I'm sure she can organise an early appointment for Jonathan. We don't want him to change his mind nor do you want any other incidents, I'm sure."

"Definitely not! I'd be very grateful if you could do that."

Stella rang back with the good news that Dr McHenry would see Jonathan the following Wednesday. Lauren then rang both Nancy and Helen to give them this good news.

"I'm pleased for you, dear," said Nancy. "You're doing the right thing."

Chapter 20

Kate was waiting in the school parking lot at twelve thirty when all hell erupted and hundreds of exuberant teenage boys burst out of every visible door. They were in high spirits and all excited about the break away from routine.

Toby was the first to reach Kate, with his little friend Miguel.

"*Buenos días, Señora O'Mara,*" said the little fellow solemnly, shaking her hand while bowing.

"Oh, please call me Kate," she replied smiling.

Miguel looked at Toby questioningly.

"Go ahead, it's okay. In Ireland it's different. You can call her Kate, or Mama Kate, if you like," Toby grandly informed him.

"Okay, Mama Kate," he said shyly.

Kate gave him a hug and his little face lit up with pleasure.

"You're one of the family now," Toby grinned at him.

Kate had heard that the Spanish were very formal and

217

Miguel was certainly behaving like a little gentleman. It was obvious Toby and he had become firm friends. The other three boys followed shortly, waving goodbye to their friends as they all headed home.

Luckily I drive a Mercedes 4x4 or I'd never fit them all in, what with all their dirty laundry and rugby gear, thought Kate.

She enjoyed their banter on the way home and watched, laughingly, as they jumped out of the car and dashed into the house, swinging their bags.

They all piled around the big kitchen table. If Danny had been there he would have insisted on eating in the dining-room but Kate preferred the informality of the kitchen. She had made a big lasagne for them which they demolished so fast she could hardly believe her eyes.

"Food, real food, at last!" sighed Justin.

"Delicious, Mom," David could hardly talk, his mouth was so stuffed.

"God, I've missed your cooking, Mom," Sam said, but his voice went down a bit as he said it.

Justin and David laughed as Sam blushed, embarrassed.

Kate hugged him. "Hey, you guys! I remember when your voices were breaking. That was very funny too."

Now it was Sam's turn to laugh.

Toby and Miguel looked bewildered.

"I really enjoy, *Señora* ... eh ... Mama Kate," said Miguel shyly.

After some apple tart and ice cream, Toby rushed away to show Miguel the house and their bedroom.

"When will Dad be home, Mom?" asked Justin. "I can't wait to tell him about our rugby training."

Her three eldest sons turned to her expectantly. She didn't know how to break the news to them. She busied herself putting the dishes in the dishwasher.

"Actually, he won't be home this weekend. He has to stay in London – on business."

She could see the shock on her sons' faces and understood what they were feeling.

"Dad's never missed a weekend when we were home before. What's so important this time?" asked David belligerently.

"You'll have to ask him that. I honestly don't know either."

She was not making excuses for Danny any more. Let him explain to his sons what it was that was more important than they were. She was still livid with him. What was he playing at? This couldn't go on. She would bring things to a head, come hell or high water, next weekend. She'd had enough. She could not believe that he would miss out on the boys' weekend home. What could be more important than that?

"I really wanted Dad to come and see me riding in the gymkhana tomorrow," said Sam, disappointment in his voice.

"Well, *I'm* looking forward to seeing you ride," Kate said, ruffling his hair.

Justin stayed on after Sam and David left.

"Mom, is everything okay between Dad and yourself?" he asked, a worried expression on his face.

"Of course, dear! This job is just very important and taking more time than he expected."

There was no way that she would upset the boys, so even though she was furious with Danny, she wouldn't let them see it.

"Can I have the car tonight, Mom? There's a disco in Maynooth and David and I would like to go. Lots of our friends are going."

"Yes, darling – as long as you drive carefully and don't have a drink, of course."

"As if, Mom!" He plonked a kiss on her head.

She wasn't worried although she wouldn't sleep till they were home again. Justin was very proud of the fact that he had passed his driving test, first time out, just after his seventeenth birthday. Most of his friends had failed and some of them twice! Danny, of course, had pulled strings to get him to the top of the list for his test and had been extremely proud of him when he'd passed on his first try.

"Ring me if you're going to be late," she reminded him, just as the telephone rang. It was Lauren.

"Kate, do you mind if we drop around? Sam and Daisy have me demented to bring them to see Toby."

"Of course I don't mind. Bring their swim gear. It's such a lovely afternoon and the boys can't wait to get in the pool."

Lauren arrived a little while later and Ben and Daisy practically ambushed Toby, jumping all over him, although it had been only three weeks since they'd seen him. Ben and Miguel hit it off immediately.

"I'm so glad. I was afraid Ben might be jealous of

Miguel and feel left out," said Kate, as they sat watching the kids cavorting in the pool.

"Oh, kids are great. Not like us adults. They have room in their hearts for many friends. And Daisy seems to be enjoying herself with all these boys dancing attendance."

"She's going to break a lot of hearts when she's older. She's becoming a flirt already and she's only ten, for God's sake! They grow up so quickly, don't they?"

"Unfortunately, yes," said Lauren sadly. "I would love to keep her a little girl forever."

"Think of the grandchildren you'd miss then!"

"Stop it! I feel old enough without talking about grandchildren!"

And they both laughed at the thought of Lauren as a grandmother.

"I don't know why I'm laughing," said Kate. "I could be a grandmother any day. Justin is almost eighteen!"

As the kids were all busily dunking each other in the pool the two women settled down on the terrace with a pot of coffee.

"What time will Danny be home?" Lauren asked, blowing on her coffee, which was piping hot.

"He won't," Kate replied, making a face.

Lauren turned in her seat to look at her friend. "What do you mean, he won't?"

"I mean he's not coming home this weekend – at all." Kate's voice was very wobbly.

"You're not serious!" Lauren couldn't keep the surprise from her voice. "But the boys . . ."

"I know, I can't believe he'd do this either," Kate sighed. "It's not like him." She gulped her coffee to stop herself from breaking down and burned her tongue. "Damn!" she exploded, letting her fury out, and went to get a glass of cold water to cool her tongue down.

Lauren was gobsmacked. This was so out of character for Danny, to miss being with his sons. Whatever else you could say about him, he did adore them. She wondered if maybe he had another woman in London, although she would never have voiced this to Kate. It must be something bloody great to keep him from a weekend with the boys. She knew Kate trusted Danny completely but Lauren wouldn't trust him as far as she'd throw him! He reminded her of so many womanisers she'd met while modelling. Married or not, they needed their egos constantly boosted. She'd also seen the lustful way he looked at Diana sometimes. He was most selfish and inconsiderate, as he was proving this weekend. Tough luck for him, she thought uncharitably. He was the one missing out, as there was such a wonderful, warm, happy atmosphere here. Not only that – he was putting all this at risk. Kate wouldn't go on taking this forever. Lauren was happy to see that she'd become much stronger lately. Danny deserved all he got!

Kate came back with her tongue submerged in a glass of iced water.

"You okay now?" Lauren asked.

Kate nodded. "How are things with you?" she managed to say.

"I spoke to Jonathan last night. He's willing to go for

counselling. He says he'll do anything to save our marriage. I think he really got a fright this time. I'm really glad that I took matters into my own hands and went to Stella. It seems to have brought things home to him and he's realising just how serious I am."

Kate lowered the glass of water. "Oh, I'm so glad for you, Lauren! I'm sure it will work out."

Lauren hadn't told her about the visit to Nancy or what she had learnt there. She felt this was confidential and should be kept within the family.

Toby wanted Ben and Daisy to stay for dinner and Kate said, "Why don't you all stay? We're having a barbecue and there's plenty for everybody. Let's make the most of this beautiful September day."

They had a wonderful evening and there was much laughter and joking as the boys told stories from school and mimicked the teachers, to the amusement of the women. Miguel was having a terrific time and Kate suspected that he would become a regular fixture in the house. Ben wanted to stay the night but Lauren put her foot down.

"No, you're staying tomorrow night and that's enough. Poor Kate has enough to cope with!"

Daisy pulled Kate aside and whispered to her, "Please, Kate, can I stay tomorrow night as well? It's such fun here."

"Of course you can, darling."

Kate felt a little sorry for her as she was the only girl but all the boys adored her. She was like the little sister they didn't have.

"Why not drop the kids over to me in the morning?"

she said. "I'll take them to the gymkhana with my lot and then they can come back here and stay the night. You and Jonathan go somewhere special. I think you could do with some time alone."

"Gosh, Kate, that's very good of you! I don't know if it will do any good but it's worth a try."

When she got home and told Jonathan, he was delighted and rang and booked a suite in Mount Juliet for the following night. He also booked two rounds of golf and dinner in The Lady Helen, where they had gone for their tenth anniversary. Lauren was a bit apprehensive about it but Jonathan was making such a huge effort and had promised to go for counselling so she tried to appreciate it.

* * *

Kate was in her element. She loved nothing better than having all her brood around her – well, all except for her husband! To hell with Danny! He was a fool. In fact, she wasn't missing him. Things were more relaxed without him around. She was amazed and a little guilty to be thinking like this.

Justin and David headed off to their disco and the young ones settled down with their PlayStations and later watched the latest Harry Potter DVD with Kate. Danny didn't even telephone and Kate was damned if she was going to ring him.

* * *

Diana couldn't contain her excitement and wondered what Michael had planned for the evening. He'd said it was something special and she couldn't wait to find out what it was. This meant that he was getting serious about her which was exactly what she wanted. She had hopes that he might dump his boring wife soon and then he would be hers. Mind you, she would have to have it out with him about the party they were throwing next week, and on a Friday. How could he do this to her?

She had taken extra care this week with her clothes and had really gone all out to look as sexy as possible. She was wearing the black Agent Provocateur lingerie and hoped it would work the wonders with Michael that it had with other men. She had chosen a deep pink Diane Von Furstenburg wrapover dress that accentuated her curves and suited her colouring. She hoped Michael would appreciate it.

He did!

"Wow! You look fantastic. God, you look so delectable I'm afraid I'll have to change my plans and take you straight to bed."

Diana was delighted. This was exactly the reaction she wanted.

"Oh, I'm sure you can wait. Believe me, I feel so hot tonight that it will be worth waiting for." She gave him her sexiest, most sultry look which worked every time. She saw from his reaction that she had him just where she wanted him – in the palm of her hand! "And where is this special place you promised me?" she asked, in her best little-girl voice.

"Follow me, my lady." He led her out front and into a limousine which was parked there. She felt like a Hollywood star stepping into it and wished that some of her friends could have been there to witness it.

There was champagne on ice and as they drove away he raised his glass to her and said, "To the most beautiful woman in Ireland!"

"Only Ireland?" she asked, raising and eyebrow.

"Forgive me – the world!" he laughed, reaching over and giving her a champagne kiss.

Even if it had been George Clooney, she thought, it couldn't have been more wonderful.

She had no idea where he was taking her. They drank the champagne which she couldn't help noticing was Roederer Cristal and Michael was, all the while, fondling and caressing her. She was glad she was wearing her wrapover dress as it took him only a minute to undo it and by the time they had got to the end of the bottle, he was making love to her, in the back of the limousine. For a brief moment she wondered if the driver could see them but then she lost herself to him and didn't care. It was the most exciting sex she'd ever had.

She was on cloud nine when they arrived at their destination. She stepped out of the car to find herself outside The K Club, one of the most prestigious hotels in Ireland. The adjoining golf club was one of the best in the country and had hosted the Ryder Cup in 2006. She felt like a princess as she entered the glorious suite that Michael had reserved.

"Oh, this is wonderful," she exclaimed breathlessly. "You're spoiling me rotten. I could get used to this."

"Why not? I'm not going anywhere and you make me *soooo* happy. You deserve to be spoiled." He was already slipping off her dress. "Very sexy underwear, I like it! You really know how to turn a guy on. I must have been hallucinating last week when I said you'd gained weight because you, my lady, are absolutely gorgeous."

She didn't let him know that she had starved herself all week but vowed that she would lose even more. It was obviously how he liked his women. She reckoned that he had probably bedded so many models that he had got used to slim, toned bodies. That was over now. She was determined to snare him and it was looking good.

After another exciting lovemaking session they went down to dinner. The maitre d' greeted Michael like an old friend and the sommelier likewise, asking him, "Your usual apéritif, Monsieur Traynor?"

"Do you come here a lot?" asked Diana, suddenly wondering if she was just one of a string of ladies that he'd brought here.

"I bring a lot of my business clients here. Don't worry, you're the first woman I've had here," he smiled, reading her thoughts.

She was relieved.

They had a wonderful meal and superb wine and Diana felt quite tiddley as they made their way back to their suite. He poured them both a cognac and they curled up on the big deep sofa, Michael rubbing and caressing her arm and leg. He couldn't keep his hands off her. All night she'd wanted to ask about the party he was having the following Friday, but she'd held her tongue. Now, this final cognac gave her the courage to broach the subject.

"I was speaking to Danny at the weekend," she said casually, "and he told me that you're having a party on Friday night." She looked at him coyly.

"Yes, that's correct," he said, taking his hand away from her leg

"Why a Friday, Michael – couldn't you have had it on a Saturday? I thought Fridays were for us." She tried to keep her voice sweet but failed. She sounded querulous.

"Darling, I know. I'm sorry, but I am a married man and my wife does have some call on my time. She doesn't demand very much of me so if she wants the party on a Friday the least I can do is go along with it."

"Do you love her?" Diana couldn't resist asking.

"Yes, of course. Marcia is a wonderful woman."

Diana felt as if he had thrown cold water over her. True, he had not told her he loved her but she'd felt it was only a matter of time before he did. She knew that she was in love with him. She had never met anyone quite like him before. Now she was terrified and scared that he was only dallying with her. She felt an overwhelming jealousy towards his wife.

"Why are you here with me then," she whispered, "if you love your wife so much?"

"My darling Diana, you appear to be a woman of the world but underneath you're just a little girl," he said, drawing her close. "I love being with you. We're really good together. I love your company and the sex we have together is just amazing. You excite me so much that there are times when I can barely concentrate on business because your body keeps floating into my mind. You know that I'm very fond of you so please try and accept that there will be times when I may have to be somewhere else. I'll make it up to you. Maybe we can get together early next week, to make up for next Friday." He cupped her face in his hand and started gently running his tongue around her lips.

Somewhat mollified, and hot for him again, Diana met his tongue with hers and he led her into the bedroom where they made love again. This time it was sweet and tender and she was convinced that, although he hadn't told her, he did love her.

They slept curled up in each other's arms all night and as she was taking her shower the next morning he entered the cubicle and they made love yet again.

She couldn't bear the thought of leaving him. She wanted to spend every waking moment with him. He brought her alive. She realised that she was only half-alive when she was not with him. She couldn't go on like this, going through the motions of life, living only for their meetings. Her life in Ballyfern now seemed intolerable.

I'll think of something, she said to herself.

Chapter 21

The younger boys were up bright and early the next morning and full of exuberance as usual. Sam was so excited about riding in the gymkhana that he couldn't eat a bite. Lauren dropped an equally high-spirited Ben and Daisy off but Justin and David had to be pulled out of bed at eleven. Kate had heard them come in at two thirty in the morning. Like all mothers, she could never sleep till she knew they were safely home.

Over breakfast Justin announced, "David's in lurve! He met the most divine girl last night. What a babe! Lucky for him, I didn't see her first or she most certainly wouldn't have bothered with him."

He ducked as David pretended to throw a punch.

"You wouldn't be her type. She said she doesn't like rugger types. She prefers sensitive guys – like me."

"Tell me more about her," asked a bemused Kate.

"Not in front of this ignoramus," replied David, taking a swipe at Justin again.

When Justin had left the room, David shyly told Kate about the beautiful girl he'd met and it was very obvious that he was smitten. This was the first girl he'd ever mentioned and she was happy for him. Young love – she thought with a sigh – how sweet! I only hope that he doesn't get hurt. She remembered her first love and the heartbreak she'd felt when it had ended. She wouldn't wish it on anybody and certainly not on her lovely sensitive son.

They all piled into the car after brunch and drove to Naas where they dropped the two older boys off. They were meeting some friends and going to the cinema later.

Kate then headed off to the stables in Kill to pick up Sam's pony, Oisín, and go on from there to the gymkhana. The weather was glorious and, as Kate and the other mothers remarked, it was the best September they could remember in a long time.

Sam was in a state of high excitement. He'd taken part in many local gymkhanas before but this was his first national one. Kate could see through his bravado and knew he was anxious. She went into the paddock to wish him luck. He looked so vulnerable, sitting astride the big pony.

"Just do your best, love. I'm very proud of you," she told him as she left to take her place in the stands with Daisy and the boys.

He rode a good clear round, as did five other riders and so they had to jump off, this time against the clock. Her heart was in her mouth as he raced around, cutting corners and sailing over the jumps. She was astonished to see the look of concentration on his face as he hurtled past. He was oblivious to everything but Oisín and the next jump. He jumped clear, with the fastest time and only one more rider to jump. Kate just couldn't watch and you could hear a pin drop as the last rider took to the ring. He was clear until the very last jump – when *thud*! – the last fence went down. They all screamed and jumped in the air, hugging each other with delight when they realised that Sam was the winner. The grin he gave Kate as the rosette was pinned on Oisín's bridle was worth all the hours she'd trekked to riding classes with him over the past seven years. The others all cheered him on vociferously as he left the parade ring and came back to be congratulated by them. Danny should fucking well be here, Kate thought savagely. It's Sam's proudest moment and he's missing it.

They were ravenous at that stage so Kate took them to McDonald's on the way home, where they stuffed themselves, as only kids can. What attracted kids all over the world to McDonald's, she wondered. She'd read that even French kids, who were brought up on superb cuisine, considered it the biggest treat. She'd never understand it but if that's what they wanted – so be it!

High School Musical was showing in the local cinema and they were all keen to see it, so Kate dropped them there. She had an hour or more to kill and decided, on the spur of the moment, to drop in on Jenny.

★ ★ ★

Jenny heard the doorbell chime and, thinking it was the coalman, answered the door dressed in the old shirt of Tom's which she wore while painting. To her surprise it was Kate.

"Hi, Jen, I hope I'm not disturbing you but I've left the kids at the cinema and thought I'd say hello." She looked askance at Jenny who had smudges of paint on her nose and chin and all over her arms.

"No, of course not – come in, come in . . ." Jenny was flustered. She was behaving like a child caught with her hand in the cookie jar.

"I take it you're painting – which room?"

"Sorry, I know I look a mess . . . actually, it's not any room, it's . . ." and she pointed to an easel, on which stood a stunning painting of two children playing on a beach.

Kate was astounded. "Jenny, this is fantastic! You painted this?"

"Well, yes. But it's not finished."

"I can see that but this is seriously good. I didn't know you painted. This is terrific!"

"Nobody knows I paint – well, except for one or two people. It's my solace. It's where I escape to from my humdrum life."

"Have you painted much more?"

"Oh yes, lots. They're all stacked up in the spare bedroom. Conor thinks I should have an exhibition but I don't think they're good enough. Tom thinks they're rubbish."

"Well, if they're as good as this you could be sitting on a fortune."

Jenny giggled at the thought. She made coffee for them both and Kate quizzed her about this hidden talent that she had kept secret.

Kate couldn't believe it. She would love to have this painting on her wall. It was way nicer than some of the stuff that Danny had paid a fortune for. Well, I'll be blowed, she thought.

She left to pick up the kids, still in awe of Jenny's artistic talent and mused all the way home about how people could surprise you. She never would have guessed — but, when she thought about it, Jenny looked like an artist with her quirky sense of style.

★ ★ ★

Lauren was enjoying the weekend. They had a beautiful suite in the old house at Mount Juliet and after a wonderful round of golf with a very nice Belgian couple, they joined up with them for a drink in the bar afterwards. They got on so well that they arranged to have dinner together in The Lady Helen that night. Lauren was pleased that it wasn't just Jonathan and her. When they got back to the suite Lauren ran a bath for herself and as she was luxuriating in it Jonathan came in with a bottle of Dom Perignon Vintage Champagne, on ice, and a velvet box which, when she opened it, revealed a magnificent diamond necklace.

"I owe you this, my darling, and much more," he said as she gazed at it, admiring its beauty and clarity.

"Oh, no, Jonathan . . . I can't possibly . . ."

"Please, my darling. Please accept it. No strings attached." He clasped it around her neck and quietly left her alone.

She felt unnerved. She wanted things to work out between them but would only commit to him again when she could be quite sure that the violence was over. Refusing this necklace wouldn't help matters so she lay there in the bath, sipping champagne in nothing but a diamond necklace, feeling totally decadent. She knew it was a bribe – she knew how Jonathan's mind worked – but it would take much more than a diamond necklace to win her back.

They had a wonderful meal and later they retired to their suite where Jonathan told her just how much he loved and needed her and promised to see this counselling through. She was happy to hear that but when he tentatively started to make love, she turned from him. She wasn't ready for that yet.

* * *

Danny had tried ringing home at least five times but kept getting no reply. Kate's mobile was turned off. Finally, someone picked up. It was Sam. He could hear the excitement in Sam's voice as he told him proudly of the rosette he'd won at the gymkhana.

"It's my first prize at nationals, Dad. I really wish you'd been there to see it."

Danny felt gutted. He should have there to share in this with his son. Next he spoke to Toby who told him all about his new school and his new friend Miguel. Danny could hardly bear it and asked to speak to Kate.

"Mom, Dad wants to talk to you!" Toby called out to Kate.

"Sorry, sweetie, just tell him that I am right in the middle of cooking dinner and can't talk."

Danny got the message. He also heard the laughter and gaiety in the house. He missed seeing his kids. God, what was he doing? Was he making a dreadful mistake? He really wished that he was there in the thick of it all with his sons hanging on his every word and Kate – he could almost smell the delicious food she would be cooking and he could just see her, glowing, happy, with those curls falling around her face. Better not think of that!

* * *

David spent almost an hour on the phone talking to his new girlfriend. Sam started teasing him but David, although blushing, took it in his stride.

"Well, I'm going to marry Daisy," announced Toby.

"What?" they all chorused. "Have you asked her?"

"Yes, he has, and I said yes," chirruped Daisy.

They all roared laughing at this and Kate hugged both of them. What innocents! She was so happy. Why was Danny not here enjoying this moment with her? He was a fool.

She lay in bed that night, feeling miserable.

He was my whole life, she thought, and I thought I was

his, but I may as well accept it – I never was. His work is his priority whereas my family is mine. We're different people with different goals in life. I never realised this until now.

She drifted off to sleep, alone again in the big king-sized bed.

Chapter 22

Lauren rang on Sunday morning to see how Kate was coping, to be told that Ben and Daisy were very good and no trouble at all. Lauren spoke to them both and they told her excitedly about Sam's win. It was obvious they were having a great time. Kate told Lauren to be in no hurry home as she was driving the boys back to school at seven and Ben and Daisy wanted to go with them. Kate would drop them off after that.

"Kate, you're an angel. I owe you one."

"Have you and Jonathan mended fences?" Kate asked, wondering if he had won her round.

"We've had a really nice time," Lauren replied, her voice non-committal.

★ ★ ★

Things were not going so well for Diana and Kevin. She had been in a foul mood since coming home the day before and Kevin had had enough. It was a beautiful sunny Sunday afternoon but she was curled up on the couch, in her dressing-gown, watching some crap on the television and sipping a gin and tonic.

"Diana, what the hell is wrong with you? You're unbearable. If you're so goddamned miserable here, why do you stay?"

Getting no response from her he became angry and, grabbing the remote control, turned the telly off.

"Hey! Why did you do that?" She put her hand out for the control.

He held on to it. "Diana, I'm talking to you. Did you hear what I said?"

"No, I zoned out when you started," she said, a bored look on her face. "It's always the same – blah, blah, blah! Complaints as usual!"

Kevin wanted to slap her but took deep breaths instead. Taking the gin glass from her hand, he said, "Diana, listen to me." He stood directly in front of her and bent down so that she had no choice but to look at him. "I've really had enough of your moods and tantrums. I just can't take any more. If you're not willing to change and make an effort then I think we should separate." His face was inches from hers.

She stared at him, shocked that he should be the one to suggest this. He'd always maintained that marriage was for life. What a turnaround! Well, if that's what he wanted – the hypocrite!

"Actually, that's a very good idea. I've wanted to do that

for quite a while," she said coolly, enjoying the startled look on his face. He obviously hadn't expected her to acquiesce so easily.

Kevin had gone quite pale and, unable to reply, went and poured himself a large whiskey.

"Make mine a gin and tonic," she said, pleased with his reaction.

He did as she asked, handed it to her and sat down opposite her.

Kevin decided to change tack. "Perhaps you'd like to tell me about the speeding ticket you got last week, coming home from Naas?"

"It's none of your business."

"It most certainly *is* my business. You're my wife and I had to hear it from a friend in the gym." Kevin had a very long fuse and rarely got angry, but he was livid now. "As long as you're my wife and living with me, you'll behave as such." He banged his glass down on the coffee table so hard that the whiskey spilt over.

"Fine! I'll leave now so!" She flounced out and up the stairs.

Five minutes later he heard her come down again, then the front door opened and slammed and he heard her car revving out of the driveway.

She doesn't mean it. She'll be back when she cools down, he said to himself.

But she didn't come back.

★ ★ ★

241

Diana was headed for Dublin. She tried Michael's mobile number but it was switched off. She rang Isabelle.

"Izzie, I've left Kevin. Can you put me up for the night?"

"Of course. What's happened?"

"I'll tell you when I see you."

She wondered if she'd been a bit hasty but she actually couldn't bear to be near Kevin any more. She kept comparing him to Michael and he was the loser every time. When she arrived at the apartment she plopped down on the sofa, saying, "Izzie, pour me a stiff gin and tonic! I need one badly."

When they were sitting comfortably she told Isabelle all about Michael and how she had fallen in love with him.

"God, that's not like you, Di! He must be something special. I'll have to meet him."

"You will. I've never met anyone quite like him. He's dynamic. I hope to God this works out. I'm scared to death."

They talked long into the night and Diana couldn't wait to see Michael and tell him what she'd done although, in truth, she was very apprehensive as to how he would react.

Chapter 23

Kate woke with anticipation on Monday morning. She had another busy week ahead of her. As she stood under the hot shower, letting the jets massage her body, she marvelled at how her life had changed in the past few weeks. Firstly, there was her new body. She could hardly believe that it could have altered so much in such a short time. Because September had turned out to be so lovely, she had been able to swim and walk every day.

This, coupled with the diet and the Pilates she had started, had all helped. Why didn't I do this years ago, she asked herself. Now that the weather was changing there would be no more outdoor swimming for her but she decided she would use the leisure club pool and gym in future.

Choosing the clothes to wear for her first golf lesson, she was delighted to be able to fit into her white Capri pants. She hadn't worn them once in the three years since she'd bought them. She was thrilled and even admitted – as she looked at herself in the mirror – that she looked much younger. That was another thing that had changed. Before now, she had avoided all full-length mirrors like the plague and had only wanted to see herself from the neck up. Now it didn't depress her any more – in fact it made her feel really good.

She was just finishing her breakfast of grapefruit and Special K when Lauren rang to wish her good luck with the golf lesson.

"Kate, I really appreciate you having Ben and Daisy over the weekend."

"How were things between you?" Kate asked her.

"Well, I think Jonathan thought that it would make up for everything but I can't forgive and forget – it's just not that easy. However, he's going for his first therapy session on Wednesday so we'll see how that goes. It's all thanks to you, Kate – you forced me into action. I was wondering if you're free tomorrow? I have to go to Dublin and was hoping that you'd come with me. I'm having my hair done by Trevor. He's a genius and I think it's time you had a hair change too – to go with this new body. How about it? My treat."

"Golly, I'm very tempted. I have my Pilates class tomorrow but I can skip that. I was just thinking this morning that I've worn my hair like this forever. I also need something new for Marcia's party on Friday but you know how I find these fancy shop assistants very intimidating. Then I can never decide what looks good or not. With you there it would be much easier – I know you'll tell me the truth!"

"Fantastic! We'll make a day of it. I'll drive. Good luck with the golf and I'll see you tonight."

No sooner had Kate put the phone down than it rang again. It was her mother and she spent fifteen minutes listening to her complaints – about the neighbours, her ailments, the local priest and the butcher. It was a fifteen-minute monologue and would have gone on for another fifteen if Kate hadn't cut her short.

"Mam, I'm afraid I have to go, I'll ring you during the week, sorry but I have an appointment . . ."

"You never have time for me," her mother started whining and Kate felt bad but she had no choice – she hung up on her – otherwise she'd be late. She turned on the answering machine straight away, thinking, I'll miss my lesson if this goes on. No sooner had she done so, than the phone rang again. Let it ring – she said to herself irritably – whoever it is can leave a message.

* * *

Danny left yet another message for Kate and put the phone down with a sigh. He was feeling guilty about not going home for the weekend and bad about missing the boys. He also had a niggling feeling that they hadn't missed him all that much. Certainly Kate seemed to be doing fine without him, which hurt his pride a little. She had always depended on him but now she never seemed to be home. Where the hell was she on a Monday morning?

* * *

Diana woke with a dreadful hangover. She and Isabelle had finished the bottle of gin and then moved on to wine, which she now conceded was a big mistake. It also dawned on her just what she had done and she wondered yet again if she had been too hasty. What if Michael wanted nothing more to do with her? What then? Could she go back to Kevin? She decided not to think about that and sent Michael a text asking him to contact her urgently. It was late afternoon when he rang her.

"Hi, babe! What's so urgent?"

"I need to talk to you." She hesitated, worried about his reaction. "I've left Kevin," she blurted out.

There was silence on the other end of the phone. Diana felt the panic rising inside. Her heart was beating like a big bird, trapped in a little cage.

"Well, well! I suppose we'd better talk. I'll meet you at nine in the Merrion. Okay?"

She felt relief flood through her. He wasn't going to dump her after all.

"Thanks, Michael."

* * *

Michael sat drumming his fingers on his desk. What a quandary! Things had been going so well between them. Their arrangement suited him perfectly. What was it with women? They always wanted to devour you. He was annoyed at what she'd done, yet as he found himself thinking of her luscious body, he felt himself getting a hard-on. She certainly knew how to push his buttons. She made him feel young again. He really needed to think this one out.

* * *

Kate was enjoying her golf lesson enormously. Phil, the young pro, was very patient with her and made her feel relaxed. By the end of the lesson she was hitting quite a few decent shots. He was full of encouragement and told her that she had a good swing and could become a good golfer if she practised hard. Feeling elated, she decided to go out and play nine holes, to practise what she'd been taught. Why did I not take this up sooner? she asked herself. She was having so much fun.

Then, coming down the ninth fairway she saw someone who looked like Kevin over on the thirteenth green. It couldn't be, she thought. He's surely at work. The guy was wearing a cap so it was hard to tell.

When she'd put her clubs in the car she went into the clubhouse and ordered a chicken Caesar salad – minus the croutons – and a glass of Perrier water. The place was very quiet, just four elderly gentlemen sitting in the far corner of the room.

Then Kevin entered the bar.

"I *thought* it was you I saw out there!" she said, surprise in her voice.

"What are you doing here?" he countered.

"I had my first lesson with the pro today and I loved it!

I could ask you the same question. Why aren't you working?"

He ordered a coffee and came over to join her. "I took a day's leave – I couldn't face work, today." His face looked grim.

"Why not?" she asked, wondering what was up.

Kevin dropped his bombshell. "Diana's left me."

"She's what?" Kate almost dropped her glass of Perrier. "Why? When?"

"Last night. She just walked out," he said, running his fingers through his hair.

"She'll come back, Kevin. She was probably just upset about something. Did you have a row?"

"Nothing more than usual. She's been hell to live with these past few weeks. To be honest, Kate, it's been brewing a long time but I didn't want to accept it. She's been making my life a misery. Now she can make some other guy's life a misery also. You see, I suspect she's met someone else although she didn't say."

"Oh Kevin, I'm so sorry! Where is she now?" She could see he was very upset.

"No idea! If not with this guy, then probably with one of her friends in Dublin. I don't know any of them very well. I've only met them casually once or twice," he said, shaking his head. "I went through her things last night and this is what's really upsetting me. I've discovered why she can't have a baby – it's because she's been on the pill. I found a cache of them hidden in her make-up drawer along with a diaphragm. So, all these years, while I thought she couldn't have children, she's been lying to me. How could she do that? That's what hurts most of all." He put his head in his hands, obviously in pain.

Kate was shocked. She couldn't imagine anyone doing that. She knew how much Kevin would have liked a child. No wonder he was in such a state. Diana had really gone too far this time.

"What can I say, Kevin? I'm so so sorry." She reached out her hand to him. "If there's anything at all we can do . . . you know we're here for you."

"I know that, Kate. At times like this you need friends. I tried ringing you this morning and Danny too, but couldn't get either of you. No doubt I'll have need of you both over the next few months. I feel so bad that I've failed with my marriage but, to be honest, Kate, it doesn't come as a big surprise. It would have ended sooner or later. It's just sooner than I expected. Now I have no choice but to accept it and get on with my life."

Kate squeezed his hand. She couldn't get over it. Diana had always been selfish but this was the end. She wondered what Danny would say. She knew what Lauren would say – good riddance!

Kate was feeling very down when she arrived home and after putting her clubs away decided to have a long soak in the bath. She saw the light flashing on the answering machine but hadn't the heart to listen to it. Probably her mother complaining again!

★ ★ ★

That evening when she called for Lauren and told her about Diana, her reaction was as Kate had anticipated.

"He's much better off without her. Kevin is such a sweetheart and he deserves better. He'll meet someone else and it's not too late for him to start a family with her. Good riddance! Thank God I won't have to watch her throw herself at every male in the golf club any more. I presume she wouldn't have the nerve to show up there again."

"I don't know. He thinks she may have met someone else."

"Poor sod, whoever he is. He doesn't know what he's letting himself in for."

They met up with Jenny and as they were going into Slimforever they met Mary from the Coffee Pot coming out.

"Jenny, you look fantastic! No wonder I haven't seen you. You most certainly haven't been scoffing banoffee pie!"

"No, sorry about that, Mary, but I just can't risk it. I often dream about it though but that's as far as it goes," she said, aware that Mary's sales must be down quite a bit as a result of her defection.

"Well, you needn't worry about being tempted by the banoffee pie any more because I no longer stock it. The girl who made them for me has left and I can't find anyone else who can make it for me."

"My friend Kate could!" Jenny turned to her. "Couldn't you, Kate?"

"Well, I have often made it. My boys love it."

"Would you make some for me?" Mary asked, her

250

hopes rising."I'm losing customers because of it." She saw Kate's hesitation. "Just to tide me over till I can find someone else?"

Kate wanted to help her. "Okay, I'll think about it."

"Maybe you'll drop in to the shop to discuss it." Mary was beaming from ear to ear. "And thanks, Kate, I really appreciate it."

* * *

The girls were in high spirits when they arrived at Moorehill Lodge for their weekly dinner treat. Kate had lost another five pounds and Jenny three and, although Lauren was still the same as last week, she was quite happy with that. Jenny envied Kate's determination and wished that she had half her willpower, but still, she was happy enough as long as she lost something every week.

As they were ordering, Jenny couldn't resist asking, "Do you think we might order one portion of chips between us? I miss them so much." The fact that Tara wasn't joining them tonight made the suggestion possible.

"Why not?" replied Lauren.

So they decided that a portion of chips between them would not be too over the top.

"Tara says we can have the odd treat. And look how well we've done," Jenny said, trying to justify the chips.

When they arrived Lauren and Kate had about five each and were content with that, but Jenny finished the lot.

"They were wonderful," Jenny said, picking the last crumbs from the bowl. "I still long for chips and potatoes .

. . and crisps and chocolate . . . how I miss chocolate! Oh, God, I find it so difficult sometimes! I really wish I had more willpower – like you two."

"You're doing fine, Jenny. Keep it up. It's not easy but you must keep trying," Lauren advised her, spearing a tomato with her fork:

"It really will be worth it," Kate assured her.

★　★　★

Diana was a nervous wreck. She hadn't been able to eat all day and had a sick feeling in the pit of her stomach. She hoped Michael would stand by her. She couldn't dare let herself think that he mightn't.

Isabelle saw the state she was in and couldn't believe it. Di had always been the hard one. No one had ever affected her like this before. They'd both started in hairdressing together and Isabelle had gone on to establish her own very successful salon. She'd had a live-in relationship for ten years with a cad who had dumped her last year – for an eighteen-year-old! Thank God they had never got married or he would have been claiming half of her very upmarket apartment and probably half of her business too. She didn't trust men any more and thought Di was mad leaving Kevin for this older guy – older, *married* guy! What was she thinking of? No good would come of it.

Diana was in such a state that Isabelle said she'd go into town with her and wait in the Shelbourne while Di went to meet Michael – just in case . . .

* * *

Diana was quaking as she walked into the bar of the Merrion Hotel. Michael was sitting at a table in the corner, looking very grave. After he had ordered a gin and tonic for her, he asked her what had happened. She explained that she couldn't stay with Kevin any more and that she was going to rent an apartment in Dublin until things were sorted.

"Diana, I hope that I have had nothing to do with this decision of yours," he told her. "You do understand that you can expect no long-term commitment from me."

Diana's heart sank but then she rallied. After all, he *was* probably a bit shocked that she'd left Kevin, she thought desperately. He just needed to get used to the idea.

"No, of course I don't expect any such thing, Michael," she said sweetly – lying through her teeth.

"Diana, I love your company and being with you but as I explained last week, I can never leave my wife. We've been through too much together. I have no problem continuing our relationship, as long as you are willing to remain as my mistress." He looked straight at her, trying to gauge her reaction.

"Of course, darling," she replied, looking up at him from under her eyes, thinking that she'd settle for that . . . for now!

"You do understand what I'm saying?" he asked her, reaching for her hand. "If you agree, I will put you up in an apartment and we can have some wonderful times together but there is no question of my getting a divorce and marrying you. Do I make myself clear?"

Relief flooded through her. He was setting her up in an apartment! That meant that deep-down he loved her. She couldn't believe that he would want to stay with that sour-faced wife of his. I'll change his mind, once he sees how happy we'll be together, she thought. I'll go along with this for the moment and when I get him really hooked, he'll divorce her and we'll be together, forever. She leaned over, put her hand on his thigh and could feel his excitement rising.

"Why don't we go and celebrate my freedom?" she whispered huskily, and she could see that she had him. She went into the ladies' and rang Izzie to tell her everything was okay. She felt elated.

They left and went to his apartment where they made love with wild abandon.

It will work out, she thought, I just know it will. He's crazy for me and it will get better.

She would ring Kevin tomorrow and tell him that she wanted a divorce and arrange to collect her things.

★　★　★

When Kate got home she checked the answering machine and found one message from Kevin, two messages from her mother, and five messages from Danny. To hell with him, she thought. He's been unavailable to me often enough. I'll ring him tomorrow. She fell into bed and fell fast asleep. She didn't even hear the phone ring at midnight.

Chapter 24

The following morning Lauren and Kate headed for Dublin. Before leaving, Kate tried Danny again, but as usual, his phone was switched off. In truth Kate hated mobile phones and as often as not left hers at home, or on silent, or switched off altogether. She'd managed perfectly well without one up till now and couldn't understand the Irish populace's need to have one stuck to their ear all day, every day. She'd even seen kids as young as six texting like mad. She still hadn't mastered that technique!

Kate was looking forward to the day. She had never been in a hair studio as chic as Trevor's before. Lauren was welcomed with open arms and, as her friend, Kate was also a privileged client. She loved it and found all the staff really sweet.

Trevor took her in hand and, with Lauren right beside him, lifted her long hair and said, "This has to go. You have a beautiful face and you must frame it. I suggest a short layered bob and I'll twist your curls into spirals. That will suit your delicate features. And then blonde highlights to bring out the blue in your eyes. Yessir!" He sounded so confident and sure.

"Go for it, Kate – remember, you're worth it!" said Lauren, encouragingly.

That was enough for Kate. "Yes. Do it!" she told him – and he did.

Two hours later, Kate could not believe that it was her face looking out of the mirror at her. She loved it! Lauren was ecstatic.

"Kate, you look fantastic! So trendy! It makes you look years younger."

Kate loved it. She adored the blonde streaks and kept turning her head left and right, loving the way her hair moved and bounced with it. She also kept feeling the back of her neck which felt bare without all that long hair.

Next Lauren whizzed her down to the cosmetic department in BT's where she had arranged a make-over with the Mac consultant, Jean-Claude.

He was ecstatic. He exclaimed in his very sultry accent, "Ooh, la la, what beautiful skin! Like a peach, golden with a rose blush. Just like Charlize Thieron!"

Kate giggled with embarrassment at his extravagant compliments. Of course, he *was* French, which probably explained it. The end result, she had to admit, was fantastic. She hardly recognised herself and Lauren was beaming like the Cheshire Cat.

"You look beautiful, Kate. He's right. Your skin is like a peach. It's luminous."

"I can't believe that my eyes are so blue!"

"It's amazing what the correct make-up can do, *chérie*," Jean-Claude said. "You are a very beautiful woman – on the inside as well as out." And he raised her hand to his lips.

With such a transformation – and flattery! – Kate decided she had to buy all the products that he had used on her.

They had lunch in The Shelbourne Saddle Room, mindful of their diet. They reckoned that they could celebrate Kate's new look with a glass of Sauvignon Blanc each. Kate had never felt so good! She felt like a new woman. Lauren seemed to know everyone and people kept stopping by their table to say hello.

After lunch Lauren took her to Richard Alan's, one of the most exclusive boutiques on Grafton Street. Lauren bought 80% of her clothes there. The sales people were all old friends of hers and they made Kate feel right at home. They were so friendly – nothing snooty here! They picked out clothes that they thought would suit her. If she liked something that they thought was wrong, they told her so, regardless of how much it cost. It was wonderful to shop with people you could trust and Kate knew that whatever she chose, they would be honest with her. Mind you, she realised that Lauren was calling the shots. They were all in awe of her!

Kate chose a beautiful Escada suit and dress and then they hit Brown Thomas. Kate had never spent so much in a single day before although Danny's accountants had often tried to convince her to spend more – in an effort to counteract his tax-liabilities. She had never done so as she just wasn't that kind of spender but today she felt she could satisfy them!

With Lauren by her side and her newly lost weight and newly gained confidence, it all felt a bit surreal. However, when she tried on the Louise Kennedy, Paul Costelloe and Richard Lewis clothes, she was hooked. Crazy! Danny had so often wanted her to shop like this and she had resisted. Now she was doing it for herself, and she loved it. She ended up putting over €2,000 on the charge-card. What the hell! He was working away from them to earn this kind of money, so why not? It only worked out at €100 a year for the almost twenty years they'd been married. The final coup was when she spotted a pair of Manolo Blahnik shoes that she fell in love with at first sight. €660! She couldn't believe it. But, God, they were gorgeous and seemingly other women spent this on shoes all the time. What the hell, she thought. They're a work of art and Danny can afford it. She bought them.

Kate had never had such a wonderful time in her life. She recognised that being with Lauren had gained her entrée to places she wouldn't normally access. They finally left The Unicorn Restaurant on Merrion Row at about eleven that evening where Giorgio had made her feel like a million dollars. They drove home to Ballyfern in high spirits, singing Abba songs all the way home. They'd both fallen in love with Abba again recently, after seeing the show *Mama Mia*.

* * *

When Kate got home she found ten messages on her answering machine.

She didn't have the energy to sort through them and went straight to bed.

Chapter 25

Kate woke with a start at around five in the morning, imagining that she heard the phone ringing, but thought that she must have been dreaming. She fell back asleep where she dreamt that the boys were babies again and that she was neglecting them.

She woke again with a horrible, uneasy feeling, afraid to go back to sleep in case the nightmare returned. Eventually, she got up and showered and finally shook the feeling off.

She was sitting having breakfast at seven thirty when the phone rang.

It was Danny.

"Kate, where in hell have you been? I've been frantic with worry. I've been trying to get you since Monday morning. I thought something had happened to you."

"No, I'm fine," she replied serenely. "I've just been busy."

"Busy? Doing what, for God's sake?"

"Don't take that tone of voice with me, Danny, or I'll hang up." God, he was something else! Seems like he

261

expected her to be sitting demurely by the phone waiting for his precious call! "Danny, you don't seem to realise that I've got my own life here now," she said. "Not that you're ever here to see it," she couldn't resist adding, for good measure.

He couldn't believe it. This didn't sound like his Kate at all. It was all that damn Lauren's fault. They've become far too friendly. I'll break that up fairly quickly, he thought. I don't want Kate becoming as bolshy as her friend. He told her that he would arrive home on Friday afternoon in time to pick her up and take her to Michael and Marcia's party.

"How kind of you," she replied, sarcasm dripping from every word.

Danny felt scared. Maybe he was leaving her alone too much. He'd have to sort her out and get her back in line.

When Kate finally got to take her phone messages, she realised that Danny must indeed have been worried. There were six messages from him, each one more frantic than the last. There was also a call from Jenny, one from Kevin and the last two were from Marcia.

"Kate, can you please ring me the minute you get this message. It's urgent!"

Kate wondered what it was all about. Could the party be cancelled? She hoped there was nothing wrong. She rang Marcia, whose words came out in a torrent.

"Kate! Thank God. I'm in an awful state. I need a huge favour from you. My caterer and her assistant were in an accident yesterday and are both in hospital. I can't get another one anywhere in Dublin. I've even tried Kildare and Wicklow, but no joy. Because it's the Rugby World Cup Final, everyone is throwing parties. I'm really quite desperate. Could you possibly cater for my party Friday night? I know you're a wonderful cook and could do it. Please say you will. If not, I will have to cancel it. I know it's a huge imposition but please say you'll do it."

What could Kate say? She could hear the panic in Marcia's voice.

"How many are you expecting?"

"Sixty."

"Wow, that's a lot of people and it's just two days away. Luckily, I have nothing that I can't cancel." There goes my game of golf today and my swim and the gardening I had planned to do tomorrow! But she sounds so desperate – I can't let her down. "Okay, but tell me what you want."

"Kate, I'm so relieved! I'll leave it completely up to you. I know whatever you do will be terrific."

Kate made some suggestions and they agreed that she would start with an Italian antipasto platter. Marcia would order all the necessary items from Morton's in Ranelagh and collect them first thing Friday morning. Kate would cook the main courses and desserts tomorrow, at home, and finish the salads and final preparations at Marcia's on Friday.

"I don't know how I can ever repay you, but I'll think of something! I'm so grateful to you, Kate. I'll be forever in your debt."

Kate finally came off the phone, wondering if she was mad. She rang Lauren to cancel the golf date and Lauren chided her for being such a softie and agreeing to do it.

Well, I have agreed to do it, so now I'll do the best job that I can, she told herself.

She took down her favourite cookbooks – Delia Smith and Darina Allen – and set to work deciding what she would do and taking note of the preparation times, as she had so little of it. Look on it as a challenge, Kate, she said to herself. You know you can do it!

Two hours later she had it all planned and, with lists as long as your arm, was ready to head into Naas to buy the ingredients that she would need. She must remember to keep all the receipts for Marcia.

Before she left she returned Jenny's call and left a message for her. She also rang Kevin.

"How are you. Any word from Diana?'

"She rang yesterday and said that she would be down on Friday to collect some of her stuff. Apparently she's moving into an apartment in Dublin. She wants a divorce."

"Kevin, I'm so sorry! How are you holding up?"

"Not well, to tell you the truth," he said, his voice breaking. "I thought she might change her mind and come home once she'd cooled down – but that's certainly not in her plans. Even if she had I don't think we could have got it together again. Not after her deceit about the contraception. I can never forgive her that."

Realising that he was probably in need of a friend to talk to, Kate said, "I've offered to cater for Marcia's party on Friday night and I'm up to my eyes at the minute but, look, I have to eat sometime so why don't you come over for supper this evening? I'll take something out of the freezer. Leave it till eight o'clock – that will give me time to get organised."

"I'd really appreciate that, Kate. Thanks. The nights are the worst – I keep going over everything again and again, wondering what I could have done differently. I think I'm going crazy!"

God help him, Kate thought. It must be hell for him. "You shouldn't blame yourself, Kevin. Marriage isn't easy. Look at the divorce rate here! We'll talk tonight."

Jenny rang her back that afternoon.

"Kate, I met Mary from the Coffee Pot and she's really anxious to talk to you about those banoffee pies."

"Oh, bloody hell! I said I'd drop in on her but I clean forgot," Kate said.

"She was hoping you would. She's really keen for you to do it. It's not like you'd be working in there – I know Danny doesn't want that. You could do the baking at home and I'd collect it from you after school and deliver it to her, so you wouldn't even need to drive into Naas. Won't you think about it?"

"Lordy, it never rains but it pours!" laughed Kate. "Okay, okay, I'll give it a go, but not till next week. I'm up to my eyes right now. You know the party I told you we were going to on Friday night, in Killiney? Well, Marcia, who's throwing it, rang me in a panic. Her caterer has had an accident and she's desperate. She asked me to cater it and, mad as I am, I agreed."

"That's fantastic," Jenny said excitedly. "I've no doubt you'll do great."

Kate sincerely hoped she was right! "Tell Mary I'll

definitely call in to her next Monday. Sorry, Jen, but I have to dash now."

"Okay! Good luck!"

Kate worked like a demon for the rest of the afternoon, making any preparations she could for the actual cooking the next day. She then put the lasagne she'd taken from the freezer earlier in the oven and prepared a salad for herself and Kevin.

She was just finishing up when she heard the doorbell.

Kevin was standing there with a bottle of her favourite Amarone wine. He almost dropped it as he let out a low whistle.

"Wow, Kate, what have you done to yourself? You look sensational! My God, you look beautiful . . ."

"Stop it, you're embarrassing me," she said, blushing and pulling him in. She was relieved to be able to sit down and take a break at last.

"Whiskey?" she asked Kevin.

"A large one, Kate, if you don't mind." He saw the surprised look on her face.

"Don't worry!" he smiled at her concern. "I walked over as I felt the fresh air might clear my mind a little, which means I can drink with a clear conscience."

"And did it? Clear your mind, I mean." She looked at him, her head to one side, as she poured a large Jameson and handed it to him.

"God, Kate, I don't know where my mind is at the moment." He took a large slug of his drink.

On impulse, she poured a gin and slimline tonic for

herself. Godammit! I need it, she said to herself. She went to check on the lasagne before joining him.

She listened as he went over the same old territory he'd covered before. She could see that he needed to talk and was happy to let him. Over dinner she listened as he wondered if he could have done things differently, unable to give him much hope or comfort. The last few months had been grim for him but she suspected that he would be happier in the long run. She figured now was *not* the time to point this out to him.

She barely said a word all night, letting him talk, and at ten o'clock she shooed him out as she absolutely had to have an early night. Tomorrow would be a long day.

"You're a rock, Kate. Thanks for everything," he said to her and then, on impulse, he bent and kissed her cheek. She wondered if it was the alcohol or his state of mind that had prompted the kiss. A bit of both, probably, she guessed.

Chapter 26

Kate couldn't believe it when the alarm went off at seven the next morning. She rolled over thinking it was a mistake and then woke with a start, remembering all she had to do today, if she wanted to make a success of Marcia's party. She jumped out of bed and into the shower which helped to wake her up. She didn't feel like breakfast so she squeezed some oranges for a juice and started into the cooking. The Italian antipasti which Marcia was getting in Ranelagh would be Parma and prosciutto ham, a selection of Italian sausage from Siciliano to Milano, olives smothered in olive oil and fresh herbs, cubed and flaked Parmesan cheese and a large buffalo mozzarella and tomato salad with fresh basil and olive oil. Parmesan cheese straws, bruschetta and ciabatta bread would round off this first course.

For the main course, Kate needed something that she could cook today and reheat in Marcia's tomorrow. Beef in Guinness would do the trick and this she could almost make blindfolded. It was comfort food of the highest order but everybody loved it. For vegetarians, she decided on a pasta dish with a four-cheese sauce. She also cooked a big chicken and mushroom casserole with cream which always proved very popular. It wasn't haute cuisine but good simple food that everyone could enjoy. If it had been a dinner party for eight to twelve people she would have made it more elaborate – but sixty people! She had to play safe. To accompany these, she would serve rice and rustic potatoes, which were easy and suitable for last-minute cooking, plus three different salads.

She went to town on the desserts as they could all be prepared today and would keep well until tomorrow: tiramisu, chocolate mousse, Bailey's cheesecake, brown bread ice cream and meringues with raspberries and cream. Coffee and wine would be Marcia's, or more likely, Michael's domain. She wished that she could have had more time. She would have liked to be more adventurous but this would have to do. The main thing was that everyone enjoyed it and went home satisfied.

Kate worked methodically all day in the kitchen, happy as a lark, forgetting even to stop for lunch. At three o'clock she was well on her way when Jenny rang to see how it was going.

"Great actually. It's all bubbling and chilling away. Why don't you call in on your way home for a cuppa?"

"I'd love to. Though I'm not feeling great. Hope I'm not coming down with something."

When she arrived she couldn't believe her eyes at the change in Kate.

"I feel like a new woman, Jenny. It's amazing. You'll have to come to Dublin with us next time."

"I certainly need something like that. Let me know when you're going again!"

She couldn't believe all the food that Kate had prepared. "Wow, this is magnificent!"

Kate gave her a little taste of this and that.

"Whoa! Stop! Are you trying to sabotage my diet forever?" she laughed, before erupting in a sneezing fit.

"Oh, Jenny! You really are coming down with something!" Kate was dismayed.

"I'm afraid so!" Jenny gasped.

Kate immediately shooed Jenny home, with instructions to stay indoors and have lots of hot drinks, and got back to work. She had been glad of the breather.

She was quite pleased with her day's work although she still had a lot of finishing touches to do. She had no intention of telling Danny what she was doing. He probably would have forbidden it. Well, to hell with him! She was enjoying doing it and it was helping Marcia out.

She then realised that she had better tell him to go straight to Michael's from the airport. She rang and as usual got his voicemail.

"Hi, Danny. I'm going to Dublin tomorrow morning so I'll meet you in Marcia's. No need to come here to collect me. Okay?"

★ ★ ★

Jenny's cold became rapidly worse.

271

When Conor called in on her later and saw the state she was in, he ordered her to bed and rang the doctor.

Luckily the doctor arrived promptly which gave Conor just enough time to rush off to the pharmacy before it closed. He arrived back with her prescription, a cough bottle, Disprin and Lemsip, all of which he insisted she take.

Trust Tom to be away when she needs him, he thought. He should be here looking after her. What a bum deal she'd got there!

"You're staying in bed, my lady! Don't dare show your face at school tomorrow or I'll shoo you home."

She giggled. "Oh, I love it when you're masterful!" she teased.

"Flattery will get you everywhere. Please hurry up and get well."

He made her scrambled eggs on toast and when he arrived in the bedroom with the tray and a rose between his teeth, she was so touched that she started crying.

"What's up, Jenny?" he asked, putting his arm around her shoulder.

"You're just so kind. I don't know what I'd do without you."

"Sshh! What are friends and neighbours for? Here, dry those tears and eat this up." She looked so vulnerable and in need of looking after that Conor felt very sorry for her.

Having settled her down to sleep, he said that he would look in on her later.

He came back and made her a cup of tea and a hot lemon drink at ten o'clock and left her sleeping peacefully.

Chapter 27

Friday morning arrived all too soon. Kate loaded all the food in the Mercedes and prepared to head for Killiney. Lauren had come over to help and wish her good luck.

Lauren was in good form. She had so enjoyed the day with Kate in Dublin. Seeing the transformation in her was marvellous. She wondered what Danny would think of it. He probably wouldn't be happy. He wanted to keep her under his thumb, and having Kate independent and – Lord forbid – attractive to men did not fit his agenda.

Jonathan had gone for his therapy session on Wednesday and although he had dreaded opening up to a stranger, he'd found the therapist very understanding and not the least judgemental. He'd spent ninety minutes talking about his past and his relationships and had agreed to attend every Wednesday.

With all this good news, Lauren was so happy and relaxed that she scored a fantastic seventy-nine at golf on Thursday, winning the President's Prize. She had just landed a very lucrative job, designing the showhouse for an up-market scheme of luxury houses in Foxrock and she was very excited at the prospect of Kate starting her own catering business. She hoped fervently that nothing would prevent her from going ahead with it, least of all Danny. Lauren certainly would be there to encourage her, all the way.

"I can't actually believe I am doing this," Kate laughed. "Do you know, a month ago I would have been quaking in my boots and would not have taken this on in a million years?"

"Well, you did, and you've done brilliantly and I know it will be a huge success," Lauren replied, hugging her.

On reaching Killiney, Marcia welcomed her with open arms.

"I'll never be able to thank you enough!"

"Well, you can start by helping me unload this lot," laughed Kate.

"Kate, you look fantastic! I'd hardly recognise you. You look so much slimmer and younger . . . and you've changed your hair."

"Oh, I've changed a lot since we last met," chuckled Kate.

Marcia was astounded by the food that kept issuing from Kate's car.

"God, this is terrific. Way better than what my usual caterer does. Kate, you're a genius!"

Kate was very impressed with the house. It was a lovely old Georgian house, quite like Lauren's, but this one overlooked Dublin Bay. The party was to take place in the beautiful Gandon conservatory. Marcia told her that they had a string quartet coming to entertain the guests before the buffet and a band for dancing afterwards. Kate thought of how impressed Danny would be by all this.

The two women worked steadily through the afternoon and at six o'clock, when all was ready, Marcia opened a bottle of champagne.

Just as she was doing so Michael arrived and gave Kate a big hug. She'd forgotten just how attractive he was.

Marcia raised her glass in a toast: "To my saviour!"

Michael's eyes twinkled as he toasted, "To Kate, who's made me a very happy man because you've made my wife happy and kept her sane!"

Kate could feel the love and warmth in their relationship. Marcia ushered her up to shower and change and she felt a million dollars as she zipped up the Richard Lewis silk jersey dress and slipped her feet into the delicious Manolo Blahnik heels.

When she came down, both Michael and Marcia's eyes opened wide with surprise.

"Wow!" Michael said, letting his eyes sweep over her body in a way that unnerved her.

"You look sensational, Kate!" said Marcia. "Every man in the room will be chasing you tonight."

Kate was embarrassed. "Oh, don't be silly!"

"Trust me, they will," said Michael, causing her to gulp down her champagne a little too fast.

Everything was ready. It all looked gorgeous and all she

had left to do was reheat the casseroles, cook the rice and pasta, stick the potatoes in the oven and dress the salads and meringues at the last moment. She felt giddy with apprehension. Better not have any more champagne till the food is served, she thought.

The guests started arriving and Danny was amongst the first to arrive. He'd been disgruntled since he'd received Kate's message saying she would go on to the party alone. He couldn't believe that she'd had the courage to go without him. Michael welcomed him and directed him into the large salon where his eyes scanned the room searching for Kate. For a minute, he didn't recognise her. Her hair, her body, even her face looked different. He took in the make-up and, in astonishment, the high heels. What's happening here, he asked himself. This is my wife and I almost didn't know her. She looks beautiful! He felt a pang of jealousy as he saw her laughing with a very attractive man.

Carlo, a suave Italian neighbour of Michael's, had asked to be introduced to her. Kate found him to be very charming and interesting company and he made it very obvious that he found her attractive. He was dark and handsome with hair greying at the temples and reminded her of George Clooney. Kate realised he was flirting with her and barely knew how to handle it. It was such a long time since anyone had fancied her that she found herself blushing at his extravagant compliments. His hand was brushing her arm as he spoke and Danny, watching, could stand it no longer.

He strode over and, kissing Kate full on the mouth, said, "Darling, I wish you'd waited for me!"

Carlo raised his eyebrows, questioningly. Kate introduced her husband but Carlo wasn't fooled. He could sense the tension between them.

"What a lucky man to have such a beautiful wife! I hope you treat her well." Then, kissing Kate's hand, he said, "*Ciao, signora*! I hope you'll save a dance for me."

Danny was beside himself with fury. "What are you doing flirting with a gigolo like that?" he hissed.

"I'm fine, thank you, and how are you – seeing as how we haven't seen each other for twelve days," answered Kate coolly.

Danny was at a loss for words. This was a Kate he didn't know and had no idea how to handle.

"I must go and help Marcia in the kitchen," she said and drifted off, leaving him speechless.

It didn't help when Michael and the two guys who had been down at their house raved on about how wonderful Kate looked. He tried to corner her again but couldn't pin her down. She was flitting about, in and out of the kitchen, chatting to everyone, laughing and joking. He couldn't believe it. Danny started to knock back the whiskeys.

Then supper was served. It was fantastic. Everyone said that they had never tasted such wonderful food. Every plate was cleared and there was not one spoonful of dessert left over. Some of the women were pestering Marcia for the name of her caterer when Michael called for silence.

"A toast! To my wonderful wife, Marcia, and to a special

lady, our friend Kate, who helped us out by stepping in at the last minute, to do the food. What a great job she's done!"

"To Marcia – to Kate!" everyone chorused, lifting their champagne glasses – except for Danny, who was too shocked to do so.

"Why didn't you tell me?" he hissed when he got her alone.

"When could I have told you? I can never get you and anyway you're not interested in what I do any more."

Before he could respond, Carlo appeared at her elbow and whisked her away to dance. He held her close and she couldn't help thinking that he was very sexy and attractive.

As the evening wore on Danny got more and more drunk and Kate could overhear him bragging about his business. He's trying so hard to impress these people but they're not in the least bit impressed, she thought. She felt embarrassed for him because he thought his money spoke for him, but these people were all very wealthy and money was not their benchmark. They could see right through him. To them he didn't fit in – he was *nouveau riche*. Danny would never understand that.

* * *

Diana was thrilled with the the apartment that Michael had chosen for her. It was beautiful. It overlooked the Liffey and was just five minutes' walk from his apartment and office. She had hoped that he could move in there with her but this seemingly wasn't an option. Not yet anyway, she thought, but just you wait, Michael! She moved in on Friday afternoon and was furious when he rang and said that he could not see her that night. His damned party!

"Couldn't you invite me as a business colleague?" she'd asked and was disturbed by the icy silence at the other end of the phone.

Instead she decided to have her own party – a housewarming party for her girlfriends. She ordered three cases of champagne and two cases of red wine from O'Brien's and then antipasti and cheeses from The Unicorn. She charged them all to Michael's account. They had a hilarious night but all the while she was thinking of Michael with his wife and friends and her jealousy was eating away at her. At one stage, when she was very, very drunk she started to call him but Izzie grabbed the phone from her and hid it. She was grateful to her the next morning. That would have been a disaster! She had hoped that he might have called her, but no chance.

* * *

Kate had a wonderful night and received at least five requests from the female guests to cater for them in the future. Marcia had suggested yesterday that she and Danny stay overnight, so she could enjoy a few drinks. Besides, she needed to take all her dishes and pots away the next day.

When she finally got to talk to Danny and told him this, he wasn't happy.

"Why can't we go home?"

"Because neither of us is in any condition to drive – we've both been drinking and it wouldn't be safe. I need to collect all my dishes tomorrow and besides I'm so shattered that I couldn't face the long trek home now. I've brought a toilet bag and change of clothes for you."

He grudgingly agreed to stay. She was worried about going to bed and leaving him at the party so she tried to get him to go to bed with her, but he wouldn't hear of it. Michael took her aside and told her not to worry. He would look after Danny.

Kate said goodnight and retired.

It was two hours and many drinks later when Danny finally hit the bedroom to find her fast asleep. Drunk as he was, he looked at the sleeping Kate and thought how beautiful she was. She looked like a cherub with the blonde curls falling about her face. She's even more beautiful than when I married her nineteen years ago, he realised. He got into bed beside her, wondering where it had started to go wrong but he was too befuddled to work it out. Within minutes he was snoring.

Chapter 28

Danny woke with a dreadful hangover. Kate was no longer in the bed. He came downstairs to find her laughing with Marcia at the breakfast table. Marcia offered him some cereal or toast but he settled for black coffee. He felt a bit sheepish and embarrassed as he remembered how much he'd had to drink the night before. He was relieved to find that Michael wasn't around – he'd gone to play golf earlier. The girls decided that, as it was such a lovely day, they would go for a walk on Killiney beach.

Danny needed to get home. He had arranged to meet up with James to review the previous fortnight's business in Ireland. He hoped to be able to get out later in the afternoon, to play golf. As he kissed Kate goodbye he marvelled to himself, yet again, at the transformation in her.

* * *

Marcia and Kate linked each other as they walked along the

deserted beach, in the warm September sunshine. Marcia was very fond of Kate and had a feeling they would become good friends. She had witnessed the tension between Danny and Kate the previous night and wished she could do something to help.

"I hope I'm not intruding, Kate, but is everything okay between you and Danny?" she asked.

"I wish I could say yes, but I don't know what's happening, Marcia," Kate sighed. "Ever since he took on this London job things have really been going downhill." She stopped and took off her shoes, enjoying the feel of the soft sand between her toes. "It's like a big chasm has opened up between us and I don't know how to close it. He's preoccupied all the time and I just can't get through to him."

"Oh, my dear, I'm sorry to hear that," Marcia patted her hand. "Business can really consume men, to the exclusion of everything else. I should know – been there, done that!"

Kate could hear the sadness in her voice.

"He seemed angry last night. I hope it wasn't because you were catering?"

"Maybe it was. He doesn't like me being independent of him, but I get so bored all week alone." Kate turned to look at Marcia, hoping she'd understand.

"Take my advice, dear, and make a life for yourself. When men get obsessed with business, they have very little time for family. Believe me – I've been through it."

"But you and Michael seem very happy."

"Well, yes, you could say that but it's been a long – and

not always easy – journey to here. He needs me and calls me his rock, yet Michael has his life and I have mine. I have my friends, my charities, my golf and bridge and, of course, I see my two daughters and my granddaughters very often. They're my life. Michael has his business and he also has a soft spot for the ladies, as you've probably noticed. He has always had a very high sex drive, which unfortunately I haven't, so when I realised many years ago that I could never satisfy him in that department, we came to an agreement. He could have his lady friends but if there was ever a chance that it was getting serious, he promised he would end it immediately and, in fairness, he has been true to his word. It may seem a strange marriage to some people but it works for us. He is very loving and kind to me and we are the best of friends. I know he would never leave me. He knows he can trust me and he depends on me a lot."

Kate was shocked and it dawned on her that Diana might be the latest lady friend. Things started getting really bad between Kevin and herself just after our dinner party, she thought. Mind you, that was the start of our downward spiral too.

Kate had often wondered how she would feel if Danny was unfaithful to her. She knew that she would be devastated. There was no way that she would ever accept it, as Marcia had done. Maybe Marcia's marriage was stronger than any of theirs, despite Michael's philandering, but it was not for Kate.

* * *

Jenny was much improved when Conor called in bringing her a delicious lunch of grilled salmon and asparagus. She hadn't felt like eating but in fact ate it all up. He was such a good cook. She loved that in a man. Tom couldn't even boil an egg – cooking was for poofs, according to her macho husband!

With all this attention she didn't feel any inclination to get up. After he left, she snuggled down in bed and drifted off to sleep with a smile on her face.

* * *

When Kate and Marcia got back to the house they loaded all Kate's dishes into her car.

"Would you like to go out to lunch, Kate?" said Marcia.

"I'd love to, Marcia, but I really need to get on the road fairly soon as I desperately want to have a talk with Danny."

"Let's have something here then."

Marcia rustled up some prawns and salmon and Kate made a delicious salad for them both.

"Kate, we have to talk seriously," said Marcia as they ate. "I have an idea. We were talking about you getting a life for yourself. Well, why not start a catering company? You have such a talent with food."

Kate stopped eating and looked at Marcia, checking if she was serious.

"I mean it," Marcia replied, her voice excited. "I'll be your first customer. I've planned a dinner party in two weeks' time and would love you to cater it. You heard all my friends last night, panting for your number. You wouldn't have to advertise – it's all word of mouth. I guarantee you'll be a great success."

Kate felt a tremor of excitement. "Do you really think I'd be able to do it? I really did enjoy doing it even though it was an awful rush."

"Of course, you can do it," Marcia stood up and came around the table and put her hands on Kate's shoulders. "I would have paid my caterer €1800 for that buffet last night. I have a cheque here, made out to you for that amount." She picked up the cheque from the counter and handed it to Kate.

Kate's eyes were like saucers. "Oh, I couldn't possibly take that!?" she said, her voice shocked.

"No argument," Marcia said, smiling. "I insist. Look on it as your first job. I really would love you to cater for me again and I've given your number to some of my friends. Please consider it. You'll be doing us a huge favour."

Kate was shaking her head, her lunch forgotten. This couldn't be happening – €1800! My God, that was a fortune! Was Marcia serious?

"This is much too much," she said, protesting.

"No argument, I said. Your food is so delicious and different to all that silly fusion food that they're all doing nowadays. You saw how much everyone enjoyed it last night. I'll gain kudos for having discovered you!"

Kate got up and hugged her. She was really excited at the prospect.

"Okay, I'll think about it but Danny won't like it." She made a face.

Marcia gave her a look as much as to say, so what? "It's time to get a life for yourself, my dear."

Kate was really excited at the idea and thought about it all the way home. She couldn't wait to tell Lauren and knew exactly what her advice would be: Go for it, girl!

Which is exactly what Lauren said when she dropped in on her that afternoon to hear all about the party.

"You're absolutely glowing!" she remarked.

"Yes, I had a really good time and everyone loved the food. I feel exhilarated. I really enjoyed it and would love to do it again. Marcia thinks I should start a catering business."

"Why not, Kate? This is a fantastic opportunity for you."

"Danny won't like it!"

"When is Danny ever here to like it? Did he even consult you about going to London? No, he just took off. Don't ask him! Just tell him you're going to do it. If it doesn't work out you have nothing to lose. It won't cost him anything. How many businesses can you start up with no investment? And trust me, when he hears you got €1800 for one night, he'll go for it!?

"I hope so. I'll talk to him tonight." She hesitated, thinking twice about saying anything then continued, "And I met a gorgeous man, an Italian, who quite fancied me, I think."

"You what?" Lauren had to sit down. She couldn't believe it! Kate was the last person on earth to look at another man. "Tell me more! Who is he? What happened?"

Kate laughed at Lauren's obvious shock. "Just because I'm married doesn't mean I'm dead!" she retorted. "He's very handsome and charming and he paid me a lot of attention. I really enjoyed his company – bit of a change from Danny's at the moment," she said, turning down the corners of her mouth.

"Are you going to see him again?" Lauren asked her, hardly able to believe it.

"No. He did ask me if he could see me again, but . . . well . . . obviously I had to refuse."

"Why?" Lauren asked her. "What harm could it do?"

Now it was Kate's turn to be shocked. "A lot. Come on, Lauren! Can you imagine Danny's reaction if I said I was meeting another man for a drink?" and she laughed at the absurdity of it.

"It would serve him right! What a pity – we could do with some excitement like that in Ballyfern."

Kate gave her friend a poke. "You're a bad influence, Lauren Smithson."

"Hopefully," Lauren replied as they both pealed with laughter.

★ ★ ★

When Michael got back from golf Marcia was in great form after the success of the party. She told him what a sweet person Kate was and how Danny was spending so much time in London.

"He certainly doesn't need to be there more than three days a week," Michael said, his brow furrowed. "I wonder does he have a girlfriend? I did hear a rumour to that effect."

"Oh God, I hope not! I think that would kill Kate. She has so little confidence in herself."

"Well, she should have. She looked bloody attractive on Friday night. Carlo was quite taken with her. He even asked me for her phone number. And what a superb cook she is!"

"I'll say! I'm going to try and convince her to start a catering business. She's so good, she'd clean up."

Their two daughters called in soon after and Michael took his three little granddaughters down to the beach. He adored them although he was secretly hoping that the baby due to his oldest daughter next month would be a boy. He'd never had a son and was dying for a grandson.

That would make life really perfect.

★ ★ ★

By five o'clock, Kate had put away all her dishes and was just sitting down with a cup of coffee when Kevin called in. She poured another one for him and they brought it through to the living-room.

"I hope you don't mind my calling, Kate? I thought I'd catch up with Danny. Is he here?" Kevin asked, looking around.

"He's golfing, but he should be home any moment," she said, curling her legs under her on the sofa.

"Good. I tried ringing him a couple of times this week, but could never get him," he said, as he sipped his coffee. "Well, how did last night go?" He saw at once from the smile on her face that it had been a success.

"It was fantastic!" she told him, her eyes glowing. "Everyone loved it and best of all, Marcia has suggested that I should start a catering company!"

"That's a terrific idea! You're such a good cook and you've been looking for something, so why not? What does Danny think?"

"Well . . . er . . . I haven't had a chance to tell him yet." She shifted uncomfortably in her seat. "I was hoping to tell him when he gets home."

Kevin could see that she was apprehensive about it.

"I really want to do it, Kevin, and I will – whether Danny likes it or not," she said, lifting her chin with a defiant air.

"The worm has turned," murmured Kevin, almost to himself. "You do it if you want to. Danny has always been selfish, Kate. That's the way he is. We overlook it because he's generous and good company and good fun but he always puts himself first. He's been my friend for a long time but even I can see how much he's changed. I probably shouldn't say this – I don't feel disloyal because I will say it to Danny too – but you deserve better. You've always put him first – maybe it's now time to think of yourself."

"You know, lately everyone is telling me to make a life for myself. It seems Danny has gone on his own way without me and now I have to find mine. I never thought it would come to this."

"Join the club. I have to find a new life now without Diana. It won't be easy but we have to move on."

She went into the kitchen for more coffee for them

289

both, asking him, through the open door, "What's happening with Diana – did she come down?"

"Yes, she came down yesterday and collected some of her stuff. She's staying with her friend Isabelle at the moment. She told me quite calmly that she has met someone else and is in love but wouldn't go into details. I can't understand why she's not moving in with him, unless, of course, he's married."

Kate wondered again if Michael was involved. She looked away, afraid Kevin could see what she was thinking. "And how do you feel? Were you very upset?"

"Surprisingly not. She was so matter-of-fact about it. It's as if our marriage never existed. She expressed no regrets, no guilt, damn-all feelings at all! It was as if we were ending a business agreement. I feel quite numb to be honest – even a bit relieved. Life is much more peaceful without her. It would have ended sooner or later – it just happens to be sooner. I tackled her about the contraceptive pills and diaphragm I found, and you won't believe what she replied."

Kate couldn't imagine what was coming next. "What?"

"'Get a life, Kevin. I don't do pregnant. Do you seriously think I would let my body be invaded in that manner? Getting a big belly and sagging breasts? Ugh! No, thank you. Everyone may say that Demi Moore looked great, posing pregnant and nude on the cover of *Vanity Fair*. *I* think she looked revolting. My vagina is for pleasure, not for pushing babies out!' Can you believe her, Kate? She's not natural."

Kate tried to stifle a giggle. It wasn't funny, but it was classic Diana. She could just imagine her saying it, in that haughty tone of hers, full of self-righteousness. She was priceless. If she hadn't been born, you couldn't invent her, thought Kate.

"Oh Kevin! Isn't she something else?"

"She sure is!"

Kate was pleased to see that he was smiling.

At six o'clock there was still no sign of Danny and Kevin had to leave.

★ ★ ★

Danny didn't arrive home from golf till half past six and she could tell at once that he'd had a few drinks. She was watching the news on TV when he came in and headed straight for the drinks cabinet. He poured himself a large whiskey and flopped down on the couch beside her.

"What rubbish I played!"

"Danny, we have to talk."

"Oh no! Not another nagging session!"

She felt the tears pricking her eyes but was determined not to cry.

"Kate, give me a break. We can talk later. I told the guys I played with today that we'd meet them for dinner at half seven back at the golf club so why don't you go up and get changed, like a good girl."

Something snapped inside Kate. She'd had enough.

"Actually, Danny, I'm staying in tonight. I've had a

hectic week and want a quiet night in. You and I need to have a serious talk."

"Not tonight. I've promised these guys I'd meet them."

"Fine, meet them. I'm staying in."

"You can't be serious?"

"Watch my lips . . . I'm . . . staying . . . in . . . tonight . . !"
And with that she marched out.

Danny couldn't believe it. She'd never done this before. She always went along with whatever arrangements he made. What had got in to her? Perhaps she was starting the menopause. He knew it affected women in funny ways. She was being so selfish. How would he explain her absence?

He was sure she would change her mind but when he was ready to leave she was still locked in the bathroom.

"See you later!" he called out.

Kate was soaking in the bath. She had used the Jo Malone bath oil and lit the fragranced candles. She put on the jacuzzi jets and after fifteen minutes finally found herself relaxing. She refused to cry although her tears were very near the surface. She had hoped that her refusal to go might bring Danny to his senses, but seemingly not. He had gone without her. She had never felt lonelier but she was determined to stay strong. She knew that things were coming to a head.

Kate had once heard someone describing her marriage breakdown. She'd said, 'Our ship had a collision and we ended up in different lifeboats'. At the time Kate had thought that was so poignant and sad. She never thought she would be saying it about her own marriage!

She dressed in her comfortable velvet kaftan, poured a glass of Guigal Côtes du Rhône, put on some Handel music and curled up with a Mary Higgins Clarke novel which she knew would keep her engrossed.

★ ★ ★

At the golf club Danny excused Kate by saying that she was unwell. Lauren stopped by his table to enquire where she was and on hearing that Kate was sick, said with raised eyebrows, "That was sudden – she was perfectly fine this afternoon." Seeing the flush of anger on Danny's face, she suspected that they'd had a row. Selfish bastard, she thought.

★ ★ ★

Many hours later Kate heard Danny come in. He stumbled on the stairs so she gathered that he'd had a bellyful. When he opened the door, the whiskey fumes filled the room. She pretended to be asleep. There was no way she wanted a confrontation while he was in this state. Thankfully, he let her be.

Chapter 29

The following morning Kate was up ahead of Danny and was showered, dressed and sitting at the breakfast table when he shuffled down, in his dressing-gown, desperate for a caffeine fix.

"Sit down, Danny. We are going to talk whether you like it or not."

"Please Kate, give me a break. I don't feel so good." He held his hand to his head as he poured the coffee.

She noticed how bloodshot his eyes were. "Not surprising, considering how much you had to drink last night."

"Well, what do you expect when my wife refuses to come to dinner with me?" he shot back, glaring at her over the coffee cup.

"Oh please, Danny. This is serious. Our marriage is in trouble. Can't you see it or don't you care? "

"Kate, you're exaggerating."

"No, Danny, I'm not. I'm really worried about us. This

London project is just not worth it. It's driving a wedge between us. I never see you and when you're home you never have time for me. We're growing apart and I don't want that to happen." Her voice was pleading now.

"You don't understand. This job is stressful. As my wife, I would expect you to understand. When I come home, I need to relax."

"You could relax – with me – here at home, but you're all the time on the go. I miss being with you. We have no time alone together any more. Do you not want to be alone with me?" she asked, her voice low.

"Now you're nagging."

"Danny, please listen to me. Our marriage is in trouble and I want to get it back on track. I can't go on like this much longer. Do you really have to spend so much time away? Are you honestly working day and night – and weekends too? Nothing is worth that. Can't you organise it so that you spend less time there? I feel you're moving away from me."

She noticed that he was very uncomfortable with this conversation and he wouldn't meet her eyes. He didn't want to hear this.

"Please, darling. I'm worried about us. Do you know how long its been since we last made love?"

He jumped up. "Is that what this is about?"

"No, of course not! But I'm beginning to wonder if you still love me and if you even want to try and save our marriage." She knew she sounded pathetic but she had to get through to him.

Still refusing to look her straight in the eye, he mumbled, "All marriages go through bad times."

"We had no bad times before you took on this London job."

"This job is very important to me." He was pacing back and forth now.

"More important than our marriage?" She turned in her chair to look at him.

"Please don't ask me to make a choice," he said.

And he walked out of the room.

She was stunned. She couldn't believe that he'd said that. She sat for a long time at the table trying to figure out if he'd really meant it. Could she mean so little to him? Nineteen years they'd been married. She realised that he'd evaded answering her when she'd asked if he still loved her. She bit her lip to stop from crying. Was it possible that he didn't any more? They had never gone so long without making love. She felt really scared.

When he came back downstairs she asked him, "Do you know that Diana left Kevin this week?" She could see that he was shocked.

"Why didn't Kevin contact me?"

"He tried, and so did I, but neither of us could get you."

"I'll go over there straight away. Then I'll head to visit the boys and from there I'll be going to the airport. I must tell you that I do not like the person you're becoming – changing your hair and wardrobe, without asking my opinion – catering for Michael and Marcia without consulting me." The coldness in his voice chilled her to the bone. "I'm the breadwinner in this family and I expect you to behave as a respectful wife. I hope that when next I'm home, you'll have come to your senses."

He walked out without so much as a goodbye, a kiss, or a backward glance.

Kate sat down, in shock, and realised that their marriage was indeed in serious trouble. She thought back on their nineteen years and realised that it was her own fault. She had let him make all the decisions, agreed with everything he wanted and in fact had been a total doormat. He was right – she had changed – but for the better. She hoped that it wouldn't be at the expense of her marriage but she knew that, no matter what, she had to become her own person.

* * *

Tom had arrived back from his two-week rugby trip on Sunday morning and within an hour had left to go and play golf. Jenny was still in bed, on the mend but feeling very weak, and if it hadn't been for Conor she didn't know what she would have done.

Conor cooked lunch for her, got her the Sunday papers and came back later with doughnuts for her afternoon tea and – sheer bliss – a large bar of Cadbury's Wholenut.

"What about my diet?" she cried.

"Fuck your diet! You need some comforting."

"I'll love you forever for this," she answered, blowing him a kiss, and ripping open the wrapper. He laughed as she stuffed the chocolate in her mouth.

She knew that Tom should have been doing these things but she was relieved that he was out of the way. He had no sympathy for her when she was ill. His attitude was, 'Get out and about and you'll feel better'. Get out and about! She barely had the energy to come down the stairs.

★ ★ ★

Diana had been feeling pretty miserable all weekend. She was sick with jealousy at the thought of Michael at home with his wife. She had expected him to call her but she hadn't heard a dickey-bird. He'd said that weekends were for his family but one phone call wouldn't have killed him. She could think of nothing but Michael and she wished that they were wrapped up in each other's arms and making love. Was he making love to his wife, she wondered. The very thought made her ill.

She would have felt a whole lot worse if she'd known that Michael hadn't given her a second thought all weekend.

★ ★ ★

Danny arrived at Kevin's just as he was coming in from Mass, his arms full of Sunday newspapers. He put the kettle on for coffee but Danny said,

"If you don't mind, I'd prefer a whiskey."

Kevin raised an eyebrow. Whiskey at eleven thirty in the morning? Well, well, he thought, pouring a Jameson for Danny and a Coke for himself.

"Kev, old chap, so sorry to hear about Diana. Kate just told me. If I'd known, I would have contacted you. What a bitch! Are you sure she won't be back?" Danny took a big slug of whiskey as they moved into the living-room.

"Unlikely. She's met someone else and besides I wouldn't have her back now. We should have called it quits some time ago but you know how it is," Kevin said, shrugging his shoulders and sitting down opposite Danny.

"Well, plenty of other fish in the sea!" said Danny.

"Thank you," said Kevin dryly, "but I'm not fishing." God, Danny could be so insensitive sometimes. "Speaking of marriage, Danny – as your oldest friend I have to say this – if you don't want to end up like me, then I think maybe you should pay a little more attention to your own marriage."

Danny glared at him. "It's Kate's fault, she should be more understanding."

"Oh, come off it, Danny! Kate has always been a wonderful wife. You're spending too much time away from her. A good marriage is the most important thing in your life. I didn't have that – you have." Kevin was sitting forward now, trying to get Danny to listen. "Don't lose it. Trust me! It's lonely on your own."

"Oh, I wouldn't be on my own. There are plenty of young girls around who appreciate what I'm doing and admire my success, unlike Kate. I know you've always had a soft spot for her but she's changed and I don't like it," He took another large gulp of his whiskey.

Of course, you don't, thought Kevin. She's not your doormat any more.

"I tell you," said Danny, "if she doesn't cop on, I'm out of there!" Draining the last of his whiskey he gave Kevin a clap on the back. "We must get together for a drink next weekend, if I'm home."

Not if I can help it, thought Kevin. He was furious with Danny. He really had become very pompous. And what did he mean by 'plenty of young girls'? It sounded like he was playing around. Was he really so stupid? Well, I'm not his keeper. I just don't want to see Kate get hurt. God, Danny and Diana are really a pair. They should get together. They deserve each other!

* * *

Kate visited the boys that afternoon but didn't stay as long as usual. She found it a strain to keep smiling when inside her heart was breaking.

David was so taken up with his new girlfriend that all he did was talk about her and Sam and Toby were oblivious to all but their own news and chatter. But she could tell that Justin wasn't fooled and she was conscious that he was watching her carefully.

"Are you sure you're okay, Mom?"

"Of course, love, just tired," she lied. Sixth Year was tough enough on him without him knowing that she and Danny were having problems. She promised to come early the following Sunday and take them into Dublin to the cinema.

"Can we go to Eddie Rocket's afterwards?" asked Sam.

"Can Miguel come too?" Toby chimed in.

She agreed and then David said that it would be great if his girlfriend could meet up with them as well. He's really smitten, she thought. I do hope he won't get hurt. When she got home she spent the evening working on some recipes for Tara, hoping to take her mind off Danny.

But although she was exhausted that night, she lay in bed, tossing and turning, trying to figure out what she could do. She finally fell asleep with the problem still unresolved.

Chapter 30

Kate's golf lesson went really well the next morning. She played nine holes with Lauren afterwards and surprised both of them by how well she hit the ball.

"I had a chat with Danny yesterday," Kate told her friend, as they walked up the fairway.

"And?" Lauren asked.

"And nothing. He accused me of nagging and said this job was very important to him. When I asked if our marriage was not important to him, he had the nerve to tell me not to ask him to choose."

Lauren rolled her eyes to heaven. "What an asshole! He doesn't deserve you, Kate."

"I'm coming round to that way of thinking myself," Kate said sadly.

They went straight home after the golf as Lauren had some work to do and Kate wanted to spend the afternoon printing the recipes for Tara.

First she rang Jenny to see how she was, assuming she

wouldn't be coming to Slimforever, but Jenny said that even if she had to come by ambulance, she'd be there.

"I couldn't miss the weigh-in," she said. "I think I've lost a lot!"

Kate had rung Jenny a few times over the weekend, checking to see how she was feeling, and had offered to come in and cook for her. Jenny told her that she had enough on her plate without having to care for an invalid as well and that Nurse Conor McCarthy was taking great care of her.

I'm really glad that Jenny has someone she can rely on, thought Kate. What a dote he is!

* * *

Jenny wasn't joking. She was 'Girl of the Week', with a whopping five pounds more gone. Though she was still feeling a bit under the weather she was delighted that she had made the effort to go along to the class.

"I can't believe it," she told the girls excitedly. "This is fantastic. I've lost a stone and a half to date. Mind you, I've eaten practically nothing since last Wednesday and what really did it was that I haven't had a drink all week. I don't advocate getting sick but it sure as hell helps you to diet."

"Did you not comfort-eat?" Kate wanted to know. "I always do, when I'm sick."

"I did break out once with a bar of Cadbury's Wholenut and a doughnut," Jenny admitted. "Conor's fault — he bought them for me and I couldn't disappoint him!"

304

"Large or small bar?" Lauren asked.

"God, Lauren, you're like an inquisitor," Jenny told her, looking offended.

"I take it it was a large one then," Lauren grinned and Jenny gave her a poke.

Kate was pleased with her three pounds which brought her down to ten stone one pound. Only two more to go to get into the nines, she thought. She couldn't believe that she had lost twenty-two pounds in the past month. What a blessing in disguise it had been when Diana had embarrassed her into joining Slimforever.

"I must remember to send her a thank-you card," she giggled.

She knew that she would never have done it without Tara's help. She was truly inspirational. It was a gift to be able to motivate people in this way. Did Tara realise the difference she was making in people's lives, Kate wondered. I must ask her later.

Jenny decided to go straight home to bed after the lecture and passed on the exercise session and the weekly outing to Moorehill Lodge. Thankfully, the doctor had given her a certificate for a week, so she did not have to return to school until the following Monday.

★ ★ ★

In Moorehill Lodge, Kate recounted for Tara the busy week she'd had and the catering she'd done for Marcia.

Lauren jumped in, "Marcia suggested that Kate start her

own catering business. She's perfectly capable of it. You know what a fantastic cook she is and she has the time."

"That's a brilliant idea," said Tara. "I'll be your first customer. I'm planning a party for the twins' sixteenth birthday at Hallowe'en and I just don't have time to cater for it myself. My friends and I are always looking for a good caterer. There are plenty of people doing it but finding a good one is another story. They're very thin on the ground. Please say you'll do it, Kate!"

"Go on, Kate. This is your chance. To Kate's Catering!" said Lauren, raising her glass.

"To Kate's Katering – spelt with a K. That sounds catchy," said Tara.

"A star is born!" said Lauren.

Kate laughed. "You two are very convincing. If you really think I could do it – then I might give it a try. I suppose I have nothing to lose."

"That's settled then. The twins will have about fifty guests and there will be about twenty family and friends, so we can reckon on seventy in total. Can you meet up with me next week, to discuss the details?"

"Okay," said Kate and she couldn't help grinning from ear to ear.

Tara looked at her watch. "Oh God, look at the time! Seán will have a fit. Sorry, girls, have to run!"

And leaving money on the table for her meal, she practically ran out the door.

Kate and Lauren looked at each other.

"Uh, oh, problems there!" said Kate. "Poor Tara!" She

felt so sorry for her.

"Definitely," Lauren agreed.

Kate was so excited that she couldn't sleep that night but lay awake, making plans and choosing recipes that she would use. If she was going to do this she would do it right and would put up a website offering her ideas for different types of parties and dinners. Kate's Katering – what a good name she thought. The only fly in the ointment would be Danny. Well, to hell with him. Everyone else was so encouraging except him.

★ ★ ★

Diana was in a tizzy waiting for Michael on Monday evening. He had rung that afternoon and said he would call when he was finished in the office, probably around eight thirty.

By eight she had candles alight everywhere, Michael Bolton on the CD player and champagne on ice. When she heard his key in the door she felt a frisson of excitement run through her – it sounded so good! They had their own home at last.

He grabbed her by the hand and, although she was dressed in a very naughty black Agent Provocateur outfit, he pulled her into the corridor outside where he scooped her up and carried her over the threshold. She felt dizzy with lust and love as he carried her straight into the bedroom and slowly peeled off her lingerie, tantalising and teasing her all the way. By the time she was naked she was panting for him, but still he teased, working his way down her body, licking and caressing her until she thought she would explode. Even before he entered her she experienced an explosive orgasm which left her crying with sheer joy.

An hour later, they finally got around to opening the champagne.

"Tell me about your party," she asked coquettishly.

"It was a great success. Kate was looking terrific too – very sexy." He smiled as he saw Diana's reaction.

"Not possible! Kate couldn't look sexy even if you gave her a makeover with plastic surgery," she sneered.

"Well, trust me she looked damned sexy last night. Every man there felt it. My neighbour Carlo, who is an Italian millionaire, even asked for her number. He fancied her like hell."

"I don't believe you," she retorted, jealousy eating her. Had Michael fancied her too?

"It's true. She stayed the night as well. Marcia is very fond of her." This was too much for Diana.

"What did the wick. . . er . . . your wife wear? Was she not the belle of the ball?" she enquired, bitchily.

"None of your business," he replied, his voice suddenly cold. "My home life is off limits. We don't discuss my wife or my family – not ever! You understand?"

She was frightened of the steel in his voice and eyes. It disappeared as suddenly as it had arrived.

"Where's my dinner, woman?" he asked jocosely.

"I thought we'd get a takeaway. I don't do cooking."

"Well, I suppose it wouldn't be fair if you were great at everything. And you're great in bed, that's enough for me. Restaurants can take care of my other appetite – only you can take care of this one."

She was blissfully happy, even more so when she realised that he was staying the night with her.

"I brought some stuff with me that I'll leave here," he said, as he emptied his bag, leaving his toiletries in the bathroom and hanging up some shirts and trousers and placing his underwear in a drawer. He changed into his bathrobe and they cuddled up on the couch waiting for their Indian meal to arrive.

They made love again before they went to sleep and as she lay curled into his body, she heard him murmur sleepily, "You'll be the death of me, woman. I'm too old for all this sex."

She could see the smile playing on his lips and knew he didn't mean it. He loved every minute of it.

Chapter 31

Kate was shocked when she saw Diana at the Pilates class the next afternoon.

The shock obviously registered on her face because Diana remarked, "Don't look so shocked, Kate! I'm not a ghost."

"I just didn't expect to see you in Ballyfern again."

"Why ever not? You don't expect me to give up my life just because Kevin and I are getting a divorce?"

Kate cringed. How could she take it all so lightly? Did the woman have no feelings whatsoever? How did she think Kevin would feel if they bumped into one another?

"I still intend to play golf here and will be down every Thursday for Ladies' Day. I'll come down for weekend competitions too. It's not the end of the world, you know."

She seemed delighted to see Kate's horrified reaction.

Poor Kevin, thought Kate. I hope she doesn't bring this new guy down with her. That would be too cruel, even for Diana. She would have loved to know who the new beau was but hadn't the nerve to ask her. Pity Lauren isn't here, she thought. She'd have no such reticence. I do hope it isn't Michael. Marcia doesn't deserve this.

She knew that Diana would stop at nothing to get her man, if indeed Michael was that man.

That evening she received a call from Mary of the Coffee Pot. She asked Kate if she could make three banoffee pies for Thursday. Why not, decided Kate. It will be the inauguration of Kate's Katering. She agreed and said she would deliver them herself as she wanted to drop in on Jenny and see how she was doing.

She rang Lauren and Jenny with the news and also informed them of Diana's visit to Ballyfern.

"The brazen hussy!" cried Lauren. "Has she no regard for Kevin's feelings? Couldn't she have waited a couple of weeks at least!"

She was disappointed that Kate hadn't weasled the name of the new boyfriend from her.

"Well, if he has any sense, he won't stay around too long," she added.

★ ★ ★

Diana laughed to herself as she headed back up to the big smoke. God, she thought, how thrilling it was to be going in this direction, away from hick Ballyfern! The look on Kate's face when I walked in was priceless. What did she think I was going to do? Bury myself? Run away and hide? Why should I? Kevin has obviously confided in her and I could see she was wondering who my mystery man was, but she didn't have the guts to ask me. She's such a wimp. I cannot understand what they all see in her. Danny, Kevin and even Michael last night, singing her praises. God, I was furious when he started that. I have to admit I did get a bit of a shock when I saw how much weight she'd lost and that new modern hairstyle was a big surprise. She is looking a lot better than she used to but she is still a long, long way from sexy. I know when Michael said last night that he found her sexy he was just trying to make me jealous. And he succeeded, she thought ruefully. Very, very jealous! Of frumpy Kate – sad!

I wish I could have told her that the new man in my life is Michael but he has absolutely forbidden me to tell anyone. I'll humour him, for now. They'll find out soon enough. Meanwhile, it's kind of exciting.

She sang to herself, all the way home, until she pulled into what she had christened, 'the love-nest'.

★　★　★

Kate met Lauren at the golf club on Wednesday morning and although she didn't play quite as well as she had on Monday, she knew that she was seriously getting to like this game. Afterwards in the clubhouse, as they were sitting chatting with the other women, she admitted that she was sorry that she hadn't taken it up years ago. They were really a good bunch and great fun. They invited her to turn up and play with them any morning at nine thirty. She couldn't believe that she had once found them intimidating. They were so nice.

Lauren had made an appointment for her, for Friday, with a friend who designed websites. She needed to work out her menus before then.

"God, it's all happening so fast. I can't believe it. Who would have thought, one month ago, that I would be doing this?"

"And playing golf," Lauren laughed. "It's amazing how you've changed, Kate. You used to be so timid. Look at you now! You've become so confident and you're about to become a businesswoman."

"Well, I have you to thank for that. If you hadn't forced me to go to Slimforever that first night, I'd still be plodding along feeling sorry for myself with too much time on my hands. Now I don't have enough of it. Losing the weight has given me a new lease of life."

"And we're not finished yet!"

* * *

Lauren was keeping busy which helped reduce her anxiety about Jonathan – this week she was caught up in her new job and was poring over fabrics and paints and furniture on the internet. Jonathan had had another session with the therapist who had taken him back to his childhood because he felt that this was where the problem lay. She knew it was very painful for him.

She had decided to give a dinner party the following

Sunday night and had invited Kate, Jenny, Tara and their husbands. She guessed that Danny probably wouldn't make the effort to stay over for it and although she asked Jenny to bring Tom, she suspected that he would cry off too. She rather hoped he would as she couldn't stand him and Jonathan certainly wasn't too keen on him either. She had also invited Kevin. Although they were both very fond of him they had rarely had him to their home in the past, because of their dislike for Diana. Now that she was out of the way it was good to be able to have Kevin there.

★ ★ ★

Kate was apprehensive about her first trip to the gym that afternoon but she had decided that she was going to make the effort. Besides, it was getting too cold for the outdoor pool and she missed her daily swim. She felt quite shy as she explained to the instructor, Niall, that she'd never actually worked out in a gym before. He was extremely patient and helpful as he explained the various machines and made out a programme for her to follow.

"Easy, easy does it," he told her. "Don't do too much in the beginning. You have to work up slowly."

"Don't worry. I won't overexert myself," she laughed at him.

Following the work-out, she decided to have a leisurely swim – nothing too strenuous!

She couldn't believe it was so quiet. There was only one other person in the pool – a man – wearing the obligatory hat and goggles, as was Kate. She watched his beautiful smooth crawl which seemed effortless as he swam length after length. Kate considered herself a good swimmer but she was nothing like this. She swam twenty lengths, then left the pool and went into the hot tub. The other swimmer was nowhere to be seen. She stood under the waterfall in the tub revelling in the powerful water force raining down on her shoulders and back. God, why have I not availed of this before? It's so invigorating. Turning around, she leaned back and closed her eyes, enjoying the sensation of the warm water cascading down the front of her body.

"Kate!"

The shock of hearing her name called almost made her topple over. She opened her eyes to find Kevin about to enter the tub. She couldn't believe it! It was Kevin who'd been swimming in the pool. He looked fantastic, droplets of water spraying from his dark curls and running down his neck and forehead as he moved. She took in his great body, toned and smooth, the tiny Speedo trunks showing off his fine physique. She felt instantly self-conscious of her own body, and sat down quickly in the tub.

"We have to stop meeting like this," he laughed, sitting down in the water. "First, I meet you at the golf club and now you're in my gym. Are you sure you're not stalking me?"

She laughed. "Don't flatter yourself!"

"What are you doing here?" he asked, surprise on his face.

"I decided to finally avail of our membership here," she

told him, blushing and sliding down in the tub as much as she could, to hide her body from him.

"How about you?" she asked. "Shouldn't you be at work?"

"I work through lunch now so that I can come here early. It gets hectic after five o'clock, but this way I have the pool all to myself – well, usually," he smiled.

"It's great here," she said, waving her arm around the complex. "I'm sorry I didn't come years ago."

"Better late than never! I try to come at least five times a week, if only for a swim, though I usually end up working out as well."

"That's why you're so fit. Gosh, Danny could do with it. He's developing quite a paunch and he's always been so vain about his looks. It's not like him."

"I noticed that on Sunday when he called over to me," Kevin looked thoughtful. "He's probably working too hard and I suspect he's drinking a lot."

"I've noticed that too and it's worrying," she replied, a frown creasing her forehead.

"Probably all that socialising – eating richly and drinking every night. He misses your good home-cooking, Kate! Have you talked to him since he went back?"

"Nope, he hasn't rung."

"That's unusual, isn't it? He used to ring you every day when he was away."

"Those days are long gone," she said, shrugging his shoulders.

When she told Kevin that Diana had been down at the

Pilates class the day before, he just shook his head. He reached across her to turn on the water jets again and she was acutely conscious of his skin as it brushed hers. She blushed, hoping he didn't notice.

"I'm just going to move on with my life, Kate. I'm not looking forward to the whole divorce process and no doubt Diana will try to clean me out but I just want to get on with it now. I'm pleased Lauren has invited me to dinner on Sunday night. Will Danny stay over for it?"

"I doubt it. I'll ask him when I speak to him. He'll surely ring by tomorrow."

Two women joined them in the tub just then so Kate took the opportunity to leave. She could see them eyeing Kevin up. Can't say I blame them, she thought. He *is* very attractive. I never realised he had such a good body and his hair is so cute when it's wet and it goes all curly. So sexy! Oh, stop it! she chided herself, embarrassed at these thoughts. This is Kevin I'm talking about. What's wrong with me? I've never thought like this before. I'm acting like a silly cow! She guessed it must be the lack of sex that was affecting her brain.

Chapter 32

The following day Kate delivered the banoffee pies to Mary in The Coffee Shop, who thanked her effusively.

"My customers will be so pleased. I almost lost some of them because they come in especially for it, so they were delighted when I told them I'd have it back in this week. I really do appreciate this."

She insisted that Kate have a coffee with her. Kate told her about Kate's Katering.

"That's wonderful. So can I order cakes and pies without feeling I'm being a nuisance?"

Kate laughed, "Of course, and you're not being a nuisance. I consider this my first order."

She bought a big bouquet of flowers for Jenny hoping to cheer her up but realised, when she called, that Jenny was as cheerful as anyone could be.

"Conor has been a gem. He's looked after me like a baby. I need your advice on what I can get him as a thank-you gift."

They had good fun thinking of various gifts for him, each suggestion getting more outrageous. When Kate suggested a willy-warmer – they ended up laughing so much that they couldn't stop.

At that very moment, Conor tapped on the door and walked in on them. Jenny never locked her door, which Kate thought was foolish.

"Oh, excuse me. Have I come to the wrong address? Is this the lunatic asylum?"

This sent them into even greater paroxysms of laughter.

Conor asked them what it was they'd found so funny, which set them off again. Their laughter was infectious and he couldn't resist laughing with them.

"You're both completely nuts," he grinned affectionately.

★ ★ ★

When Kate got home she started into her recipe books immediately. When the phone rang, she thought that it might be Danny, but to her surprise it was Diana.

"Hi, Kate, I need a favour. I need to collect my stuff from Ballyfern and as you know I have only a sports car. I was wondering, seeing as you have such a big car, if you could collect my stuff from Kevin's tomorrow and take it to my new place in Dublin for me?"

Kate was dumbstruck. She couldn't believe it. The sheer nerve of her!

"Sorry, Diana, I can't," she answered, putting the phone down.

Kate was quite proud of her response. In previous times she would have agreed, even if it had meant changing her own plans to accommodate Diana, but no more. The gall! She thinks she can walk all over me, thought Kate. Well, let her find out that she can't!

* * *

Bitch! Diana said to herself. You'd think she'd help out an old friend. She's probably jealous – knows I'm living the high life while she's stuck in hick Ballyfern. Now, because of her, I'll have to hire a van. I badly need to collect my computer as I miss not being able to email my friends. And I absolutely *must* have all my shoes. I'll definitely need a van to fit them all. Now it will have to wait till next week – thanks to stupid Kate!

* * *

When Danny hadn't rung Kate by Thursday night, she decided that she had better ring him. Surprisingly, he answered straight away but he was very cool with her. Still sulking, she thought. She passed on Lauren's invitation which Danny irritably rejected, as she'd suspected he would.

"Couldn't she have had it on Saturday? She knows I fly back on Sundays."

"You and Jonathan have the Lion's Club dinner on Saturday night. I think Lauren hoped you'd stay over

Sunday night for the dinner."

"Well, it's out of the question."

He hung up without any other conversation.

Kate felt sad that it had come to this.

★ ★ ★

Jenny had got exactly the same reaction from Tom when she told him of Lauren's dinner.

"We've a Town's Cup match on Sunday and you know we always come back to the rugby club afterwards."

"Could you not give up one night there to come to dinner in my friend's house?" she asked him.

He looked at her as though she'd asked him to go to the moon. "Are you serious? It's a Town's Cup match!"

She left it.

When she rang to tell her, Lauren said, "Jenny, I wonder if Conor would like to come? If you give me his phone number, I'll give him a call."

She rang him and apologised for the short notice and was pleased when he said he'd be delighted to attend.

★ ★ ★

On Friday, Kate and Lauren made their way to Dublin. Lauren was meeting the builders to discuss what it was they wanted for their new development. She got a huge buzz from this. They always had their own ideas but after a little while talking to her they inevitably gave in to her vision and gave her free rein to be as creative as she wished. She was always exhilarated after these meetings. She felt confident that she could make this a beautiful living space for whoever would buy it and she liked to think that in some small way she brought happiness and serenity to their lives.

After a quick lunch in the Powerscourt Centre they met up with Clarissa, the website designer. She listened carefully to what Kate wanted and came up with so many different ideas that Kate's head was buzzing. She promised to e-mail Kate over the weekend with some samples, so that Kate could get an idea of what they would look like.

"Kate's Katering! That's a brilliant name."

"Yeah, I'm getting used to it."

They then went shopping for Lauren's dinner party. First they went to Sheridan's for cheese, then to Searson's of Monkstown for wine and finally to Morton's of Ranelagh – for almost everything else.

"I'm not as good a cook as you, Kate, so I have to cheat a little," she laughed.

When Kate got home there was a message from Mary on the machine.

"Kate, I can't tell you how successful your banoffee pies were! They sold out in one morning. Everyone loved them. They're even better than my old ones. I'll double the order for next week, if that's okay with you. Thanks so much. I'll be eternally grateful."

It's certainly okay with me, thought Kate, smiling. She went to bed with a nice warm feeling. It felt good to be doing something for herself – at last!

Chapter 33

Danny arrived home at ten on Saturday morning, much to Kate's surprise. He grabbed a bite to eat and headed off to meet James and his accountant. He was polite to her, but distant. Kate knew she would have to tell him about Kate's Katering sooner or later and was dreading his reaction. Better to wait until after he'd had a few whiskeys and maybe he'd receive it better.

She could tell he'd had a few when he arrived home at six thirty. He'd obviously come home via the golf club. He went upstairs to shower and change for the Lion's Club dinner and when he came down he poured himself a large whiskey and plonked down in the armchair. When had he started drinking so much, Kate asked herself – as she sipped her Diet Coke.

He shouldn't be driving but if I say that to him he'll explode.

She had to tell him about Kate's Katering before he heard it from someone else. Now is as good a time as any, she figured. Here goes!

She plunged in and told him about her plans.

He said nothing for a long moment – just looked at her coldly. She felt herself quaking under this scrutiny but was determined to stay strong.

"You know my feelings on you working but I don't suppose it will make any difference, will it?"

"No, Danny, not this time."

He threw back his whiskey in one go, got up and left for the dinner without another word. She was sleeping when he came home, well after midnight.

★ ★ ★

When she woke on Sunday morning, he was not in the bed beside her. He had slept in the guest-room. Right! That's it, she decided. Why am I making such an effort here when it's obvious he doesn't give a damn? If he's not interested in making a go of it, why should I worry? I'll be like him and live my own life. That seems to be what he wants. All the same she felt sad.

She had arranged to pick the boys up from school at twelve thirty and take them to Dublin for the afternoon. Danny refused her request to join them, saying he had to get back to London early. He dropped in on the boys on the way to the airport. She arrived at the school to find her sons in high spirits and looking forward to the outing. Miguel was joining them and David had arranged to meet up with his girlfriend. Kate was keen to meet this young girl who had so entranced her lovely son. He'd arranged to meet her in Burger King.

"You'll love her, Mom. She's cool and very pretty."

He was so impatient to meet her that he couldn't even wait for Kate to park the car and asked to be let out at the entrance.

When they caught up with him, Kate looked at the girl in amazement.

"Mom, this is Melissa."

She was a miniature Tara. Everything about her, the golden hair, intensely green eyes and sweet smile, were exactly like Tara's.

And approaching them was the lady herself.

"Tara!"

"Kate, what on earth are you doing here?"

"You two know each other?" cried Melissa while David stood there, his mouth open in shock.

"Of course, we do. This is my friend Kate who I meet every Monday night and who's going to cater for your party, Melissa!"

"You're what?" exclaimed Justin and David together.

"It's a long story. I'll explain later," laughed Kate, realising that she hadn't yet told her sons of her new venture.

"Wow, Mom, you're full of surprises lately!" said Justin.

There was much laughter at the coincidence of David and Melissa getting together and the two mums not knowing it. Kate was not surprised that her son was infatuated with Melissa. She was stunning and a very sweet girl besides.

They had a lovely afternoon together. After the boys had stuffed themselves with massive burgers and fries, they went into the cinema. The three younger ones wanted to see the latest Disney movie while Melissa, David and Justin opted for the latest Batman. Kate was relieved that she didn't have to sit through either and went for a coffee with Tara. This gave them a chance to plan the forthcoming party.

After some shopping, where the boys picked up some sports gear, Tara and Kate were anxious to get going so as not to be late for Lauren's dinner party, but the boys wanted to go to Eddie Rocket's for another feast before returning to school, so Kate obliged. She marvelled at how much they could eat in one day but she supposed that if she had to put up with school food all week, she would also stuff her face on her day out.

She told them about Kate's Katering in the car on the way back and was delighted with their reaction.

"That's brilliant, Mom."

"Go for it, Mom!"

It was great, they all agreed. She was very moved when Miguel presented her with a box of chocolates and a thank-you card on which he had written: *To my Irish Mom, Kate.* She included him in the big hug she gave the boys when she was saying goodbye.

She had to rush to get back in time for a quick shower and change before Lauren's dinner party.

Kevin picked her up and was stunned at how glamorous she looked.

"Kate, you're a wow in that dress!"

She was very pleased with his reaction. She felt great.

Lauren and Jonathan were superb hosts and put everyone at ease. The drawing-room was looking splendid. Logs were blazing in the large white marble fireplace, reflecting their light on the polished brass surround. There were big vases of peony roses everywhere and candles glowing in crystal sconces on the walls. It had such an air of elegance, yet was warm and welcoming. Daisy and Ben were brought in to say hello to the guests and were chuffed to see two of the teachers from their school there. Daisy was especially pleased that Conor was there. All her friends had a crush on him and she couldn't wait to get to school on Monday to boast that he had been to dinner in her house. Lauren smiled as she watched her little daughter flutter her eyelashes at him. Amazing the effect he had on females, from eleven-year-old Daisy to the almost-seventy Maggie, who became quite coquettish when he addressed her.

Tara was stunned by the beautiful house and elegant furnishings. Looking at Lauren and Jonathan she thought how perfectly they matched the surroundings. They could have doubled for Grace Kelly and Cary Grant. Tara was wearing a stunning emerald green, silk jersey, wrap-over dress which clung to the contours of her wonderful body and complemented her colouring perfectly. She had on incredibly high heels in the same emerald silk and wore an emerald and diamond choker and earrings. Daisy asked her if she was a film star!

"Wow, you look fantastic!" Kate told her as they kissed.

Jenny and Lauren concurred.

"Well, you only ever see me in track-suits or leggings and they do nothing for any girl," she laughed. "Lauren, what a beautiful home you have! Thank you so much for inviting us. I'm really looking forward to the evening."

She was funny and witty and totally unaffected and added greatly to the success of the night. Her husband Seán was very quiet and totally her opposite. They appeared to be like chalk and cheese. He had a worried look about him. Did he resent her beauty and personality, Lauren wondered.

"Tara looks sensational, doesn't she?" whispered Kate to Jenny and Lauren.

"She looks so sexy," said Jenny. "All the men are attracted to her but I don't think she realises it."

"Her husband does," remarked Lauren wryly.

"He has a vaguely worried look about him, doesn't he?" said Kate.

"A man who is married to a woman who looks like Tara will always be vaguely worried," replied Lauren, sounding like an expert on such matters.

Jenny was her usual bubbly self and had everyone in stitches with her funny stories. She was one of those people who have a vast array of jokes, can remember them and then can deliver them with perfect timing. Kate thought this was a great gift. She could never remember jokes and if she did, then she messed up the punchline. It used to annoy Danny enormously. He was a gifted joke-teller also. Like Jenny, he was always the life and soul of every gathering. They were all laughing uproariously at another of her stories when Kate noticed the way Conor looked at Jenny. It was obvious that he was mad about her.

Conor was having a wonderful time. This was the house he would buy if he ever won the Lotto. Everything he could see had an air of good taste and quality. When Beth had been alive they had spent many weekends scouring antique shops and auctions so he recognised and appreciated the genuine Georgian pieces that filled the rooms. He had always had a huge interest in art and went over to inspect one particular painting.

Jonathan joined him. "Do you like it?"

"Is this a genuine Sir Joshua Reynolds or a copy by Romney?"

"It's a Reynolds. It's been in our family for generations."

Jonathan was very surprised at Conor's knowledge and they started discussing eighteenth-century art. That led on to Georgian furniture and Old Irish Silver and Conor astounded Jonathan with his depth of knowledge and interest. They got on famously and Jonathan was reluctant to leave their discussion when Lauren signalled she needed him.

"Ladies and gentlemen, can I have your attention please?" Jonathan announced, tapping on his glass. "We have a very special occasion to celebrate tonight."

Maggie had entered the room carrying a tray laden with glasses of champagne which she passed around.

"To a very special lady and the success of Kate's Katering!" announced Jonathan.

Kate found herself blushing furiously. Lauren gave her a big hug as they all raised their glasses to her.

"To Kate's Katering!"

Tears came to her eyes. Danny should have been here. She gulped at her champagne, praying that she wouldn't make a show of herself by crying. She caught Kevin's eye as he winked at her and she felt better.

They filed into the dining-room and Kate thought how lovely everything looked. Lauren's special touches were evident everywhere.

Jonathan was pleased to find he was sitting close to Conor.

"How come you don't play golf?" he asked him.

"No offence, Jonathan, but I've always felt that golf is an old man's game. As long as I can still chase a squash and tennis ball and surf, ski and rock-climb, then golf will have to wait."

Jonathan tried to convince him otherwise, to no avail, much to the amusement of the others.

"Mark my words! You'll regret it some day."

Tara smiled as she watched them banter. They were both so handsome, in different ways. Jonathan was tall and distinguished with his dark hair showing grey at the temples. Quiet and reserved but obviously very intelligent. She liked his sense of humour. Conor, on the other hand, was exactly the opposite – an outdoors guy and very laid back. He still had the tan and long blond-streaked hair that he'd picked up during his two months in Australia that summer. And yet, these two seemed to hit it off really well. As for Kevin – he was such a pet. Kate had told her about his marriage and her heart went out to him. He looked a lot like Antonio Banderas, well, not exactly, but near enough to make the comparison. He had the same dark good looks, curly hair and dreamy brown eyes that you could drown in.

She was aware that her husband was feeling unhappy with all these very good-looking men present. How she wished Seán could just relax and enjoy himself. They were all so loving and warm but she knew he was watching her. Every look, every word – she dare not put a foot wrong. She knew that with so many handsome men around he would be jealous and feel threatened.

The meal was – like everything Lauren did – perfection. Kate was amused to see that she had used some of her low-calorie recipes, which suited Jenny and herself. They did not want a weight-gain tomorrow night! They both tried to watch their wine intake but it was difficult as Jonathan poured a different wine for every course.

Towards the end of the meal Lauren raised her glass, looked towards the girls and said, "To my good friends! May we all have a truly happy, wonderful life . . . because . . ."

"We're worth it!" the others chimed in.

The four of them dissolved in giggles.

The men exchanged glances with each other, as much as to say – 'Women! Are they all mad?' But then they too joined in the laughter.

Kate had a wonderful time though she didn't feel quite as comfortable with Jonathan as before, now that she knew how he'd treated Lauren. She confided in Jenny that she actually had enjoyed the evening more because Danny hadn't been there.

"I certainly had a better time without Tom," was Jenny's reply.

Kate told this to Kevin on the way home and he laughed, saying, "I'll add to that, because I certainly had a better time than if Diana had been there. Doesn't say much for marriage, does it?"

"Dear God, we're terrible. Please don't punish us for this!"

★ ★ ★

Lauren and Jonathan were sitting by the fire having a nightcap.

"It was a great success, darling, and the meal was superb, as always. I really enjoyed the company tonight. Your friends are lovely and Conor is a smashing guy. I'd really like to have him around again and I will persevere until I get him playing golf. I've a feeling he'll be a natural."

"Yes, the girls are terrific. We're all so different yet we get along so well. Mind you, I think the fact that Danny and Tom and Diana weren't there made a difference. I think maybe if Tara had come alone she would have been better off too. Seán seems very strange."

"I noticed. He's very possessive of her. Can't say I blame him. She is very attractive. I think she has a lot of problems with him."

"I couldn't bear it if you were like that. We all thought she had a perfect life."

"Nobody has that, my dear," he sighed. "It doesn't exist. Life is all about problems."

★ ★ ★

Conor was happier going home that night than he'd been since Beth had died. For the first time he'd felt that he was letting go of the past and was moving on. He would never forget her and the good times they'd had, but he was now ready to look to the future and the good times that he knew lay ahead. He said this to Jenny as they drove home.

"I'm really glad to hear that," she said.

"This is in no small way due to you, Jen," he continued. "You're a very special person and it felt so good tonight, being with you and your friends."

She smiled as she patted his hand, thinking it was time his grieving period was over.

He, meanwhile, was hoping that he would be included in her warm circle of friends in the future.

★ ★ ★

Meanwhile Tara and Seán were having a major row. He accused her of flirting with not just one, but all of the guys.

"That's ridiculous. The girls are my friends and I would never do that."

"Conor is a widower. He's not with Jenny."

"Don't be ridiculous!"

"What about Kevin? I saw you smiling and talking to him."

"Oh, for God's sake," she said, exasperated. "Of course I spoke and smiled at him. I was being sociable. His wife just left him last week. Do you think he's looking for someone else already? Seán, I can't take this jealousy any more. You promised you'd stop. I'm sorry I accepted the invitation. Every time we go out, it's the same story. I've had enough."

* * *

While the girls and Kevin were enjoying themselves in Ballyfern, Diana had been sitting alone in her apartment feeling sorry for herself. Although her evenings and nights with Michael were still sensational, there were not enough of them. She bitterly resented the fact that he insisted on spending every weekend with his wife. He had now started to talk about his granddaughters, in a doting voice that really pissed her off. I'm only thirty-two, for God's sake, she thought. I don't want to hear talk of grandchildren.

He had spent Monday night with her. Mondays were always good because he was obviously sex-starved after his weekend with The Wicked Witch, as she now called his wife. He wasn't too pleased when he heard her say it for the first time but it drove her crazy when he spoke about his wife with affection and especially when he called her Marcia. She tried to push that part of his life out of her mind. She was quite sure she could change all that.

Tuesday, she had rushed back from Ballyfern hoping he

would drop in but he hadn't. They met on Wednesday and went out to dinner – he stayed the night and that was blissful. She went to Ballyfern on Thursday and played golf with the ladies where she found even some of her old cronies were avoiding her. Silly old cows! She was glad to get back to Dublin.

On Friday, Michael dropped in at around five o'clock. They went to bed and made love – twice – but then he had to leave as he had promised to take The Wicked Witch to the opening of an art exhibition. How she wished she could be by his side at these functions. This was the second Friday night in a row he'd spent with his wife. She heard not a word from him Saturday or all day Sunday.

To make matters worse, Kevin was acting the prick. He had cancelled her credit card and her access to his account. He had set up a separate account for her and told her he would deposit €250 in it every Friday. €250! That would barely see her through a weekend! She suggested to Michael that he might give her an allowance but he only laughed and reminded her that he was paying for the apartment and its upkeep. He suggested that she should think about going back to work. God, getting up early every morning – she couldn't bear the thought of it. She had been rather hoping that he would offer her a credit card, but no such luck. But, as she reasoned, it was early days yet!

★ ★ ★

It was no coincidence that Marcia was finding reasons to have Michael by her side on Friday nights. She suspected that he was seeing someone new. She had discovered, years ago, that he became twice as caring and considerate to her whenever he had a new 'bit-on-the-side', as Marcia called them. She actually felt sorry for these girls. She knew some of them fell hopelessly in love with him but she knew her husband well. As soon as they became too demanding, which they always did, he would dump them. She felt secure that he would never let any bimbo threaten their marriage. To him, it was sacrosanct. However, as an extra insurance, Marcia was clever enough to involve him more in her life whenever she suspected he'd found a new lady-friend. To this end, she had booked a cruise across the Atlantic on the Queen Mary and five days in New York, as a birthday present for him. She had presented it to him on Friday night. They would leave the third week in November.

He had been delighted. He loved cruising and the Queen Mary was the tops. He also adored New York. It was his favourite city in the world.

"Darling, what a wonderful birthday present! We need a break and this is just perfect. Thank you, my sweet. You always know exactly what pleases me!" He'd given her a warm embrace. He had a momentary thought that Diana would probably go ballistic, but so what? He certainly wouldn't mention it to her until the last moment.

Chapter 34

Kate woke on Monday morning to the realisation that she had a manic week ahead of her. Clarissa had e-mailed her ideas for the website which were very exciting. She had asked Kate to photograph everything that she cooked for the catering business. I suppose that means Mary's banoffee pies and Marcia's dinner party and I shouldn't forget Tara's birthday buffet, Kate thought. Luckily, she had a digital camera.

Before she left for her golf lesson she rang Marcia, who asked her if she could cook the same meal for the dinner party that she had served, five weeks previously, in her own home in Ballyfern.

"My God, is it only five weeks since that dinner? So much has happened and changed since then," remarked Kate.

The dinner was for twelve and they agreed that Kate would buy everything required and come to Marcia's at noon the following Friday. She would prepare as much as possible on Thursday, in her own kitchen. She realised that if this was going to be a proper business she would have to invest in some stuff for conveying the food: a small portable freezer and fridge, cool boxes and other cartons, which she would need for safe transport. Luckily, she had a big car.

There was so much to do. Clarissa had said she would have her business cards ready for Friday and had agreed to have them delivered to Marcia's. They showed a female cook, in a chef's hat, tossing up a pancake, as well as Kate's details.

The golf lesson went well and afterwards she played nine holes with Lauren during which they held a post mortem on the dinner party the previous night.

"Conor is a pet. Jonathan was very taken with him. It's a shame he and Jenny can't get together. They're so obviously meant to be. If only she could dump Tom. We can't stand him."

"Neither can I! He's so ignorant. And I felt sorry for Tara. Her husband is very strange, watching her all the time like that. I tried to engage him in conversation but he really wasn't interested."

"Yes, he's a strange one indeed. Jonathan and I think that he's very possessive and that she must have a difficult time with him."

"God love her. She's such good company and I don't know why he should feel that way. I wasn't aware of her coming on to any of the guys."

"Of course not, it's all in his head. She's just so damned attractive. I feel sorry for her – and for him in a way."

They grabbed a quick salad in the clubhouse and Kate headed home to work on her menus and shopping list for Marcia's dinner and Mary's pies. She decided she would go shopping early on Tuesday morning, take in her Pilates class in the afternoon and then go for a swim. She was determined to try and keep exercising as much as possible even though she would be busy catering. But firstly, and most importantly, she had a Slimforever class tonight to get through.

At the weigh-in, Kate and Lauren had lost two pounds each but Jenny had lost nothing.

"Your Cadbury's Wholenut is still telling on you!" said Lauren.

"I'm afraid I was even bolder this week," Jenny admitted, making a face. "Mars bars were 'chocolate of the week'." She swore that she wouldn't touch a bite of chocolate during the coming week.

Kate was disappointed she hadn't lost more even though she was into the nine stones, which was a landmark for her.

When Tara saw her disappointment, she explained to her, "You've done fantastically well up to now, Kate, but there's no way you can keep up that massive weight loss indefinitely. As this stage, you should be happy to lose just two pounds every week. It still means that you'll be at your target weight by Christmas, which you didn't believe possible five weeks ago. So please be patient and consider anything more than two pounds a bonus."

Kate was somewhat mollified after this little speech and agreed that she would settle for that.

"Sorry I can't join you in Moorehill tonight," Tara whispered to her. "My husband is getting pissed off with me coming home so late." She threw her eyes to heaven.

Kate understood.

★ ★ ★

Diana was in a very bad mood. She had been all prepared for Michael to visit her as usual but he rang to say he couldn't make it. He had a business dinner to attend.

"Can't I come?" she asked him.

"Are you crazy?" he replied. "Most of these guys know Marcia. It's out of the question."

That didn't exactly put her in a good mood.

"Well, can we meet somewhere afterwards?" she'd asked.

"No, babe. These things can go on all night. I don't know what time I'll be finished."

"Can't you come and stay the night?" she asked in a wheedling voice.

Michael had in fact considered doing just that but now she was pissing him off so he changed his mind.

"No. I'll see you tomorrow night. Okay?"

She was furious with him. She wanted him so badly – she needed him tonight! She'd never needed anyone as much. Her longing for him was intense. All her energy went into making love when he was with her and yearning for him when he was not. She needed him, couldn't he see that?

He did indeed see that and this was worrying him. She was becoming very demanding and needy, which he didn't like one little bit. He needed this like a hole in the head! He had to make her understand that he had his life, she had hers, and let them enjoy the shared moments they could snatch in between. This was not how Diana saw it. She had no life outside of him. She didn't want one. He *was* her life.

* * *

Jenny was in the staffroom on Tuesday eating a salad for lunch when she heard the commotion.

One of the sixth formers came running in, "Please, sir, come quickly! Miss Delaney has fallen in the school yard," he said to Conor, who was standing at the microwave.

Conor ran, followed by the other teachers, Jenny included. The poor dear was lying on the ground moaning, her leg twisted under her and her face as white as a sheet.

"Okay, you're okay," Conor told her gently. He then started barking orders at the rest of them. "Jenny, ring for an ambulance! Ciarán, go get me two blankets! Jimmy, water!"

All the while he was soothing Miss Delaney, who was obviously in a lot of pain. He was rubbing her head and talking to her, reassuring her that help was on its way.

"We can't move her. She may have broken something. Let's just keep her warm and comfortable." He noticed the frightened children's faces crowding around. "Jenny, get the kids back into their classrooms!"

She was still busy doing this when she heard the siren.

343

Within minutes they had Miss Delaney in the ambulance and on her way to Naas Hospital. Conor had gone with her. He arrived back just as school was finishing for the day.

"The poor thing," he told them as they crowded around him to hear the news. "She has a broken hip, but she's comfortable now and in good hands. I also rang her sister, who came to the hospital straight away."

Jenny marvelled at how calmly he had dealt with and organised everything, with a minimum of fuss. 'A good man in a crisis' – as her mother used to say of her father.

* * *

Kate met Diana at the Pilates class the next afternoon but Diana completely ignored her. Oh, well, you can't win them all, Kate thought ruefully.

Kevin rang her that night to say that Diana had arrived, with a van, to collect her belongings and that she hadn't appeared too happy.

"Yeah, she cut me dead at Pilates today."

"She's still very discontented. She doesn't seem to be too happy with her new life either.'

* * *

When Michael arrived at the apartment that night Diana tried to play it cool but once he'd taken her in his arms and started kissing her all over, she relented. Within five minutes she was panting for him, everything else forgotten except for the pleasure she found with him. As they lay in bed later, curled around each other, she started to complain but he shushed her by caressing and kissing her and arousing her once again. Afterwards, she fell into a happy sleep, wrapped in his arms.

Later he woke her up and they made love again.

Things are back on track, Diana thought happily.

Then, just before they went back to sleep – he dropped the bombshell.

"Darling, I won't be seeing you on Friday night. Marcia has invited some friends for dinner. I'll see you Monday night."

She was so disappointed she couldn't help herself. "This is not good enough, Michael. Two nights a week is all you can spare for me? You used to see me every Friday night, before I left my husband for you. Now The Wicked Witch needs you every Friday night, as well as every weekend!"

"Don't ever talk about my wife like that again," he said in an icy voice. "And you didn't leave your husband for me. I asked you that at the time and warned you not to take me into the equation. You assured me that I had nothing to do with it. I laid my cards on the table from the outset. Now, if you don't mind, I'm leaving. I'd rather sleep alone tonight."

With that he was gone.

She was stupefied. Did he not love her or care for her at all? She'd messed it up. She felt so alone. She'd thought that he'd felt the same as she did but now she was scared. She had seen a side to him that she didn't know. Obviously, to be as successful as he was, he had to have a ruthless streak, but she didn't think that it extended to her. It frightened her.

She half hoped that he would relent and come back, but he didn't. The whole weekend was stretching ahead of her and she didn't know how she would fill the time. It was all very well living right in the middle of the action, in the centre of Dublin, but it was expensive to go out and money was in short supply. Another thing that bugged her were the young things in the trendy bars and clubs that she liked to frequent. They all looked like models, with their skimpy tops and bare bellies. She reckoned that most of them were no more than sixteen or seventeen. The young guys all looked like boy scouts and the older men were not interested in her but were chasing these teenyboppers. It was most disturbing. They made her feel like an OAP. Goddammit! She was only thirty-two. She knew Michael frequented these bars and clubs regularly and she was sick at the thought of these young girls throwing themselves at him. She knew she didn't stand a chance against them.

Scrutinising her face in the mirror, she could see some tiny lines around her eyes and mouth. Oh God, I really need to do something, she thought. Cosmetic surgery is very expensive but maybe some Botox? I could afford that. I'll ask Izzie about it tomorrow.

She went back to bed, hoping and praying that Michael would ring her tomorrow.

Chapter 35

Lauren was very taken up with this new interior design job she had started and so was unable to play golf with Kate on Wednesday.

"Why don't you go up and join the girls at nine thirty?"

"Maybe I will. I'll be a nervous wreck though."

"You'll be fine. They're very nice."

So it was that Kate joined the ladies on Wednesday morning. She did fine although, as she joked with them, "You needn't worry that I'll be taking any prizes from you for quite some time. You're safe for at least three years."

She had lunch with them after golf. Yet another salad!

"I swear to God, I'll turn into a rabbit if I eat much more salad," she laughed.

"I'd live on salad if I thought I could lose weight like you, Kate. You look terrific," remarked Mabel, the Lady Captain.

After lunch she hurried home as Jenny was collecting the banoffee pies to deliver to Mary in Naas. She had photographed the banoffee pies from every angle and Jenny helped her choose the best shot for the website. She spent the rest of the evening working on it and choosing the best recipes to use. It was a nightmare pricing everything and to this end she had gone online to see what other catering companies were charging.

Kevin had offered to help her work out the costings and she gladly accepted his offer. Danny would have been a great help with this, she thought sadly.

"Why not come over for supper and we can work afterwards?" he suggested.

"This is becoming a bit of a habit – having supper together, I mean," she said.

"Why not? It makes sense. We're both alone and we have to eat and besides I enjoy your company. You're my best friend now that Danny seems to have resigned that position. And I certainly owe you for all the meals I've had in your house."

"Yeah, well, I just hope the neighbours don't get the wrong idea," she laughed.

* * *

Jenny and Conor went to visit Miss Delaney on Wednesday afternoon, to find her sitting up, eating grapes and smiling. She couldn't thank Conor enough for his help and told all the nurses who came in how wonderful he was. Jenny could see that they thought so too as they kept popping in and out to see how Miss Delaney was doing, smiling at

Conor as they did so. Jenny felt invisible!

"You'll have to stay here with me, Conor. They don't normally pay me this much attention," Miss Delaney laughed.

Conor was enjoying himself and Jenny noticed that one particularly pretty nurse seemed to come in and out more often than the rest. She was tall and very slim, with tanned smooth skin, and long blonde hair caught up with a clip. She smiled at Conor, her startling blue eyes looking up at him from under long lashes, reminiscent of the look Princess Diana used to such effect. Jenny had no doubt that Cassandra, which was the name on her name tag, probably spent hours in front of the mirror, getting the look down pat! Even her name was gorgeous, Jenny thought irritably.

As they left the hospital, Jenny asked him, "Do you fancy a pint? I have something to tell you."

He wondered what it was and, sitting in Lawlor's bar, drinks in front of them, he found out.

"I have some news for you," she announced. "I've been offered the principal's job, starting next January."

"Wow! Congratulations! I'm really pleased for you, Jenny," he said, smiling and lifting his glass to her.

"Well, actually, I've turned it down – so I'm sure they'll be offering it to you next."

He looked at her to see if she was joking, but saw that she was serious.

"But why did you turn it down?" he asked puzzled that she would do such a thing.

"Oh Conor, I'm not really principal material. I'd hate all

that paperwork and administration. The very thought of dealing with the board of managers and Father Murphy gives me goosebumps." She rolled her eyes. "No, thank you, you'll do a much better job. Besides, I'd miss the children too much – I really do love teaching." She lowered her voice then and her shoulders slumped as she continued, "I also feel that with the state my private life is in, I've enough to think about."

"Are you sure you've given it enough thought? What did Tom say about it? I'm sure he'd want you to take it, what with the rise in salary." Conor was concerned that she'd made a rushed judgement. After all, it wasn't everyday that a principal's job became available!

"Probably, but to be honest, Conor, I didn't even tell him. It's nothing to do with him anyway. It's my choice. I honestly don't know how long more I'll stay with him. Things are very bad between us," she said, her voice breaking.

"My poor Jenny! You deserve better. He's a fool." He put his arm around her shoulder and gave her a squeeze. "Well, if they offer it to me, I'm taking you out for a swanky dinner to celebrate. Okay?"

"That's fine with me. I won't refuse – as long as I can have chips and chocolate mousse," she replied, smiling.

Conor was happy to see the twinkle back in her eyes.

★ ★ ★

First thing Thursday morning Kate started on the desserts

for Marcia. It took up most of the day and then she had to haul herself into Naas to collect the meat and vegetables that she had ordered – Marcia was picking up the scallops in Cavistons, on Friday morning. This catering is more than just cooking, she thought. It's the time and the planning, ordering, shopping, driving and then, of course, the cleaning up. Maybe I'm not being as overpaid as I thought.

She prepared as much as possible and sank into bed, setting the alarm for seven o'clock. She had hoped that Danny would ring to wish her well, but no such luck. She was on her own there.

However, Lauren, Jenny, Tara, Kevin and even Conor had rung – but the best phone call of all had come from her sons.

"Hi, Mom," said Justin. "We're all here to wish you the best of luck tomorrow night and we know you'll do a great dinner. Okay, guys?"

"*Good luck, Mom!*" they all roared.

She spoke to each of them briefly and even Miguel who was one of the crew now. She had a lump in her throat and tears in her eyes as Sam said, "Mom, I really wish I was going to that dinner. I know it will be yummy." "Me too, me too!" she could hear the others in the background.

They were wonderful. No matter how bad things were now with Danny, they had produced these four fantastic people.

★ ★ ★

Conor had visited Miss Delaney twice on Thursday. Jenny wondered if it was Miss Delaney or the good-looking nurse that was the attraction. She found out soon enough.

"I've been invited to a party tonight in Naas," he told her at lunch in the staffroom on Friday. "Ciarán and Jimmy are coming with me. Should be fun!"

Jenny wondered why he hadn't invited her. "Whose party?" she asked, as she made a pot of tea.

"Some nurse from Naas Hospital. I don't actually know her, but Sandra – you remember Miss Delaney's pretty nurse? – invited me and asked me to bring some friends."

I certainly remember Little Miss Blue Eyes, Jenny thought uncharitably. She was quite miffed that he hadn't asked her although no doubt Sandra had stipulated male friends only. Jenny felt let down but knew she was being irrational.

"Enjoy it!" she said to him, walking off to sit with the girls.

What's wrong with her? Conor wondered.

★ ★ ★

On Friday, Kate packed up the car and headed for Killiney. Marcia was all of a dither. The house looked gorgeous. The florist had just finished arranging the beautiful flowers all over the house. He joined them for a cup of coffee. Kate was shocked to hear that he came every week and changed all the flowers. This wasn't just for a special occasion, although he did admit that he pulled out all the stops when

Marcia was entertaining. Kate headed for the kitchen which was stocked with every conceivable pot, dish and utensil, even though Marcia never cooked. Marcia offered to help but Kate shooed her out of the kitchen. She preferred to work alone.

Marcia headed for the beauty parlour and hairdresser's and was back in time for lunch, which she had brought from the local deli.

"You're priceless," laughed Kate, over lunch.

"My talents lie elsewhere," responded Marcia jokingly. "On a more serious note, how are things with Danny?"

"Couldn't be worse! He's furious that I'm starting this catering business."

"That's too bad. He'll get over it. Men! Why do we put up with them? I'm sure Michael has a new lady friend. I can always tell, you know. I was wondering if it was that girl you had at your dinner party. You know who I mean, the one who was all over Michael like a rash. The black-haired, hard-faced one."

"Diana? I couldn't say. I do know she's left her husband and I believe she's met someone else. She's not too bad, you know. She had a very rough childhood."

"Not too bad? You're always so kind. Whatever her childhood, she's a bloody bitch!"

Kate was shocked to hear Marcia, who was always so ladylike, talk like this. Then she figured that it must have hardened her, having to put up with Michael's philandering for all these years.

"I don't know how you can be so forgiving. I couldn't

be. If Danny ever cheated on me, I'd be gone. *Finito!* Marriage vows are for life. To me, it's the ultimate betrayal."

"Oh, Kate! I wish it were so simple. Men unfortunately are not born to be monogamous whereas it seems most women are, despite what most feminists and lesbians will say. It's God's little joke! Propagation of the human race — that's what it's all about. Man must sow his seed!"

Kate didn't know what to say. This cynicism was not like Marcia. Obviously she was hurting but was making the best of a bad situation and had spent all her life putting up a brave front. Kate could see past that to the deep, hidden hurt in her soul. I could never accept what she does, thought Kate. How can Michael do this to her? I don't understand it.

Everything went well in the kitchen and Kate resisted tasting, except when absolutely necessary. She realised that this catering lark could play havoc with her diet if she wasn't careful.

Marcia had employed two teenagers to help with the service and by the time the guests arrived at seven all was ready to go.

Marcia had asked Kate to come and have a drink with her guests but Kate was adamant.

"No way! I'm working tonight and besides I need to watch things in the kitchen."

Michael arrived home just then and Kate was amazed to see how loving he seemed to be with Marcia. He kissed her deeply and kept putting his arm around her and touching her gently. They seemed to share an intimacy and Kate just couldn't figure out how he could be having an affair with another woman. He obviously loved Marcia a lot. She'd never understand it. After the guests had arrived, Michael came into the kitchen with a glass of champagne for Kate. It was very thoughtful of him and she was chuffed. He was so charming that one couldn't help but be bowled over by him.

Everything went swimmingly and, after the main course, Marcia came into the kitchen to tell Kate how wonderful it all was. Everyone was raving about her food, she said. Kate was delighted.

"I've promised them all I'd give them your card before they leave. You're going to be very much in demand. I hope you won't be too busy to cater for me in the future."

"You'll always be my premier client. If it wasn't for you, I wouldn't be doing this at all," Kate smilingly told her.

They hugged and said goodbye as Kate wanted to get home as soon as the dessert trolley was out. Marcia handed Kate a cheque for €600. This was almost too good to be true, thought Kate. Getting paid for something she loved doing so much. She supposed that she would have to start thinking about keeping books and accounts. She was useless at that sort of thing but Kevin had said he would help her.

Driving home she wondered when Danny was coming home. He hadn't called her all week so she was in the dark as to his plans. After his behaviour last weekend she was determined not to make the first move. She was looking forward to having a nice rest tomorrow. On Sunday, she'd arranged to take Ben and Daisy to visit the boys. She couldn't wait to see them.

★ ★ ★

On Saturday there was no word from Danny and no sign of him either. Maybe it is my fault, she thought. Maybe I should have seen it coming and averted the danger, but what could I have done differently?

Kevin rang her late on Saturday afternoon and when he discovered that Danny wasn't home insisted on taking her out for dinner in Naas. Despite his best efforts and a whole bottle of wine, he couldn't cheer Kate up. She felt like it was the end of the world.

Chapter 36

If Kate thought she was having a bad weekend, it was nothing compared to Diana's. Izzie had a date on Friday night so Diana had rented two videos, stayed in, and knocked back two bottles of wine on her own, thinking of Michael in his cosy home with his cosy wife, entertaining their friends. Oooohhh . . .! She felt like screaming. It was so unfair!

She woke on Saturday with the worst hangover of her life. She stayed in bed till three o' clock and met up with Izzie for an Indian meal that evening. Izzie was full of excitement over this new guy of hers, Simon, who was a doctor in St. James' Hospital. He was taking her to meet his parents the following day, so she didn't want a late night.

"This is it, Di! He's my Mr Right. I just know it." She could talk of nothing else.

Diana was bored. God, why is it women get so infantile when they meet a guy, she asked herself, conveniently forgetting that she was just as bad about Michael. Izzie just went on and on about how great he was, till Diana had to ask her to shut up talking about him. Izzie was annoyed at her lack of enthusiasm and left soon after.

It was back to the apartment and another bottle of wine alone. She wondered where Michael was and what he was doing.

He was, in fact, having dinner with Marcia and his daughters and their husbands in Dalkey. He was in his element, surrounded as he was by these wonderful women who all adored him and he hadn't given Diana a thought.

* * *

Jenny didn't see Conor all weekend. On Friday she'd gone straight from school to visit an old friend who'd retired from teaching, and when she got home at eight thirty, Conor's car was gone. There was still no sign of it when she hauled herself up to bed at two thirty, having watched a late-night film. On Saturday morning there was still no sign of his car and she supposed that he'd spent the night with Little Miss Blue Eyes. His car was missing all weekend and somehow Jenny felt lost and lonely. Tom went to Limerick on Saturday to watch Munster play and he hadn't come home either. Not even a phone call!

Jenny rang Kate on Sunday morning and she sounded so down that Kate asked, "What's the matter? You sound terrible."

Jenny sighed. "Nothing really, I'm just feeling very depressed. I've been on my own all weekend and I'm asking myself what the hell I'm doing with my life."

"You poor love! Can I do anything?"

"Well, I was wondering if you're doing anything this evening?"

"No, nothing planned. Do you want me to come over?"

"That would be great. I don't know what's wrong with me but I'm feeling really down. My life seems so pointless. I warn you I won't be great company."

"You obviously need someone to talk to and I'm your woman. What are friends for? How would you like to come with me to see the boys this afternoon? Daisy and Ben are coming with me."

Jenny laughed. "Thanks, Kate. You'll have enough on your hands with that pair, but I look forward to tonight." She sounded a lot brighter than she had earlier.

* * *

As Kate was driving to the school with Ben and Daisy in the back, Danny rang her on her mobile.

"Hello. Sorry I couldn't get home this weekend. I tried ringing you but couldn't get you."

Bloody likely, thought Kate. When she didn't say anything, he continued. "Are you going to see the boys?"

"Of course, I am. I go every Sunday. I'm on my way now."

"Give them my love."

"You should be here to give it to them yourself. You know next weekend is Hallowe'en and the boys are home for the midterm break. I suggest that if you want to keep your relationship with them strong, you come home and spend some time with them. "

"Yes, of course I'll be home."

Kate hung up without another word. She was afraid she would say something she would regret and Ben and Daisy had already heard enough.

When they got to the school, Daisy and Ben were whisked off by Toby, Sam and Miguel to look around and be shown everything: the dorms, the ref, the playing fields and even the classrooms. Toby was so proud and felt ever so grown-up. Ben and Daisy thought everything was cool and decided they were going to refuse to go to any other school but this one.

"They don't take girls, silly," said Ben.

"Well, I'll cut my hair then," she smartly replied and the oh-so-grown-up boys laughed at her.

David was in seventh heaven as Melissa had persuaded her older brother to drive her over to visit.

"You don't mind, Mom, do you?" he asked, his eyes aglow.

"Of course not, say hello to Melissa for me."

He was gone like a bat out of hell and so she was left alone with Justin. They went for a walk through the grounds and when they sat down on a bench he took her hand.

"Mom, I don't like to talk in front of the younger ones, but things are not right between Dad and yourself, are they?"

She sighed, "I don't want to worry them either, but

you're right, sweetheart. Things are not good."

"Dad is so stupid," he said vehemently. "Sometimes I want to punch him." He then reminded her of nasty things in the past that Danny had done – things which even *she* had forgotten. She realised with a shock that her little boy had become a man and saw much more than she had ever given him credit for. Their relationship changed that afternoon – they became friends. She knew she could confide in him and rely on him. He was in her corner. She felt a huge surge of love for him, as she had the first time they'd placed him in her arms, eighteen years ago.

★ ★ ★

When Kate saw Jenny's face that night she realised that she was very down indeed. The sparkle was missing from her eyes. Jenny opened a bottle of wine and they sat down to chat. Kate eventually got to the crux of the matter. Tom hadn't come home – so what's new, she thought – but Conor had seemingly gone missing too.

"It's not like him," Jenny confided in her. "You know we've been friends forever and we always know what the other is doing. But he's met a nurse from the hospital and went to a party with her on Friday night and hasn't been seen since."

Kate knew from her tone of voice that this was what was bothering Jenny, much more than Tom being missing. Lauren and she had often speculated that Jenny was a little in love with Conor. She'd even asked Jenny about it once.

"Don't be ridiculous!" she'd answered. "We're just great friends. Don't forget Beth and I were best friends." But Kate wasn't convinced. Lauren was certain that Conor felt the same way about Jenny and as far as they could gather he hadn't even been on a date since Beth had died, two years ago. Now it appeared he was getting back into the swing of things and this was obviously bothering Jenny. So, maybe they were right. Perhaps love *was* behind it! If that was the case then it was no wonder Jenny was so down in the dumps. Conor had been her rock and confidant and now that might be whisked away from her. Kate's heart went out to her.

Jenny was in full flight. "You should see this nurse. She's perfect. Tall, slim, tanned, blonde hair and blue eyes – and boy does she know how to use those eyes! And you know men. They can't resist a pretty face and they lap it up, the idiots!"

Kate let her rant on, trying to hide a smile. "Sounds to me it's bothering you that Conor might be interested in this girl."

"Of course not! He's a free agent but he should have let me know that he'd be away for the weekend." Jenny couldn't see the contradiction here.

Kate let her talk on, hiding her smile behind her glass. She drank just the one glass of wine as she was driving but Jenny kept topping up her own glass, unaware that she was doing so. Uh-oh, somebody's going to have a hangover tomorrow, Kate thought.

Jenny had calmed down by the time Kate left, and

smiled as she said, "Well, now I've got all that off my chest, I'm feeling better."

Kate thought that the four and a half glasses of wine she'd consumed were probably more responsible for the good feeling.

"Sorry for going on so much. I'm in a bit of an anti-men mood at the moment," Jenny said sheepishly.

"So I noticed," Kate said drily.

"Sorry. It was a boring night for you. I appreciate your coming over and listening. Thanks, Kate."

"It's okay. As I said before, that's what friends are for."

Chapter 37

Jenny arrived into the staff room on Monday morning in very bad form and more than a little hungover. Her mood wasn't helped when the principal came in, leading a gorgeous young blonde who looked as if she had just stepped out of the pages of *Heat* or *OK*.

"Hello, everyone, I'd like you to meet Kirsten, who'll be replacing Miss Delaney for the next couple of months."

Kirsten flashed a dazzling white smile at everyone and, shaking her long silky blonde hair, said, "Hi, everyone! Nice to meet you all." She threw an especially dazzling smile at Conor, Jenny noticed. My God, there were gorgeous blondes coming out of the woodwork and throwing themselves at Conor. What was happening? Could it be that now he had decided to move on, he was giving out vibes to women that he hadn't been doing previously? In fairness to the girls, she couldn't blame them – he *was* very attractive. Still it rankled.

During her lunch break she rang to apologise to Kate.

"Forget about it," said Kate. "I was happy to listen."

Jenny breathed a sigh of relief.

At Slimforever that night Kate had lost two pounds and Lauren one.

Jenny had thought of crying off the class but Kate had persuaded her to go, and she was glad she did, as she had lost another three pounds. She had made a huge effort the past week although she'd been sorely tempted to indulge over the weekend and, of course, the wine last night . . . she didn't want to think about that . . . and poor Kate, who'd had to listen to her moaning!

Kate had made out a menu for the twins' party the following Saturday night which she gave to Tara in Moorehill Lodge, suggesting she should decorate the room with candles in pumpkins, witches and broomsticks to tie in with Hallowe'en. Tara was delighted with everything.

"It's crazy, isn't it? Hallowe'en has become as big a circus as Christmas now," remarked Lauren.

Tara only stayed long enough to have a coffee.

"She's definitely having a problem with that husband of hers," Lauren remarked when she had left.

"Haven't we all?" Kate said as Jenny raised her eyes to heaven.

★ ★ ★

Diana waited nervously on Monday night, praying that Michael would come, and her relief when she heard his key in the door was overwhelming. She fell into his arms and within seconds they were naked and making love on the floor of the foyer.

"Someone is pleased to see me," he whispered in her ear, as he started probing it with his tongue, arousing her once more.

She put her hand down and felt his hardness growing again.

"And you must be pleased to see me because you have no pocket and that's no gun!"

He roared laughing. She was a tonic! Lifting her off her feet he carried her into the bedroom, her legs wrapped around him. There, he took her again, more gently this time, and his tenderness reduced her to tears.

"Why are you crying, my beauty?"

"Because I love you so much."

Michael froze. Oh, no, he thought. Not again! This is not what I wanted to happen. I thought she was cool enough to just enjoy the moment. I was wrong. Damn! Why didn't I see this coming?

Diana could feel him stiffening and realised she'd made a mistake. She should never have told him that she loved him. Well, it was done now but he hadn't said anything. Certainly not that he loved her. She was distraught. Why had she let him know how she felt? She was frightened of his reaction. He was very quiet after that and she had the strangest feeling that he had detached himself from her.

★ ★ ★

Kate went to her Pilates class on Tuesday and couldn't believe how flexible she'd become, in just a few weeks. Of course, she'd lost a lot of fat, which helped.

This week Diana spoke to her. She's looking for something, was Kate's immediate reaction, surprising herself with this uncharitable thought. One never knew where one stood with Diana. She was so unpredictable.

"Kevin tells me you've started a catering business. How quaint!"

"Maybe, but I enjoy it. I started a couple of weeks ago when I catered a drinks party for Michael and Marcia – you remember them from the dinner in our house? They were my first clients and I did a dinner party for them last Friday also. They were a great success so it's catching on and –"

Kate stopped mid-sentence. She couldn't believe Diana's reaction. Had she said something wrong? Firstly, Diana went deathly pale, then her face became suffused with anger and she turned on her heel and left the room. What's that about? Kate asked herself, stunned. Then it dawned on her. Marcia's suspicion that Diana and Michael were having an affair was perhaps true. There was no other explanation for Diana's reaction.

* * *

Diana was shaking with fury. Kate had catered for his party and he never even mentioned it! She was consumed with jealousy. The thought of Kate there in his house, meeting his friends, being chummy with his wife filled her with anger. Frumpy Kate! Couldn't he have got someone else and why hadn't he told her? She was livid and if he had been there with her at that moment she would have lashed out at him physically. She tried ringing him on his mobile but couldn't get him. She left a message.

He rang her back that night.

"What is it, Diana?"

"Why didn't you tell me that Kate catered for your parties?" She could hear the accusing tone in her voice.

There was silence on the other end. Then Michael replied, in a very cold voice, "My domestic arrangements are my own and my wife's business. I don't have to share them with you. I warned you that my home life was off limits."

She could tell he was very angry. Maybe she should have waited till they were in bed to discuss this. They were never good on the phone.

"Will you be around tomorrow night?"

"No, I'm going to London first thing tomorrow morning and don't know when I'll be back."

Without elaborating, he hung up.

★ ★ ★

I've got to get out of this situation, Michael thought to himself. He knew now that Diana was trouble. She was too intense, too possessive. He didn't need it. He didn't know how he would extricate himself. He felt a bit like Michael Douglas in *Fatal Attraction*. Thankfully I have no pet rabbit

– he allowed himself a smile. The quicker he got rid of her, the better. God knows what she was capable of. He must protect Marcia at all costs. Maybe he was getting too old for all this larking about. Maybe it was time to hang up his boots, or in this case, his trousers. He had such a wonderful wife and family and he did not want to jeopardise that.

★ ★ ★

Diana was bereft. She wished she hadn't rung him at all, or mentioned Kate but she couldn't help herself. She had been beside herself with jealousy and now she'd made matters worse. She even doubted that he was going to London at all. She'd have to figure out a way to find out if he was lying to her.

She did.

★ ★ ★

Kate played golf with the ladies on Wednesday morning and the rest of her waking hours were spent in the kitchen cooking. Mary from Naas had asked her to make cheesecakes also this week, as well as the banoffee pies. She did a big cook-in for the freezer so that she would have plenty of food prepared for the boys' weekend and, of course, she had Tara's party to cater. She was busy but happy.

She had received four enquiries from friends of Marcia asking her to cater for them and she promised to notify them when her website was up and running. Once she had finished her price list and photographed the buffet for Tara's party, then she would send the final draft for it to Clarissa. It was all very exciting.

* * *

The school in Ballyfern started its Hallowe'en break at lunch-time on Wednesday, two days early because of a problem with the central heating that needed fixing. The kids and teachers were all delighted. Conor was heading off that afternoon, surfing in Mayo in the west of Ireland with some friends. He was in high spirits in the staffroom at the break and Kirsten monopolised him for the whole time saying how she'd adore to surf and asking him all about it. Jenny half expected her to insist on going with him. These young ones – they were so brazen! He came over to say goodbye to Jenny but she practically ignored him. He didn't know what was bugging her but she'd been avoiding him since last weekend. He had tackled her about it but she'd denied it. She definitely wasn't herself but, if she wouldn't talk to him, he could do nothing about it. He hoped she'd be in better form when he got back from Mayo.

* * *

Jenny had arranged to go to Dublin on Wednesday afternoon to meet her friend, Emma, who was also an amateur artist. They were going to an art exhibition together.

What Jenny didn't realise was that Emma thought Jenny's work was good enough to exhibit and with that end in view intended to introduce her to people who could make it happen.

At the exhibition Jenny found herself talking to a particularly persuasive guy who made her agree to let him come and look at her paintings.

"Great! Let me introduce you to our co-ordinator. She'll arrange it."

Taking her hand, he brought her across the room to meet a very attractive brunette, who looked familiar. When Jenny heard her name – Valerie – she realised, with a shock, that it was Tom's ex-wife. She recognised her from old photos that Tom had showed her.

"Nice to meet you. Actually, I think we have something in common. I'm married to Tom, your ex-husband," she said shyly.

"Of course! I should have recognised your name. My son, Mark, has told me a lot about you. He thinks you're quite a woman. He's very fond of you but he never told me that you're an artist."

"No, well, I've kept it a bit of a secret. I don't think I'm very good," Jenny said modestly.

"That's not what Emma says."

"How is Mark? He's such a nice boy and Tom doesn't see nearly enough of him. You know Tom," she added lamely.

Valerie caught the unhappiness in her voice. "Don't tell me he's still the same old smart-ass. I'd hoped he might have changed when he got married again. I hope he's not making your life as miserable as he made mine."

"Well, it's no bed of roses," Jenny admitted ruefully. "I think if we'd had a baby, it might have made a difference —"

"Yes, I'm sure that's true. It's unfortunate that he can't."

"He can't?" Jenny was startled. "What do you mean?"

Valerie looked at her, alarm showing on her face. "Tom can't have a baby," she said. "He had a vasectomy after Mark's birth. He never wanted another baby. Don't tell me he didn't tell you?" She saw from the shock on Jenny's face that she hadn't.

Jenny thought she was going to faint.

"Oh, you poor thing!" said Valerie, putting her hand out to steady her.

Jenny was in shock. Was she hearing right? Was Valerie saying that Tom had had a vasectomy? No wonder she couldn't get pregnant! That's why he wouldn't come to the specialist with her. She thought she was going to throw up.

"Sorry, I have to go to the bathroom," she mumbled.

Valerie put her arm around her and guided her there and Jenny did indeed throw up. What a bastard, thought Valerie. He obviously hasn't changed. Poor Jenny! She's much too nice for him. I can't believe he didn't tell her about his vasectomy. What a rotter!

When Jenny finally got herself together she asked Valerie to locate Emma and tell her she needed to go home.

★ ★ ★

Late on Wednesday afternoon Diana drove to Killiney and located Michael's home. She parked her car nearby and walked up the Vico Road, taking in the beautiful house and gardens. There was no sign of his car but there was a Mercedes parked in the driveway which she presumed was his wife's. She went down to the hotel and dawdled there, ordering a meal.

At eight thirty she drove by his house again. Still no sign of his car. She hung around till ten o'clock, by which time she decided he wasn't coming home, so she drove by his apartment in the city centre. No sign of life or his car there either.

★ ★ ★

On the drive back to Naas Jenny thought about what Valerie had told her at the Art Exhibtion. The shock was beginning to wear off and she was starting to feel angrier than she ever had in her whole life. How could he? To think that he had suggested it was her weight problem that was hindering her ability to get pregnant and all the time he knew the reason why. He knew how much she wanted a baby. How could he have been so cruel?

She arrived home in a daze and went inside and threw herself on the couch, waiting for her husband. She had no idea how long she sat there but when she heard him come in, she was ready for him. He was surprised to find her sitting there, in the dark.

"What's up, Jenny?"

"I have one question to ask you and if you don't tell me the truth, I'll find it out anyway. Have you had a vasectomy?"

"Where did you hear that?" he mumbled, and she realised she'd caught him on the hop.

"It makes no difference. Answer me! Yes or no?"

He had never seen her so steely. She didn't look like his Jenny.

"Yes or no?" she demanded again, with menace in her voice.

"Well, yes, but I didn't know how to tell –"

"Get out! This minute! Pack your bags and leave my house, now!" she screamed at him. She wanted to lunge at him and strangle him.

"Oh, Jenny, I'm sorry but I knew you would –"

"Damn right! We're finished. I'm divorcing you. You're a cheat and a liar. You've betrayed me. I never want to set eyes on you again. Now get out!"

He was scared. He'd never seen her so angry. He decided he'd better do as she asked. She'd maybe come round later but it wouldn't happen anytime tonight. He sheepishly packed a bag and left.

When he had gone, the anger drained out of her and she started sobbing. She had no idea how long she cried for, but it was a long time. All the wasted years of hoping and praying and longing were washed away with her tears. She could never have believed that any person could betray another like this – let alone someone who was supposed to love you.

The phone was ringing but she let it ring. She put the lock on the door in case he came back.

Then there was a knock on the door but she stayed sitting in the dark and didn't answer. She guessed it was Tom coming back to try to make amends, as if that were possible! He obviously gave up because the knocking stopped. She crawled into bed and fell asleep.

Chapter 38

The moment Kate heard Jenny's voice on the phone next morning, she knew something was wrong.

"What is it, Jenny? Why aren't you at school?" Her voice was fearful.

"We started the midterm break yesterday, luckily," said Jenny.

Then, tearfully, she told Kate what she had discovered. She cried as she told the story and Kate found herself crying too.

"You poor darling! Would you like me to come over?"

"No, Kate. I know how busy you are with Tara's party, but if you get a chance this evening, I could do with some company. I'll come to you, if you like."

"Great. We'll meet up then. I'm supposed to be going to Lauren's for dinner, but I can cancel that, no problem. Do you mind if I tell Lauren?"

"Of course not, but I don't want anyone else to know. I feel enough of a fool for being deceived by that rotter, without the whole world knowing it."

"Don't worry. You know your secret is safe with us. Oh, you poor thing! How cruel of him!"

When Kate told Lauren the story, she too was shocked and upset for Jenny.

"God love her! What a bastard! Frankly, I'm glad that at least she's rid of him. She was always too good for him. I feel so sorry for her. But who knows, maybe it's for the best. Tell you what – I'll ring and see if she'll come to dinner tonight."

"Good idea. She needs all our support now."

★ ★ ★

Diana was back outside Michael's house on Thursday but still no sign of Michael. As she was parked there his wife drove by. Diana thought that Marcia gave her a strange look but reckoned that she was probably imagining it. She could be anybody after all.

★ ★ ★

Jenny declined the invitation to dinner at first but Lauren insisted she come. She was grateful to both Lauren and Kate. She needed distraction right now and it would help to share her pain with the girls.

She stayed in bed for most of the day, barely able to function. She heard the phone ringing and the doorbell too but ignored them both. She couldn't face anyone. She felt ashamed that she'd been taken for such a fool.

When she arrived at Lauren's that evening, her two friends hugged her and told her how sorry they were.

"It helps a lot to have friends like you," she told them tearfully, "but I still can't get over the lie that Tom lived. I should never have married him – it was a huge mistake – but now I've just got to get on with my life. I feel such a fool. Thank God I own the house, so I was able to put him out."

"He won't make any trouble for you, will he?" Kate asked, a worried frown on her face.

"He'd better not. I'm changing the locks tomorrow. He's a coward at heart and knows what he did was wrong. I doubt I'll ever see him again, except in court."

It was a very subdued dinner although Jonathan kept them entertained with stories of the courtroom. When dinner was over he went into his office to give the girls time to talk, in private. Jenny was so grateful for their concern and support.

Chapter 39

Marcia had, in fact, got a good look at Diana outside her house on Thursday and knew exactly who she was. She now knew for certain that Diana was her husband's latest fling.

On Friday, she noticed Diana parked outside the gate and, as she drove out, took down the number of her car.

Marcia pondered the best way to approach this with Michael. Accusing him outright was out of the question. She had to be much more subtle.

After a little thought, she knew what to do.

When Michael arrived home from London, late that night, she lost no time in putting her plan into action.

"I was a bit nervous this week. I feel maybe there is a burglar casing the house. I've noticed a BMW sports car, parked outside for the past three days. I got the number . . ." She handed it to him. "I didn't like to notify the police until you came home."

"You did right, dear. I'll look into it. Don't worry."

I bet you will, said Marcia to herself, with a satisfied little smile. This would be curtains for the hard-faced bitch. Michael would never tolerate her infringing on his home.

★ ★ ★

On Saturday morning, Kate took David and Justin shopping in Naas to choose gifts for Melissa's birthday. The previous day she had collected the boys, plus Miguel, from school. They were all on a high, looking forward to nine whole days of freedom. Lauren had offered to take the three younger ones in order to give Kate a chance to finish the preparations for the party. She'd planned to take them riding in the afternoon and then they would stay the night with her. They were thrilled with this, as were Ben and Daisy. Lauren had made up costumes for them all to go trick-or-treating and then they were having a party with Hallowe'n games afterwards. Miguel's eyes were popping out of his head with excitement. They didn't have anything this exciting in Spain. Toby got the ring in the barmbrack and promptly put it on Daisy's finger.

Danny had arrived home that afternoon to find that all his sons were out. He was furious.

"We didn't know when you were coming!" Kate told him. "You can't expect everyone to put their life on hold when you don't let us know your plans. You'll have tomorrow with them." He really was too much!

"I was planning on working with James tomorrow," he replied sulkily.

"Well, then, I suggest you get James in today," she told him coolly.

He couldn't believe it. Nobody seemed to care whether he was there or not. He seemed to have lost all control in his own home. He admitted to himself, grudgingly, that he should have let them know when he was coming but he would never admit this to Kate.

Then he saw the mounds of food in the kitchen and asked what it was all in aid of.

"I'm catering for a party tonight. It's David's girlfriend's sixteenth birthday. Both David and Justin are going to the party."

He was speechless. David's girlfriend? Since when did he have a girlfriend? He realised that he was losing touch with his family. So what, if there was a big rift between Kate and himself – but he didn't want the same thing happening with his boys.

"I'd hoped you'd come with me to the golf club tonight for a meal."

"Out of the question! I've got this food to deliver."

He felt adrift. Everything had shifted. Kate was so ... he searched for a word to describe it ... self-contained. That was it! Where had this self-confidence come from? He looked at her closely. She looked terrific ... different.

Feeling abandoned and alone, he sat in the office with James, all night, working through the many problems that had accrued since his last visit home, two weeks ago.

* * *

Jenny went through the weekend in a daze. She felt detached from reality – just going through the motions. The doorbell never stopped on Saturday night with kids trick-or-treating. Normally, she had a cache of sweets for them and enjoyed their antics but tonight she couldn't hack it so she curled up in bed and watched TV.

Tom rang on Saturday afternoon and she informed him that she was filing for divorce. She packed up all his belongings and told him that she would leave them at his brother's house, over the weekend. She never wanted to see him again. She planned to spend the coming week immersed in her painting and meeting with her solicitor. She wanted her marriage ended as quickly as possible.

Chapter 40

Tara's party for her twins on Saturday night was going with a bang. The atmosphere was electric, the music terrific and the food awesome, as all the kids and the adults present agreed. Kate was pleased and Tara delighted. Melissa was wearing a stunning royal blue, very, very short, silk chiffon dress which showed off her beautiful tanned limbs to perfection. When she took to the dance floor she brought the room to a standstill as she shimmied and twirled to the music. She reminded Kate of the professional dancers on her favourite programme, *Strictly Come Dancing,* and Kate thought she was just as good as any of them. She and David were joined at the hip for most of the night as Kate and Tara looked on happily.

"Young love. Isn't it wonderful?" Tara exclaimed. "Wouldn't it be lovely if it lasted and we'd be in-laws?"

"We might be in-laws twice over by the looks of it. Justin hasn't left your daughter Naomi's side all night."

"Well, they both want to study medicine next year so I

suppose they've a lot in common. They do make a lovely couple."

Kate immediately took to all of Tara's seven children. They were so friendly and outgoing and the girls were stunners, like their mother. Seán, her husband, was another story. Kate couldn't make him out although she suspected that being surrounded every day by all this beauty and personality must be very daunting. Eventually, towards the end of the night, she found herself sitting beside him and they started to chat. She found him to be very shy and she identified with him because she used to feel like that too. However, she could see that his eyes followed Tara everywhere and she began to understand that he was afraid of losing her.

"She loves you very much, you know." Kate didn't know what made her say it.

"She's so lovely," he replied. "I can never understand why she stays with me. I feel so inadequate beside her."

"Don't be silly. She needs you. You're her rock, her stability. Stellar people like Tara need someone like that, to ground them."

"Do you really think so?"

Kate's heart went out to him when she saw the hope and vulnerability in his eyes.

"I know so. Now come on and let's have a dance."

"Delighted!" He gave her an old-fashioned bow. "Now I know why Tara is so fond of you. She says you're a gem. And you are." With that he twirled her onto the floor.

It was after two when they left. David was in seventh heaven.

"Wasn't Melissa gorgeous tonight? I thought she looked beautiful."

"Naomi was pretty fantastic looking too," said Justin. "And she's also a lovely person and very intelligent."

"God, is this what I have to listen to for the next ten years?" Kate cried, in mock horror.

"More like twenty," replied David. "Sam and Toby are still to come."

"I'll never survive it!"

"Course you will, Mom. Think of all the daughters-in-law you'll be gaining – and the grandchildren!" Justin laughed.

How she adored them! They filled her with love and warmth. She was so lucky.

Danny was sleeping in the guest-room when she got home. If that's what he wants, she thought, so be it!

★ ★ ★

The following morning Danny woke Justin and David at eight and asked them to go golfing with him.

"Ah no, Dad, it's too early. Can't we go later?"

"No, I'm going back to London later."

"Well, I'm not up to it," said David, turning over.

Justin agreed and Danny left the house in a temper.

Lauren arrived at noon with the younger kids and she and Kate took their coffee out on the terrace.

"Danny was furious that the boys wouldn't go to play golf with him at eight this morning."

"What does he expect? They're teenagers and they were out late at a party last night."

"I know, but he expected to spend some time with them this weekend. He's going back this afternoon so he'll barely get a chance."

"Then he should have missed his golf," said Lauren, showing Danny no mercy. "My, how quickly they're growing," she murmured, watching them all playing about in the garden with a football.

"I don't know where the years have gone," said Kate. "They're young men now. Even my baby, Toby. He's grown so much since he started in Hayworth and I can't believe how independent he's become. I hated letting him go but I have to admit now that it was the right decision."

"And maybe for you too. Look how much you've grown in the past two months."

"Yeah, but look at how my marriage has deteriorated."

"That would have happened anyway, Kate, sooner or later. Once you became your own person."

"I suppose so," Kate replied, a little wistfully.

* * *

Danny had exactly one hour with his sons before he set off for the airport. He found Justin very distant.

"Have you said anything to Justin about our relationship?" he asked Kate before he left.

"I didn't have to. He told me last week that he knew things were not right between us. He's not stupid, Danny.

He can see for himself what's going on. He's a young man now, not a child. Speaking of which, his eighteenth birthday is in three weeks. We have to decide on a present for him and I'm organising a party for him on the Saturday night. I think we should buy him a car. I know that's what he'd really like."

Danny couldn't believe that Justin was almost eighteen years old. Where had the years gone?

"Yes, of course. I've always planned to give him a car for his eighteenth. What do you think he'd like? A convertible?"

"I think not. I think he'd prefer something that he could take his friends around in and, let's face it, a convertible is pretty limited. I think we should let him choose. Financially within reason, of course."

"Yes, of course. I'll go and propose it to him now and he can go look at them during the week. Then I'll take him to buy it next Saturday. Great idea! With luck he'll have it for his birthday."

Kate realised that Danny had had no idea that Justin's birthday was coming up and hadn't thought of a car either.

"It might be a good idea to leave him your car this week to get around. He can drive you to the airport and meet you next weekend. That means he won't be depending on my car all the time. Please mark in the date of his party in your diary. It's Saturday the first of December, when he's on his next weekend break. Can you be here for that?"

"For my eldest son's eighteenth birthday? Are you crazy? Of course, I can be here for that."

"Just thought I'd make sure," she said in an exasperated voice.

* * *

Kevin called in later that evening and was surprised to find that Danny had already left. He had thought that, as it was a Bank Holiday, Danny would have stayed over till Monday. He had offered to deliver the photos and menus for Kate's website to Clarissa's office the following day, en route to visit his parents in Rathgar. Kate persuaded him to stay for supper and he was secretly delighted as he loved her boys and enjoyed spending time with them. He would never understand how Danny could bear to be away from them so much.

* * *

Diana woke on Sunday with the now customary hangover. Her week had consisted of eating chocolate all day and drinking wine all night. She knew it was crazy but she couldn't help herself. After a couple of black coffees, she headed out to Killiney again. She felt like a woman driven. She had to know where Michael was and she couldn't relax until she saw him again.

She drove past his house and with relief saw his car parked there. She drove on down to the beach and parked her car, intending to go for a walk. To her horror, she saw Michael, not a hundred yards away from her, holding two little girls by the hand. He had his trousers rolled up and was paddling at the water's edge with them. Every time a wave broke, they ran back in, giggling and shrieking. His wife was standing on the beach with two beautiful girls, one heavily pregnant, and the other pushing a buggy. They were obviously his daughters. With a shock she realised that they were about her age. The little group walked away from her, up the beach, and she saw Michael put an arm around his wife and the other around his pregnant daughter, while the other daughter chased after the two little girls. They were obviously happy together and she could sense the love between them. When he bent and kissed his wife, Diana almost went crazy. She wanted to scream at him, but, of course, she couldn't.

* * *

Michael would never know what made him turn around at that exact moment but he did, and saw Diana standing on the path. He froze, then turned around and tried to behave as normal. Luckily, Marcia hadn't noticed. That decided him. He would end it right away.

* * *

Diana drove back to her apartment, admitting to herself for the first time that maybe it was not going to work out as she wanted. She really had to get a grip and work out a plan of action.

391

As she opened yet another bottle of wine to dull the pain, she had a Scarlett O'Hara moment: "I'll think about it tomorrow."

Chapter 41

As Monday was a Bank Holiday there was no golf lesson for Kate and no Slimforever meeting that night. On the spur of the moment Kate decided that they should meet and weigh-in anyway. "Otherwise, we'll never survive till the following Monday," was how she put it to Jenny and Lauren.

She hated to admit it but she was relieved that Danny had gone back, as the atmosphere in the house was much less tense. She felt like having a party and so decided to have her friends over for supper. She had enough food, ready to serve, in the freezer.

Jenny was alone and so was delighted to be invited. Jonathan had gone back to Dublin with his mother so Lauren said she'd love to come with Ben and Daisy, who were yelling like wild Indians with delight. Then, of course, David wanted to invite Melissa.

"And why not Naomi too?" asked Justin.

"Well, if Tara has to drive them over and collect them,

I'll invite her also." Kate did ask Tara if Seán would like to come but it was his poker night and, as she explained, that didn't stop – not for Bank Holidays or anything else. "But if it's okay I'll bring Melissa's twin, Scott. Otherwise he'll be on his own."

"No problem. I'm pleased actually, as otherwise we would have been thirteen. I never like to sit down thirteen at a table."

"Kate, I can't believe you're superstitious. You're so down-to-earth."

"Ha, ha! You don't really know me. Maybe I'm a witch."

"You're crazy! See you later."

"Bring your scales. We need to be weighed."

It was a jolly little group that enjoyed the scrumptious food that Kate dished up. Before they sat down, Tara weighed them and again Kate had lost two pounds, Lauren nothing and Jenny two pounds more.

"I don't believe it! Two more pounds and I'll be in the eight stones! That lout has done me some good!" Jenny laughed.

"What do you mean?" asked Tara.

Jenny told her about Tom and Tara hugged her saying, "You're worth so much more. Put him behind you. Move on."

"I intend to," she announced, which gave rise to a questioning glance between Kate and Lauren.

They had so much fun over dinner. The kids kept them entertained with jokes and stories and Kate thought how fantastic they all were. They loved Jenny. She had such a good way with them and Kate thought how awful it was that she would never have any of her own. She'd have made a wonderful mother.

After dinner they played charades and the antics of the kids, trying to get their message across, made the women laugh till they cried.

Wiping her eyes, Kate said, "Ladies, I can't take any more. Let's retire to the terrace for a coffee."

"It's so cosy in here and still you feel like you're in the garden," Jenny commented.

"It's all double glazed and we have underfloor heating, that's why," Kate told her. "It's my favourite room in the house, summer and winter."

"It would be mine too," Tara agreed.

"It's been a wonderful evening, Kate," said Jenny. "I feel privileged to have been a part of it – such wonderful kids and so much happiness."

"They are so funny and they all get on so well. We're blessed," Kate said, smiling.

Lauren turned to Jenny, "I was just thinking, Jen. How much have you lost to date?"

"One stone eleven pounds. Why?"

"Well, it strikes me you're still wearing the same clothes as you were almost two stone ago. It's time for a change. How about a makeover? You deserve it after all you've been through."

"Because I'm worth it?" laughed Jenny.

"You certainly are. I'm serious. What do you say girls that we take her to Dublin this week and work on her?"

"Fantastic idea!"

"Count me in," said Tara.

"There's no way you'll make me look as good as Kate did, after her makeover. You can't make a silk purse out of a sow's ear," retorted Jenny.

"Let's give it a bloody good try!" said Lauren. "Friday suit you all?"

"Absolutely."

They sat chatting for another hour or so, till Lauren realised it was almost midnight and broke up a game of blind-man's-buff, which was just as well as it was getting very boisterous.

* * *

After they had all left and the young ones had gone to bed, Kate sat having a chat with Justin. David had already gone to his room to phone Melissa.

"I don't ever remember any boy ringing me as often as this when I was young."

"Times have changed, Mom. You didn't have mobiles then. Mom, I really enjoyed tonight and so did Naomi. Your friends are great fun. She says her mum is really pleased she met you all. She doesn't have many friends."

"They're a very nice family. I hope we stay friends."

"Me too. For sure!" Justin said with enthusiasm.

* * *

Diana hated Bank Holidays. The whole world seemed to have something exciting planned but she had nothing. Izzie was at the Jazz Festival in Cork with her new boyfriend and all her other friends were involved with either their husbands and families or boyfriends. She was feeling very sorry for herself. She dared not think of what Michael was doing. He's probably dancing attendance on The Wicked Witch and his stupid daughters, she thought. She decided that this week she would tackle him, and insist on more of his time and attention. Yes, that's what she'd do. She'd give him an ultimatum. In the meantime she just wanted to get today over with. She was sure he would be in touch tomorrow and she planned to go all out to ensnare him when he arrived the next night. That cheered her up as she planned what she would do to him.

She resisted the temptation to drive out to Killiney. It made her feel closer to him but she knew she couldn't risk him seeing her again. Instead she went out for a walk down by the Liffey but all she could see were couples walking, holding hands and laughing together. It depressed her so she bought yet another box of chocolates and retired to the apartment to watch television.

When Michael rang at nine thirty the following morning, she was exhilarated. He wanted to come and see her at lunch-time. Yes! I knew it, she thought gleefully. He can't wait to have sex with me again. Poor lamb, he's been starved – a whole week without it! She was getting aroused just thinking about it. He would be ravenous for her and she imagined just how he would take her. Better not wear anything too expensive. There's a good chance he'll rip it off, she thought, getting more excited by the minute.

She was wearing just a black, see-through, baby-doll negligée and her highest Manolo Blahnik heels when he came in the door.

"Darling, it's so good to have you back," she whispered huskily, as she wrapped her arms around his neck.

Despite himself, he wanted her. God, she looked sexy! Just one last time, he thought. Before he could stop himself his hands were all over her body and his lips on her nipples. She was pulling off his shirt and then his trousers. Not able to wait – he entered her. Ohhhhhh . . . it felt so good. Within seconds he had climaxed.

Feeling a bit of a rotter, he decided that he couldn't finish it like this. He'd taken his pleasure, he couldn't just walk out. Carrying her to the bed he started kissing her on the neck and made his way down her body till he came to the spot which he knew gave her most pleasure, driving her into a frenzy which excited him further. He let her have her orgasm and then came into her once more and they both climaxed again, together. It was the best sex they'd ever had.

She was in a daze of happiness. This was what it was all about. They were meant to be together, she felt sure of it. He would just have to accept that. She knew how to make him happy.

He looked at his watch. "Oh Lord, look at the time! I've got to get back to work."

He couldn't bring himself to tell her that they were finished. Not after that lovemaking. That would be too cruel. He knew he could not risk coming here again to meet her. It would always be the same story. His insatiable lust would mean he would not be able to resist her. No, far better to finish it over lunch somewhere. Lunch was safe. That way he couldn't jump her and she could hardly make a scene which he had no doubt she would if he ended it here. It didn't bear thinking about.

"Diana, honey, can you meet me in the Waterfront, Thursday, for lunch?"

"Yeah, sure, as long as you come back here and screw me, like you just did."

He winced at this but didn't reply. He'd got himself into this and now he had to get himself out. What an idiot I am. Always thinking with my prick!

* * *

Jenny was having a calm quiet week at home. She was painting every day, sometimes for up to eight hours, and somehow, the hurt she had gone through seemed to bring an added dimension to her work. She was amazed at what was appearing before her. For the first time in her life she was happy with what she painted. It had more depth and feeling than anything she had ever done before. All her loss and yearning seemed to find its way onto the canvas. She lost herself in it and didn't hear the phone ring nor the messages left on it. She was in another world and it was helping her cope with the pain.

She was exhausted every night, mentally and physically,

as she fell into bed and slept like a baby. She missed Conor dropping in and wondered how he was getting on with his surfing, but was glad of this time to herself, to put the pieces of her being back together again.

By Thursday night she had finished the painting and stepped back to view it. With mounting excitement she acknowledged that it was in a different league to anything she had done before. She cleaned her brushes, poured herself a glass of wine and and relaxed, happy with what she'd achieved. She was now ready for her makeover tomorrow and looked forward to the day with the girls in Dublin. It was just the tonic she needed.

One of the messages on the answering machine was from the Art Gallery in Dublin. Oscar, the dealer she'd met, wanted to come down and view her work. She agreed to see him the following Tuesday afternoon. Conor had rung a few times too. Well, she'd see him when he got back.

* * *

The week flew by for Kate, looking after her sons and Miguel and making sure they had a good time. Kevin called around most evenings and he sometimes ended up staying for dinner. Kate suspected he was trying to make up to her sons for Danny's absence.

Justin was over the moon about his new car and spent every day trawling the garages trying to decide which one he would choose. He also made a few trips with David to Tara's house. He was becoming as smitten with Naomi as

David was with Melissa.

My oh my, did I ever think the day would come when they would be more interested in girls than messing around with their friends, mused Kate. She also noticed a distinct improvement in their dress and toiletries. The whiff of after-shave overwhelmed her as they passed by and they had taken to spending hours in the bathroom before going out. It was definitely a change for the better.

Chapter 42

Diana was up bright and early on Thursday morning to prepare herself for her lunch date with Michael. The horny devil, she thought, he can't wait till tonight. She planned to drive him so crazy today that he would come back tonight and stay the night. He was in love with her, she could tell.

She soaked in a scented bath before going to have her hair done. She agonised for an hour over what she would wear. Today she needed the wow factor. Eventually, she settled on the Armani suit with the short skirt. It would not look out of place in the restaurant which was mainly frequented by businessmen from the Financial Centre, but underneath she chose to wear a flimsy shirt with the top buttons undone. It left nothing to the imagination. She also wore black fishnet stockings and suspenders and her highest black patent Christian Louboutin shoes. No one could say she didn't know how to turn her man on, she thought smugly.

When she walked into the restaurant, every male head

in the place swivelled to stare at her. She was aware of the effect she was having on them and it turned her on.

Michael kissed her cheek, very much aware of the envious glances he was receiving. He didn't blame them. She took off her jacket and he couldn't take his own eyes off her voluptuous breasts. They were straining against the flimsy top. In spite of himself he had a hard-on, and she knew it. She loved teasing him.

He longed to reach across, unbutton her shirt and fondle those beautiful breasts. He tried to get a hold of himself but found it difficult. After they'd eaten, while they were waiting for their coffee, she excused herself and went to the Ladies'. She came back with a smile on her face, wearing her jacket again.

"Why are you smiling?" he asked, as he sipped his coffee.

"I have a surprise for you," she replied. "I've taken off all my underwear." And she casually opened her jacket so that only he could see. The bra was gone and he could clearly see her breasts.

"Downstairs too," she laughed, seeing the lust in his eyes.

"Let's go," he said, ushering her out. He couldn't wait to get her back to her apartment.

There, the sex didn't take very long and he felt terrible after it. This had to stop! He just couldn't see her any more. He couldn't risk it because her body seduced him every time and he was powerless to prevent it.

He was about to tell her when he got a text message on his phone:

'*Congratulations, we have a beautiful new grandson. Call me asap. Love you, Marcia.*'

He couldn't believe it, a grandson at last! He had hoped and prayed that Nicky would give him the grandson that he longed for, and now she had. He was over the moon. He loved his granddaughters, of course, but every man wanted a grandson. He had not been blessed with a son but now he would have a little boy to play ball with, to teach rugby and golf to and just talk boy-talk. He couldn't believe it. This had been his last chance as he knew neither of the girls wanted more children. Halleluiah!

"What is it?"

He had forgotten all about Diana.

"I have a grandson! I can't believe it," and he punched the air while letting out a whoop of joy.

"Congratulations," she said sarcastically, but he was gone out the door like a bat out of hell.

Bloody hell, I suppose that's tonight fucked, she thought angrily. Stupid child! What bad timing.

* * *

Michael rang Marcia who told him she was in the hospital with Nicky. She sounded thrilled also.

"I'll be right over," he said. "How is he? Is everything okay? Who does he look like?"

"He's perfect and gorgeous. Come and see for yourself!" she laughed.

He stopped off on the way and bought two dozen

yellow roses for Nicky. He also bought four cases of champagne. Two for Nicky, who would need them for all the friends who would be visiting her in hospital, and two for himself as he certainly would be wetting his grandson's head with his friends. He wheeled half-a-dozen champagne glasses from the salesman, who also lent him an ice bucket filled with ice. Michael generously tipped him €50.

He ran up the steps of the hospital, precariously carrying the roses and the champagne on ice. Passers-by smiled at him indulgently, thinking he was a new father. When he entered her room, Nicky was propped up in bed with the baby at her breast. She looked tired but was glowing with happiness. Her husband was beaming with pride, delighted with his new son, and Marcia and Alex, his older daughter, were beaming from ear to ear also. He kissed Nicky, congratulating her.

"Hi, Dad, meet your grandson, Michael."

He looked at his tiny grandson, suckling greedily, his eyes closed and his oh-so-tiny-hand splayed on his mother's breast.

Michael couldn't help it. Tears started to flow down his cheeks. He looked across at Marcia and saw she was crying too. He was so happy and so proud of his little girl and her son.

She took the baby off the breast and handed him to Michael.

He was terrified that he might hurt him or drop him.

"It's okay. He's tough, like his grandpa."

They all laughed.

He held him gently, crooking his arm around the little blond head and, when he put his finger in the tiny hand, he couldn't believe the strength with which he grasped it. The baby wouldn't let go.

"No doubt about it! He'll play rugby for Ireland one day!"

Then they all got busy, opening the champagne and putting the flowers in water, but Michael wouldn't relinquish this new, tiny human being whose blue, unseeing eyes looked up into his. Baby Michael! He was so proud that Nicky had called the baby after him. I've got to be a role model for him, he thought, feeling shame for his behaviour, even this very afternoon as his grandson was coming into the world. He looked at the little group: his wife Marcia, who looked at him so lovingly, his two beautiful daughters who had grown up to be women of whom he was very proud and now this little bundle who touched his heart as no one ever had. This is my family, my life. I love them and they love me. This is all I need. And with that he made a promise to his little grandson that he would change. From now on, family was everything. As he looked up at Marcia, she smiled at him and he felt that somehow she knew.

★ ★ ★

Diana was expecting his call. She'd known he'd be back for more. What a stud! He was insatiable. She'd even wondered if he was on Viagra, but decided not. He was just a fantastic, very horny lover.

"Hi, sexy," she began but he cut her off.

"Diana, I'm very sorry but it's over. I can't see you again. Our affair is finished."

She didn't believe him. He was joking with her.

"Very funny, but I know you can't stay away. You need me like other men need air. Are you coming round?"

"No, and I am sorry, but you won't be seeing me again. That's final and, don't worry, I will survive. You can stay on in the apartment until you find another one, but I want you out by Christmas at the latest. I'll pay the bills till then. Goodbye."

"Michael, please . . ."

But he was gone. She stood looking stupidly at her phone. This wasn't happening. She felt like she was in a nightmare and would wake up soon and it would all have been a dream. But it was no dream. Michael had finished with her. She couldn't take it in. She was in shock. He needs me, I know he does. He'll be back. He's probably overreacting because of that damned baby. God, what bad luck! Opening a bottle of wine and a box of chocolates, she took solace in both.

★ ★ ★

When, finally, Michael and Marcia went to bed, having liberally toasted their grandson's birth with the family and their friends and neighbours, they cuddled up to each other. Marcia was a little tipsy from all the champagne and he was surprised when he found out that she had dispensed with her usual nightie and was naked. He was even more surprised when she started to caress him and murmured, "Make love to me, Michael!"

In all their thirty-four years of marriage, she had never once initiated sex. They made love and he felt more fulfilled than he ever had with Diana or any of the multitude of women he'd had in his life.

As they lay snuggled up afterwards, he couldn't resist asking her, "How come you wanted to make love to me tonight? You've made me so happy."

"I was very wrong opting out of the sexual side of our marriage for so many years. I've started taking HRT and it's made me feel sexier and more alive than I ever have. I should have done this from the very beginning. I should never have sent you to other women. I was wrong."

"I love you and I need only you. The others are over, darling."

"I know, and I love you too, Michael." Smiling, she fell asleep.

Chapter 43

Friday had finally arrived and with it the shopping expedition to Dublin. Kate had arranged to drop the three young ones over to Maggie, who would look after them for the day, along with Daisy and Ben. They were all hyper as Maggie had promised to make them lunch in her little cottage before going up to the "Big House", as she called it. They adored Maggie's place which seemed to them like a doll's house, compared to their own, even though they all had to squash around the table. Kids!

"Probably because it's much more their size, like a house in a fairytale. You know, a bit like Goldilocks loving the Baby Bear stuff," remarked Lauren.

"God, you should have been a psychologist!" replied Kate laughing.

"Actually, I'd have made a great one," said Lauren, with a straight face. "I might even consider studying it one day. It's never too late. And you might just be my first subject!"

"Don't even go there!"

"Seriously, Kate, isn't it fantastic? We can do just about anything we want nowadays. Start new careers – like you – change careers, start studying just about anything we want. How lucky we are! Our mothers and grandmothers never had this chance. We are the luckiest generation of women."

"You know, ten – even five years ago – I would never have considered doing what I'm doing," said Kate. "Jenny would not have considered divorcing. Well, she couldn't have because there was no divorce in Ireland then. You're right. We are the lucky generation. I hope our daughters have it as good."

"Does it bother you not having a daughter?"

"It's what I would have loved, more than anything in the world but Danny decided that four kids was enough. So that was that."

"How selfish of him! It wasn't as if you couldn't afford another baby."

"I think he would have been jealous of the love I would have given a daughter. He was always jealous of the boys when they were babies. Crazy, I know, but true."

They had arrived at Jenny's by then so all conversation of babies stopped.

Jenny was in good form. The sadness surrounding her the previous Monday seemed to have disappeared.

"I am soooo looking forward to today."

"You won't know what hit you, girl!" said Lauren. "Hope you took a good look in the mirror before you left because that girl is gone – forever!"

"I won't miss her," Jenny giggled. "Today is the first day

of the rest of my life and I plan to live it to the full."

"That is such a good philosophy," Kate agreed.

"Nearly as good as 'Because we're worth it'!" said Jenny.

"They're both great and sum us up exactly," declared Lauren.

"Well, what is the programme for today?" asked Jenny.

"Firstly, I have to drop something in to Jonathan in the Law Library. He forgot it and needs it for a court case this afternoon."

"I've never been there," said Kate. "Can we come with you? I'd love to see it."

"Of course. It will be about coffee time so maybe we'll persuade Jonathan to take us for coffee in the restaurant there."

"Oh, I'd love that," said Jenny. "I've never been there either."

"That's settled then and I'll reveal the rest of the day's plans over coffee."

* * *

Lauren led the way across the courtyard and into the melée that was the Law Library foyer. The girls couldn't believe it and stood with their mouths open and eyes wide. There were about two hundred people squashed into a room about big enough for forty. People rushed in and out and the many barristers in their flowing black gowns and white wigs kept coming and going so fast that they felt dizzy just looking at them. People stood around in little groups and

Lauren explained that these were solicitors and their clients. There was an unbelievable buzz and hum about the place. Everyone seemed to be carrying big folders of papers and it was all very exciting.

Jonathan came out, looking extremely handsome in his wig and gown. Smiling at their obvious amazement at the place, he invited them to join him for coffee, which they happily accepted.

"And what's on the menu for today, girls? Off to spend all our money?" he joked.

"Hopefully," replied Lauren. She outlined her plan for the day. "We're heading to Trevor's first where we will all get our hair done, then to BT's to Jean-Claude's salon where Jenny will have her make-up done. We're meeting up with Tara for lunch and then we'll hit the shops."

"God help the shops and the credit cards," he laughed.

★ ★ ★

Trevor welcomed them with open arms and Jenny couldn't believe her eyes when he opened a bottle of champagne for them.

"Nothing is too good for my best client and her friends."

Lauren is certainly that, thought Kate. She's brought him two new clients! He handed Kate and Lauren over to juniors, to be shampooed, while he took Jenny in hand.

"You've very good hair texture and it's a beautiful colour," he said. "What colour do you put in it?"

"It's my natural colour. I don't use anything."

"Lucky girl! Most of my clients would die for hair like this."

Taking her hair in his hands, he fingered it, taking it up and back off her face whilst deciding how to style it.

"I really don't want it too short. I've always worn it long," she ventured timidly.

"I understand perfectly and I think long suits you, but this is too long and much too heavy on top."

He then told her what he would like to do and she was happy to go along with it. When he was finished she viewed herself in the mirror and couldn't believe the change. It fell just to her shoulders but he had layered it so there was so much more shape to it and the tight curls had become glossy waves. He had also given her a fringe which she loved. Her hair looked and felt great – shiny, glossy and so much lighter on her head. She loved it so much she bought all the products that he had used, and promised herself that she would return every six weeks to maintain it like this.

When Tara arrived to greet them, Trevor exclaimed, "What magnificent hair! Even I couldn't improve on it. Wow! You girls look like the *Sex and the City* girls – four sexy, glamorous women!"

They all found this very funny and laughed wholeheartedly at the compliment although they were secretly flattered.

Next on the list was Jean-Claude, who was delighted that Kate was using the make-up as he had shown her. He also complimented Jenny on her wonderful colouring and suggested a light natural look for her which was exactly what she wanted. She had been a bit nervous that she would end up today scalped and looking like a painted doll, but she was more than happy with the result. These guys really knew their stuff. She should have realised that Lauren would only have brought her to the best.

As they walked up Grafton Street to the Shelbourne for lunch, feeling on top of the world, they were aware that they were turning heads. In the Horseshoe Bar, they decided to order four Cosmopolitans, just like the *Sex and The City* girls, for a laugh.

As the young barman served them, he asked, "Okay, which of you is Carrie and where's Samantha?"

They roared laughing and tried to decide who was who.

"Lauren's definitely Miranda. Tall, elegant and smart-assed," said Kate to the amusement of the other two.

"Jenny is Charlotte, and Kate's definitely Carrie, everyone's confidante," replied Lauren.

"Well, thank you very much," said Tara. "Does that mean you think I'm Samantha?"

"I think she's fabulous — so sassy!" Jenny protested. "Okay, a bit promiscuous, but what the hell, nobody's perfect!"

This remark by Jenny brought more gales of laughter.

They had a superb lunch, being very choosy about what they ordered and very aware of Tara's watchful eye. They ordered a bottle of Sancerre between them.

"This is my problem," Tara told them. "I make people nervous about eating in front of me and if any of my members catch me eating anything not on my diet sheet, they really give me a hard time."

"But that's ridiculous – you're not overweight. You don't need to diet."

"I know, but they don't seem to understand that. It makes my life bloody difficult. I was once in a cake shop, buying a cake for the birthday of one of the kids, and this really massively overweight member of mine was also there. She acted like she had caught me committing a crime. She was delighted and kept saying, 'Ah, ha, caught you out!' I wanted to punch her. Actually, what I would really like to have done was to say to her – 'I'm not twenty stone like you and, if I was, I wouldn't be in here like you!' – but, of course, I didn't. I had to grin and bear it."

The others understood but had to smile at her confession.

After lunch, they hit the shops. Lauren insisted that Jenny, first of all, visit the lingerie department of BT's and get measured for a good bra.

"You've got big boobs and the right bra can make such a difference to your clothes. I bet you've never been measured before."

Jenny sheepishly admitted she hadn't. When the saleslady had finished with her, she realised that she had been wearing the wrong size bra all her life. Three new bras later, she could see that her credit card would have a field-day today. Bloody hell, I deserve it, she thought.

They then hit the other departments where Jenny kept veering towards the hippy-type kaftans that she always wore but Lauren adamantly refused to let her try them on. Instead, Jenny eventually chose a suit from Wallis and a Karen Millen dress. They were both fitted and she couldn't believe that she actually had a figure in them. It was then that Tara spotted an Issa dress and insisted she try it on. It was a green silk jersey and when Jenny saw the price tag of €320 she almost fainted but to please Tara she tried it on. She couldn't believe it when she looked in the mirror. It was perfect. She actually looked slim and it curved with her body beautifully.

"I can't believe it. I don't look like me."

"It is you – the new you," said Lauren. "It's gorgeous on you. You have to buy it."

Jenny didn't need much persuasion.

"Oh, Jenny, you look stunning! I think I'll try one on as well. They have it in blue," said Kate.

"As long as you check with me whenever we're going to the same do. I don't want us turning up in the same dress!" laughed Jenny.

"Of course! You'll have first option of wearing it," agreed Kate, and when she tried it on she loved it so much she bought it.

"Well, there's no way you're wearing boots with this dress," said Lauren, who then herded her into Fitzpatrick's shoe shop. There Jenny bought a pair of green suede, peep-toe stiletto shoes, which matched the dress perfectly.

"God, I look so much taller in these."

She also fell in love with a pair of black suede ankle-boots, which just about got by Lauren.

"Okay, they're like shoes. They'll look great with black tights."

Then they headed to Marks & Spencer's where Jenny bought tights, sweaters, shirts and two knee-length skirts for school. Everything she bought was fitted, not a kaftan in sight! It was a complete change from her normal wardrobe and she loved it. The final purchase was a forest green, crushed-velvet fitted jacket which was very pretty and feminine and didn't break the bank.

"That's it. I'll be bankrupt if I buy any more. That's the most fun I've had in years. I've always hated shopping but you girls sure give it a whole new meaning. I would never have chosen these clothes. They're completely different to what I'd normally buy."

"That's the whole point of a makeover," said Lauren.

"Well, I certainly look and feel like a new woman, thanks to you all."

Kate had to pick up some cooking equipment that she had ordered and they met up again in the Westbury to have a snack before heading home.

The girls had a surprise for Jenny. Kate presented her with a beautiful black lace La Perla lingerie set and sheer black stockings. Lauren gave her an ivory satin chemise and robe, which was very short and very sexy, and Tara gave her a set of Jo Malone bath oil, body lotion and scented candles.

Jenny felt the tears come to her eyes. She was so touched.

"You're the best friends any girl could wish for, but I

suspect you're setting me up for some serious seduction," she said, blushing as she hugged them.

"Why not? Worse things could happen to you," Tara suggested.

Lauren and Kate exchanged sly smiles.

Jenny was blissfully happy. It was one of the best days she'd ever spent. She was ready to face the future.

Chapter 44

Diana was on tenterhooks, waiting for a phone call from Michael. He would ring, she was convinced of it. She spent hours deciding how she would react when he finally did. Should she refuse to see him? That would drive him crazy, for sure. She suspected that she wouldn't have the willpower to do that, so decided that she would agree to see him but would put him off for a day or two. That would show him!

As the hours passed and she didn't hear from him, she began to get scared. She was missing him so much. She was feeling hot and needed him in her bed. She masturbated, thinking of him. She was desperate.

Eventually, she could wait no longer and started calling him. His mobile was always on message mode and when, in desperation, she rang him at the office, his PA told her that he did not wish to speak to her. His home number was unlisted and the only one who had it, that she knew of, was Kate. She rang her.

"Hi, Kate. I wonder if you could give me Michael Traynor's home number?"

Without hesitation Kate said, "Sorry, it's an unlisted number and so I can't do that. Frankly, from what I gather, he doesn't want to hear from you."

Diana was furious with her and banged down the phone.

She called into Michael's office but there was no way she could get past his dragon of a PA, who politely but firmly showed her the door. She was very protective of her boss.

Diana eventually realised that it was hopeless and decided the only thing for it was to catch him coming out of the office.

She stood outside his office that afternoon, in the biting cold, knowing that he generally left early on Fridays. Her persistence was rewarded when he eventually came out – but he was not alone, he was with a group of his staff. Seeing her there, he simply ignored her and, to her horror, got into a taxi with a beautiful leggy blonde. Has he already replaced me, she wondered, feeling as though he had plunged a knife into her heart.

It began to dawn on Diana that perhaps he wasn't coming back, not ever. If he'd cared for her even a little, he would surely have acknowledged her.

She felt wretched and to top it all she'd caught a cold, standing in the freezing rain, waiting for him.

She went home to bed, feeling very sorry for herself, and pondered what she should do. She couldn't survive on what Kevin was giving her and also pay for an apartment and its upkeep. She wasn't about to live in a grotty place, in a bad area, no matter how badly off she was. She was used to better than that. After mulling over it, she decided she'd give Michael another week before she made any decisions. Ever optimistic and egotistical, she thought he'd come round.

* * *

All week long Justin had been visiting car showrooms and had narrowed his choice to a Golf GTX or an Audi, which he felt might be a bit over budget. Driving around in his father's BMW convertible, he had fallen in love with it but he knew any kind of four-seat convertible was out of the question, much too expensive. He couldn't wait for his father to come home on Saturday, to show him.

Danny arrived in at nine thirty Saturday morning, much to Kate's surprise.

"I got the first flight," he explained. "James is having lots of problems here. Have to sort them out."

"You haven't forgotten that you're taking Justin to buy his car?"

"Of course not!"

But she knew from the way he said it, that he had.

"Is he up? We'll go straight away."

Justin was still in bed but was downstairs in two minutes flat when he heard Danny was home and ready to go. He even refused breakfast, a first for him. Two hours later, they were back, Justin the proud owner of an Audi convertible. As Danny retired to the office with James, Justin told Kate excitedly what had occurred.

"Well, Dad asked me what car I really wanted and I told him I preferred the Audi but it was too expensive and I'd settle for the Golf GTX. He asked me if I didn't want a convertible and I told him, of course, but I wanted a car with four seats and they were really too expensive. As it turns out there was a demo Audi four-seater convertible for sale with only 3000 km on the clock. We took it for a spin and five minutes later Dad had bought it! 'Only the best for my son, the future doctor,' he told the salesman. Oh, Mom, come and have a look! It's silver, beautiful! I can't wait to show Naomi. Dad is getting James to sort out the insurance and tax on Monday, so I won't actually get to drive it till I'm home next. That's cool. It will be on my birthday, actually."

He dragged her out to see the car and she had to admit it was gorgeous, but much too flash for an eighteen-year-old student. Trust Danny! She would have preferred to buy him something more modest and let him work his own way up to the flash cars. Well, it was done now.

Kate was busy emailing the women who had enquired about her catering when Marcia rang with the good news about her grandson. Kate could hear a happy lilt in her voice that hadn't been there before.

"Michael is over the moon about it and the fact that they've called the baby Michael. He's quite a changed man. This little boy seems to have affected him greatly. Of course, we'll be having the mother of all christenings for him and we'll want you to cater for it. We haven't decided on a date yet but I'll let you know as soon as we do. It will be January sometime. By the way I have some more clients for you. I'll email their addresses to you."

"Congratulations, Marcia, and tell Michael the same from me. I'm delighted for you. You sound really happy. I've put up a website but as I'm useless at computers, and even have problems emailing, Kevin is going to help me. You remember him from my dinner party?"

"The poor man married to you-know-who? By the way, I found out for sure that she was the one, but Michael has finished with her now, as I knew he would sooner or later."

"Oh, I am glad for you! That's why you sound so happy."

"Maybe! And then we have our cruise to New York which I hope will be like a second honeymoon."

Kate was pleased for Marcia. She had given her so much help and support with the catering business. If it wasn't for Marcia she probably would never have started it. She planned to get her something really special as a thank-you gift. She was such a lady and a good wife and deserved to be happy. How was Diana taking it? Kate wondered. She had never told Kevin of her suspicions that Michael was the man Diana was involved with. Now he didn't need to know.

★ ★ ★

In Mayo, Conor was worried. He had rung Jenny almost every day and even left messages but she hadn't rung back. He'd thought that maybe she'd decided to go away for a few days during the break but she hadn't said anything to that effect and anyway she would surely be back by now. He couldn't settle and it put a pall on his week, not knowing where she was. They'd always kept in touch with each other before this. He started to worry that something had happened to her and by Saturday morning, when she still wasn't answering her phone, he couldn't stick it and decided to come home a day early.

* * *

Jenny had had a very stressful day.

First off, she'd had to write out the full history of her marriage for her solicitor, and it had left her devastated. She tried to be fair to Tom but whatever way you looked at it, it made a sorry tale. Writing it, she asked herself why in the name of God she hadn't got out sooner. But then there had always been the hope that she'd conceive. That's what kept her there and now she realised what a farce that had been.

Then she'd met Tom's sister in the supermarket in the afternoon and she'd practically attacked her for putting poor Tom out on the street. He was seemingly staying with them so the sister was obviously a bit put out.

After her dinner – a mushroom omelette – she went for a long soak using the Jo Malone bath oil and scented candles the girls had bought her. Then, in her dressing gown, she lit a big fire and all the candles in the living room, poured herself a glass of wine, put Frances Black on the CD and sat down to wallow in her misery.

She had almost finished the second glass of wine when she heard the rap on the door and someone coming in. Damn! I forgot to lock the door as Kate is always saying I should. She froze, in a panic. Could it be Tom?

She got up, expecting to see Tom's big bulk filling the doorway, but collapsed in relief when she saw it was Conor.

"Jenny, what's wrong? Are you okay?" He came forward towards her.

"It's okay. I was scared. I thought you were Tom," she said, her voice breaking.

"But why are you scared of that?" he asked, puzzled.

"Oh, Conor!" she let out a wail and started sobbing.

He reached for her and took her in his arms. "Jen, Jen, it's all right. I'm here now. It's okay."

He didn't know what the hell was going on but she was obviously distressed and it had something to do with Tom. I hope that bastard hasn't hit her, he thought to himself. If he has, I'll fucking kill him.

He held her close, crooning to her and gently rubbing her hair until her sobs subsided. He led her to the couch, offered his handkerchief and said, "Okay, sweetheart. You're safe now. Tell me what's happened.

"Oh, Conor, I can't begin to tell you. I threw Tom out. It's over. I'm divorcing him," she whispered.

"What happened?"

She told him the whole sorry tale. He couldn't hide his shock.

"Oh, my poor love! How awful! How could he have been so deceitful?" He put his arms around her. His concern started her crying again and she sobbed in his arms as he stroked her hair, over and over. "Oh Jenny, I'm so sorry." His kindness opened the floodgates and Jenny let out all the anguish that she was feeling at her husband's betrayal. Conor sat holding her, stroking her hair, till her tears stopped but she stayed there in his arms feeling comforted and loved.

"There, there, my darling. It will be okay. I love you and I'll keep you safe."

Through her tears she heard what he was saying. He was kissing her tears away and before she knew it his lips were on hers and she was kissing him back and she let go of her pain as she gave herself up to him. They kissed passionately and she wanted him to make love to her more than she'd ever wanted anything. He saw this and he felt the same but he also knew that tonight was not the right time. She was too upset and vulnerable. He'd waited a long time for her – he could wait a little longer. Instead he lay with her on the sofa, his arms wrapped around her. She was shocked at her longing for him and how right it had felt. She had known for a long time that Tom was not the man for her and she had loved Conor as a friend. Now she realised that it was not just platonic love. She remembered that he had said he loved her but perhaps that was only to comfort her. She couldn't be sure.

"What about Little Miss Blue Eyes?" she asked, looking up at him.

She saw the puzzled look on his face as he said, "Who?"

"Nurse Cassandra, with whom you spent the weekend after her party," she replied, not able to keep the jealousy from her voice.

He roared laughing. "Sandra? You silly twit! I didn't spend the weekend with her. We went to the party but they were all kids so I left and went to Dublin to stay with my friend, Steve, for the weekend. I had planned to go there on Saturday anyway." He saw the relief that flooded Jenny's face. "Don't tell me that you thought . . ."

He started laughing again and Jenny joined in, relief and exhilaration mixing together.

"You crazy woman! I meant what I said – I do love you," he said, as though reading her thoughts. "I've loved you for a long time but because you were married . . ." he trailed off, kissing her again.

She couldn't believe it. This wonderful man was saying he loved her. He knew her so well, better than almost anyone, certainly better than her worthless husband. She felt her confidence returning but she still mourned the wasted years when she had hoped that she would become a mother. That dream was gone now. Maybe it was never meant to be.

She fell asleep in his arms and he watched her sleeping. She was adorable. He loved her love of life, her sense of humour and twinkling eyes that captivated all who met her. He loved her enthusiasm for everything, how she became so animated when she spoke. He had always had a soft spot for her and Beth had understood.

As he watched her sleeping he thought back to a conversation he'd had with Beth. She had just found out that she was dying and Jenny was still single, and she'd said to him, "Darling, if I can't beat this cancer, I want you to get married again. Not too soon mind – wait till after my first anniversary – but you would have my blessing. Not some floosie or bimbo but someone genuine, someone like Jenny. She's such a good woman and maybe she could give you the child that I never could."

He had tried to shush her and reassure her but she had looked him squarely in the eye.

"Conor, don't bullshit me. I know I'm dying and I want to be sure that you'll be okay when I'm gone. And let's face it – it's the ultimate power trip for me, choosing your next wife." And she had laughed so heartily that Conor had joined in. "It's a true sign of my love for you that I want you to be happy when I'm gone."

At that, he had wept uncontrollably.

"Don't be such a baby!" she'd said with a tear in her eye. "Come here and give me a hug. I've had a very happy life. I've been so lucky."

He never told Jenny about this conversation and then just two months before Beth died, she upped and married Tom, just like that! Conor and Beth were shocked. They had both known Tom for a long time and knew he was not the right man for Jenny. If they'd known of her plans they would have tried to stop her, but before they had a chance it was a *fait accompli*.

Beth had obviously known him better than he'd known himself because he'd never imagined he'd fall in love again. No doubt Beth was smiling down on them tonight!

He got a duvet and covered Jenny up, then blowing out the candles he quietly let himself out, locking the door after him. They had plenty of time. They had a whole life ahead of them.

* * *

All that Saturday afternoon and evening, Danny was ensconced in the office with James. They didn't even emerge for food and when Kate took them in some sandwiches she could feel the tension and knew that something was wrong.

Sunday morning, James was back and even Danny's weekly golf game was abandoned.

Something was seriously wrong.

After lunch, during which Danny was unusually quiet, he asked her to come into the office with him.

"Kate, we have a major problem here. The Irish market has gone to hell. Too much supply and not enough demand. Besides that, there seems to be a substantial amount of money missing from our accounts but the auditors will find that. I've had to call them in. What I really want to say is that business is booming in the UK and I have two more big contracts pending. If I get them, and I'm sure I will, it would mean us moving to London, permanently."

Kate looked at him, disbelieving. She was shocked to the core.

"Are you saying that you want us all to up sticks and move to London?" She asked him, her voice a whisper.

"Yes, I can't keep commuting like this."

"Danny, it's out of the question. What about the boys and their schooling? We can't just move them like that. And I couldn't survive in London."

"Of course, you could and there are plenty of good schools in England."

"No. No way. This is not on."

"I may not have a choice, Kate. It's too good an opportunity to miss. I can't turn it down. Look, I have to head for the airport now. I won't get home next weekend but please think about it."

She sat there in shock while he said goodbye to the boys and got his things together. She couldn't believe that he was asking this of her. She would not disrupt the boys' lives like this. And what about her life here: her friends, her golf, and now her catering business? Was she to leave all this behind, because he wanted to work in London? Kate was adamant. He could go if he wanted. She was staying put. They had more than enough money. He could sell some of his properties in Dublin – even this house for all she cared. She didn't need a house this size with a housekeeper and gardener and pool cleaner. No!

No way was she locating to London!

With a heavy heart she drove the boys back to school but she didn't mention anything to them. She didn't want to upset them. Time enough for that.

Chapter 45

Conor called into Jenny on Sunday morning and she came down to let him in, still in her dressing-gown. He had brought her the Sunday newspapers and some hot croissants for breakfast. She felt shy in his presence, afraid that maybe she'd imagined the night before.

"No, you didn't imagine it," he told her, reading her mind as always. "Come here," he said, taking her in his arms. "I meant everything I said last night. I love you," and to show her he kissed her long and deeply.

Her head was in a spin and her heart was singing. How had she not realised before now that she was in love with him? She was some idiot. Now she felt relief that Tom was gone. Conor and she would probably never have got together otherwise.

"We're going out to celebrate tonight," he told her, coming up to kiss the back of her neck as she stood making the coffee.

"Celebrate what?" she asked, not able to stop smiling.

"Your freedom and my being next principal of Ballyfern School."

"Conor, you're not serious? Have they offered it to you?"

"Yes, there was a letter waiting for me when I got home," he said joyfully, swinging her off her feet.

They kissed again and she wanted to drag him straight up to bed but she still felt a little shy about making the first move.

"So, my lady," he said, when he'd put her down, "get your glad rags ready because I am taking you out for a very special meal tonight!"

She looked at him, thinking, this can't be happening. He looked so gorgeous, his face tanned after his week's surfing. The tan made his eyes bluer and his teeth whiter than usual. His hair seemed even more blond-streaked than before. She loved him so much.

She spent the whole day smiling to herself and even pinched herself, in case she was dreaming. Ouch! It was real!

Thank God I bought those new clothes last Friday, she thought. Now I have something decent to wear tonight. That evening she soaked in a Jo Malone bath again and then put on the silk chemise and robe that Lauren had given her. It was all so luxurious that she felt truly pampered. She vowed to look after herself like this in future.

Having used both Tara's and Lauren's presents, she felt she had to use Kate's as well and felt really sexy in the beautiful black La Perla underwear. The stockings and suspenders felt strange but they made her feel deliciously bold so she decided she'd better get used to them as she loved this strange new feeling. Slipping on her new Issa dress and green heels, she could feel her excitement mounting.

Checking herself in the mirror, she was amazed, yet again, at the difference her new hairstyle made. She loved it! What would Conor think of her transformation? He'd only seen her in her dressing-gown last night and this morning and she'd looked a mess then. She took great care with her make-up and was a bundle of nerves when Conor arrived at seven to pick her up.

He stood stock-still as he came into the room and saw her and for a moment she was afraid.

"Am I okay?" she asked him nervously.

"Okay? . . . Jenny, I've never seen you look more beautiful. My God, you look stunning! What have you done to your hair? and your figure looks fantastic and you look taller . . ." He could hardly take it all in.

"Yes, well, that's the heels," she grinned as she turned and lifted her foot for him to see.

"I've never seen you in heels before," he said, his voice husky. "I want to take you to bed this minute," he reached for her and she came into his arms.

"I want you too," she said, pressing herself against him, her body on fire.

"Oh, God, I can't go out like this," he said, talking of his erection. "Stop it, woman! You're too damn sexy! We have a restaurant to go to."

"Later, much later," she promised, looking at him over her shoulder, as she went to get her green velvet jacket and her bag.

"Hang on," he said. "I have something for you."

Out of his pocket he took a jewellery box and inside was a silver necklace with a Claddagh heart, set with a green stone.

"I saw this in a jeweller's in Westport and had to buy it for you. It matches your dress perfectly. Turn around and let me put it on."

She was so touched by his kindness that she had tears in her eyes as he clasped it on, kissing her neck as he did so. He turned her around to see it and through her tears she said softly, "I love you, Conor."

"Oh my Jenny, I love you too," he said, gently kissing her tears away

He took her to Barberstown Castle, a very romantic restaurant, about twenty minutes away. On the drive over she told him of her day in Dublin with the girls and the make-over they'd insisted on.

"I must thank them personally," he grinned.

He had pre-ordered champagne which was on ice, waiting for them in the beautiful drawing room. They could barely keep their hands off each other and their fingers were entwined for most of the night. Jenny couldn't ever remember being this happy before. The food she was eating barely registered except that she knew it was wonderful. They didn't dally over coffee but left straight after the dessert. They were both high with anticipation and desire.

They were hardly in the door when they started kissing and taking off each other's clothes. They left a trail of them up the stairs and into the bedroom.

She drank in his beautiful body and he was even more aroused when he saw her lingerie. He couldn't wait for her to take off her stockings and entered her straight away. It was the most glorious sex either of them had ever experienced.

Later that night, when she had lit the candles in the bedroom and they'd had more champagne, they made slow, sensuous, gentle love and they fell asleep, their naked bodies entwined, both sated and blissfully happy.

* * *

Kate was feeling totally miserable. She couldn't come to terms with what Danny had proposed. She knew she'd hate living in London. She loved visiting but living there was another kettle of fish. She'd never survive in a city that big. Hell, she didn't even think she could survive in Dublin. She was a country girl at heart. She wasn't just thinking of herself but also of her boys. To uproot them, at this stage of their education, could have devastating effects on them. She knew they would not want to leave their home and friends. No, there was no way she could consider this. Danny would have to see the impossibility of what he was suggesting. She knew she'd have to convince him.

Kevin called in on Sunday night and knew immediately, from her glum expression, that something was wrong. She told him of Danny's proposal and he was as incredulous as she had been when she'd first heard it.

"You can't disrupt the boys' education at this stage. The English system is completely different and I don't think you'd want to raise them there."

"Definitely not, and leaving them in school here, while I uproot to London, is most definitely not on. I couldn't visit them every Sunday and what about long weekends and midterm breaks?"

"I can't see you settling there either, Kate, and what about Kate's Katering? It would be a shame to leave it now just as you're getting it off the ground."

"I know. Danny has given no thought to anyone but himself. What's new? He's so restless, always wanting more, bigger and better. Well, this is one time he won't get his way. This is too important to me."

Kevin left, kissing Kate on the cheek as he did so. This was something new that he had started and she had to admit that she quite liked it. It unnerved her a bit when he came so close. She remembered how he'd looked in the Jacuzzi but put it out of her head, guiltily. God, what would Kevin do if he knew what she was thinking? He might stop calling around and she'd really miss that. She supposed it was because of her sexless life that she was having these thoughts.

She'd taken to going to the gym at least three times a week and she occasionally bumped into him there. She couldn't help but like what she saw. He was devastatingly attractive. She wasn't the only one who thought so.

She'd shared the Jacuzzi one day with a strikingly handsome woman.

"Hi, I'm Randy," she'd introduced herself to Kate with an American accent. "I'm a writer and I'm renting a house outside Naas. I just love Ireland and Irish men. They're dolls!" she'd drawled. "I've just divorced my fourth husband and I came here to find me a nice Irish husband. They're so cute!"

"God, four marriages and you want to go again?" Kate had laughed.

"I'm like Elizabeth Taylor. I like being married," she'd replied, "and I have my eye on just the guy. You see that guy with the fab body just getting out of the pool," she'd continued, "I believe he's about to be divorced and he's hot as hell."

Kate followed her gaze and to her dismay Kate saw that it was Kevin she was talking about. Kate felt a bit miffed.

"What a body! I bet he's great in the sack," Randy continued.

Kate excused herself and left the Jacuzzi. Honestly, American women were the end. Randy is right, thought Kate. She's well named and she must be fifty at least! All the same she felt a wave of jealousy as she saw Kevin get in the Jacuzzi and saw him smile and talk to Randy. Her Kevin! He'd never – would he?

Chapter 46

The following night, on the way to Slimforever, Kate told Lauren what Danny had proposed.

"He wants us all to move to London," Kate said forlornly.

Lauren almost crashed the car as she swivelled around to look at Kate.

"Careful!" Kate cried, reaching for the wheel.

"Sorry," Lauren mumbled. "You're not thinking of going, I hope."

"Not in a million years. I've thought about it and it would be a dreadful move, not just for me, but for the boys as well. I have to think of them."

"You have to sit down with him and talk it out. This is serious, Kate."

"Who are you telling? He dropped this bombshell at one o'clock on Sunday and at ten past he was gone. I just can't get him to sit and talk with me any more. He's always busy or going somewhere."

"I have an idea," said Lauren. "I'm going to London on Thursday to buy some fabrics. Why don't you come with me? We can do some shopping and you can surprise Danny. Make him sit down and discuss this and tell him how you feel."

Kate thought this was a great idea and Lauren offered to go online and book the flights for her. She felt much better, now that she had made a decision to do something about it, and relaxed with the girls at the meeting and in the restaurant afterwards.

Kate wasn't surprised to find that she'd lost only one pound. With the boys home last week there had been much more food in the house. She determined to be extra good this coming week. She had ten more pounds to lose.

Lauren herself had lost one more pound and had just one more to go to reach her Target Weight. The others thought she looked fantastic, so slim and willowy. No matter how much they lost they'd never look like her. She was one of those God-given, naturally beautiful women. Lucky for her!

Jenny was on a high as she'd finally broken the nine-stone barrier. The others laughed at her exuberance which continued in the restaurant.

Tara was unusually quiet, not her usual bubbly self, and the girls wondered if there was something wrong but she didn't confide in them and they didn't like to pry.

"I'd love to be going to London with you," she said. "In fact, I'd love to get away on my own for a bit, but, of course, I can't because of my slimming classes."

This remark really worried the girls. It was so unlike her. Again she had a coffee and only stayed for ten minutes. The girls were very concerned about her.

When she was gone Lauren turned to Jenny and looked at her quizzically.

"You look positively glowing tonight. Has something happened?"

"Yes, what happened to down-in-the-dumps Jenny from last week?" Kate wanted to know.

Jenny blushed, "Please keep this between ourselves. I wouldn't want it getting around, but . . . I don't quite know how to say this . . ."

"For God's sake, Jen, out with it! I can't bear the suspense," Lauren cried.

Jenny was grinning from ear to ear. "Well, the fact is, Conor and I got together over the weekend." She looked at her friends to see their reaction.

Shocked, to put it mildly. They both stared at her open-mouthed. Lauren was the first to recover her composure.

"Do you mean you . . .?" and she waved her hand back and forth.

"Oh, it's not just sex," Jenny clarified it, "although we did . . . eh . . . make love, but we've discovered we *are* in love."

Kate couldn't utter a word – she was completely dumbstruck – and even Lauren, who was never lost for words, couldn't find anything to say.

"Aren't you pleased for me?" Jenny asked, bewildered at this silence.

Getting over her shock, Kate squealed, "I knew it, I knew it! Oh, Jen, I'm thrilled for you!" and she jumped up to hug her.

Lauren who was not normally demonstrative, did the same.

"Tell us, tell us, how did it happen? I don't believe it!" Kate was laughing. Jenny, relieved, told them the whole story.

"I always said you'd make a great couple," Lauren announced. "Best thing you ever did was turf Tom out."

"Oh, Jen, I'm so happy for you both," Kate said, tears in her eyes at this happy outcome. Jenny deserved some happiness.

★ ★ ★

Jenny was on cloud nine but was in a state all day Tuesday, the day Oscar was to visit, at the thought of a stranger looking at her paintings. However, it was too late to back down now. Conor was delighted when he heard that an art gallery was interested in her paintings and tried to reassure her but she was still very nervous.

Oscar arrived that afternoon and was silent as he looked at one painting after another. He hates them, she thought, regretting that she had invited him to view them. Still he said nothing. Eventually, he broke the silence.

"Jenny, these are seriously good. Why haven't you shown them to someone before now? I particularly like this last one you've done. I will have no problem selling any of these, if you'll allow me to exhibit them."

Jenny couldn't believe it. People would actually pay for her paintings? She painted because she loved it. Now she was being paid to do it! Why not? Before she knew it, she had agreed to let him do it.

Conor came over the minute Oscar had gone and twirled her around the room when he heard the news. She rang Kate and Lauren and they were both delighted for her too. She still couldn't believe her good luck.

★ ★ ★

Isabelle called in to see Diana at lunch-time on Wednesday and was shocked to find her friend still in bed and looking a mess.

"Oh, come on Diana, pull yourself together! This guy is not worth it. You knew he was married and he did say that there would be no future in your relationship."

"I know," she wailed, "but I thought he would come round! We were fantastic together. You can't begin to imagine how hot the sex was."

"That means nothing. To men, sex and love are two completely separate things. Just because he has fantastic sex with you doesn't mean he loves you. I should know!" Isabelle snorted. "Men can compartmentalise their lives. You know the old saying: 'Love is of men's life a thing apart, 'tis woman's whole existence'. I hate to say it, but I reckon he was just one horny guy, you gave him great sex and that's where it stops with him."

447

Diana put her hands over her ears. She didn't want to hear this.

"If I were you," Isabelle continued, "I would accept that it was just a fling, go back to Kevin and say you're sorry. You had a really good life with him – lots of money and the freedom to do what you wanted. Many girls would kill for that. You can still have your little dalliances and if Michael does come back, which I strongly doubt, you can still meet him for sex."

After Izzie had gone, Diana thought about what she had said. Maybe she was right. Perhaps she had put too much pressure on Michael. When she'd lived with Kevin, she'd seen almost as much of Michael as she had while living in Dublin. In a way it was even more exciting then. She'd certainly had a better social life and none of that hanging around, wondering if he'd come to her.

That's what I'll do, she decided. I'll go back to Kevin tomorrow evening, say I'm sorry and that I've made a dreadful mistake.

She felt much better having made that decision. Michael might even come back crawling, begging her to return, once he realised that she wasn't hanging around waiting for him.

Chapter 47

Lauren and Kate arrived in London City the following Thursday at about ten thirty in the morning. Lauren had two calls to make, after which they met up for lunch in Selfridge's. After lunch they shopped there and then made their way down South Molton Street, enjoying the boutiques there. Kate bought a pair of boots in Russell and Bromley and gorgeous red stilettos in Faith. She was finally beginning to get the hang of this shoe fetish that other women seemed to have been born with. She could quite get into this. They made their way to Bond Street and she couldn't believe the prices of the clothes and jewellery there.

"Are there really women who spend this kind of money?" she asked Lauren.

"Oh, yes, and not just celebrities. You'd be surprised."

Kate loved Fenwicks as the prices there were more reasonable and the clothes gorgeous. She flashed the credit card there, maybe too often. God, it felt great! Finally, happy but with sore feet, they made their way back to their hotel where Kate sank into a delicious bath.

They planned to have something to eat and then at about nine she would make her way to Danny's hotel. She wanted to surprise him and reckoned he would probably be out eating till then.

Lauren wanted to accompany her as she was apprehensive about the outcome but Kate insisted on going alone.

"Just wish me good luck," she said to her friend anxiously.

She rang the hotel number from the taxi and asked if he was in.

"Yes, Mr O'Mara is in his room. Shall I put you through?"

"No, thank you,"she replied, quickly hanging up. She didn't want to alert Danny to her presence and she knew that reception wouldn't let her up to his room without notifying him.

Arriving at the hotel she slipped past reception and took the elevator up to his floor, rehearsing what she had prepared to say to him. She hoped that the shock of seeing her here like this would bring him to his senses and impress on him the seriousness of their problems. She found his room and knocked timidly. No one answered, so she knocked louder.

The door was opened by a very young, very tall, voluptuous blonde, wearing only a man's shirt. Kate started to apologise, thinking she had got the wrong room, when she heard Danny's voice from inside asking, "Who is it, sweetie?"

Kate pushed past her and into the room, only to find Danny lying on the bed, as naked as the day he was born. He jumped up, shock on his face, and reached for his trousers. She watched as he struggled to put them on, getting all tangled up in the process. She resisted the urge to laugh hysterically. Of course, she should have recognised Danny's Charvet shirt, barely containing the blonde's ample, siliconed breasts.

"*Ooh ees thiz voman?*" squealed the blonde, in what sounded like an Eastern European voice.

"I'm his wife!" Kate replied, amazing herself at how calm she sounded.

"*Yorr viffe?*" she screamed at Danny. "*Yoh tehl mee yorr a divvorrce mahn!*"

"Oh, believe me, he will be, very soon," Kate said to her.

"Please, Petra, I can explain. Please listen to me!"

Wham! One designer shoe whizzed past his head.

"*Yoh basstaard!*"

The second shoe just missed him, because, luckily, he'd ducked. It found a target, however, as bottles of whiskey and vodka went crashing down, spilling their contents all over the place.

Kate watched this whole scene as if in slow motion. Her eyes scanned the room slowly, as if it was a scene from a movie. The girl's clothes and shoes, lots of them, were scattered all around. She could see into the bathroom where jars of make-up crowded the shelves and bras hung from the shower rail. This was no one-night stand – this girl was a permanent fixture.

She watched Danny plead with the girl, who wouldn't heed him, but grabbed his Burberry coat, slipped into heels, and stormed out of the room.

One Charvet shirt and one Burberry coat down the Swanee, Kate thought, repressing a giggle.

Danny turned to Kate accusingly. "Now look what you've done!"

Kate came to her senses. "Look what I've done? You lying, cheating bastard! So this is what's been wrong with our marriage. This is what it's all been about; all the working weekends, not getting home till Saturday. This is what has kept you here and you hadn't even the guts to be honest with me!"

"You wouldn't have understood."

"Bloody right, I wouldn't have understood and neither would your sons! Just answer me one question and have the grace to tell me the truth. How long has been this been going on?"

With his head in his hands, Danny mumbled, "Not long."

"Tell me the truth, you bloody liar! Since when?" She moved closer to him, a murderous look in her eyes.

"Since the first week I came to London," he whispered.

Her fury knew no bounds. Afterwards, she couldn't explain what came over her, but she picked up one of the blonde's shoes and hurled it at him. She was a better shot and it found its mark. Danny put his hand to his head, feeling the blood, shock registering on his face.

"Kate, please, I'm sorry!"

"You're a pathetic piece of shit and you can tell your

bimbo that, yes, you are getting a divorce, because I'll be filing for one just as soon as I get home!"

With that she turned on her heel and, with her head held high, walked from the room.

She had no memory of going down to the lobby, leaving the hotel, hailing a cab, or arriving back at their hotel. She was in deep shock.

Lauren was surprised to see her back so soon. Realising that Kate was in shock she asked no questions but took care of her. She had thought that she would be spending the night with Danny. So had Kate!

"Oh, Lauren," Kate said, her voice shaking.

Lauren got two brandies out of the mini bar and handed one to Kate as she sat her down. Kate's hand was shaking so violently that she could barely get the glass to her lips. After a few sips she felt better and she recounted what had happened with Danny. Lauren couldn't believe her ears.

"The bastard, how could he? My poor darling, how dreadful for you!" She put her arms around Kate.

"It was so strange. Everything appeared to be happening in slow motion. I felt like I wasn't a part of it. I felt detached, like it wasn't reality. He looked pathetic and he obviously cares for her more than he cares for me. That's what got to me most. He was only concerned about her walking out. He didn't care what he was doing to me or what I might have been feeling. How did I never suspect?"

"Well, they say the wife is always the last one to know . . ."

Kate went through it again and again as if trying to

convince herself that it had actually happened. When she told about the blonde storming out in just his shirt and coat, she started to laugh and Lauren could see that she was getting hysterical. She calmed her down and finally, after numerous retellings and another brandy, convinced Kate to take a sleeping pill.

"What are you going to do now?" she asked Kate.

"Look for a divorce, as soon as I can. There's no going back. My marriage is over. I could never live with him again. I could never trust him. He doesn't care for me. That was the worst part. He was more concerned about her than about me."

Lauren wished that there was something she could say or do, but of course there was nothing, except to be there for her friend. If she could have got her hands on Danny at that moment, she was sure she would have strangled him. What an idiot he was! Kate was better off without him. Lauren thought it strange that she had not shed a tear, not once. The old Kate would have been in floods, but she had become a very strong woman or maybe the hurt went too deep for tears.

★ ★ ★

The following morning Lauren slipped out, leaving Kate fast asleep. She left her a note saying that she was going to look at some fabrics and would be back for lunch and then at three they would leave for the airport.

Kate slept right through till midday and had just showered and dressed when Lauren returned.

"How are you feeling?"

"I'm not. I'm just numb."

"Maybe that's best for the moment. The body has a great way of coping."

"Could you ask Jonathan to get me a good solicitor, to handle my divorce? I want to get it over as quickly as possible. I want Danny out of my life, asap."

"Of course, he knows them all and will make sure you get the best. He'll make Danny pay dearly for this."

They checked out, had a very subdued lunch, and left for home.

★ ★ ★

Kate walked through the house as if in a dream. She felt like a zombie, completely detached from reality, as if she wasn't there. She kept seeing Danny and that blonde together. To think he'd been cheating on her for almost three months. No wonder he hadn't wanted to make love. He couldn't bring himself to do it. She couldn't bear to think about it, so she switched off.

Lauren rang to say Jonathan had already organised someone for her.

He came on the phone. "Kate, honey, I'm so sorry. You don't deserve this. Danny's a bloody fool. I've been on to the best divorce lawyer in Dublin. He has a waiting list of clients but he owes me, so he has agreed to see you tomorrow morning, at eleven. Can you make that?"

"Can I what? Thanks, Jonathan."

He gave her the name and address and she recognised it from some high-profile divorce cases she'd read about.

Lauren came back on. "This guy is the very best there is, Kate. I'm so glad he's going to take you on. He'll get Danny where it hurts most – his pocket."

I don't want revenge, Kate thought., I just want to be able to look after my sons properly. Mostly, I just want peace. I want to forget about this humiliation and his betrayal. I want to put it all behind me and move on and the sooner I can do that the better.

* * *

She rang Kevin on Friday evening.

"You're back!" he said. "How did it go with Danny? I hope he saw reason."

"It's a long story. Can you drop over?"

"Sure, I'll come right away. And boy, do I have news for you!"

"Well then, it looks like we're going to have an interesting evening."

Chapter 48

Kevin had indeed a lot to tell Kate, he thought, as he walked over to her house.

It had started with a telephone call from Diana. "We need to talk. It's urgent."

She wants more money was the first thought that came into his head. Money was always the most urgent thing with Diana. They arranged that she would come down to Ballyfern on Thursday, play golf with the ladies and that he would meet her in the golf club afterwards. He preferred that. He didn't want her coming to the house. When he walked into the golf club he got quite a shock. She looked dreadful. Her eyes were puffy and she had definitely gained weight, which was most unlike her.

She was sitting on a banquette in the corner and he had no option but to sit in beside her. She smiled at him, came closer and planted a kiss on his cheek. He knew his wife too well. She definitely wanted something from him.

"You're looking great, Kevin."

Now that was a surprise. He couldn't remember the last time he'd heard her say something that nice to him. He waited, letting her sweat it out, making small talk, until she eventually got to the reason for her visit.

"I've been thinking, Kevin," she said, snuggling up to him, "that maybe we should give it another try. I was too hasty, rushing off like that after we had that row. I'm sorry. Forgive me, darling. I want to come back home."

Kevin was so thunderstruck that he couldn't utter a word. Was she serious? Did she really think she could sail back into his life, just like that? She mistook his silence for delight.

"I know this is a surprise. I'm so glad you're pleased about it. We can be happy again," she said, batting her eyelashes at him.

She was using that husky voice that he detested as she snuggled even closer. He finally found his voice.

"Diana, you can't be serious! What about your new boyfriend?"

"Oh, he was just a fling, nothing important," she said, shrugging her shoulders.

"Well, it was bloody important to me!" The truth dawned on him. "He's dumped you, hasn't he?" and he almost laughed because he saw from her expression that he had hit the nail on the head. "And you seriously think that you can waltz back here and take up where we left off? I'll say this much for him. He's obviously much brighter than I am because it took me eight years to see through you. Frankly, my dear, I don't want you back. I'm much happier without you and want to go through with this divorce." He moved a little further away from her on the banquette.

"But I can't manage. I can't afford the upkeep on an apartment with the measly pittance you give me. Dublin is very expensive," she pouted.

"You don't have to live there. Find somewhere cheaper. How about a job? Has working ever even entered your mind?" He raised his eyebrows.

"You're so horrid!" she cried.

He left her then, but he would always remember the look on her face. She couldn't believe that a schmuck like him wouldn't be waiting with open arms. Well, I'm a schmuck no longer, he decided, smiling grimly.

★ ★ ★

Kevin had read Diana like a book. That's exactly what she'd thought. She had even been planning a 'welcome home party' on the way down in the car this morning. She couldn't believe it. He didn't want her back. In her wildest dreams she had never expected this. He actually seemed happy and he was looking great. He'd always had a great body and he was obviously looking after it. She had watched Antonio Banderas in a movie on television the other night and Kevin's resemblance to him was even more pronounced now than when they were younger. It was so unfair, she pouted – how come men got better-looking with age while women deteriorated. God was most definitely a man, despite what the feminists said!

Looking at Kevin now, she had to admit that he was getting more attractive with the passing years. Attractive but still boring. If she didn't know how boring he was, she could quite fancy him again. What now? She'd have to look at all her options. She'd make him sell the house and give her half the money. That would be a start. Oh, well, she'd worry about it tomorrow.

★ ★ ★

Kate put the kettle on and listened as Kevin recounted all this to her. She was equally flabbergasted at Diana's brass neck although she should not have been surprised at anything she'd stoop to. She was secretly pleased that Kevin had turned her down. He'd been much happier since she'd left. "Right, that's my stunning news. Now let's hear how things went in London?"

"I think maybe we need a drink before I go into it."

"That bad, huh?"

"Worse!"

She poured the drinks and he sat down opposite her, his face full of concern.

"Well, I didn't tell him I was coming as I wanted to surprise him and, boy, did I surprise him!" She gave a hollow laugh. "The door was opened by a tall blonde with big boobs wearing just a shirt – one of Danny's Charvets, by the way!"

Kevin's face registered his shock. "What?" he exclaimed.

"Danny was bollocks naked – excuse my language –

when I walked into the room."

"I don't believe it." He almost dropped his glass with the shock of it all.

"You'd better believe it," Kate continued. "Anyway, she is apparently Eastern European, her name is Petra and she was under the impression that he was divorced. When I told her I was his wife she went ballistic, hurling shoes at him."

"Maybe she was just a one-night-stand," Kevin said quietly, hoping that's what it was.

"Oh, no, she's a permanent fixture there. Her clothes and shoes – lots of them – were strewn all over the place. Jars and jars of her creams in the bathroom, she's been around for a while. Since the first week he arrived in London, he told me later."

Kevin had gone pale. "Oh my God! How could he? That explains his recent behaviour."

"It sure does! The worst part was that he was more concerned with her finding out about me than me finding out about her. That's when it hit me that he doesn't love me any more."

"What did you do then?"

"Well, I started throwing shoes at him too but I was a better shot than her," she smiled at the memory. "Then I told him that I was filing for divorce, which I've already started."

"That selfish fucking bastard!"

Kate was shocked. She had never heard Kevin swear before. He punched his fist into the palm of his other hand.

"I'll kill him when I see him. I swear I will!"

"Oh, he's not worth doing time for," she laughed, trying to calm Kevin down. She couldn't believe how angry he was. "I should have known what was happening. Things had got so bad between us. I just never thought, for a moment . . ."

"You can't blame yourself Kate. You couldn't have known. You don't deserve this."

"Well, we don't always get what we deserve in life. Maybe it's a lesson for the future. We never know what's in store for us. One good thing," she continued with a little laugh, "it's helped my diet. My appetite's gone! Anyway, Jonathan has got me an appointment with a top solicitor in Dublin tomorrow."

"Gosh, you're not exactly letting the grass grow under your feet."

"No," she said, her face serious. "I mean business."

"Good girl! You'll come through this better than ever. Danny's a bloody fool! He never deserved you."

As he left he put his arms around her and for one wild moment she thought that he was going to kiss her on the lips. Instead, he kissed her lightly on the cheek and said, "You take care, Kate, and you know where I am if you need me."

When he was gone she put her hand to her cheek, where he's kissed her, and wondered what she would have done if he had really kissed her. She didn't want to go there. Oh, stop being ridiculous, she told herself. Kevin sees me as just a friend. I'm just a frustrated old biddy with too vivid an imagination!

* * *

Lauren had arrived home from London to find a problem of her own. Jonathan was in an irritable mood and she sensed his underlying anger. After dinner, when the kids had gone to bed, she sat him down and confronted him.

"Darling, you're getting angry with me. I can feel it. You promised that you would listen to me and do something next time to avoid a conflict."

"I'm fine. I'm fine," he replied, brushing away her concern. "I'm just a bit tense. I have a big case next week and I'm not sure we'll win it."

"Why not ring your doctor? Didn't he tell you to contact him if you felt like this?"

"There's no need, I'm fine I tell you," he said irritably.

Lauren wasn't convinced. She knew the signs too well. Her heart was heavy and she was very apprehensive.

* * *

Kate was very impressed with the solicitor when she met him. He certainly seemed to know his business and her head was swimming, listening to him.

"Well, you'll get the family home, no doubt about that, and I'll need a list of all his other properties and bank accounts as soon as possible. Do you have access to his business and bank accounts? Can you get copies of these to me as soon as possible?"

"Yes, everything is in the office at home."

"Good. As you want this over and done with as quickly as possible, I suggest you apply for a UK divorce which will be much quicker than an Irish one. As a director of your husband's company you're in a very strong position. You have been a full-time wife and mother and also contributed to the business. You will certainly be entitled to a very good settlement and a portion of all his future earnings. He is a very foolish man indeed. This dalliance of his is going to cost him a fortune. We'll take him to the cleaners."

"I don't want to do that. I don't want to destroy him!" Kate protested.

"This has nothing to do with vengeance. You're simply seeking what you're entitled to."

Her head was reeling when she left him. Danny would go mental.

★ ★ ★

Lauren rang Kate in the afternoon to find out how things had gone with the solicitor and tell her of her fears about Jonathan.

"Things went great. He's so thorough, he scared me," Kate told her. "I'm not surprised he's one of the best divorce solicitors around. I wouldn't want him against me, that's for sure. I was with him two full hours and he took me through every detail of my marriage. I'm quite exhausted after it."

"He is the best, no doubt about it. Danny won't know what hit him." Lauren paused. "Kate . . ." she hesitated.

"Is everything okay, Lauren?" Kate asked, sensing something was wrong.

"It's Jonathan," said Lauren. "He's simmering with anger again. I know the signs so well. I'm really worried, Kate. I've asked him to contact the doctor, which he's supposed to do if he gets like this, but he won't hear of it. I don't know what to do."

"Oh Lauren, no!" Kate's heart sank. "Be careful please. I'm scared he'll do something to you."

"So am I," Lauren sounded worried. "He's not here tonight. He's staying in town, thank God."

"Listen, Jenny has just been on to me asking how London went. I told her everything and she's asked me to supper tonight. Why don't you come too? I know she'd love to have you, and Maggie can look after the kids, can't she?"

"Yes, that's not a problem. I'd love that. Will you ask Jenny if it's okay? You can tell her I need to be around friends."

Three minutes later, Jenny rang her.

"Lauren, you're more than welcome. I'm so upset about Kate and Danny and I know you're going through a rough time too. God, life is tough."

"My problems are nothing compared to Kate's and she's being fantastic. I'd love us to be together tonight. Thanks, Jenny."

★ ★ ★

Kate told Lauren exactly what the solicitor had said as they drove to Jenny's that evening. When Lauren heard that the solicitor had said they'd take Danny to the cleaners she gave a little yelp of glee.

"Yippee! That's no more than he deserves. Bastard!"

"I told him I didn't want that," Kate protested.

"Are you mad, Kate?" Lauren demanded. "Look what he's done to you. You're far too soft."

"Yeah, well, we'll see," Kate mumbled as they arrived at Jenny's.

Jenny had prepared a tasty chicken stir-fry. It was good to be together and they shared their thoughts and hopes for the future. They all agreed that having each other, in these tough times, made all the difference. Jenny had invited Tara to join them but she had declined, giving no reason.

"I get the feeling something's wrong there too."

"I got that impression last Monday night," said Kate. "I hope she's okay. She has said she doesn't have any girl friends. I do wish she could see that we're here for her."

"It's strange that she has no girlfriends – she's so nice," mused Jenny.

"It's not strange at all," remarked Lauren. "She has that elusive sex appeal that draws men to her, like bees to a honey pot. You saw how all the men were attracted to her the night of my dinner party. They can't help themselves, any more than she can't help attracting them. It's why her husband is so possessive of her. It's not just her looks or her great body – she has sex-appeal. Women find her a threat so they keep her at a distance. They're afraid their husbands will fall for her. Simple."

"None of us feel that way," Jenny said.

"No, because whatever problems we've had with our husbands, falling for another woman wasn't something we were worried about."

"Well, that was one big mistake I made, obviously," said Kate ruefully.

No sooner had she said this than the doorbell rang.

Tara was on the doorstep.

"I hope you don't mind my bursting in like this, Jenny, but I needed to be with friends."

Jenny could see that she was upset.

"Of course not, love. We've just been saying that we missed you. Come in and hear all our tales of woe. We're like the misery sisters here."

"Well, I'm about to make it worse."

Jenny took her hand and led her into the cosy living room which was glowing with all the candles she loved so much. "Look who the Good Fairy sent us!"

Lauren and Kate jumped up to embrace Tara who promptly burst into tears. The others all crowded around her trying to comfort her while wondering what the hell was going on. Eventually she stopped crying.

"I'm so sorry. I'm making a fool of myself but I just didn't know where to turn. I'm at the end of my tether. Seán is pushing me over the edge. I honestly can't take any more." She sniffed, blowing her nose noisily.

"There, there," Kate said putting her arms around Tara's shoulders.

"He has become so possessive that I can't even go to the shops any more," Tara continued. "He's convinced I'm meeting a man every time I leave the house. I don't know what to do!" She looked to the three girls hoping to find an answer.

"You poor thing, how awful," Kate said giving her a squeeze.

"It's an awful predicament," Lauren added. "Has he always been like this?"

"Pretty much," Tara answered her, "but it's got much worse lately."

"I couldn't live with that," Jenny said. "It's soul-destroying."

"I had a friend whose husband was like that," Lauren told her. "He was convinced that she would leave him. She eventually got him to go for therapy where they worked on his feelings of insecurity. That was his problem and once that was sorted out, they had no problems after that. It's worth a try, Tara."

"I suppose so. I just know I can't live with this any more."

They talked some more and eventually all agreed that she should give him an ultimatum – either he goes for therapy or she would leave him. They reckoned that might have the desired effect. She rang him and told him where she was and with whom and what she had decided. He pleaded with her to come home to him and that if she did, he would go to see a therapist. She felt much better after talking with him.

"Lord, is there any such thing as a happy marriage?" Lauren asked.

"Well, I thought I had a happy marriage but obviously

I was deluded," Kate said with a grimace.

Tara looked at her in surprise. "Why do you say that?"

Kate told her what had happened with Danny during the week.

"Oh God, here I am, with my silly problems," said Tara, "when you have much more to contend with!"

"It's all relative," said Lauren. "When you're going through something horrible you think it's the worst thing in the world, and then you hear of someone who's much worse off. It happens to all of us."

"So says Lauren, our philosopher. Any which way, it seems to be always bloody men who are the root of all our problems," declared Kate.

"They're not all bad. We just seem to have got more than our share of bad ones," said Jenny who was feeling a little guilty about being so happy when her friends were having a rough time.

★ ★ ★

Danny rang Kate on Sunday morning.

"Kate, we must talk. We must sort this out."

"It's too late for that, Danny. I've wanted to talk for weeks, but you couldn't spare the time. Now I've nothing to say. It's over, Danny. I've already started divorce proceedings. I'll pack up your things and you can let my solicitor know when you're coming to collect them."

She gave him the name and phone number of her solicitor. Danny groaned audibly. The solicitor was known as the divorce shark of Dublin because he chewed up so many husbands.

"I never want to speak to you again," she continued. "Anything else can be dealt with by my solicitor. If you want to see the boys, you can contact Justin and he'll arrange it. Goodbye, Danny," and she hung up.

Kate was shocked at the iciness and steel in her own voice.

* * *

Danny heard it also and it shocked him to the core. He had been so sure that she would come around and forgive him. He knew she had loved him. He had expected her to be in tears and wanting to start again. He certainly hadn't bargained for this cold, detached, unemotional woman. What had happened to her? She had always been so gentle and sweet. Just shows you, he thought to himself bitterly, you can't trust women!

He knew a way to get to her. He rang Kevin.

"Kevin, I need a favour. I need you to talk to Kate for me and tell her I'm sorry. Tell her I promise it won't happen again if only –"

Kevin cut him off mid-sentence. "You selfish fucking bastard! If I was near you now I'd kill you! How could you do this to her? What has she ever done to deserve this? I don't want to fucking know you any more! You're a little shit and I wouldn't dream of asking Kate to forgive you. Why should she? You don't deserve it!" And he hung up.

Danny stood looking at the phone in disbelief. In all their years as friends, he had never heard Kevin swear once. This was his oldest friend. They went back a long time. Now it appeared he'd lost him, as well as his wife. But Kevin had always been sweet on Kate. God! They were all overreacting. Millions of men cheated on their wives but were given a second chance. She'd come round. I'd better get over there and talk to her this weekend, he decided.

Chapter 49

Diana was determined to have a whale of a night. She had coerced Izzie to get a few of the girls together for a blow-out night. They'd started at seven o'clock in the Shelbourne. All of the others, with the exception of Izzie, were drinking sparkling water.

"Hey girls, loosen up! We're meant to be celebrating my freedom. Have a decent drink," said Diana, ordering her third margarita.

"Cool it, Di. We have to drive home, you know," said Chloe. "We'll have a glass of wine in the restaurant."

"Some blow-out! Haven't you heard of taxis?" She was speaking a tad too loudly.

"God, Diana, you know it's impossible to get a taxi on a Saturday night in Dublin," Jasmine said, looking at Diana as if she was from the sticks.

"Leave off, Diana. We're all living in the suburbs now, with husbands or partners. Our clubbing days are behind us," Chloe said, a supercilious look on her face.

"By the way, how's that gorgeous ex-husband of yours?" asked Rita, the only other unattached girl there. "Is he dating anyone? You don't mind if I give him a call?"

"God, you're like vultures. We're not even legally divorced yet," Diana looked at them, disgusted. They were pathetic!

"Well, with such a dire shortage of eligible men in Dublin, one can't miss a chance. All the men over twenty-one are either hooked or gay," Rita said and Diana could hear the desperation in her voice.

Diana sensed that this was going to be a bummer of a night. When they'd met, Izzie had warned her that Simon would be collecting her when he came off duty, so there would be no clubbing. It would not be the night Diana had hoped for.

They went to a small Italian restaurant where Diana downed a bottle and a half of wine. Everyone else had just a glass. After the meal, the others all baled out leaving Diana and Izzie alone. They moved on to Doheny and Nesbitts, where Simon was waiting for Izzie. They had one drink and then Simon said it was time to go. By this stage Diana was quite drunk.

"Diana, come on. You've had enough. We'll drop you home," Izzie tried to coax her.

"Piss off, Izzie. I'm a big girl. I can look after myself," Diana told her, ordering another gin and tonic.

"You're a big girl all right but I'm not so sure about the next part," replied Izzie grimly. "Have it your way." And she turned and left.

Diana had noticed a guy eyeing her up earlier and, drunk as she was, she recognised that he was a bit rough. What the hell! Here was someone who wanted to party. She bent down to give him a better eyeful of her cleavage and within a flash he was beside her.

"Can I buy you a drink? I'm Frank."

"Hi, Frank. I'd like that. I'm Diana."

"What's a gorgeous creature like you doing on your own? I've been admiring you all night. You have one hell of a body," he said, leering at her breasts.

She leaned towards him giving him a better view.

"Wow!"

This was fun. He was so nice and he bought her three more drinks. Then they started snogging.

"What do you say, you take me home and show me the rest of that fantastic body of yours?" he smiled. "I have my car outside."

"Are you married?"

"No."

She knew that he was lying. It didn't matter one way or the other. She was very drunk by this stage and on the way out she fell against a young teenybopper who was sporting a bare midriff with a big emerald stud in her bellybutton and a micro mini-skirt.

"Get off me. You're totally drunk," said the girl in disgust.

Diana turned on her slurring her words, "Yesh, but you're shure ugly – hic – and I'll be shober in the morning, hic." She thought this was hilariously funny and Frank laughed at her witticism too.

★ ★ ★

The following morning Diana woke with the worst hangover she'd ever had. She couldn't remember how she'd got home and when she turned and saw the sleazeball on the pillow beside her, she couldn't remember where she'd met him or how he'd got here. She shook him awake.

"You have to go."

"Oh my God, what time is it?" he said, leaping from the bed.

He pulled on his clothes – no shower needed, she noticed – and as he left the apartment he grinned at her.

"Wow, you were a hot bitch last night!" he said, leering at her.

She couldn't remember a thing!

"How about meeting me next Friday night for more of the same? Six o'clock in the Four Seasons' Ice Bar?"

"Okay ... ummm ...."

"My name is Frank."

She had no intention of meeting him. He didn't look so good in the morning light. He had to be fifty, if he was a day, but then Michael was over fifty too. Oh, how she longed for him and missed him. She tried ringing Izzie and left three messages, but Izzie didn't return her calls. She knew that her friend was very annoyed with her.

★ ★ ★

It was a very forlorn Kate who made her way to the school to visit the boys. She couldn't decide whether to tell them about the divorce. She discussed it with Kevin. They would have to know sooner or later. In the end she decided to tell only Justin. He was old enough to understand and she would tell the others when they came home for their next midterm break, in two weeks' time.

Justin went very quiet when she told him about it. She didn't go into details but Justin wanted to know why.

"He must have done something awful on you, Mom, for you to go down this road. Is it another woman?"

Kate looked at her eldest son in surprise. Had he known something she hadn't?

"Well, yes, actually. It is."

"Oh, I could kill him! He's such an idiot. I hate him. Are you okay?"

She felt like crying when she saw the tears in her son's eyes.

"I'm fine love, really, and you shouldn't hate him. He is your father. He's just weak."

Justin agreed that it would be best not to tell the others until they came home. Driving home, she marvelled, yet again, at what a fine young man her son had become. Worth ten of his father!

The following morning, just as Kate was about to go for her golf lesson, there was a call from Danny's auditors, asking if they could come and collect all the books and accounts.

"Could you leave it till tomorrow afternoon, say five

o'clock?" she said. "Today doesn't suit me nor does tomorrow morning."

They agreed.

She rang Kevin straight away. She had no idea how to copy onto disc or how to retrieve files from the computer and he had promised to help her download all the stuff required by her solicitor. Now it needed to be done urgently before the auditors took everything away. Kevin told her he would take a half-day and start on it after lunch.

He worked all through the afternoon making copies of everything he found. He was not sure if they would be needed but decided it was better to be safe than sorry. He couldn't believe the extent of Danny's business empire. He had his finger in a lot of pies. By the looks of it, Kate would be a very wealthy woman.

At six thirty Kate called him out for dinner, his favourite – shepherd's pie. She ate nothing as it was her Slimforever night. He still had a lot to do so he stayed working and said he would come back in the morning to finish.

She went into the office to say goodbye to him and, resting her hands on his shoulders, told him, "You're so kind, Kevin. I don't know what I'd do without you."

He put his hands on hers and squeezed them. "You're welcome!"

She smiled. "See you later then."

"Good luck with the weight loss!" he said softly as she left.

★ ★ ★

Not surprisingly, considering she had eaten practically nothing since that fateful night, Kate had lost four pounds, Jenny one and Lauren had lost that last pound reaching her target weight. In spite of all their troubles it was a happy group that met in Moorehill Lodge that night.

"Congratulations, Lauren! Your meal is on us tonight. You're the first one of us to reach her target," Kate insisted.

Lauren protested. "Come on girls, I only had ten pounds to lose! You've lost almost two and a half stone, Kate, and Jenny, you've lost how much?"

"A stone and a half," Jenny said proudly. "But it's been a hard struggle. I've don't have your willpower!"

"It's fantastic," said Kate happily. "I can't believe we're almost there. I have only six pounds to go and Jenny, you'll be there in no time."

"It's all thanks to you, Tara."

"No, girls, you did it all by yourself. I wasn't home with you watching what you were eating. I wasn't walking and exercising in your place. You deserve the credit."

"I am not looking forward to this week," said Kate. "I have to travel to Donegal on Wednesday to see my mother. She's back from a two-month visit with my sister Teresa in Australia. My peace is over. I'm dreading it. It's such a long drive and I have to tell her that I'm divorcing Danny. At the best of times it's all moans, groans and complaints but when I drop this bombshell, all hell will break loose."

"Would she not come and visit you? It might be easier to tell her on your own home ground," suggested Tara.

"You don't know Kate's mother," grimaced Lauren.

"She expects to be waited on, hand and foot. She thinks Kate has nothing better to do. She's a dragon. I don't envy you, Kate. My mother is nearly as bad. She's in a nursing home in south County Dublin and expects me to trot up there two or three times a week. She just doesn't understand that I can't." Lauren raised her hands in frustration. "She's a terrible snob," she continued. "If I arrive wearing all my jewellery and bringing expensive gifts, she gives out to me, saying I'm showing off. If I arrive less than perfectly groomed, I'm letting her down. I can't win." She shrugged her shoulders as the others made sympathetic noises. "She still treats me as if I'm six years old!" Lauren was in full flow now. "She wants to show off to all the other residents and I have to do the rounds of the nursing home, every time I visit. She's dreadful but she's my mother and she makes me feel guilty all the time."

Kate laughed. "That reminds me of something I read once in a Cathy Kelly novel about a fridge magnet that said 'My mother is a travel agent – for guilt trips'." They all pealed with laughter at the truth of this.

"Why do they do that? I'll never do it to my kids," vowed Tara.

"Well, I'm glad my mother isn't alive to see me getting a divorce," admitted Jenny. "She just wouldn't accept it. Though she warned me not to marry him. 'Marry in haste, repent at leisure', were her words. How right she was!"

★ ★ ★

Diana couldn't face Ballyfern that week. She knew the women at her Pilates class and in the Golf Club regarded her as a Jezebel. They were all avoiding her and she came to the conclusion that she had no friends there. Even Izzie was not taking her calls and she had always stood by her. She was bored, she had no money and she realised that she would have to start looking for a job and an apartment, and soon.

* * *

Kevin finally got all Danny's records copied in time before the auditors called to collect the originals. He dropped the copies off with Kate's solicitor the following day, on his way to visit his parents. He was gearing himself up to tell them of his divorce. They were as usual delighted to see him and he thought how lucky they were to have had such a wonderfully long, happy marriage.

He finally told them that Diana was gone. They didn't seem surprised and he was amazed at how calmly they took the news. Their only concern was for him.

"The problem is that I will have to sell the house to give Diana her share of it. If I can then afford it, I will buy a small apartment in Naas."

"But you love living in Ballyfern," his mother said sadly.

"Yes, but there are no apartments there and I couldn't afford a house. I don't fancy taking out a mortgage. You know how I hate owing anyone anything, least of all banks."

"Well, maybe this is all for the best," said his father, glancing at his mother. "We have been thinking of moving to a retirement home. This house is much too big for us now and too much work for your mother. It will be yours anyway so this is as good a time as any for us to sell. The market is buoyant, you'll be able to keep the house in Ballyfern, pay off Diana and even buy another place as an investment if you so wish. Your mother and I can then move into the home which, as it happens, is in Kildare quite close to Ballyfern – and we'll all be happy. What do you think, Doris?"

"The perfect solution, dear," said his mother, beaming at him.

He hugged them both. They had always been such wonderful parents. He was glad they would now be living close by so that he could see them more often

★ ★ ★

Kate took delivery of her huge new freezer, mobile freezer and fridge on Tuesday. Now she was all set to go. She had decided not to start until after Justin's eighteenth birthday in December. She already had four definite bookings and many more enquiries. She was going to be busy but now, with the freezer which was like the ones used in professional restaurant kitchens, she could start cooking and building up a stock. She was glad to have this to keep her busy and take her mind off her personal life but first she had to survive the visit to her mother.

Kate was very tired arriving in Donegal as the rain had

been pouring down since the moment she had left Ballyfern, making driving on the country roads treacherous. It had taken her longer than she had expected. She hadn't even stopped for a coffee.

The first words her mother spoke when she walked in the front door were,

"You're late. What on earth kept you?"

It was all downhill from there as Kate listened to one complaint after another, moan, moan, moan! She put off telling her mother about her divorce for as long as possible but eventually had to broach the subject. Her reaction was even worse than Kate had expected.

"I'm not surprised. You never could do anything right. Now you can't even keep your marriage intact."

"It was Danny who strayed. He was the one who had the affair," Kate protested, in her own defence. Why was she always on the defensive with her mother?

"That's because you couldn't hold on to him. What's all this nonsense about starting a catering business? I don't blame the man," she said, her thin lips in a tight line.

"But Mum . . ."

"A woman's place is in the home. He wants you at home looking after *him* not cooking for other people," she continued pontificating.

It was useless. Kate gave up. She let her rant on and on. She was even glad when her mother got on to her favourite subject, her health. She was as healthy as a thirty-year-old but went on and on about all her imaginary aches and pains and illnesses.

It was with a sigh of relief that Kate kissed her goodbye the next day. She had invited her mother to Justin's party.

"Are you mad? Travel all that way for a party? At my age?"

Her mother was sixty-eight years old but behaved as if she was ninety. Secretly, Kate was relieved that her mother wasn't coming. She would have expected to be the centre of attention and everyone would have had to dance attendance on her.

Kate was very happy to be back in Ballyfern.

★ ★ ★

Justin decided that he didn't want a huge party in a hotel – he wanted a more intimate affair at home. He had invited about twenty friends and they would bring sleeping bags. This suited Kate and she had already planned what she would feed them. Justin didn't want Danny at the party, so that would be another hurdle to jump!

Marcia rang to book the baby's christening party and to say goodbye. She and Michael were heading off on Saturday on their cruise to New York. She sounded happy and very much looking forward to it. Kate told her that she had left Danny and, strangely, Marcia didn't seem surprised.

Chapter 50

Danny arrived in Dublin on Friday to meet with his auditors. There was a major problem. It seemed that his trusted aide, James, had been siphoning off money from the company for years but it had accelerated greatly in the past few months since Danny had been working in London. It would become a matter for the Fraud Squad. Danny remembered, ruefully, that Kate had warned him not to trust James. He should have listened to her. She'd always had a great intuition about people.

* * *

Diana was so bored by Friday that she decided to keep her date with Frank. She could barely remember what he looked like but he would recognise her, she was sure. She propped herself up on a high stool at the Ice Bar of the Four Seasons and ordered a Cosmopolitan. She was trying to sip it slowly as she didn't want to have to pay for it. God, the prices they charged here! She was wearing the silk Gucci dress that she'd worn the night she had first met Michael. She hoped that it would bring her luck tonight. She was aware that her nipples were standing big and erect, obvious through the fine silk material. She could see some men staring at them lustfully. Her long slim legs were getting attention too. They were prominently on display as she had hitched her skirt up as high as she dared.

There was no sign of Frank and her glass was almost empty when she heard a familiar voice call her name.

She turned and was surprised to see it was Danny.

"Danny, what are you doing here?" she beamed at him. They kissed.

"I'm staying here for the weekend, on business. You look ravishing, as always," he remarked, staring at her nipples. "And you?"

"I'm meeting someone but he's late."

"In that case will you join me for a drink, until he arrives? I'm alone."

This was her lucky night. He ordered a large whiskey for himself and another drink for Diana. She wondered why he was staying in this hotel and not driving down to Ballyfern.

With another Cosmopolitan in hand, she crossed her legs *a la Basic Instinct*, enjoying the effect she was having on Danny. He had always lusted after her but because of his friendship with Kevin, he had kept his distance. She knew however, that with a little push from her, she could have had him any time. She hoped now that the sleazebag, Frank, wouldn't turn up. Danny was a much better proposition. And rich . . . very rich! Just then she saw Frank approaching. Oh no!

"Diana, babe, sorry I'm late. The traffic . . ."

She didn't give him a chance to continue. "Sorry, I never wait longer than ten minutes for anyone," she said with hauteur.

"I apologise, but there was an accident . . ."

"Too bad! As you can see I'm otherwise engaged. I've had a better offer. Now get lost, jerk!" She nodded towards the door.

He glared at Danny, muttered, "Bitch!" and walked out.

Danny roared with laughter. She laughed with him.

"God, Diana, you're priceless. You treat men like shit and they keep coming back for more. I love it."

That jerk was right – she was a bitch. She had such balls but he admired her for it. He had no time for sweet-as-pie women who behind it all were hard as nails. At least Diana was upfront. You knew where you stood with her. Wow, those nipples were driving him crazy and she knew it!

"Now that it looks like *Madame* is free for the evening maybe she would care to join me for dinner?"

"*Madame* would be *enchantée*."

He called the waiter over, ordered two more drinks and asked him to book a table in the restaurant for them, for eight o' clock.

"You know, the first time I saw you in that dress I wanted to rip it off you," Danny said lasciviously, putting his hand on her thigh.

"Someone else once told me that," she said sadly.

"Michael? Are you still seeing him?"

"He's history," she said coldly.

Danny raised his eyebrows. "I suppose you've heard about Kate and me?"

"No. Don't tell me she's pregnant, sweet little earth mother that she is."

"I wish. No, she's divorcing me."

Diana almost fell off the stool with the shock. She even spilled some of her Cosmopolitan on her beautiful Gucci dress. Damn!

"You are joking me! Kate would never do that. You and the boys are her world!"

"Exclude me from that now," Danny said, the hurt showing in his voice and face.

"What happened?"

"It's a long story. Anyway she's filed for divorce."

"I just can't believe it."

"You better believe it. She's changed. She's not as sweetie-pie as she used to be."

"About time! You know, I never had much time for her but, in fairness, I think she really loves you." Diana was being uncharacteristically nice.

"Loved. Past tense," he told her. "She won't even talk to me now."

"Honestly, forgive me, but I find this so hard to believe. What on earth brought this on? What did you do?" Diana was gobsmacked.

"She found me in bed with a nineteen-year-old Russian model."

"Oh my God! Oh Danny!" Diana doubled up with laughter. She could just imagine Kate's face when this happened. "You're not serious?"

"Deadly." Even he started to laugh with Diana at the preposterousness of it all. "I've been an idiot. I know that now. I should have kept Petra in an apartment not somewhere that Kate knew about. Anyway it was a bloody awful scene."

"God, I can well believe that." Diana was still shaking her head in disbelief.

Danny ordered two more drinks.

"Where is this girl now?" she asked.

"I wish I knew. She was bloody gorgeous." He sighed, thinking of Petra's body. "She ran out in just my shirt and my coat, can you imagine it? My bloody Charvet shirt and Burberry coat at that!" he grinned.

Diana started laughing again and even he could see the funny side of it.

"She spoke to me once since then and said she would come back when I could show her my divorce papers and an engagement ring. God, I liked her – she was great in the sack – but not that much. She's a porn star, not the makings of a good wife!"

"Porn star? You said she was a model."

"Yeah, well, that's what they all call themselves. She wants to be a fashion model but it's difficult to break into. She has done a lot of topless work for men's mags and she's earning a fortune. You wouldn't believe how much they pay her just to bare her tits. You could make a fortune there, Diana, with those whoppers."

He ran his hand over her right breast and she felt excited at his touch. He ordered two more drinks. By this stage they were both enjoying themselves enormously.

They went in to dinner and Danny ordered a bottle of Chablis and a good red Burgundy. Diana hardly noticed what she was eating but it was delicious. Danny was great company. They knew each other so well that they were easy together. It was inevitable that he would ask her to stay the night. She didn't need much persuading.

He was a skilful lover. Not as good as Michael, but then nobody ever would be. He adored her body and especially her breasts. What's new, she thought? She felt very comfortable with him and eventually had an orgasm. God, she loved this sensation. The following morning they made love again and he ordered breakfast from room service.

"Why don't you relax and enjoy yourself in the hotel today? They have a great beauty and spa centre. Just charge it to this room and whatever you like to have in the restaurant. I'll be gone all day. My last meeting is here with your ex, Michael. We should finish at six, so why don't you meet me in the bar at ten past. Here's a little something. Go buy yourself a really sexy outfit for tonight. I'll bring you to my favourite restaurant."

He casually deposited money on the coffee-table. When she counted it, she found €500. Yes, sireee! Danny was her kind of guy. God, they made a good pair! She wished she could let Kate know that she was screwing her husband. But how? She'd have to find a way.

She had a great day. Firstly, she helped herself to the

champagne in the mini-bar. Then she booked appointments in the beauty salon and hairdresser's, charging everything to Danny's account. Three hours later, she felt rejuvenated. She sent Izzie a text saying, *Please forgive me and let me treat you to lunch in the Four Seasons, today, 12.30. Love you. Diana.*

She waited in the bar, sipping a glass of champagne and was relieved to see Izzie walk in. They hugged and made up. After all, they did go back a long time. They had a brilliant lunch with Diana insisting on ordering lobster for them both and a bottle of Meursault.

Diana was happy that their friendship was back on track. She kissed Izzie goodbye and headed to Grafton Street with Danny's €500 burning a hole in her pocket. She found a beautiful black dress in Oasis, which clung to her curves and showed a lot of cleavage. It was very short – simple but devastating. She also invested in a Newbridge Silver choker and bracelet which completed the ensemble. She took a taxi back to her apartment where she collected her make-up and sexy nightwear, lingerie and stockings. She also packed her Manolo Blahnik shoes.

At five fifty she walked into the bar of the Four Seasons. Her stomach contracted when she saw Michael sitting with Danny. God, she loved him so much and her body ached for him. He gave her a glassy stare as she walked up to Danny and kissed him full on the mouth. Put that in your pipe and smoke it, she thought, as she watched for Michael's reaction. Nothing! She had thought to make him jealous but it wasn't working.

"Michael, you know Diana." Danny pretended to know nothing of their affair.

"Yes."

"Hello, Michael," she leaned forward, ostensibly to shake his hand, but actually so he could ogle her breasts. He ignored her.

"Danny, can we get on with this? I have to leave soon," he said in an icy voice.

"Sure thing, Michael. Diana, honey, order yourself a drink and I'll join you as soon as I can."

Danny was aware of the tension between them and he didn't want to alienate Michael. He needed him.

Diana was mortified. Michael was a shit. She walked away cursing him in her own mind. Had she never meant anything to him? She felt tears stinging her eyes. Damn him! She decided that love was a waste of time. Better to use people and take what you want. That seemed to be what everyone was about nowadays.

Michael left the bar without even a glance in her direction. Danny came over and seemed to recognise that she was upset. Many drinks later they went out to Roly's for dinner and then back for another night of passion. Even though she must have had at least ten drinks, Diana felt as sober as a judge. It didn't help matters when Danny told her that Michael and his wife were heading off to New York on The Queen Mary the next day.

Their lovemaking was even better than the night before. Diana tried to put Michael out of her head but thinking about him made her feel even more horny. Danny loved her underwear. God, he was easy to please!

As he undid her bra, he remarked, "Diana, you have the most fabulous breasts I've ever seen. Way better than Petra's, which were all silicone. You could make a fortune with these in London," and he kissed and caressed them until she could no longer feel them.

When he had collapsed beside her, she started thinking. Why can't I get a piece of this cake? Danny says my boobs are even better than his nineteen-year-old girlfriend. I should cash in on them. He had given her an idea.

The next morning over breakfast, Danny said, "I've really enjoyed this weekend, honey. Why don't you come and visit me in London next weekend? I promise I'll give you a good time."

Diana played it cool. "Maybe – I have to see what else is on. I'll give you a call."

In fact, she had made up her mind. She was going to London and what's more she was going to stay there. Danny was her ticket to the good life.

Danny enjoyed Diana. She was so transparent. She only wanted money and a good time. That was easy, he could provide both. No complications.

Now he had to face Ballyfern and the ogress.

He rang Kate and left a message to say that he would be down to see her on Sunday morning at eleven o'clock. He was dreading it.

* * *

When Danny tried his key in the door of his house he was surprised to find that it wouldn't open. Damn, he thought, she's either bolted it or changed the locks. He rang the bell and was a bit put out to find it opened by Lauren. When he came inside and saw Kevin there, he realised that Kate had called in the troops.

"I see you have your bodyguards here," he remarked sarcastically.

"What do you want?" she asked coldly. "I told you to communicate with me only through my solicitor."

"Please, Kate. We need to talk."

"Danny, I told you. It's finished. Read my lips: o-v-e-r. Your stuff is all packed away and waiting for you in the garage. Please have it removed as soon as possible. I left your suits hanging up on a rail so they wouldn't get creased."

"Ever the good housewife!" he smirked.

"Just be glad they have all their sleeves intact."

This remark floored him and took the smile off his face. She was referring to the wife who had cut off the sleeves of her cheating husband's suits. He didn't recognise this new spirited woman. She looked terrific and her figure was fantastic. Wow, she'd really lost weight! No longer a doormat! She was turning him on. He knew that he had been a fool. He'd had his head turned by a silly young girl while this magnificent woman was at home, waiting for him. I went out for a burger when I had fillet steak at home, he thought, ruefully. Now it was too late. Kate had made her mind up and wouldn't change it. 'The lady's not for turning' went through his mind. There was nothing for it but to leave. He could feel Kevin and Lauren's resentment. Kevin hadn't said a word. Danny was glad. From the murderous look in his eye, he feared Kevin might have killed him.

Feeling very despondent he drove over to visit the boys. He stayed only an hour with them. Justin was very cool with him and, having said hello, pleaded a study project that he had to complete. Danny knew from the accusing look in his son's eyes that this was just an excuse. He drove back to Dublin with a heavy heart.

★ ★ ★

When both Danny and Kevin had left, Kate and Lauren sat having a coffee.

"Phew! I'm glad that's over," Kate said. Despite her composure in front of Danny she was shaken.

"You did great. I was terrified he'd win you round," Lauren confessed.

"Not a chance! Kate grimaced. "How is Jonathan? Has he calmed down at all?"

"Still the same," Lauren replied a worried look in her eyes. "He's still simmering with anger but no matter what I say he keeps insisting he's fine and won't ring the doctor." She was twisting her wedding ring continuously, which was something she always did when she was nervous.

"Didn't he see the doctor last Wednesday?" Kate asked.

"That's the problem. I'm not sure he kept his appointment because I think the doctor would want him to

admit himself into the clinic if he saw how agitated he is."
She sighed.

Kate was anxious for her friend. "Look, Lauren, if he
starts anything, come straight over here. Promise?"

"I will."

That afternoon Kate went to visit the boys and made
the final plans for Justin's party the following weekend. She
had already started baking and cooking and thanks to her
new freezer she would have it all done before they came
home for their weekend break. In the meantime there was
still a lot to do.

Chapter 51

The following Monday night at the Slimforever meeting, Jenny had gained a pound but she was so happy with her new-found love that it didn't bother her too much. Conor had said that he loved her feminine roundness and curves so she reckoned if he was happy with her body, she should be too. Kate had lost three pounds more and Lauren had stayed at her target weight.

At Moorehill Lodge they shared a bottle of wine but Jenny declined as she was suffering with a tummy bug. She was barely able to eat half of her omelette.

"You really should go to the doctor if this doesn't clear up," said Kate.

"Yeah, there's a terrible tummy bug going around," Lauren told her.

Tara was in much better form and not rushing off as she usually did. She told the girls that Seán had been to see a therapist who said that she could help him.

★ ★ ★

Lauren arrived home on Monday night and Jonathan met her at the door.

"Lauren, did you see a file marked 'O'Leary'? I distinctly remember leaving it on the hall table but it's not there now. I've been searching for it all evening!"

Lauren felt an iciness creeping into her stomach. It was coming – she knew it! "I might have put it in your office," she replied, her voice shaking.

He was clenching his hands and his face had a murderous look. She realised that he'd been drinking. Please, God, please, let him not start, she prayed.

"I told you not to touch my things," he growled and she shrank back against the door as he advanced towards her.

"Please, Jonathan, I'm sorry," she whimpered. "Please, let me look for it."

Wham! His hand struck out and before she could move he unleashed his fury on her. She put her hands up to protect her face and head as he pummelled her body, knocking her to the floor. She tried to get up but he kicked her back down. She tried to crawl away from him and he gave her one last kick in the abdomen. The pain shot through her and she was sobbing when as quickly as he'd started, he stopped.

He strode from the hall and in agony she pulled herself up, opened the door and dragged herself out to her car. Luckily she had her keys still in her hand. Her hand was shaking so much she could barely get the key in the lock but she managed it, got in and locked the doors. As she started to drive away Jonathan came running out and tried to open the passenger door. In a panic she revved up and he had to jump out of the way as she careered down the driveway. She zapped the gates open and turned towards Kate's house. As she moved into the road she heard his car starting up and realised that he was going to follow her.

Terrified, she found her mobile phone and pressed 5, Kate's speed dial number.

Luckily Kate answered on the first ring.

"Open your gates, Kate, quickly, and close them the minute you see me coming through! He's following me!" she gasped, her voice panic-stricken.

Kate ran outside to meet her and when Lauren reached the house, she almost fell out of the car into Kate's arms.

"Have you closed the gates?" she asked Kate, hysterically.

"Yes, yes, they're closed. You're safe. He can't get at you now." Lauren collapsed in her arms sobbing and Kate led her inside.

"Oh my God, what has he done to you?" she asked, tears in her eyes when she saw the state of Lauren.

"I really thought that he was cured and that he'd never touch me again," Lauren said, her sobs subsiding. "But you were right, Kate. He'll never stop. I was deluding myself."

The bell on the gate was ringing. It was Jonathan.

Kate went to the intercom.

"Please, Kate, please let me in! I have to talk to her. I have to tell her how sorry I am."

Kate's fury lashed out at him. "You bastard! You're an animal! How could you do this to your own wife? You're a bully and you'll talk to her over my dead body. You should be locked up!"

"Please, Kate," he was begging now.

"Go to hell, Jonathan!"

He obviously left as they heard no more from him and they turned off their mobile phones. But he rang the house phone continually and left umpteen messages for Lauren. She didn't want to hear them.

She rang Maggie.

"Maggie, sorry for ringing so late. Something's happened. I'm staying in Kate's tonight. Could you get the children up and out to school in the morning? Tell them not to worry. I'll pick them up after school and I'll call round to you in the morning and explain."

"Lauren dear, there's no need to explain. I hope you're okay. I'll do anything I can to help you. Just let me know. I hope this time you'll do something about it," Maggie said sadly.

Lauren thanked her and wondered how long Maggie had known what was going on. Probably always.

"Even Maggie," Lauren told Kate, "who's looked after Jonathan since he was born, thinks I should do something about it. It's over, Kate. I'll never give him the chance again.

Kate ran a bath for Lauren and after it, wrapped in Kate's dressing-gown – which looked comical on her, as it was much too short – she sat drinking cocoa by the fire and talking about what she would do.

"First thing, I'll ring Stella, my solicitor, and then we'll take it from there. She mentioned a barring order before which is probably what I'll have to do. I can't believe he did it again, I really can't. He knew it was his last chance!" She started crying again.

Kate let her cry and then, giving her a sleeping tablet, put her to bed, where despite everything she slept soundly.

The following morning Jonathan was still leaving messages on Kate's phone, which they ignored.

Maggie then rang to say that the children were fine and in school and that Jonathan had had to go to work as he was in court all day. Kate drove Lauren over to the house to see Maggie and to collect some clothes for herself and the children. Maggie was there and was shocked when she saw the bruises on Lauren's face. She put her arms around Lauren who cried out with pain as her bruised ribs came into contact with Maggie's arms.

"I'm sorry, my dear," Maggie apologised, tears in her eyes. "He's really done it this time, hasn't he? Have courage, my dear. You must think of yourself and the children."

Both Maggie and Kate helped Lauren to pack for herself and the children, doing the donkey work while she gave directions.

"I'll be here waiting for you," said Maggie as she saw them off, "and I'll look after you and the children for as long as you need me,"

"Thank you, Maggie!" Lauren smiled gratefully at her.

Kate then drove her up to meet Stella who said that the first thing to do was apply for a barring order so that Lauren could stay in the house with the kids and Jonathan would have to stay away. She insisted that Lauren go to the doctor immediately and have her injuries looked at. She was black and blue from his beating and feared her nose was broken as it was bruised and swollen and very painful. She had to ask the doctor to take photographs which was very humiliating but which had to be done. She went to a lady doctor in Naas, who was a friend, knowing that she would be discreet and not talk about it.

She and Kate arrived back in Ballyfern just in time to pick up the kids. Kate's heart went out to them as she saw their worried little faces, full of anxiety for their mum. They were so relieved to see Lauren that they threw themselves at her and she winced with the pain, trying not to cry out and alarm them.

"We're all going to stay with Kate for a while. What do you think of that?"

"Will Daddy be coming too?" Ben asked.

"No, just us." She saw the relief on his face and it broke her heart that it should have come to this. She hoped it wouldn't affect his relationship with his father but who knew? Kate had seen the look too and threw Lauren a sympathetic glance.

They had quite a jolly evening, all things considered.

★ ★ ★

Kate invited Jenny over for supper on Thursday night and she cried when she heard what had happened to Lauren. She got up and gave her a big hug. "God, I've never had so many hugs lately and they're all agony," Lauren cried.

"Sorry, sorry," Jenny said, but then she saw that Lauren was smiling.

She was still suffering from her tummy bug and felt ill after just a few forkfuls of the stir-fry Kate had prepared. Even the wine was upsetting her tummy and she stuck to mineral water.

"You really should get that looked at," Kate told her. "There's a bad gastric virus going around."

"I guess I've caught it. I feel sick all the time. I can't eat a thing. At least I'll have lost a few pounds this week. I'm sticking to crackers and Seven-Up with the fizz gone out of it. They say that's the best thing for an upset tummy. I'll definitely go to the doctor if it hasn't cleared up by the weekend."

★　★　★

Stella had managed to get a court appearance to apply for the barring order for Friday morning. To Lauren's relief Jonathan didn't appear but sent his assistant. It took all of two minutes for the judge to grant it. She guessed the doctor's report had clinched it. Stella left to serve it on Jonathan straight away. It meant that Lauren could move back into her own house that evening. She was happy to go as Kate had enough on her hands what with all the lads home and Justin's party. Maggie insisted on staying in the house with her. Lauren knew she was afraid Jonathan might turn up but there was no chance of that. He was a barrister, after all, and would never defy the court order but she was happy to have Maggie's company in the big house when the kids had gone to bed.

* * *

Kate had spent all day Wednesday and Thursday cooking for Justin's party. Although they had given him the car, she had also bought him a beautiful Piaget watch. She wanted him to have something special as a keepsake of his coming-of-age. She collected the boys on Friday and, that evening, they all helped her decorate the house for the party the following night. She half-expected Danny to turn up on Saturday, but there was no sign of him. She suggested to Justin that he ring his father but he refused.

"I don't want him here, Mom. If he turns up, we'll deal with it, but I'm not ringing him. It's up to him. After all, it's my birthday and if he's not coming he could at least ring to wish me a happy one."

By the time the party started at eight Danny had not appeared nor rung. Kate was too busy after that to worry about him. It was a wonderful party and Justin told her afterwards that he would never forget it, as long as he lived. She loved his friends and she suspected that having Naomi by his side had made it extra special for him.

She lay in bed that night wondering why Danny had not appeared, nor even contacted Justin. He wouldn't have done that just to punish her – would he?

Then it dawned on her that he had, most likely, forgotten all about it. Although he'd known about the party for the past six weeks, he had probably been relying on her to remind him. Well, there was no way she was going to contact him again. They would meet in court. Life with Danny was over. She had to put it behind her and move on. It wouldn't be easy but she would do it.

* * *

On the night of his son's eighteenth birthday, Danny was squiring Diana around London. He took her to The Met Bar for cocktails, then Nobu for dinner and finally to Club Colosseum where she sat sipping champagne, looking out over the Thames. She was all agog, recognising some of the celebrities that she loved so much to read about in her magazines. A rumour went around that David Beckham had arrived and Diana practically had an orgasm at the thought of seeing him, but it was only a rumour. She saw no sign of him.

She hadn't had such a good time for as long as she could remember. Even Michael hadn't shown her the town like this. She was really grateful to Danny and showed her appreciation when they eventually got between the sheets.

Danny was in the seventh heaven. My God, this woman was insatiable and she knew all the right buttons to push. It was the best sex he'd ever had and to think that she had been right under his nose for all those years. All that time wasted!

He had moved into a new penthouse apartment in Chelsea. He needed a new home since Kate had chucked him out and he had decided, definitely, that his future lay in London. He was tired of hotel living and when this apartment came on the market he had snapped it up.

As for Diana, she adored it. She walked around the massive apartment with the spectacular views and every luxury and determined that this was where she would stay. She had hooked Danny with her sexual prowess and she had lots more in store for him. She had big plans.

They shopped on Saturday and he enjoyed buying her things. He particularly enjoyed Agent Provocateur and spent a fortune on sexy lingerie for her but he reckoned that he would get more pleasure from it than she would.

On Sunday night she told him that she couldn't bear to leave him so he simply said, "Then don't. Stay here with me."

"All my clothes are back in Dublin."

"I'll buy you new ones."

This was getting better and better!

"Well, I'll have to go back and pack up the apartment there before Christmas. I suppose I can pick up my things then."

To celebrate, he opened a bottle of Cristal Champagne and they made love on the rug in front of the window.

It was on Monday morning, while Diana was hitting the shops, that Danny realised he had missed his son's birthday. He tried ringing him but, of course, Justin was in class. He rang later that evening and when Justin answered Danny wished him a belated Happy Birthday.

"Sorry, I couldn't get home for your party, son. Did your car arrive?"

"Yeah."

There was an awkward silence and Danny continued, "Did you have a good party?"

"Wonderful. Mom, as usual, excelled herself. We all had a great time. You weren't missed." He wanted to punish his father for what he'd done to Kate.

Danny winced.

"Have to go, Dad. Bye."

Danny wondered how they would take it when they found out he'd shacked up with Diana. Not well, he was sure. His boys adored Kevin but had never liked Diana. She didn't like children and they knew it. Well, he'd cross that bridge when he came to it. Meanwhile it was nice to know that she would be waiting for him tonight, probably dressed in her new naughty undies. He couldn't wait. Kevin was a fool not to have held on to her.

* * *

At the Slimforever meeting that evening there were whoops from the girls when Kate reached her target weight. She had lost two stone nine pounds in total. What an achievement! It was a very happy group who met up afterwards. She decided to treat herself and ordered chips with her steak but found she couldn't eat half of them. She also decided to have a glass of wine.

"Seeing as how you're all paying!" she laughed.

To their surprise Jenny didn't touch the chips that Kate left and in fact had eaten very little and refused a glass of wine.

"Don't tell me you still have that tummy bug," Kate

said. "I thought you said you'd go to the doctor if it hadn't cleared up."

"I rang this morning but he couldn't see me today. I have an appointment tomorrow at four thirty."

"Good, make sure you keep it!" Kate ordered her.

"Yes, Mummy," Jenny said laughing and they all joined in. Kate was forever the mother hen!

"What happens now that we've reached our target weight?" Lauren asked Tara.

"Well, you have one free meeting every month, to ensure you keep that weight off. If you feel you need help maintaining your loss or if you'd like to lose a little more then you can come more often."

"I'd like to keep coming just to make sure I don't regain anything, especially with Christmas coming up," said Kate.

"Well, I'm not going to miss out on these Mondays so I'll keep coming too," remarked Lauren.

"I'm relieved because I would miss you all so much and these Monday nights," Tara said wistfully.

"Don't worry. We'll still keep meeting every week, sometime. You're our friend now so we'll be in regular touch, even when we're finished with Slimforever. Not to mention the fact that my two sons are madly in love with your daughters!" laughed Kate.

Tara hugged her and the others. She had been really afraid that they'd stop coming and that she'd lose them. She should have known better.

★ ★ ★

Conor was also very concerned about Jenny. There was a serious virus going round and, like Kate, he had been insisting that she go to the doctor.

He was relieved when she eventually went on Tuesday afternoon. Dr Brown was an old friend whom she'd been attending for years. She told him how she was feeling and he took a urine sample and blood test. He then asked if he could examine her breasts which she thought a bit strange.

"Hmmm . . . How are your periods? Are they regular?"

"Pretty much."

"When was your last one?"

"Let me think . . . I don't really count any more . . . mmm . . . let me see . . . I suppose it's almost six weeks now."

"As I thought. It's not a tummy bug, Jenny. You're pregnant."

"I'm what?" she asked, feeling the blood draining from her face.

"You're expecting a baby. Aren't you happy? Isn't this what you've wanted for years?"

"Of course. Are you absolutely sure?"

"Certain. Your baby should arrive . . . let me see . . ." he counted the weeks, ". . . next July. Congratulations!"

She left in a daze. She couldn't take it in. Was it possible? Was her dream finally coming true? She drove home and tried to make sense of it. Counting back, she realised that she must have conceived the night that she had first made love to Conor. She wondered how he would react to the news. God, what if he didn't want to know? She didn't dare contemplate that. He said he loved her and if he truly loved her then he would be happy for her. She was overcome with happiness and excitement. She was pregnant at last! The thing she'd been dreaming about and praying for had happened and even if Conor didn't want to know, she would have this baby and love and cherish it. She fervently hoped that he would feel as she did.

The reality began to sink in as she let herself in to the house. I'm going to have a baby. I'm going to have a baby, she shouted, when she'd closed the door, laughing and crying as she realised it was really happening.

Conor dropped in shortly afterwards to find out what the doctor had said.

He saw the excitement dancing in her eyes. "What's up?" he asked with a puzzled frown.

"You'd better sit down and prepare yourself for a shock!"

He sat down, apprehensive, wondering what was coming.

She paused, looking at him anxiously. "It's not a tummy bug, as we thought." She took a deep breath. "I'm pregnant."

He *was* shocked. She could see it written all over his face. She held her breath, grasping the table so hard that her knuckles went white.

"Are you sure?"

"No doubt about it. The doctor confirmed it. The baby's due in July."

"Then it happened . . . ?"

"Probably the first night we made love," she said,

desperately wanting him to say he was pleased.

"Jenny, are you serious?" he said, frowning.

Oh dear God, he doesn't want it, she thought, feeling she might faint. Then she saw the smile spreading across his face like the sun coming out from behind a cloud.

He jumped up, lifting her off her feet, and swung her around, kissing her as he did so. He put her down and wrapped her in his arms.

"Oh, my darling, this is the best thing that could ever have happened. I can't believe it! We're going to have a baby!" and he swung her round again.

Relief flooded through her.

"I'd open a bottle of champagne," he continued, "but there's no more drinking for you while this precious bundle is inside you!"

She placed her hand on her tummy and he did the same. She started laughing with the relief and excitement and he joined in.

"I really can't believe it," she said when the laughter had finally stopped. "After all these years of longing, and then, just when I'd given up hope, it's happened. I'm so glad it's yours and that you're pleased."

"Pleased? That's the understatement of the year. I'm over the moon. I'll take care of you both. I'll never let you down and I want to marry you just as soon as you're free."

He stayed the night and they made wonderful, gentle love. He held her close as she drifted off to sleep and she thought that never in her whole life had she known such happiness.

Chapter 52

Kate's divorce was moving swiftly along. Jonathan hadn't been joking – this guy was the best divorce lawyer in the world, not just Ireland! He was now in negotiation with Danny's solicitor. Kevin was her rock and she saw him most days. Once a week he cooked for her and she had him over for supper another night and every Sunday for lunch. She enjoyed his company and they often went to the theatre or cinema together. It was good to have him in her life. He'd heard that Danny and Diana had shacked up together in London. Good riddance! They deserved each other.

Kate was busier than she had ever been in her life. The bookings for Kate's Katering were coming in fast and furious. They were so numerous that she had to turn some down. She decided to hold off on the website. She had more than enough business without it. She realised that she had found a niche for herself. There was more demand than supply for good-quality caterers. She reckoned that there was great potential for growth, if she so desired. She wasn't sure she did. She liked to be in control and doing things herself. She wasn't sure she could delegate. After all, her reputation was at stake. Everything that went out of her kitchen would have her name on it.

She had employed a woman from the town to help her with the basic stuff and Naomi and Melissa came in at weekends to help out also. They were pleased to earn the extra pocket money and, as she came to know them, Kate grew very fond of them both. There weren't enough hours in the day for her, but she was happy.

★ ★ ★

Lauren surprised herself with the ease with which she settled into single life. She felt at peace for the first time ever, knowing that Jonathan was gone for good. She realised now that she should have left the very first time that he had touched her but hindsight is a fine thing, as she told the girls two weeks later in Moorehill Lodge.

To their surprise Jenny had lost five pounds that night to bring her to her target.

"This calls for champagne!" Tara announced.

"No, not for me, thanks," Jenny said.

"Do you still have that tummy bug?" Kate asked her. "Don't tell me you didn't go to the doctor," she said angrily.

"Actually, I did and it's not a tummy bug. Brace yourselves, girls!" Jenny's eyes were shining. "I'm pregnant!"

You could have heard a pin drop. "You're what?" Kate practically shouted at her, making the other diners look around to see what the fuss was.

"Conor and I are going to have a baby – next July," she said, her face aglow and then all three girls were on top of her, hugging and congratulating her.

"What wonderful news!" said Kate. "And we thought you were sick!"

"Some tummy bug!" Jenny laughed.

"Why didn't you tell us immediately?" said Lauren.

"I wanted to keep it a secret for a little while but who can keep anything secret with you Nosey Parkers around!" she said, grinning at all of them. "Actually, I've been dying to tell you all. I'm so happy."

"You look it. So that's why you've not been eating or drinking," Lauren said.

"I'm as sick as a dog. All day, every day."

"Don't worry," Tara assured her. "It's pretty awful but it should pass at about four months."

"So says mother-of-seven. And she should know," said Lauren.

"It is awful but I don't mind," said Jenny. "It's worth anything to have this baby."

The girls agreed with her.

★ ★ ★

To celebrate their baby news, Conor took Jenny to The Abbeyglen Hotel, in Clifden, County Galway. She loved the wildness of Connemara. She couldn't eat very much but that didn't bother her.

The best moment of all came when Conor took her into a little chapel and produced two wedding bands.

Slipping the ring on her wedding finger, he brought tears to her eyes when he said: "I, Conor, promise to love honour and cherish you, Jenny, till death do us part. I will repeat these vows the day you legally become my wife, but as far as I'm concerned you're now my wife."

She was so touched. She placed the ring on his finger and promised the same. Then they kissed. They followed this with a very romantic evening in The Abbeyglen. Jenny was ecstatically happy.

She and Conor had decided to move in together and rent out his house. It made sense. He was spending all his time with her anyway. She was a little worried about what the neighbours might think but Conor's response was 'to hell with them'. In fact, all the neighbours were delighted that they had found happiness together. They had all loved Beth but no one could stand Tom. He'd had rows with many of them and they were glad to see the end of him.

Conor moved his things over to Jenny's the following week and advertised his house for rent. Within a week he'd found very nice tenants. Jenny was happier than she'd ever been in her life. Sometimes she had to pinch herself to make sure that she wasn't dreaming.

They discussed her divorce.

"I would prefer if you tried for an annulment, Jen – that means we could get married in a church," he told her.

He was strangely old-fashioned in ways, she thought fondly. Jenny didn't give a damn where they got married as long as he loved her and they could be together.

She checked it out and discovered that she had a very good chance of getting an annulment, given that Tom had married her under false pretences. They said she had a good case so she went ahead and applied for one. She hadn't seen Tom since the day she threw him out and she wasn't sorry. She wondered how she could have been so foolish as to have married him in the first place.

Chapter 53

Kate's fortieth birthday was coming up the week before Christmas and she was not looking forward to it. Besides the boys, Kevin and Lauren were the only ones who knew about it. Her sons would still be at school on the big day but had offered to take her out for a special birthday dinner during the holidays. Kevin invited her out for a quiet meal on the night itself. The Ballyfern Inn had been renovated and had just reopened, so he suggested they go there.

The boys rang her that morning to wish her a Happy Birthday, as did Lauren. She heard nothing from Danny. Theirs was obviously not going to be an amicable divorce.

She dolled herself up for the birthday dinner and Kevin arrived with a beautiful bouquet of coral roses, her favourite. He also gave her a bottle of Chanel 'Mademoiselle Coco', remembering she had mentioned that she loved it.

"How thoughtful of you, Kevin! What would I do without you?"

For some unknown reason, she started to cry. She felt vulnerable and sad on this her 40th birthday. She supposed every woman felt the same as the big four-oh became a reality. Somehow, it felt like her youth was gone. She felt she was being silly but he understood and put his arms around her shoulders. They arrived at the Ballyfern Inn and he led the way up the stairs.

"Oh, this is new. I didn't realise they'd moved the restaurant upstairs."

"Yes, strange decision," he agreed, as he opened the door for her.

The room was dark and then the music started up – *Happy Birthday to You!*. The lights came up and in a state of shock, Kate saw all her friends and even her boys – and Miguel! – smiling and singing. She couldn't believe her eyes. She turned to Kevin.

"Happy Birthday!" he said, kissing her on the cheek.

Like a fool she started crying again and then they were all upon her, friends and family, kissing and hugging her. She started laughing through her tears.

"How on earth did you do this?" she asked him.

"It wasn't easy. I was terrified you'd find out," replied Kevin. "Lauren was my co-conspirator!"

Laughingly, she shook her fist at Lauren. "And the boys, how come they're here?"

"I got permission from the principal to have them out for the night, even Miguel. He insisted you were his Irish mother! Lauren collected them from school and was a great help with everything."

Toby was clinging on to her. "You look beautiful, Mom," he whispered.

She ruffled his hair and planted a kiss on his head.

Miguel, not to be outdone, said, "*Eres muy bonita, Mama Kate!*" She ruffled his black curls and kissed his head, laughing at their childhood rivalry.

She turned to Lauren. "How did you keep this from me, you witch?" she demanded as they hugged.

"With great difficulty," replied Lauren, beaming from ear to ear. "We had to keep it secret until the very last minute from Toby and Miguel, and Ben and Daisy, as we were afraid they'd let it out!"

Jenny and Tara were there with Conor and Seán and they embraced her, as did Tara's girls. Daisy and Ben were high with excitement and danced around her. She was thrilled to see Marcia and Michael there also and managed to have a quiet word with Marcia on her own later.

"How was your cruise?" she asked her.

"Fantastic!" Marcia replied. "We had a truly wonderful time." Lowering her voice, she confided in Kate. "Michael is a changed man since Mikey's birth. It's like a miracle. All he cares about now is the family. I'm very happy."

Kate took this to mean that he had stopped his womanising. Probably due to Diana, she thought. Marcia did indeed look blooming. Kate was happy for her. She was a lovely woman.

It was a wonderful night. Kevin had organised a superb hot and cold buffet and there was champagne and wine flowing. There was also a huge cake with forty candles which Toby and Miguel helped her to blow out. She had so many presents that she decided to wait till she got home to open them.

There was a wonderful band and Justin asked her for the first dance. She was afraid that she would cry again but managed to restrain herself. She was so full of emotion. Kevin danced with her next and she twisted and jived the night away non-stop after that. It was the best night of her life.

Taking a breather, she sat in a corner with Lauren, Jenny and Tara.

"You've all been so good, helping to organise this. Thank you, from the bottom of my heart."

"You're worth it!" they chorused, laughing.

To the surprise of the girls, Tara's husband was circulating, talking to everybody and seemed to be in great form. He wasn't watching her all night and things were obviously much better between them.

On the way home in the car Kate remarked to Kevin, "After a rotten year things seem to be turning out well for all of us."

"Yes, every cloud has a silver lining," he replied softly.

* * *

When they got home the boys all scampered off to bed, tired but happy.

"Kevin, this was the most wonderful night," Kate said to him as he was leaving. "How can I ever thank you?"

"Just stay in my life. That's all I need." He gazed at her thinking how radiant she looked and before he could stop himself, he blurted out, "I think I've fallen in love with you, Kate!"

She thought she was hearing things and looked at him, her eyes wide.

"What did you say?"

"I said that I've fallen in love with you. In fact, I think I've always loved you."

"Oh Kevin, how sweet! I wish it could be, but it's too late for us," she said sadly.

"It's never too late, Kate," he said softly, pulling her to him and kissing her gently on the lips.

"I need time, Kevin," she replied, but she couldn't resist kissing him back.

Somehow, since she'd heard Danny and Diana were a couple, she'd felt free.

* * *

Diana and Danny were indeed together. Very together! The first week that she was in London she contacted an agent about a career as a topless model.

"You're a little long in the tooth for it," he said.

She peeled off her top, gave him one look at her breasts and he decided that, yes, he could probably get her some work.

"Some men like older women. If you'd be prepared to do full nudity, which pays very well, then I'm sure I can get you some work."

"The nerve of him! Older women indeed!" she complained to Danny later. However the chance to make big money was too tempting. Why not? She was very proud of her body. Danny thought it was great and encouraged her all the way. He was proud to have this sexy Page 3 Girl on his arm. He felt it boosted his image.

★ ★ ★

Kate basked in the afterglow of her birthday party for quite a while and had a wonderful Christmas. She was exhausted by Christmas week but recovered in time for Christmas Day. She and Kevin had grown ever closer. His mum and dad both adored Kate and could see that their son was very fond of her. They secretly hoped that love would blossom between them.

★ ★ ★

Michael and Marcia rang Kate on Christmas Day.

"Happy Christmas, Kate! Sounds like you have a big crowd there," Marcia shouted into the phone, afraid that Kate couldn't hear her with all the din.

"Yes, indeed," Kate laughed. "Kevin is here and his parents – Jenny and Conor too, as well as Lauren and her two children, not to mention my four. That made us unlucky thirteen but lucky for us Maggie, Lauren's housekeeper, was able to join us, so we're fourteen in total."

"Gosh, I don't know how you cope with that crowd,"

Marcia said, feeling faint at the very thought of it.

"It's no problem. Everyone is mucking in. We're having great fun," Kate replied, trying to shush the boys. "We're going to Tara's tomorrow, so I'll have a nice rest there. How about you?"

"Well, as it's Mikey's first Christmas, Nicky wanted to stay home so we came over to her for Christmas dinner and Alex and her family are joining us later. Michael hasn't left his grandson out of his arms since we arrived. He's a doting granddad!" she said, smiling fondly at the two men in her life. "I'll be in touch in the New Year about Mikey's christening party."

This would be the christening party to beat all christening parties, by the looks of it.

★ ★ ★

Diana and Danny started drinking at ten in the morning on Christmas Day and both got so drunk they fell into bed at seven o'clock. Their Christmas dinner had been a Chinese takeaway!

Chapter 54

One Year Later

Kate stood, once again, looking at herself in the mirror. Gone was the trim waistline that she had sported a year ago. Her boobs were bigger than ever and she was a stone heavier. She lowered herself into the bath and enjoyed the feel of the warm silky water on her body. She was preparing to meet the girls, for her hen party.

She'd already had her divorce party, two months ago. The divorce had taken only nine months to come through the British courts. Poor Jenny would have to wait six or seven years, though, for her annulment to be finalised.

The divorce had been anything but amicable. Danny had fought her hard but her lawyer had secured her a really good settlement. She was now a very wealthy woman. Not that Kate needed much. She liked a simple life. The house in Ballyfern was now hers and she had a very healthy bank balance. Yes, indeed, life was good.

'Life begins at forty' went the saying and Kate couldn't agree more. The previous year had been her '*annus horribilis*'

PAULINE LAWLESS

but this past one had more than made up for it.

It had taken her a little time to realise that she loved Kevin. Not the crazy mad way that she had fallen in love with Danny (look where that had got her!) but a gentle deep caring love which was what she needed at this point in her life. He had moved into her house in July – after she had discussed it with the boys, of course. They all loved him and he was a far better father to them than Danny had ever been.

As Kate soaked in the bath now, she thought back on the amazing changes that had happened in her friends' lives also.

Lauren was very content and in the year since she'd left Jonathan she'd taken the opportunity to do something she'd always wanted to do – write a novel. Her first book had been accepted for publication and would be in the bookstores by summer. The others were eagerly waiting to get their hands on it.

"Of course, you'll all recognise yourselves in it," she teased them.

They hoped not.

But Lauren was truly happy and at peace with her life.

Jenny was now the very proud mum of two beautiful babies. When her twins were delivered, six weeks prematurely, she was terrified that she would lose them. Jenny and Conor had suffered a few anxious weeks but happily, the babies thrived, and all was well.

Nothing had prepared Jenny for the intense love she'd felt when she held her babies in her arms for the very first time.

"I've heard so much of this bonding between mother

and child," she told Kate as they stood over the incubators in the hospital "but nothing could have prepared me for this feeling. It has surpassed anything anyone has ever described."

Kate nodded, knowing exactly what she meant.

"Can you believe how tiny they are, Kate? And still so perfect," Conor said, awe in his voice. He adored his babies and when they came home was a real hands-on dad.

* * *

Kate looked at her watch with a start. She'd been lost in her thoughts, the bath water was getting cold and if she didn't hurry she'd be late for her own hen party. Stepping out of the bath gingerly, she dried herself and then dressed once again in her black silk tunic and pants but this time, as she surveyed her image, she smiled. Patting her tummy, she spoke gently to the baby in her womb,

"I swore I'd never gain weight again but this is different – this is all you and you're worth it. Your mommy will be nice and slim again, once you're out in the world."

Kevin came into the room and coming up behind her put his arms around her, nuzzling her neck. He placed his hands on her tummy and asked, "How are my two girls doing?" She met his eyes in the mirror and the love she saw in them touched her to the core.

Kate had been overjoyed to discover, at her latest scan, that the baby she was carrying was a girl. The little girl she'd always dreamed of.

Just then the baby kicked and the look of wonder on Kevin's face as he felt it melted Kate's heart.

"Are they sure it's a girl? This seems like a footballer to me!" he joked.

"Girls play football and rugby, nowadays," said Kate.

"Not my daughter! She's going to be a girly girl, like her mum," he said proudly.

Kevin's parents were over the moon at the thought of their first grandchild. They had moved into a nursing home only ten minutes from Ballyfern so Kate and Kevin saw a lot of them.

Kevin's divorce from Diana had come through two months ago and he had decided to sell his house in Ballyfern, give Diana half the proceeds and hold on to his parents house in Rathgar – Justin was now studying medicine at UCD and, as it looked like the other three boys would follow him there, they would need accommodation in Dublin.

It was all working out perfectly.

* * *

Meanwhile, across the pond, things were not working out as well for Danny and Diana. Danny's Irish business had come to a standstill. James had done a lot of damage and had gambled away all of the money that he had stolen. Danny had brought the boys over for a few days after Christmas. When they'd found out that he was shacked up with Diana, they returned home at once. She didn't like kids and none of them could stand her.

Diana had made the most of her time in London. Danny had given her an American Express and a Visa Card so she had set to work with a vengeance, flashing them whenever she could. Exhausted from all this shopping, she discovered Ebay, which opened up a whole new world to her. She could shop without even leaving the house! She never spent her own money. She had invested the money that Kevin had given her from the sale of the house. This, added to the big money she was now earning meant she would be able to afford a nice little pad in Dublin or London when the time was right.

Life was good with Danny for a while. He was great in the sack and he was great fun and incredibly generous. But then he started drinking too much and getting hooked on cocaine and things started going wrong. Not that I don't like to drink and snort, she thought to herself, but I can stop. Danny can't.

The agent she had hired was as good as his word and got her many assignments as a topless model. She was a refreshing change from the usual pneumatic blondes, who all looked alike, and for a while she was very much in demand. Many photographers, when they saw her breasts, exclaimed, "Real tits, at last!" Diana was even something of a C list celebrity with all this exposure. Danny was extremely proud of her and bought every magazine that she featured in.

Then the fashion changed and they were looking for boyish-looking models. Boyish, Diana was not. They were tired of her and so the work dried up. At that stage the only option left to her was porn films.

This was when the rows started with Danny. He didn't want her having sex with other men, not even for work. It all came to a head one night when they'd had a party. Too much drink, too much cocaine, and near naked women offering themselves in exchange for another line of coke. There was a little blonde with pneumatic silicone tits – which had always attracted Danny – and somehow he'd found himself in bed with her. Diana had walked in and that clinched it – she left him.

She had in fact, already started an affair with Rocky, the most famous of the male porn stars. She had enjoyed working with him so much that she had carried it over into real life. It was just for sex, she told herself at first but eventually she got hooked on him. She had made the big mistake of falling in love again and had to endure the agonies of knowing that he was screwing women on the film-set and, she suspected, probably off it as well. This was where she was at now.

★ ★ ★

Kate was ready and waiting when Jenny, Lauren and Tara arrived. She'd been reluctant to have a hen party at all but Lauren wouldn't hear of it.

"You can't get married without a hen party," she had insisted.

"Oh God, please spare me!" Kate pleaded. "I'm too old and too pregnant to be dressing up in a veil and tiara and all the other shenanigans that hen parties get up to!"

"What? No male stripper? Oh, Kate, don't disappoint us!" Jenny cried.

"We'll save the stripper for yours, Jen," Kate promised her.

"How about a nice elegant meal in The K Club?" Tara suggested.

It was all arranged. Just the four of them and a nice civilised evening with definitely no male stripper.

Kate had intended driving to the K Club but at the last minute Kevin insisted on driving his "two girls" to and from the venue to make sure they were safe and sound.

"He treats me like a china doll," Kate laughed with her friends later.

"Make the most of it – once your baby is born he'll go back to normal," advised Tara.

They started with champagne and Kate allowed herself one glass.

"Who could have imagined that we'd be sitting here, just a year after we came together at Slimforever, with so many wonderful changes in our lives?" she sighed happily. "Let's drink a toast to –"

"Allow me!" Lauren interrupted, raising her glass to Kate. "To you, Kate, glowing with happiness, seven months pregnant, about to marry Kevin who worships the ground you walk on – enjoying your hen party with three friends who love you too!"

"Well said, Lauren!" Jenny clapped.

"And let's not forget Kate's Katering!" added Lauren.

"Not to mention her wonderful weight loss," said Tara. "And that goes for all of you — between the three of you, you lost over five stone — and we're not counting your baby weight, Kate — and you all look years younger than the first night you walked into my class."

"And Jenny's painting and her sell-out exhibition last March!" said Lauren.

"And hey, what about Lauren's novel?" Kate clapped Lauren on the back and it was her turn to blush. "What a surprise to have a real author in our midst!"

"It's quite amazing what you've all achieved," said Tara. "You've turned your lives around. And I've found three wonderful new friends!"

"Let's drink to that," Kate said. "To us!"

They raised their glasses, smiling at each other and all together chorused, "Because we're worth it!" before dissolving in laughter.

THE END